LIPSTICK IN AUSCHWITZ

Miriam Nick

Producer & International Distributor
eBookPro Publishing
www.ebook-pro.com

LIPSTICK IN AUSCHWITZ
Miriam Nick

Illustrations: Miriam Nick

ISBN 9789655754872

Lipstick *in* Auschwitz

The Unbelievable True Story of a World War II Holocaust Survivor

Miriam Nick
Born Marysia Sperling

Contents

Tel Aviv, Spring 1985

My Dearest grandchildren,

It is for you that I venture into this masochistic orgy of recording my memories, registering coolly and objectively all that I saw, observed and went through — on the "other planet", that of the Holocaust.

It is not intended for you now, tots that you are, but for later, much later, when you will be able to comprehend. But will you ever be able to understand? How will you ponder over all this material when I shall not be here to answer your questions...? Can anybody who wasn't there indeed comprehend? Still, I have this compulsion, this heavy obligation, to try, try very hard.

It is late, perhaps too late. It is exactly forty years after the nightmare ended, but my memories are with me, day and night, they never left me. Contrary to most my fellow sufferers, I never tried to forget, I even made a tremendous effort to memorize and thread this necklace of my recollections. Still, the question remains: why I did I wait, why did I postpone it for forty years...? I am known to be a born extrovert, quick with my pen and never at a loss at expressing my thoughts.

I can prove it. I have written and published thirteen books and booklets (and one more, still unpublished, in five volumes), a great number of articles (one of them for the 'Encyclopaedia Judayca'), an open letter which appeared in the Time Magazine, one play and what not. If so, why didn't I dare, for forty years, to publish my memoirs? The fact that I have been too busy working as an art teacher and simultaneously as an anthropologist and museum curator — this is no excuse.

I happen to be an "excellent and reliable" witness of the Holocaust period... I have gone through the first stages of the German occupation, hiding in a convent, going through life in a village and experiencing its total liquidation... I have gone through the total liquidation of a ghetto, taking part in three escapes, hiding in the woods and keeping contacts with the underground.

I "also" passed through seven concentration camps and participated in two "Death Marches".

With such a balance-sheet, why didn't I hurry to record my experiences? What was the reason and what were the reasons?

Most astoundingly, the very first is the reality, the facts, the truth. It doesn't help, it disturbs. It is such a heavy responsibility to be honest, truthful, factual... and to do justice to all the figures involved. To reveal all that is relevant and not to twist certain aspects of the complexity of the full picture — this is the duty. The knowledge of bare facts, imposing a heavy obligation, can turn into an impediment.

The other reasons for this self-imposed silence are not much easier to explain. There was for many years a mutual pact of silence and non-aggression between those who weren't there and those who went through it, through the Holocaust. Those who weren't there estimated that it must be tactless to bring up this painful subject in front of the survivors; the survivors didn't dare or try to impose the subject...

Among the additional reasons, there was this heavy suspicion, never expressed, but hanging in the air: "What did you indeed do to survive, while six million perished? You must have done something, something ugly, you must be tainted". This attitude is best expressed in one sentence of an Israeli woman who said about my friends: "They are such sweet, cultured and honest people, even though they are Holocaust survivors".

I experienced this kind of a shock much earlier, shortly after the liberation, when my own uncle wrote from America. "We in the U.S.A. know well how demoralized and inhuman you have become, there in the camps, but it is about time to return to the right path".

Even when we were socializing with people of our own kind, there was a barrier of silence on this subject. Whenever one of us mentioned something concerning this period, the hostess would quickly suggest to "let us change the subject" (so that it wouldn't spoil the taste of the cake she was serving).

Most of us survivors have indeed certain problems of conscience. Our sense of guilt is well understandable. Each of us asks himself the same eternal question: Why did I, the little man, survived while my nearest and dearest, while my betters, so worthy and noble — perished in the mouth of Moloch. Consequently, feel each of us, like bowing and saying — "pardon me that I survived...".

I, Miriam Nick, born Marysia Sperling, still feel guilty that I have lived twice.

Miriam Nick

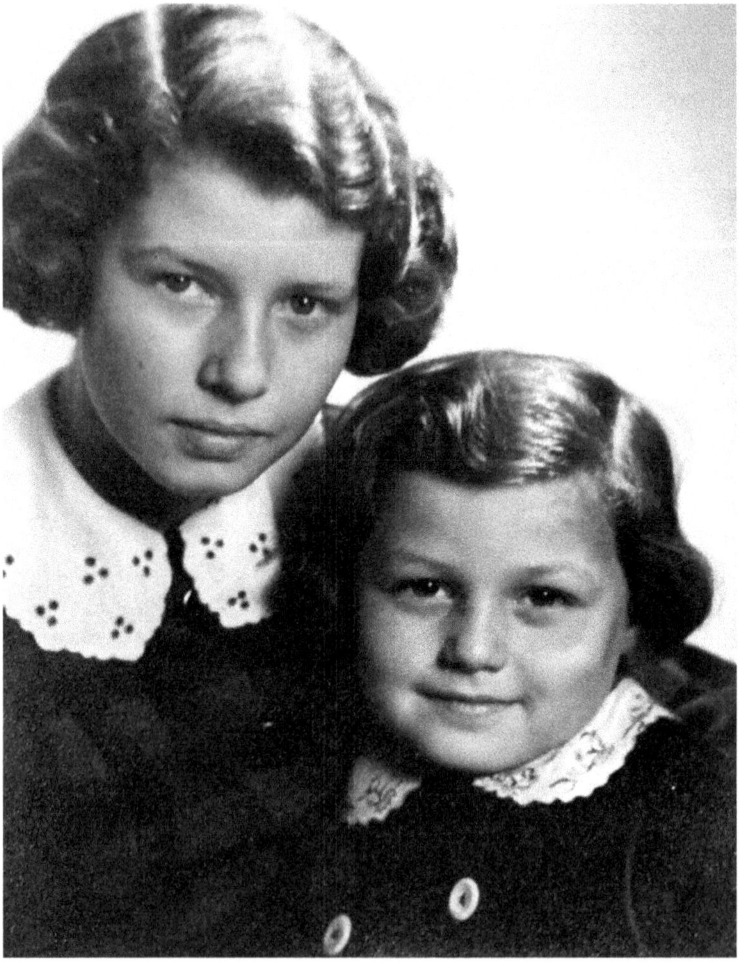

The author (age 13) with her little brother, Witeck (then 3 years old), who perished (age 14) in the Gas Chambers of Auschwitz.
The photo was acquired, after the war, from relatives living in America

"CATCH 22" — REIGNING IN THE "EMPIRE OF THE ABSURD"

A catch 22 is a paradoxical situation from which an individual cannot escape because of contradictory rules or limitations. The term was coined by Joseph Heller in his 1961 novel "Catch-22"

The phenomena of the Holocaust cannot be approached rationally, logic doesn't apply to them. Aiming to expound the paradoxes, I shall have to slaughter several "sacred cows", to bleach what has been tarnished and to reveal "Catch 22" wherever it shows its horns. Even behind the saber-rattling slogan "fight for freedom" hides a "Catch 22".

Let us now take under the microscope the main aspect of our problem. It took more than twenty years to wipe out this unfortunate expression: "You people went to your death like sheep to slaughter". This generalization wasn't true, that much history has revealed.

Let us analyze the problem of the historic heroes, of the Jewish underground and the uprisings in several ghettos. Take for example a certain ghetto, full of families with children. Let us assume for a moment that fifty young underground members can prepare a brilliant action and set the whole ghetto free. They, the young heroes (who probably have their families already placed in security, outside the ghetto), can escape into the woods and become partisans. What will become of the whole population...? It would be killed in reprisals and the whole ghetto would eventually be totally liquidated. Can they, the young leaders, take it upon their conscience and live with this crime?

Let us now dissect the scenario of a potential liberation of a whole concentration camp... Let us suppose for a while, that the leaders of such an uprising overpowered the guards (including those on the watchtowers), cut off the current, cut the barbed wires and set free ten thousand Jews. The question is — where would such ten thousand turn to, or for that matter — where would one thousand, or one hundred, or ten Jews find refuge…? Who would shelter them? How many Polish gentiles would risk their necks and those of their whole family to hide a Jewish fugitive…? The answer I got to this question, from a person very close to me was: "So what, so you would, all of you, die in dignity"… But the sheep didn't and couldn't believe that everybody would be killed by the Germans, stage by stage, so they hoped to survive and refused to die "in dignity" by tens of thousands.

You, the innocent people, know nothing about the high hopes nourished daily by fantastic and optimistic rumors. You, the innocent people, know nothing about the wild instinct for survival and the game of playing for time. Do you follow me, do you get my point? I am not so certain that I can convince you, now when one knows so much about the gas-chambers and crematoria. And that is exactly why I kept silent for forty years.

In spite of all such most serious apprehensions, I would perhaps have written or recorded my memoirs many years ago, if it weren't for one more hampering experience:

"Why didn't you people organize a general uprising? After all, you must have known that you are all doomed. You must have known that the transports are sent to death" — returns again and again the same accusation. I have now to prove, that in our seclusion, we didn't know for certain. Let me try to explain and reveal the constant "catch 22".

There were, in the year 1942, some vague rumors about the existence of extermination camps. It seemed preposterous. Massacres and mass-murders were committed right there in our presence. The Germans were not ashamed of it. Why would they go to all the trouble of sending multiple trains of thousands of Jews to some imaginary extermination camp? It must be a bad joke of the vicious Poles. Indeed, the Germans had a ready explanation for the transports. These Jews were allegedly sent to Ukraine. Over there, behind the Russian front — so they spread the rumor — "every pair of hands is needed, so as to unload and unpack many trains of supplies for the German army. The Jews will be employed there to prepare thousands of first-aid kits and tens of thousands of battle-rations for the German soldiers…" (They had to be distributed all over the long front line). "A mere tot" — went on explaining the SS-men –"could prepare a packet of biscuits, one corned-beef can, some tea, a little sugar. The mother, sitting next to the tot, would check and pack the units…" Sounds plausible? Anyhow, we wanted to believe it.

In May 1944, a general selection in the Plaszow camp netted all the emaciated prisoners and the last children. It was now known that this transport was sent to Auschwitz and there was no more chance for nursing any illusion. Still, some people claimed having seen personal greetings from the beloved ones, scribbled on some planks, sent from Auschwitz. The Capo of the kitchen got them, allegedly, from his children.

Let us suppose for a moment, that at this late stage, a general uprising was still an option. How could those heartbroken people participate in it, those depressed people who didn't know where their next meal would come from, who suffered from diarrhea and had no toilet paper, no shred of newspaper nor even a leaf… Such trivialities could break a giant. This uprising had no chance: it would certainly fail and end in a massacre of the total population of the camp.

The Germans had still other means of peeping order. Way back, when many Jews fled the cities, so as not to be trapped in a ghetto, they streamed to villages. The Jewish inhabitants of every village were counted, and the Germans imposed collective, mutual responsibility; would one Jew escape from the village — ten Jews would be executed in reprisal. This threat was implemented. Later, the same policy was applied to the working groups that returned to concentration camp from an outside job. Would one be missing, its Capo and ten members, picked at random, would be executed… Many men perished after one escaped from the group.

How could the Jews bear such calamities? Did they still have a shred of hope? Oh, yes, great hopes. There never was a week without some stupendous, good news. The poles and the Jews became brilliant war-strategists; before the southern European front became a reality — some "Napoleons" knew already that soon a great offensive would be launched from Greece and Yugoslavia, and shoot like an arrow straight to Poland… while The Russian bear will move and strike a decisive blow from the east.

As for the atomic bomb — the Poles and the Jews knew all about a top-secret lethal weapon, which would, with one stroke, devastate, annihilate and wipe all of Germany from the map of the world… Were such global false news detrimental to the morale of our people? Yes, the higher the hopes — the deeper the fall into depression.

IN THE "EMPIRE OF DEATH" — THERE IS NO PLACE FOR APOLOGETICA

"Qui s' excuse s'accuse" — states a French proverb, meaning "Who makes excuses — himself accuses". But De la Rochefoucauld wrote in his "Maximes" that "Nothing is as white or as black as it seems". Thus, we have already slaughtered some sacred cows when we inspected the issue of the fight for freedom; we have now to bleach certain ugly phenomena tarnished by sheer lack of information and comprehension.

A great urge drives me to try to explain, right at the beginning, how was it possible that Jews were willing to serve in the "OD" — the Jewish police (which was charged with most horrible missions)? How can one explain that Jews acted against brother Jews? I shall have also to explain the odious phenomenon of Jewish spies and informers acting on behalf of the Gestapo.

Let us start with the OD (service of order), which was to become later, the Jewish Police. It started in a most innocent way...

Here I have to go back to the beginning of the German occupation. All of a sudden, the same old "community council" — now called the Judenrat, found itself charged with many activities, well beyond its capacity. It was ordered to supply, day by day, squadrons of workers to be employed in changing numbers, in different labors and at different emplacements. All this had to be supervised. The food rationing coupons were also delivered by the Judenrat. There were long queues in front of its building and somebody had to keep order so that the weak and old would not be disadvantaged. The Judenrat appealed to the population asking young energetic men to volunteer for this service. The young men received a badge of "Civil Service". What can be more glorious than giving good services to the public…

The young volunteers never suspected what function this activity will turn to… It never crossed their minds that they would eventually become the Jewish Police, and what an odd police. After the ghetto was established, they received a cap with distinctions, afterwards they got a smart uniform, and eventually… a whip. The moment they realized what is happening to them — it was too late to retreat… When one of them saw the kind of missions imposed on the OD and tried to ask the commander, Symche Spira, to be relieved and released — Symche would shrewdly let him understand that if discharged, he would not be able to protect his family from dangers, in fact he himself would become endangered (He already knows too much, he cannot be discharged). It was further implied, that if he was depressed and felt like committing suicide — It will not help his family; his family might be even punished. Checkmate! Thus, our noble young man is trapped. There will come a day when he will be handed a list of people to be delivered by him for transport or for execution… As far as I know, only one OD man succeeded in extricating himself from OD with the help of medical certificates.

I am not claiming that all the OD policemen were innocent. Not all of them were recruited as Civil Service volunteers. Some joined the ranks of police at a later stage, but I had to make this attempt at objectivity.

Now you can ask the obvious question: Can anybody be objective in his judgment of the informers? Here too I have to write a scenario of sorts, which is far from being imaginary.

Let us take, for example, an imaginary man. Let us call him Mr.F. He is a respected lawyer of excellent reputation and irreproachable character. One day, this Mr.F. is accosted, in one of the ghetto streets, by an unknown little man of a non-descript type. "You are Mr.Friedman, aren't you?" The man asks politely. "I have a request to you, Mr.Friedman… and let me explain it without interrupting… You are kindly requested to accompany me to a certain person who wishes to talk to you. You understand that you cannot refuse… If you try to shake me off and flee, you won't be able to. You are being followed by a strong man. Now let us part, and follow me please from a certain distance, I shall lead you".

The speech is over. Mr.Friedman is helpless, has no choice. He is brought to a secret office of a Gestapo official in civilian clothes. The man opens politely. "Good day, Mr.Friedman. Please be seated... There is nothing to be afraid of. All I have to do is to explain what I am expecting of you. It will take no more than ten minutes, and then you can go and do whatever you had to. Nobody will know a thing about our meeting. You are a respected person, you are involved in many matters, you know many secrets. We hope to receive from you information on several subjects. First: who are the rich men that have still preserved their resources? Second: Who has connections with the communists? Third — who is known to be active in the underground...? Don't interrupt me, there is nothing you can do about your situation, you have no choice. You are not going to endanger your whole family, your wife and children. If you plan to escape, forget it. You could never take in one sweep all your next of kin, including your parents, your sisters and their families. So, you see the point... don't hope either that you will sell us some malarkey, providing names that we know of. You have to deliver the goods or... So now just take this paper listing your contacts and meetings with my people. You are now free to go, and our conversation did not exceed seven minutes. Good luck".

Here is another pattern of a checkmate, and the nice Mr.Friedman, who seven minutes ago was an honest citizen, turns under coercion into an informer. Such informers were many in the ghetto and in the concentration camps. Some of them were browsing in the city and denouncing Jews with forged identity papers, who tried to pass for Arian Poles.

We have now to deal shortly with the capos (the commanders of working groups) and the "Blockalteste" (the barrack commanders). It's simple. They didn't have to volunteer; they were hand-picked, being visibly young, energetic and athletic.

One such barrack commander explained to his friend why is he, sometimes, beating his own people. He drew out of his pocket a tiny slip of paper on which he recorded the statistics of death cases in each barrack. His barrack had the lowest number of victims. He then explained: "When I see on the rollcall an SS-man watching one of my men stepping out of line — I instantly beat him up, so the SS-man wouldn't shoot him..."

Exactitude and truth are dangerous words. Sometimes the absurd can parade as a travesty of the famous German exactitude in planning.

Does the Guinness book have an entry for the "Absurd", for the top of the absurd? Max von Sydow, the Swedish actor (who appeared in most of Ingmar Bergman's films), asked me this question once, while visiting my museum in Tel Aviv:

"You tell me that you went through seven concentration camps. As we know, the Germans had a hard problem with the scarcity of trains to carry supplies to the Russian front. How could they engage hundreds of trains to move millions of Jews like you, to transport them from distant lands and to move them between distant concentration camps?"

What was I to answer? That the Jewish appraise department of the Gestapo had the highest priority... That it provided jobs for thousands of the SS bureaucrats (so as to avoid sending them to the front?) The main answer is that it happened in the "Empire of the Absurd".

Another absurdity is "autonomy". It is an empty word, elastic like rubber. The Germans bestowed autonomy upon the Ruthenians (Ukrainians), the Lithuanians, the Latvians and whoever was willing to collaborate. They engaged them to serve as guards in all concentration camps.

So, the Ukrainians were naive — you will say. How naive could we, the Jews, have become? What lies were we ready to swallow? What illusions were we willing to cherish? Let us see.

PROLOGUE

The first episode will deal with an innocent fairy-tale. It concerns the prophecy of my survival, declared well before the outbreak of the war. I wouldn't dwell on it if it weren't probable that from this prophecy stemmed my fortitude, which might have influenced my fate.

Before I describe this trifling episode, I have to relate to a certain story. During the last years preceding the war, my dear father suffered two heart-attacks, and we lived in constant strain and anguish. One day a young aunt of mine came running to my mother and literally forced her to visit a miracle-working, wandering rabbi. My aunt, who was as far from religious circles as we were, had an astonishing experience with this rabbi. While talking about her family, the rabbi interrupted and asked, "Your husband, what has he here in his cheek?" — and he held his hand to his twitching cheek, as if a spasm would contract it. Indeed, my uncle suffered from "facialis", which disfigured the left side of his face. At the end of her visit, the rabbi said to my aunt: "You have only thirty-three zlotys in your purse — pay me, it will be enough".

When my mother, dragged along by my aunt, came to this rabbi, he declared immediately that her problem is her heart-ailing husband, but critical as his condition seems at the moment, it will greatly improve. (It did.) He, the rabbi, will help with his prayers. Then he insisted on seeing my mother's children. My mother obligingly brought my own humble person and my eight years younger brother Witek. I must have been fifteen, my brother seven. He was a brilliant child compared to me. Yet looking into his eyes the rabbi became sad, dropped his hands, swayed his head and in heavy silence moved over to me. He gripped me by my shoulders, shook me and exclaimed: "Oy, is dus a mazl kind" — meaning "oh, she was born under a lucky star". He repeated it twice more. I was stunned. I, who was in my eyes plain and certainly not a lucky child, why should I be so distinguished by this rabbi with x-ray eyes? I did not believe it, but I was impressed. I still am. How could he have known that I would survive and my little brother would not?

Later on, a gypsy woman whom I met in the Plaszow concentration camp, went even further in her prediction concerning my fate, but that will be related in the proper context of time. I wouldn't bring it up if it hadn't a bearing on my story. I also believe that coincidences are not incidental. A real mystery shrouds the so-called coincidences, as I shall be able to prove by many instances.

After this interlude, I now have to stick to facts and depict the entrance of the Germans into the picture. The drama that history played on us, in a mere couple of days, is best illustrated by this popular pre-war slogan and its parody coined in the aftermath of the short war. The gist of the slogan chanted in the streets was:

Strong and steady in determination
to defy Hitler — is this nation.

Its parody:
Strong and steady in determination
to sell out to Hitler — is this nation.

The rumors about the possibility of an imminent outbreak of war reached us while we were vacationing in a pastoral mountainside village called Rabka. We left Rabka in haste and returned home. We couldn't realize at this instance what role this lovely resort was to play in our lives a year and a half later.

THE FIRST STAGES OF THE GERMAN OCCUPATION

My story begins from the point of our return to Krakow. This is the story of the German occupation and the Holocaust — as I saw it.

Though over the years I told my daughter, Sigalit, many episodes from my experiences, I never put them in the right context and the right sequence. We actually never sat down, for a couple of hours, to tell the whole story in its general outline and in a cohesive way.

It is now time to put order into my relation. Still, introducing the Germans into my report means showing their policies and attitudes, well before we were to meet them face to face. We got the first taste of the German cruelty and intransigence as early as 1938. In that year, Hitler's Germany expelled all Jews who were born in Poland, robbing them of all their possessions. The Germans deposed them, with one suitcase, on the Polish frontier. Some were snatched and carried away in their pajamas.

Destitute as they were, they reached, most of them, the first south-western city in Poland, which happened to be Krakow. The Jewish Community council placed them in schools and synagogues and appealed to the Jewish population to accommodate them in private homes. My parents turned our magnificent living room, decorated with brocade wallpaper, into a shelter for three refugees. My parents provided them with meals, heating, cleaning and linen-washing, like in a good hotel. All that, over a period of four months, until they were able to find work and move out.

Five years later my mother came across one of them in the Plaszow concentration camp. He was in a fairly good condition, working in the glasses workshop in the camp. When my mother asked him kindly to repair her eyeglasses, he was not ashamed to ask an exaggerated price, even though he saw how emaciated we have become. That was for us some lesson in human relationship, but it failed to harden my mother's soft heart.

We got another such lesson on the very second day of the war. Though only one little bomb was dropped on Krakow during this short war of a couple of days, the alert sirens began wailing from the first day of the outbreak of war. Hungry for credible news, such as not disclosed in the Polish radio broadcast, we came, Mother and me, to my father's bank, which was situated in the heart of town on the main square. The news were confusing, but it was clear that the front was broken. Many people considered fleeing the town. We left father's bank in the company of a distinguished, refined gentleman, a family friend, Mr.M. When we crossed Grodzka street, our fine gentleman marched between mother and me gently cupping our elbows as a gentleman should. Before we reached the middle of the crossing, a shrill sound of alert pierced our ears. At that moment, our distinguished companion dropped our elbows and ran like a rabbit, leaving us in the middle of the crossing... Believe it or not, we laughed like crazy.

That was our first encounter with a new pattern of behavior, one that can only be experienced in a crisis, when a man drops his mask. Years of friendship would have never revealed it.

Over the next days the exodus began. It was believed, at that point, that if the Germans conquered west of Poland, Jewish men would become the endangered species. It couldn't possibly apply to the womenfolk. But the Poles too were touched by this fever, so that single men and whole families with children started the march eastward. Whoever had a car or a horse and carriage, started the journey with piles of personal belongings. Others started on foot. Soon the fleeing Polish army overtook the thousands of civilians, and Polish officers confiscated from Poles and Jews, all cars, horses, carriages, motorcycles, bicycles and prams. The perplexed civilians dropped their belongings and marched on foot.

Over the long distance between Krakow and Lwow, food became so scarce that one had to exchange a gold ring for a loaf of bread. People paid with dollars for a glass of water. Everyone was running and the Russians too. The Russian army coming from the opposite direction, moved in, and occupied eastern Poland. Many civilians returned and related about their exodus, others reached Lwow, but were received there less hospitably than the German Jews in Krakow, two years before. Those in Lwow who applied to the Russian authorities for a return visa to the German occupied part of Poland, were transplanted into the depth of Russia, being considered by the Russians as suspected elements. In spring 1941, the Germans conquered all eastern Poland. As for us, we were spared the very trepidation of reaching a decision. With my ailing father, leaving was out of the question for us. Thus, here we were in our beloved, marvelous historical city, Krakow, when the German army moved leisurely in, encountering almost no resistance.

Let me describe now the entrance of the German army into our town. Grown-up people cried openly in the streets. Here they are in the very center of the medieval quarter, filling the whole ancient market with their tanks and equipment. They are spread out on both sides of the splendid "Sukiennice" building, erected in pure Renaissance style. I had a special sentiment for this old market, where as a child, jumping on the cobblestones polished by centuries, I used to browse among squatting poultry sellers and flower stands.

You may wonder what did the Germans do, first thing after their deployment on the market...? Being covered with a thick layer of dust, they formed a queue to the old cistern pump, and started washing thoroughly their bodies and shaving their faces. Minutes after their deployment they were clean and presentable... Thus, we saw them, regiment after regiment, and that was our first encounter with the Germans. Some Polish women or tarts started fraternizing with the soldiers... otherwise everybody kept his distance. And what about the Jews...? The older generation remembered the good years of the Austrian occupation, most favorable to the Jews. The younger generation could not, in their wildest dreams, foresee into what hell this German occupation would turn.

It has to be stressed here, that there was a great difference between the army and the Gestapo in their conduct toward the Jews. But even the "SS" men were, at this stage, quite innocent and not well versed in the art of vicious persecutions.

I am no historian, but as far as I remember, the first official evil decree issued by the Germans concerned the filling of the ditches of anti-aircraft defense. Days before the outbreak of the war, all the population was engaged in digging those ditches that were to serve as shelters. Now, the filling of the same trenches was imposed on the Jews. We were but a few Jews in this quarter of the town, and we had to fill a long, zigzagging line of ditches, while the Polish gentiles stood watching on the ramparts, humiliating us with their remarks. A fat Polish boy stood above me with his hands on his hips and quipped: "It is high time to see the Jews do some work at last." I had some other qualms while filling the ditches with earth. I was working arm to arm with my former best friend Halinka Korngold. It so happened that just before the war, our parents, who were good friends, turned into mortal enemies. Here we were working side by side, silently, avoiding even furtive glances. But I shall soon return to this painful subject.

The schoolyear began this autumn much later than usual, only when things began to settle under the occupation. There were changes in the curriculum, and there was a plan to advance the date of the final exams of matriculation, because the future was so uncertain. Two classes were fused into one, the second being from another school. That was an additional hardship for a class facing the matriculation.

I made new friends that I have to mention briefly, because both were to play a role in my story. One of them was Ala, who behaved in a somewhat strange way. She sought friendship, but at the same time avoided more personal contacts. I lived not far from our school, and whenever I invited Ala to visit me or to do homework together — she flatly refused. She also refrained from inviting me to her place. It so happened that once I urgently needed some material that had remained with her. I knew her address and had to seek her out. It was somewhere in the Jewish quarter of the town. I am ashamed to admit that for the first time in my life, I visited the poor quarter — in my own town. The house was huge, ugly and had a whole annex behind its front, which was even more dilapidated. Around the inner courtyard ran endless galleries reachable over back-stairs of iron and giving access to little one-room or two-room flats. There was one toilet for every floor of many apartments. The whole house smelled of urine, dirt, suds of washing and putrefying vegetables. That's where Ala lived, and you can now understand how ashamed she was to receive my visit there. I was probably more ashamed to discover, so late, the world of poverty. I must have been raised in a cocoon.

My second new friend was Mirka, who will play a role in my story when we reach the stage of our life in the ghetto.

The school year turned for us into a short-lived episode. We, the Jewish students, were expelled from all high schools and primary schools. It was a hard blow, but sometime later, all high schools were closed. By that time,

I was much preoccupied with the situation at home. There were drastic changes in our apartment. Our lodgings consisted of five rooms, an eleven-meter-long corridor (in which we children played ball), two tiny servants' rooms and one storeroom. Now, the German housing office limited us to the occupancy of one room, all the others to be occupied by the Germans. We were almost lucky, I dare say, because many Jewish families were evicted from their apartments. We were even luckier; being able to declare two more rooms as already occupied, so that only two were seized by the Germans.

In one of the non-sequestered rooms, we accommodated the couple Likiernik, distant acquaintances, fugitives from Sosnowiec. The other room was already occupied by Olga, the former nanny of my little brother Witek. She functioned now in a new, elevated status. She was a pure German, raised in the Polish part of Silesia. She spoke a funny sort of Polish, her mother-tongue being German. She was a spinster, devoted to my brother with a possessive, jealous kind of love. Olga stayed with us, having nowhere to go, but my father noticed how uneasy she had become. She held my father in great esteem, so that one day he could dare to address her with these words: "Fraulein Olga, we have not forgotten that you happen to be a real German, and we realize your problem of loyalty. While many Poles turn their coats and declare themselves as Volksdeutsche, sons of the German nation — you, the real German, keep silent and fret. You have nothing to be ashamed of. If you feel like claiming your rights and apply for a Volksdeutsche identity card, do it, by all means — we shall understand". Olga felt as if a stone fell from her heart. She quickly applied for a new identity card. Thus, she became a protected lodger, entitled to keep one room out of our five.

Two years later, when asked by mother to shelter my brother Witek in the house of her old mother in Silesia, Olga flatly refused, even though her mother had 15 grandchildren and nobody would guess which one he was... But all that relates to a later period. Right now, her situation became quite profitable, as a German she was appointed 'Treuhander' (trustee) to a Jewish owned shop.

The two other rooms of our apartment were seized by the Germans, one for an army officer by the name of Ochs (bullock) which he really was — the second for a German female secretary, with a squirrel head imbedded in virginal frills of her many blouses of identical pattern. All together there were four capricious strangers, if you count the Likierniks, who were a couple of pampered egoists. And who was to serve all these people gathered now in our lodgings? Me, the tender hot-house plant, who never before had to use a broom, wash linen or dishes... The very sight of dishwater used to be nauseating to me.

I am sorry that I must register on the following pages very many trivial things. Life happens to be composed of so many trivialities. The most dramatic events were interwoven with them. When we shall eventually reach the point of the story where you, the reader, will expect a whole concentration camp to revolt and get free — I shall ask again the same question: how and what, do you suppose, will prepare and start the rebellion of an emaciated person, who doesn't know where his next slice of bread will come from. How will a man who doesn't have toilet paper, or any sort of paper for sanitary use, start this rebellion? You will maintain nonchalantly that by that time he is used to the lack of both. He isn't, it bothers him. Lesser trivialities can break the spirit of a person — and that is why you will bear with me, while I report on all the little hardships and miseries of this early period.

There was a time when we had three people engaged in the service of our household: a cook, a housemaid and a governess. After the losses of my father in the Korngold affair there were just two. Now our dear and funny cook Anna had to leave us. Gentiles were not allowed to serve Jews; anyhow we couldn't afford to pay her wages anymore. I missed her sound sense of humor. Being an illegitimate child, raised in an orphanage, she used to say of herself: "I am the fruit of free love".

Now, with my father incapacitated, mother became the minister of exterior affairs and cook, I became the housemaid. I had to clean the whole huge house, wax and polish the wooden parquets, wash the linen by hand, hoist up pails of coal from the cellar to make fire, in five stoves and one kitchen oven. Before the war I didn't even know who darned father's socks or how the maid put the coals into the stove, reaching with her bare hand over the flames.

I was not a kid anymore, almost 18... but I had to learn all this, from the very beginning, very quickly. I also had to peel vegetables and wash the dishes after eleven people, because the Likierniks brought one more couple to stay with them. They were rich and they were the paying lodgers entitled to get good service. The refined and spoiled Mrs. Likiernik, though raised in a poor family, was very fussy, demanding and capricious. The German secretary had special claims, I had to wash, starch and iron the frills of her countless blouses, but the officer Ochs surpassed everybody. He detested the army officers' mess, being a reclusive misanthrope. He ordered from us Jewish food, to be prepared according to his minute specifications. He was quite knowledgeable in this subject. So as to "keep the beast happy", we had to buy for him on the black market, a feat that we could ill afford. Once he threw a boot at me, when it was not polished like a mirror.

Somehow, I quickly adapted myself to the role of Cinderella. The worst were the morning hours; Provisions became scarce, because the Germans confiscated food for the army and the peasants started to hide their produce. In order to buy the essentials, we had to get up very early and stand in queue hours before the shop opened. Minutes after the shops opened, everything was sold out, the rest being stocked away to be sold on the black market. It was a severe winter and standing in queue from five o'clock was not enough. People were hoarding whatever was obtainable. Eventually the queue started forming at four or even earlier. My brother Witek, who was eight years old, volunteered to queue up, but was pushed and ousted by the Poles. We wouldn't let him do it anymore.

In all these gloomy circumstances, I was still aware of social injustice before the war, which only now became leveled. The janitor of our building lived with his three children in one room, while we lived in five rooms. This caused me a "sense of guilt" all the years of my adolescence. Wasik, the janitor, was drinking heavily. When in high spirits, he used to beat his wife black and blue. Once, after a drinking bout, he took an axe and bashed in and smashed all the furniture. His little boy, hiding in a corner, was probably greatly amused by this scene because he ventured from his corner: "Papa, you have forgotten the wall-clock".

Right now, Mr. Wasik was faring much better. He offered his services to the Germans and got a job as parquet layer. He had to submit formal bills for his work, bills written in German. He turned to my father, who typed for him his bills in perfect German. When it came to spell the janitor's name — Leon Wasik ("wasik" meaning a little moustache) father had a problem. There is no way of writing Wasik in German, after all it has to sound like Vounshick. But my father, with his clipped sense of humor, invented a solution and turned it into Von Shick, which is a titled name of German aristocracy. The solution so pleased Mr.Wasik that it gave him ideas. He became bold enough to ask for new identity papers on the grounds that his name is good old German name — Von Shick. Thus, thanks to my father, we had now another 'Volksdeutsche' living in the same house, this one presenting some danger.

When I was nine years old, I used to play with Wasik's vulgar daughter Helka. I was so impressed with her free manners that I started to wipe my nose on my sleeve and to curse in saucy language. I was very proud of my emancipation. Mother was of course shocked to the core, but my liberal father solved the delicate problem, "Let them play together, and let my daughter distinguish between the bad and the good manners" — he said, and that's the way it was, after her father became a "volksdeutscher", Helka snubbed me without shame. She passed close to me, turning her head away as if I smelled. She was a 'Volksdeutsche' now and I was a stinking Jewess…

Our connections with the Dr.Korngold family, the owners of the building, were no less ambivalent. As I mentioned before, the relations between the two families, linked with ties of friendship over a long period, turned into enmity and downright hostility. Three years before the war, it transpired that Dr.Korngold was heavily indebted, not only to my father (a fact that my father concealed from my mother). He, a witty but unreliable lawyer, speculated on coins and currency and lost all his money (including my father's money).

There was a long lawsuit which probably caused my father his heart attack. Living as tenants in their building, we were no longer on speaking terms. This infected on us, the children of both couples, and my dear friend Halinka passed me on the staircase without looking at me. We both suffered agony but had to be loyal to our parents. Thus, two girls, two friends of mine avoided me in our house.

Now, under the occupation, Dr.Korngold made a pathetic move. He came down from his apartment, rang at our door and said to my parents: "Dear Henry and Rosa, let bygones be bygones… Whatever passed between us should have no bearing on our relations now, in war time, when we are all sitting ducks. Please, let us renew the old friendship and spend the evenings of the curfew together like we used to in the old times." And so it was. We all became friends again and discussed politics throughout the long evenings. The crazy dear Halinka was so relieved that she bit my ear. Halinka had an inimitable language of her own. She said: "Without you I was so eaten up by spleen and 'weltschmerz' that I felt my fingernails aching".

So far, I have depicted only the inner world of our house. But the outer world started to penetrate our lives, more and more.

One day, Dr.Korngold was seized by the Gestapo in the street, taken to the Gestapo main station and forcibly fed huge chunks of raw pork-fat. He, who liked ham, who never ate "kosher", had to swallow now raw fat of swine just because he was a Jew. He vomited, was beaten up and fed again this abominable fat. Whatever he threw up he was made to lick up from the floor.

To me it was the first case of German persecutions I had known of. But it has to be stressed that we lived far from the Jewish quarter, the theater of German oppressions. As I said before, the Germans were still "innocent" in this game, they only started inventing persecution. At this stage, on the general play they only claimed a contingent of young Jewish males for forced labor. Sometimes they seized Jews from the street, some of them never to return.

The Jewish community council, now called the "Judenrat" had to cope with the situation by supplying daily the required number of Jews for work. They were called up by the "Judenrat", applying the rotation system. Rich Jews could pay for a replacement. Sometimes, the Germans ordered to supply them a squadron of girls. I was called up several times and it turned out to be great fun. We were taken to the "Blonia" fields and ordered to pick the sweet-smelling lime-tree blossom, which is used for medicinal tea. We worked singing and it turned into a lovely picnic. As said, it was all very innocent at the beginning.

Eventually, the Germans took forces of men far away to labor camps, and some of them escaped, returning very sick and heart-broken. But that was later. Otherwise, the Gestapo took its pleasures in catching pious Jews and cutting off their beards and side curls. Many bearded Jews took to walking the streets with bandaged beards, pretending toothache. Sometimes drunk hordes of SS-men played their games in the Jewish quarter, smashing furniture and beating up Jews without distinction of age or sex. Gradually, only gradually, the situation grew worse and worse. The way you acquire good skills, they started to acquire vices.

The next formal hostile edict imposed on the Jews was the wearing of the Jewish badge, the stigmatic white armband with a blue Shield of David. In the provinces it was a yellow star but in Krakow it was this band, worn on the upper arm. I made a protest against this discrimination in my own very personal way. One day Halinka and I took out ski-equipment, and without the Jewish badge, we went to the hills and slopes in the vicinity of Krakow, for a real skiing spree. Mother was in despair. "Look" — she said — "what you are risking for the mere pleasure of skiing. If just Helka Wasik were to denounce you, you would be arrested and..." We had to promise never to try it again. Thus, I remember with nostalgia my last ski outing. I was so good at this sport, so good at slalom, telemark and two styles of Christiania. I loved the smell of snow, the sparks on snow and the ecstatic feeling of falling on the soft quilt of snow. Father understood that I needed this little demonstration which helped me to bear the drudgery of enslavement.

In this long sad winter, I had to do something with myself. I decided not to succumb passively to stagnation. I got in touch with some girls from my class. We decided to form a group and prepare for a clandestine secondary school exam. In our case it was doubly dangerous.

There were two traitors among our former teachers. Fraulein Theresa "Something", who used to teach German, was still in town holding a high position in the German administration. She was allegedly planted as a spy before the war. The sweet old principal of our high school, Prof. Julius Ippoldt, was of German origin. He allegedly said that he is too old to change his Polish skin, anyhow, his daughter and son did declare themselves Volksdeutsche. Thus, the Ippoldt family played it safe on both sides. Dear old Ippoldt, professor of Germanists at the University, was a real humanist and a brilliant pedagogue, but his sour spinsterish daughter posed a problem... We thought her quite capable of denouncing us. Under such circumstances who of the teachers would dare examine us? Who would dare sign such clandestine certificate without the ministry's formal questionnaires, supervision and blessing? The problem was solved — we would prepare and wait what happens in the big world... Didn't everybody predict that this war couldn't last long. The Germans would surely run out of raw materials and supplies... In fact, only six years later I was able to present myself for the French baccalaureate and pass it.

I made several other plans and decided to reach their parameters on my own. Otherwise, what should I do with myself withering as a housemaid? How could I better myself? I made a threefold plan: 1) I must improve my English .2) I must learn typing. 3) Learn shorthand writing. There was a fourth mission; I had to teach my brother Witek, so that he wouldn't fall behind, now that the school expelled Jews. But that was a real trifle. He was so gifted that he needed a bare minimum of instruction.

In my high school curriculum, I received good tutoring in German, French and Latin, the three were compulsory for final exams. I took English for one year in private lessons and reached the level of the first stories by Oscar Wilde, like "The Swallow", "The Happy Prince". From here to the mastery of English was a long way. I picked at my uncle's house no more and no less but "The Pickwick Papers" by Ch.Dickens, one of the most difficult books in English. I started to read it. At the first reading I understood nothing, absolutely nothing. Still, I kept reading it to the very end. I refrained from using the dictionary. With my good ear and facility in assimilation of foreign languages (I was excellent in all three taught at school) I knew that I shall overcome the difficulties by perception, by conjecture and by guessing. I forced myself to read this difficult book for a second time. I have begun to see the light. After I read it patiently for the third time, word by word, I became capable of reading any book in English... It was achieved at a high cost, but it was a breakthrough, a great victory, perhaps the greatest of my educational career.

To learn typing was a child's game. My third venture — learning shorthand — I became a dead duck. I never used it and forgot without regrets. Later on, when I studied in France, after the war, I could apply it. Typing was to prove a great asset in several instances. When I sat down to a typewriter after an interval of full twenty years, it took me half an hour to recapture this skill. Thus, you can see, my dear grandchildren, that whatever you learn — is yours! Nobody can take it away from you, not even the Germans... and I am not sermonizing. It is a treasure and a source of pride. Losing eventually 30% of your acquisitions — is a trifle and a good price to pay for self-esteem. I am not being sanctimonious or preaching, my whole life proves it, stage after stage.

My only recreation, if one can call it that, were our evening chats with the Korngold family. She, Mrs. Korngold, was pessimistic by nature. Her husband, though crushed after his incident with the Gestapo, tried valiantly to preserve his optimism in spite of all. She would say: "We shall never get free from the German yoke. Read it for yourself in the newspaper. They are all over Europe and advancing in North Africa. Trace it on the map and you can see their astute deployment". "No" — interposed my father — "learn to read between the lines. Take one sentence at a time and analyze it. Take this sentence: 'Our army is being deployed along the lines planned in advance.' — What does it mean? It is an exercise in escapism. It either means a standstill or a partial retreat". Thus, we were taught to read between the lines.

In reality, the political situation was critical. Immersed as I was in relating our personal affairs and the atmosphere in our house, I failed to describe the main events of this period.

The Jews of pre-war Poland constituted a very sizable part of the general population, almost nine percent. Under the German occupation, the Jews of Krakow were counted and registered already by the end of November 1939. The new "Judenrat", the elected Jewish Community Council, was responsible for the distribution of ration coupons issued to the registered Jews. But these food coupons allotted to the Jews, were considerably limited in quantities as compared to the rations granted to the Arian Poles. The Jews received only the most basic victuals, and even these were reduced by half — as if a Jew possessed only half a stomach.

A Jewish family needs probably less living space — decided the German Housing Office. Already in December 1939, many Jewish families were evicted from their tenements. They didn't get a written order to vacate the premises at a certain date. The Gestapo officials just knocked at their door and ordered the unsuspecting family out into the street, immediately. When I shall speak later of "years of life with a toothbrush as only possession", I shall be exaggerating... These people were not even given the time to take a toothbrush with them. When freezing downstairs, they dared to ask permission to fetch a coat — they were beaten up and driven away.

By this time, the Gestapo people were already quickly pilfering the apartment before sealing it off on behalf of the Housing Office. Now you will understand how lucky we were, our family, to be squeezed into one room of our apartment.

The sporadic cases of eviction and extradition, resettling whole families, were quite marginal in the general outline of the German plans for the Jews. Somebody had already tried to resettle all the Jews of Poland as early as 1937. At that time, the Polish government engendered a brilliant idea of transferring all its Jews to... Madagascar. This colonial French island had a mild climate, and caring for the good fate of its Jews, the Polish government engaged in negotiations with the French government. In fact, this plan was even older, and Theodore Herzl was not adverse to it at a certain stage, hoping that eventually the Jews would 'hop' over from Madagascar to Palestine — or so my father explained this matter to me. Hitler merely picked up the idea, but somehow had to abandon it. Perhaps Madagascar was too good for the Jews... perhaps it had some strategic importance.

Hans Frank, the Governor of the "General Government" of Poland, would like to see the Jews leave for Madagascar. It would spare him (who represented the civil rule) the most unpleasant contacts and collaboration with the elitist (in barbarism) formation of "Einsatz–truppen", a branch of Heydrich's "Sicherheitsdienst" — the "SD" in short.

Frank, the civilian authority, had to comply. Thus, in this first "Aktion" against Jews, which was executed in the Jewish quarter of Kazimierz — several inimical formations took part acting in a concerted move. These formations drove into Kazimierz on December 4th, 1939. Their aims and tasks were different. While the SS-men evicted whole families from better apartments and searched thoroughly for diamonds, gold and furs, the brave knights of the "Einsatztruppen" diligently destroyed and burned the ancient synagogues of Krakow. They were already well versed in this art, having passed their internship in destroying the synagogues of Silesia, turning the praying Jews into living torches. While the SS-men were not above cutting off a Jewish finger together with a ring that wouldn't come off — the independent Einsatztruppen knights, acting without Frank's orders, "took care" of the oldest historic "Stara Boznica" synagogue, constructed in the 14-th century. They acted in their own way and style. Though the Jews got a secret warning before the "Aktion", and many moved out for a couple of days, the Orthodox Jews sought salvation through prayer. The Special Commando of the SD was not satisfied with the few people encircled in the synagogue... so they just caught Jews from the vicinity of the building, among them many liberal, assimilated Jews which were dragged into the synagogue. Now this strangely mixed crowd of different backgrounds, was ordered to file next to the Ark and to spit on the precious, fragile parchment of the Torah scrolls.

There was in this crowd a notorious Jewish gangster by the name of Max Redlich, who most probably had never crossed the threshold of the synagogue. The orthodox Jews, suffering hell, spat obligingly, believing that the Almighty would surely forgive this desecration of His holy scroll, performed under duress. The profane gangster, Max Redlich, refused to spit on the Hebrew letters. He even made a statement, reported later by a drunk participant of this orgy. He remarked pensively: "I have done many a thing in my life, but that is one I wouldn't do". He was shot on the spot. All the others were to share his lot, only the old synagogue was not shot. It was set afire.

Hans Frank was not amused. He wanted Krakow, the lovely capital of his "General Government" preserved intact. He too wanted to render Krakow 'Judenrein', cleared of the Jewish vermin, but he would do it along a different pattern. He would relocate the Jews somewhere to the Lublin region. Instead, he was stuck with more and more Jews and Poles because the SD and its "Einsatztruppen" cleared off Jews and Poles all of western Poland, annexed now to the "Reich" — the German homeland. "Wehrmacht", the German Army, also hated this imposed traffic. In fact, they hated the SD and the SS. This was a public secret, we all knew it. These relocations engaged the whole railway system, cutting the army off from its vital train services.

The "Jew traffic", run by these abominable formations, paralyzed the war efforts of the Army. This absurd situation was to last to the very end of the war. There is a possibility, that the German Army, the "Vehrmacht", would have won this war if it had not been deprived of the railway network, because of the huge transports of thousands of Jews. (Thirty years after the war, Governor Frank's son wrote a biting criticism of his father's action.)

As for the Jews, they became as pragmatic as they could, under the given circumstances. They had their flirt with the civil authorities. When the former Jewish Community Councils were turned into the "Judenrats", responsible to these civil authorities, they found it in their best interest to supply, as quickly as ordered, Jewish labor squad to these bodies. Their secret was, that by seemingly collaborating, they spared the Jews the anguish of being seized from the street, beaten, mutilated or sent to work in some distant region, unable to inform the worried family regarding their whereabouts. Shoveling snow or digging ditches around Krakow was not so bad after all. The rich Jews could pay for a voluntary replacement, the sick could be exempted. This policy was "nolensvolens" adopted by the honest Marek Biberstein (my friend's father), the first president of the "Judenrat" under the German occupation.

Another wise policy of the "Judenrat" was rendering the Jews useful and essential to the German industrial effort, and especially to the Armaments Inspectorate. The Jews, being skilled in many trades and enmeshed in the Polish net of industry, became indeed indispensable to the German administration. Soon the time would come when Frank would do everything to reduce the numbers of Jews in his kingdom. Yet, he would have to leave in Krakow those who had documents signed by German industrialists or "Treuhanders", thus testifying to the importance of these Jews to the German war-effort.

In spite of the influx of provincial Jews to the "General Government" territory, the exodus of Jews from Krakow started well before the publication of the edict pertaining to the establishment of a ghetto. Between April and November 1940, Frank got rid of some 23,000 Jews, out of some 80,000 before the war — if my sources are reliable.

Before the ghetto was formally opened on March 20th of 1941, the Jewish population withdrew or was reduced to 15,000, even though Frank planned initially to limit its residents to 5,000 specialists with their families.

The head of the "Judenrat", Marek Biberstein, prompted by good advisors, tried even bribery to grant the permit of residence in Krakow to ten thousand Jews, more than allotted so far. Though I worked for a while at this registration office — I was not aware of this secret. It is hard to imagine the straightforward Marek Biberstein, offering a bribe to a middleman who was to divide this sum among several German officials, posted in key positions. He must have been so clumsy and gauche in this attempt, that he got arrested and was sentenced to two years prison...

But before we reach the prospect of the institution of a ghetto, I must cover many other subjects. Beside my little personal world, and this of the Jewry of Krakow, there was also somewhere the big world that had a bearing on our existence.

How can I describe what the fall of Paris meant to us! All I can say is that the whole population of our city cried openly. You saw people in the street with tear-stained faces and red eyes. Thus, they cried when the Germans entered our town, when Warsaw fell, and thus, they cried when the statue of Adam Mickiewicz, the national poet, was toppled by the Germans.

Did the Jews cry contemplating the fallen statue of Adam Mickiewicz? Yes, they did. He was a symbol, we were raised on his poetry which was greatly valuated. Mickiewicz was sympathetic to the Jews, and probably initiated into the world of the Jewish Kabbala. He even used some veiled Kabbalistic hints.

The statue of Mickiewicz was facing my father's bank, which was situated in my grandparents' house. My grandfather was famous for his hospitality and love of merry company. There was even a jingle on this subject, passed from mouth to mouth; "Why is Mickiewicz standing there so lonely and sad? Could he take a glass at Rose's, he would be merry and glad". Here is one more example of our ambivalent relations with our Polish compatriots.

As I said, the general atmosphere was glum. But then, you do not know the Poles and their vivid imagination. Throughout the six years of war and occupation, they were forever diligently inventing and concocting imaginary, secret, excellent news. A whole year before America even considered entering the war, there were already rumors about the American army allegedly being concentrated in Yugoslavia, on the rear of the German army... There was no end to the variants of such good news. They had an ambivalent impact on the morale of the population. Wild hopes would flare up in an instant, and the moment this wonderful news were disproved — the hearts sank even deeper.

Never underestimate the psychological effect of this seesaw. When you ask why all the Jews didn't rise up in a rebellion, knowing that they were condemned to death — keep in mind two things; They never believed that they were all going to be killed, and they were almost daily fed such magic, excellent news. Four years before the atom bomb was conceived and produced, there were apocalyptic rumors about a most secret weapon that could annihilate whole Germany in one stroke. Please, make an effort to understand these shifting moods fed by fables that were believed. Throughout my whole life, I have always wanted to know the bare truth, all the bitter truth, but most people prefer soap-lather of illusions, and they are probably right. We need illusions like oxygen. When they evaporate — it is as dangerous as cutting off oxygen. At the time I am speaking of, the year 1940, we had one more source of information, this one a very pragmatic and reliable — the B.B.C.

Did I mention that all the wireless receptors in Poland were confiscated by the Germans? No, I didn't, I forgot. Well, the very possession of a wireless was punishable by death. How then can I speak about listening to B.B.C.? There was a way. My mother's sister, the diminutive Helcia, her husband Olek Klein and their daughter Rutka (who was like my sister), had a small, sunny apartment. There was only one lodger, the good German of the old generation, bank director Mr.Forber. He was so friendly to the Klein family that he told them to use his room whenever he was away on his weekend visit to Berlin. Did he imply that they could use his wireless? Who will ever know?

Anyhow, taking the greatest precautions, we tuned his wireless to B.B.C. and listened avidly to the news in Polish. Often my aunt invited me to stay with them overnight between Saturday and Sunday and listen with them. Sometimes they invited my brother Witek, who was nine years old by then. This brilliant boy was capable of reporting to us, word by word, the whole long news without taking a single note. He was able to point out on our maps all the movements of the armies.

My weekends with the Kleins were a treat for me in this different atmosphere. Somehow, there was a lot of fun going on. My uncle Olek was endowed with a ribald brand of humor. His wife had none and Rutka was merely receptive. Olek missed a son. Now, during the war, a son of sorts was sent to him. It was the son of Cousin Sarah of Lodz. When the ghetto was established in Lodz, Sarah decided to send her son Eddie to her mother in Krakow. But the grandmother and the domineering great grandmother were not able to manage this wild horse aged seven, and so he was placed with Olek and Helcia. Both, uncle Olek and Eddie were in seventh heaven. They played wild games and turned the house "topsy turvy". When I stayed with them for a weekend, it happened one evening, that Rutka and I took off our clothes and went to the bathroom. After we emerged from there, what did we find? Our slips and bras were hanging high on the lamp, while Olek and Eddie were dancing around them the dance of wild Indians... We had to pay ransom to redeem them. These were the best moments I remember from this drab period. But even there, amidst this merry and warm atmosphere, the privations were tangible. When my aunt Helcia eventually bough sometimes a cake of butter, she tried to make it last for a long time, so long that it became rancid. With my aunt it was like in this proverbial joke: When does a Jew eat an orange? When it is rotten or when he feels rotten.

At home, the situation became more and more depressing. There was only one change for the better. A sweet man moved in, instead of the abominable Likierniks. He was the small, rotund Mr.Brandt, a prominent Jew from Berlin. One day the German housing office sent an inspection to check if there was one more room disposable in our apartment. The inspectors passed from room to room, and my father had to inform them about its occupants. In what used to be my room now lived Mr.Brandt. He was taking his afternoon nap, covered with a soft thick quilt. "Who lives here"- asked the inspector, opening the door. "Herr Director Brandt" — answered my father in a whisper. -"Is he a "Reichsdeutscher" (a German from the homeland)? Father did not bat an eyelid answering in the affirmative: "Jawohl, of course he is"- still in a whisper, so as not to awake him. The inspectors clicked the heels in honor of "Herr Director" and my father closed the door softly. If only the inspectors could have caught a glimpse of the well-hidden Jewish nose of "Herr Director" — that would have been the end of us.

While the Germans evicted many Jewish families from their homes, we remained still more or less safe in our lodgings. Soon, another hostile edict took us by the collar. The Jews had to deposit all their valuables in foreign currency, as well as in silver, gold or platinum. The Jews were to hand them over to a certain bank against a formal receipt. I only mention this worthless receipt because it could have proved of great importance ten years later, when the sums of German restitution were settled. Had we been able to retrieve this receipt, we would have been very rich in the last twenty years.

Right then, when this edict was published, our financial situation was bad enough, in fact it was bad from the very beginning of the war. Why did we, rich people, fare so badly? It must be explained. My father was most punctilious and scrupulous in his business affairs, as a banker he also had a representation of the Polish National Lottery. When the outbreak of war became almost a certainty, my father had to send his whole cash capital to the Center of National Lottery in Warsaw. Friends tried to dissuade him, but my father argued that he, the good citizen, must not fail to pass the funds to Warsaw — "it's a question of honor", and besides, he may lose his license... He mailed the whole sum, and even received the whole lot of National Lottery tickets, that became worthless two days later... Thus, we were left without cash the very day the war broke out. We had to sell our possessions from the first day. It so happens that even now very old people from Krakow mention my father as a very rich man. He wasn't. We possessed nothing except what was in our flat. Mother liked to live well, but my parents acquired nothing except art objects. My father had to support three families — ours, and these of his two sisters. His mother lived with his younger sister and her husband. This husband was an "almost lawyer", who never took his final exam. Because he had a cultivated flowery handwriting, my father kindly employed him as bookkeeper, with a real bookkeeper checking his work. My father also financed the studies of his older sister's son in Italy, and the expenses of this divorced sister's cures. He was lucky to have only six siblings and to be the richest of them.

My granny had eleven siblings. I asked my father once how many they were indeed because I had heard more than twelve names mentioned. He answered in his jocular way: "I really don't know, I once tried to count them, reached the number of sixteen, not including miscarriages and... lost count". Forgive me this anecdote out of context — the account of father's burdens and all this family background... I inserted them only to prove that my father was not a man of means. My mother had one most regrettable idiosyncrasy, which I unfortunately have inherited: she had no respect nor attraction to diamonds, rubies, emeralds or gold. Consequently, she possessed only some antique rings and bracelets of silver and a watch. She would not let father buy her even one gold brooch or similar trinket.

Thus, we found ourselves impoverished from the very beginning. We had very valuable pictures and carpets, and these had to be rescued before the Germans made a list of sequestered art objects in our flat. Then they were ours no more, they belonged to the German state. There were other objects of art to be rescued. We had, for instance, whole scenes of court and boudoir society, depicted on Sevres and Maissen porcelain, of the 18th century. I could stand for hours studying every expression, every finger of these exquisite porcelain personages. There was also a collection of miniatures and ivory objects. To hide them, to replace the paintings on the walls, and to eventually sell them at great loss — was now my mother's task.

Now comes the main feature: My father had a numismatic collection of rare historic coins. Some of them were ancient Greek and Roman, most were old European. Among the old Polish coins there were some white ravens, like the ones minted in 13th century Poland and bearing a Hebrew inscription. How possible? The Jewish money lenders of this period got for some time a minting license (to finance the wars of a Polish king) and proudly minted part of them with Hebrew texts, like "To Metshialav (Mieczyslaw), the King of Poland".

When the aforementioned edict concerning the deposition of foreign currency was published, my father was in despair. How could he part with his dear collection? Nevertheless, he claimed that the acquisition of all these coins was registered in his books, and the day the Germans claimed them, he would have to prove that they were duly deposited at the appointed bank. Our remonstrations were to no avail. Father insisted, and father's health was so precarious that we could not endanger it. Thus, mother and I took the whole numismatic collection, together with shares linked to the dollar, to the main bank in city center. You should have seen the face of the clerk who received us. He changed all his colors at the sight of such rare coins. It took hours to register each and every coin. Finally, he handed us a receipt. This receipt, with all the lists of specifications, was then hidden in our private safe built in the bottom of a cupboard. There was nothing else left in this safe when we left our flat. In 1947 mother came back to Poland and tried to retrieve the receipts. They could have served as evidence and achieved very high payments. It was not to be, but that is a story that belongs to the aftermath of the war.

What did we live on between the autumn of 1939 and the spring of 1942 — don't ask me. I don't know how mother managed it, I really don't remember. My maternal grandmother, Felicia Rose, possessed fabulous diamonds. Living alone, she was afraid to keep them, and one day asked my father to take them over and hide them. She knew that we had hidden some valuables in the outer wall of the kitchen for the case of a sudden and unexpected eviction. We could have hidden her diamonds there, walled in. Any other son-in-law would jump at this opportunity — not my father. He remained adamant, explaining to her: "One day, when you have a bad dream, you will come running and ask me to break this safe and... No, please, release me from this heavy responsibility". Thus, the diamonds remained with my granny, and their further story will be told in this recording.

You may wonder why my grandmother didn't offer some of her diamonds to her daughter, knowing how badly we fared. The truth is that even she didn't know how impoverished we had become, and my mother wouldn't ask for help. She was too proud. There was a very peculiar relationship between my grandmother and my mother. The two didn't agree even whether it is day or night. They had such diametrically opposed characters, and both had hot tempers.

At this point of time, with the Likierniks gone, with Ochs sent to the front and replaced by a more lenient officer, I could start a new career. I volunteered to work for the Jewish Social Welfare. It was subjected to the Polish Main council of Welfare, both bodies being financed by the International Red Cross, both being controlled by the Germans. The office I worked in was responsible for the District of Krakow, covering the South-Western part of former Poland. Our rooms and storeroom constituted an annex to the main offices of the Jewish Social Welfare. The president of this body was Dr. Weichert, a distinguished figure from Warsaw. His was in a very high position that automatically put him into contact with the occupation authorities. The whole budget of this institution depended on the whims of these authorities, and he had to wheel and deal with them. In the aftermath of the war, Dr. Weichert was prosecuted for his allegedly murky dealings with the Germans. He was exonerated, but a shadow of suspicion remained hanging over his head.

I shall reduce the problem to a few sentences. The question is how his personal privileges were obtained. Were they granted by German goodwill or was a price attached to them? When the whole Jewry of Krakow was clustered between the walls of the ghetto, Dr. Weichert and his family were free to live in town... But his main problem of conscience was the following (to reduce it to the basics); how to deal with the German conditions so as to allow and support the existence of the Jewish Social Welfare.

Let us assume that the Jewish population in Poland constituted thirteen percent of the general population. In that case, the Jews were entitled to receive thirteen percent of all the funds and goods provided for distribution by the International Red Cross. The Germans turned to Dr. Weichert, with more or less these words: "we have no intention of remitting to you Jews your due of 13%. Either you will accept some five to seven percent and confirm with your signature the receipt of thirteen percent — or you will receive nothing... and the Poles will be quite happy about it". Here you have, my children, a real problem of conscience. What would you do, my children, if you were in Dr. Weichert's boots? Would you proudly refuse, while part of the Jewish population was starving and shivering in rags? But then, who in the whole world seemed to care if the Jews of Poland received thirteen or five percent of the help offered by the International Red Cross? Dr. Weichert gave in, allegedly accepted these conditions. This acquiescence became the pivot of the accusations raised against him in the trial after the war.

But let us return to the office. I received this job thanks to the recommendation of Dr.H.Hilfstein, our distant relative. He was a great Zionist, the founder of the primary and secondary Hebrew school. He himself never learned Hebrew, a fact that he diligently concealed by opening his speeches with a hefty "Shalom". Whenever he came to us for a visit, he would variably greet me: "How are you, goya". He never forgave my parents that they didn't send me to Hebrew school. It was the same Dr.Hilfstein who placed in the main office of the Jewish Social Welfare his favorite, young Dolek Liebeskind, who was to become the leader of the Jewish underground. I know now that Dr.Hilfstein remained in touch with Dolek Liebeskind till the death of this hero. This pale young man was later to organize several famous actions of the underground, among them the Cafe Cyganeria attack, in which many Germans were killed. It has to be noted that to this very day the Polish underground takes credit for this action, without actually having had a part in it.

At this stage we were a family of sorts, and I was on excellent terms with Dolek Liebeskind and all the people employed in the main office. My boss, presiding over the Krakow District, was Dr.Richard Lowenherz (Heart of Lion and... Richard of course). He was the former head of the Jewish Community Council in Gdansk (Danzig). The man was highly responsible, honest, dry and more of a German than a Jew in his conduct. These traits of his character are best illustrated by the situation he created several months after I started my work as his secretary.

It was a very cruel winter in 1940, and our office was in possession of a storeroom full up to the ceiling with warm clothes and solid food. Yet, Dr.Lowenherz distributed them most sparingly to the district institutions, depending on us. He claimed that he had to preserve the main bulk of our treasures for the next winter. It became a grave problem to me because nobody seemed to be aware of this strange policy of my boss. I had to do something, but I couldn't... me, the little mouse, I could not go to Dr.Weichert and turn informer against him. I suffered agonies. Almost daily, poor people in rags knocked at our door and asked for help, which they didn't get elsewhere. Dr.Lowenherz dismissed them, stating flatly that we were the district office, and there were various institutions dealing with individual problems... What did I do at such instances? All I could do was ask my parents to give me some wardrobe items. I handed them out behind Dr.Lowenherz's back, often together with the sandwich I brought for my lunch.

Once, a blind beggar-woman in stinking rags, painfully climbed the stairs to our office, sat down and asked my boss for help. According to her statement, she left her two small children in the cellar where she lived, closing the door with a key. She supported her children and herself by begging in the streets. Dr.Lowenherz gave his usual answer that we deal only with institutions... At this instance I and Fela, the second secretary, interceded as by accord, and implored Dr.Lowenherz to do something. At least, will he let us, please, take her address. He said: "Oh, well, you can verify her claims if you wish to". After working hours, we went straight to the given address. And indeed, what we saw was most appalling. We discovered in this cellar poverty beyond description. Peeping through a narrow window on ground level, we discerned inside this hovel two pale, emaciated children on straw. The children wept and we wept, we felt utterly helpless. From the next day on we brought food, clothes, money — whatever we could collect for them. We didn't let the poor blind beggar become ground by the wheels of bureaucracy before we contacted the appropriate institution. But I was crushed after this experience. Fela, who was a poor widow's daughter, was touched to the core but did not feel guilty. I emerged from this episode with a deep sense of guilt. Guilt, because I had not been made aware that such poverty could exist, that I only read about it in books... believing it to be the cruelty of past ages, or literary creations of some Victor Hugo or other. As in classic manuals of psychology, I projected my guilt on my parents. Finding no better solution, they were willing to plead guilty.

The next episode of this kind was absurdly tainted by romanticism. There appeared in our office two former students, fugitives from a forced labor camp in Debica. They came not in rags but in tatters, that made whole shivering parts of their body visible. If you had seen it in a theater, you would not believe it possible or authentic. I got a "coup de foudre". Instantly I fell in love with one of them, the one with fiery black eyes, shaded by deep blue circles. I fell in love with his peachy, prominent cheekbones, painted red by consumption fever. Dr.Lowenherz told them to come back the next day, he would by then have prepared a warm letter of recommendation to a welfare institution. Dr.Lowenherz had respect for students. This time I didn't ask my poor father for some more articles of clothing — I stole them.

But the two students never came back. The next day the janitor told my boss: "Do you remember the two young men who came to your office at a late hour yesterday? Well, when they left your room, I saw them piss all over the staircase".

I felt deeply humiliated, as if it concerned me personally. This case ridiculed my idealization, my compassion, but mainly my romantic nature. I decided on the spot to better control my emotions. Still, I remained for years incorrigible in this respect. I wasn't cured. Many a time I came home, weeping over victims of the German oppressions.

Meanwhile, that winter, thousands in the Jewish quarter suffered from lack of food and a heavy cold, lacking fuel. Yet, here, we in our office were 'sitting' on a storeroom full of food, warm blankets, woollies, sweaters and what not. These were still distributed to institutions in negligible quantities. Something had to be done — it was already February.

At last I had an idea. There was to be held in the main office a very modest tea-party celebrating I don't remember what. I wrote a pamphlet for this occasion, which in an astute way, had to convey and disclose the bitter truth about the miserly policy of my boss. Taking advantage of the announced absence of Dr.Lowenherz, I prepared my pamphlet by innocently ridiculing some of his habits. Only in its second part did I turn to the main problem. As for his habits, they were a legend. This crazy pedant happened to be very absent-minded. He smoked a pipe, and often saliva mixed with tobacco dripped from it on a signed letter or protocol. He never felt it. I used to snatch such a stained letter, copy it once more and submit to his signature. "Miss Marysia" — said my boss icily — "I distinctly remember having sighed this letter, why do you submit its copy to sign?" I had to improvise. "Oh" — I said innocently — "I rumpled it by mistake and had to copy it, excuse me". He never guessed the truth. He was even quite capable of taking some pages... to the toilet. Thus, many important documents were missing and I wasn't even able to reconstruct it.

Now, In front of the committee, I parodied it all in my pamphlet, and read it in the main office over a cup of tea... in presence of Dr.Weichert and other bosses.

And who do you think laughed like a child of my innocent jokes? The so serious, the intense, dedicated future leader of the underground — Dolek Liebeskind. At this instance I could have no idea that two years later, somebody sent by Dolek would try to recruit me for the underground organization Z.O.B.

I don't know what passed at the next committee meeting with Dr.Lowenherz, I only know that all of a sudden, the distribution became highly accelerated. Two or three weeks later, my most pessimistic forecast became a catastrophic reality; the whole contents of our store room, lock, stock, and barrel — was confiscated by the Gestapo. It was the end of the whole operation. But before I close this chapter, I have to tell you of one more episode from the end of this period.

A week before the total sequestration of our stock, an ugly incident took place. Dr.Lowenherz signed the papers for a delivery of a huge transport to Debica, where the most sever labor camp was situated. The truck was expected at an appointed hour, but it failed to keep the appointment. Dr.Lowenherz said that he could not wait any longer. He gave an order to our young porter, Marcel Goldberg, to stay and load the truck when it arrived. Fela and I volunteered to check the list and to help out. The porter, Marcel Goldberg was a very special kettle of fish. He must have felt frustrated and denigrated by his humble job of a porter, and minutes after the boss left our office, Marcel declared: "I am not a fool to wait longer for this blasted truck..." We remonstrated with him, explaining how costly this transport was for the Jewish Community Council of Debica, how needy its community — a stone would melt, but not Mr.Goldberg. We implored him, we threatened him — it was a lost effort. He left without a word. Fela and I stayed at the office, hungry and freezing, but eventually rewarded. The truck did indeed arrive after dark. We worked as porters, Fela and I, carrying huge crates, because the truck driver was already furious after the unpaid delay caused by a puncture in one wheel.

The next day we complained to Dr.Lowenherz and he fired Marcel Goldberg on the spot. Dr.Lowenherz couldn't have guessed how greatly he would improve Mr.Goldberg's lot by this speedy dismissal. It transpired later that Marcel Goldberg volunteered to the ranks of OD, the Jewish police, and rose rapidly to a high rank and high brass of this abominable service. He was to become a notorious monster of the ghetto, and later on, of the concentration camp in Plaszow. When you read the "Schindler's Ark" book, you will discover that it was not Oscar Schindler, the good crazy German, who took exorbitant sums for putting somebody's name on the life-saving Schindler's list — it was Marcel Goldberg who cashed it all, and put a lion's share into his own pocket.

All that was not yet written in the cards, while he worked as our porter. I couldn't possibly foresee how much I endangered my own life by denouncing Goldberg and how he would, two years later, seek his revenge. I couldn't foresee that I should always have to hide from him in the ghetto and the concentration camp. The epilogue of this 'Marcel Goldberg episode' will be played out in Paris, in 1946. He will appear there with a bunch of his minions, denounced as a collaborator, be arrested and... But about that I shall relate at the proper place, at the end of my recordings.

Let us now return to the story in the right sequence of events. The Jewish population of Krakow was constantly regrouping and shifting. Those evicted from their flats were moving in with relatives. Those from the provinces streamed into Krakow, hoping to get work or peddle more easily in town. The German authorities of the "General Government" made new plans; They ordered the registration of the whole Jewish population of Krakow, with the aim of sifting it out and granting residence only to positive elements, while eliminating the influx of marginal groups.

As it eventually transpired, all was planned to prepare a quota of population to be enclosed in a ghetto, which was to be situated in the Podgorze suburb of the town. Somehow, I received a job right at the office of this registration. It was considered special luck, but it didn't turn out that way.

I entered a huge room, where everybody was seated at a long table and establishing personal cards with references for every Jewish citizen and family. The employees worked in pairs. The manager of the office asked me if I would rather work with that young man, or with that elderly gentleman. Shy and inhibited girl that I was, I chose to work with the solid old man.

But the old gene soon proved to be very, very naughty. Bending over the material in front of us, he manipulated under table, passing his long hand over my legs. I noticed the furtive glances of many people directed at us. They quipped knowingly, and I understood that I got myself into a trap, and that the manipulations of the old goat were open secret. He was a notorious lecher. I got up and asked to be transferred to work with another partner.

One can believe at this stage, that being so well placed, I should be able to manipulate the personal cards of our family in such a way as to provide the fateful blue seal-stamp — the desired permit to stay in Krakow. But fate decided differently; I had no protection, no access to our files and in the final outcome of this sifting operation, my whole family got the blue stamp... except me. My application was rejected.

Finally, it had no influence on our lot. My parents were decisively averse to the idea of being trapped in a ghetto, they decided to look for another solution. Until such was found, it was published meanwhile that people without the blue stamp had to leave Krakow. I became an illegal resident in my own town, where I was born. I had to go into hiding, at least temporarily. Otherwise, I could be seized in a house-search or in a document control in the street, and sent to a labor camp. My parents had found me a hiding place. It was no more and no less than in a convent of Catholic sisters of mercy. We had for years a deeply religious Christian seamstress coming to our house every month for a day or two of mending jobs. Now my parents turned to her and implored her to hide me in her room in the convent. She was not a sister of mercy or a lay sister, she had a room as protected adherent. There was no safer place, at least for a couple of days.

HIDING IN A CONVENT

Kazia — that was her name — could not refuse, she acted as befits a good Christian full of mercy. She took me to her almost bare room with a huge crucifix. There was no toilet, no running water, only a washstand with a jug, basin and pail. She shared with me her bed. The big, cold room was never aired and had a musty smell. Even Kazia and her bed smelled. She was also sweating with fear — for a good reason. She was aware of committing a mortal sin. The sin of smuggling me into the convent. She did not dare to ask mother superior, it was too late, I had already been smuggled in. Poor Kazia was torn by pangs of remorse. She sought a way to appease her bad conscience. She eventually found a trick.

She asked me timidly if I would consider becoming a Christian. Not at once, but gradually, by the sheer persuasion of the real truth of the Christian religion. Do I not know — asked Kazia — that the Jews use Christian blood as ingredient in matza-baking? Oh, she read that... I am not guilty, but I must surely know that it is one of the sacred Jewish commandments. Is it not abhorrent to me? I felt like yelling "It is not true, it is a lie spread by your sisters of mercy". I could only utter in a hoarse whisper that she was misled by somebody. Surely, she heard it from a poor soul, an ignoramus — I said. At that moment I got a brilliant idea. "Ask your nuns, ask your mother superior" — I ventured — "if she can point out in the Holy Scripture common to both religions such a passage". And then I added shrewdly that the nuns couldn't possibly utter such a lie, she must have got it from a wrong person. Poor Kazia could not reveal what I guessed: that it was the nuns who fed her such abominable infamy. She averted her eyes but kept her own ground. Couldn't I make at least an effort to come closer to Christianity? she asked.

What was I to do, what would you do, my grandchildren, in my place? You, the blood of my blood… I said: "Dear Miss Kazia, you have known me for years… you know that I never tell lies. I couldn't possibly promise you such a thing just because I need a hiding place, right at the moment. But I want you to know one thing. I adore the churches… I am full of admiration for the Christian mercy, for the humility it teaches, for the peace of soul it provides. But I happen to be born Jewish, and I wouldn't forswear my religion while Jews are persecuted under the German yoke. Would you prefer me to pretend and to play a false game?" Kazia accepted silently my effusive apology, and appeased her conscience by silent hope, hope that someday I would see the light. Still, every day she prepared for me a question on ethics, trying to bend my mind.

I remained adamant but tactful in my responses. I was totally dependent on her goodwill. I could never leave this bare room, not even for a while. If I felt nature's call, I had to wait till all the nuns were at prayers, or I had to sneak out at night to the toilet. I thought that I should never leave that convent. I was actually imprisoned for weeks on end.

We used to get up before dawn. At six o'clock, Kazia was already at the church for morning prayers. I wouldn't dare to stay in bed. I had to sit all day long behind a screen. The screen was there for customers who had to undress when trying on a dress repaired by Kazia. I had to be invisible to a potential visitor. Not that she had many visitors, but it was a simple and basic precaution. I caught a cold in that early spring and was afraid to sneeze behind the screen in the presence of a customer. The screen was placed close to the window, so at least I could read, read for endless hours, read, and shiver.

Meanwhile, my parents were seeking a solution for our whole family including Grandma Rose and the Kleins. Grandma Sperling and her daughter Hela with her half-lawyer husband had relatives in a village close to Krakow, in Borek. Where could we go? Where, if not to the places indicated by the Germans? Where was a quiet secure place for a Jew? There must be one, and naturally my parents thought of Rabka, the lovely hamlet Rabka, where we spent the last vacations before the war. There were in Rabka private pensions and huts-to-rent. The Germans must be certainly concentrated somewhere far from this heavenly hamlet.

Do you realize what it means to liquidate secretly a whole household, and snitch out some valuable items registered by the Germans as German property? How does one find a cart with a coachman willing to transport clandestinely a Jewish family with all its belongings, loaded on a cart? Can one dare to do it openly by daylight or should one execute this exodus under the darkness of night. The time was set before twilight.

While I was hiding in the convent, my mother, the eternal hero or Cossack, as papa used to call her, made desperate last efforts to sell some of the art objects that would prove unsalable in Rabka. Most paintings registered by the Germans had to be left in their rooms, the rest was sold or left in custody of the faithful noble Mr.Poraj Chlebowski, the gentile friend of my father. There were two more Persian carpets of great beauty, temporarily hidden in the cellar. These had to be sold immediately. My mother turned to the old firm of Stieglitz, dealing in antiques. We had been their clients for years. Papa also bought from them many coins for his collection. They answered that they were very busy and they have of course a German appointed Treuhander (trustee), but they would send two representatives. The two envoys proved to be shady types, kind of emancipated gypsies. The bargaining started. In the middle of sharp haggling, with my mother remaining very firm, the older gypsy said whispering to my mother: "My son is quite drunk, as you can see — who knows what he will do when he gets angry. He may denounce you to the Gestapo that you are selling requested German property. You better reach an agreement; you do not want to be dragged to the Gestapo..." My mother didn't bat an eyelid, she remained adamant. Whereupon the son "lost his temper" as his father predicted, stopped playing drunk, and said in a clipped tone: "If that is your last word, you will kindly accompany us to the Gestapo". "That I shall do" — answered my mother, took her coat, and went out with them. The headquarters of the Gestapo were situated quite a distance from our street. Here was my tiny mother, marching proudly and resolutely between the two Gypsy giants, and not saying a word. Midway, they started to work on her and tried once more to persuade her. "No" — said mother — "to the Gestapo we shall go". A block before the Gestapo building the two types retreated and disappeared. But they uttered the last threat: "You are going to hear from us".

Indeed, the threat was not empty. The next day they reappeared with a civilian blond giant identifying himself as a secret Gestapo agent. Olga opened the door and said that the Jews were gone and she, Olga, a Volksdeutsche, was occupying this house. Meanwhile, mother was hiding in a cupboard. They didn't come back anymore. What became of the carpets — I do not remember. They too must have been left with Victor Poraj Chlebowski, of whom we shall speak a lot, but later.

As you know, I was still hiding in the convent and I left it only a day before we went to Rabka.

What would a sentimental girl like me have to liquidate or take care of before the exodus? Family pictures of course. A short time before the war I had sifted out photos and snapshots and pasted the chosen ones into a lovely album. The rest remained in shoeboxes. In whose trust should I now leave my precious photo-albums? There was only one person, my beloved aunt Hela, father's sister, the round, full-bosomed auntie, in whose arms I spent many of my best hours of my childhood. She was going legally, as I mentioned, to the 'safe' village Borek. Aunt Hela was like me, or more than me, a compulsive and avid collector of family pictures. Endowed with a lapidary brand of humor, she developed her own style of collecting. Having no children of her own, she was crazy about us and cherished every snapshot. Whenever she paid us a visit when I was a child, she demanded, of course, to be shown new photos. After a careful scrutiny she would pick one or two pictures, and then... she would sit down on them. The pictures were lost to us, her heavy bottom was like a fortress defending the precious photos. I could tell many anecdotes about her, but I won't, now that I have to proceed with my story.

As I said, I decided to confide the family album to her care. Unfortunately, this album was to share her cruel lot and tragic end. Auntie Helka with her husband and my dearest granny Rachel Sperling perished, eventually not in the "safe" Borek but in Bochnia, where they were driven. The details are unknown to me, but one source knew to relate that when the massacre at Bochnia started, my aunt and uncle decided to flee. Granny, afraid to be a burden and impediment in their flight, chose to stay and die on the spot.

My heart is aching while I give this matter-of-fact report. I dearly loved my witty aunt and my sunny grandmother Rachel. I want you to know, my grandchildren, that the real heroes among your ancestors were the women. Though my grandfather used to lift a table, holding it by one leg, my tiny grandmother was left widow with seven children. She earned their upkeep and raised them to honorable citizens. She worked from dawn to midnight, and whatever she did, she always sang when going about her chores. Father remembers from his childhood that on Fridays his mother baked a cake at three in the morning, took it to her parents to the furthest suburb, and was back at home before seven.

My mother painted a portrait of her mother-in-law, that sweet mother-in-law, who before my parents' wedding equipped my father with two dozen of socks, so that the new bride wouldn't have to start her marriage by darning hubby's socks... But wait a moment; I forgot to mention that my mother was an excellent portrait painter. In this portrait, granny's velvety eyes were the most distinct feature. The wandering spark was there, and a song seemed to be dancing on her lips. I realize now that my brother Witek must have inherited granny's fascinating eyes.

But I have to return to the album. In the traumatic outcome of this tragedy and loss, you will perhaps understand, my dear grandchildren, why did I never dare to start a new album, after the war. Why are all the pictures of you stored in a box and never affixed in a photo album. It is clearly the outcome of this traumatic experience. This and many graver psychological blocks. In this actual photo-box of mine there are also many very old pictures. Among others, some of my maternal grandparents, pictures that are now a hundred and three years old. How possible? The answer is very simple. Those double of rejected pictures, that were not pasted into the album, I confided to the custody of Grandma Rose's house janitor, the good Julian. This sweet old man handed them to my mother, seven years later when she arrived in Krakow, in 1947.

These photographs are still in a huge box of old and new family- pictures, placed in the cupboard. Were a fire to break out in my house, the only thing I would try to save would be this picture-box.

The lot of the album and the background of my idiosyncrasy led me away from my story. Let us return to it.

Here we were all packed, sitting on a cart drawn by a horse, and moving to Rabka. I was already longing for the fresh air and pastoral landscape of Rabka. Here I have to make a confession. While I was sitting thus on the cart my thoughts returned to my last vacation in Rabka. A young romantic girl can have some queer thoughts. I am much ashamed to admit, but I remembered right then a friendship and flirt that I had got enmeshed in during that last week of vacations. I was getting on seventeen; he was a young medic working in the Jewish hospital in Krakow. He had to go back to work after his weekend in Rabka, so he asked me to meet him the next Saturday in the same spot in the park, at the same hour. But that next Saturday we were already back in Krakow, facing the possibility of the outbreak of war. Sitting on the wobbling cart, I remembered this missed rendezvous. Actually, I don't even remember his face or his name.

THE DELUSIVE PARADISE

If you were in our shoes, you would rationalize along the same lines — the Germans cannot be spread everywhere and penetrate every village... They may send to this summer-resort some convalescent soldiers, but nothing much beyond that. The German politicians are flirting with the Gorals (tribe of the mountains), they offered to grant them autonomy, they wouldn't interfere much in the Goral territory. The local Jews, far from any municipal concentration are a very marginal factor. Thus, we thought that we have found the real paradise.

We arrived at Rabka with Grandma Felicia Rose, aunt Helcia and Rutka. The Kleins had split up, uncle Olek decided to stay in the ghetto of Krakow and try to earn some money, so as to sustain his wife and daughter. Granny Rose came with us, but was not expected to live and stay with us. One would find her a good accommodation, a boarding house, she could afford it. It is a sad fact that my mother and grandmother were hardly on speaking terms. They had both extremely strong personalities and saw everything from a different angle.

A pragmatist like my grandmother and an artist like my mother (who was realistic and quite pragmatist herself) couldn't get along. It sometimes happened that they were both right in their controversy (if such a thing is possible) and each defended her own position, in hot dispute and open hostility. I shall give one example right here, because I want you to judge from the perspective of the given situation.

Grandmother and mother owned in partnership a tenement house (after my father paid off my grandfather's debts). This was one of the finest houses in our town, besides being situated in its center, and facing the Mickiewicz statue. It was the third house from the famous historic St.Mary's church, a church built in exquisite pure Gothic style. Grandma lived there and she was very proud of her house. My father had his bank there. Now, under the occupation, the German authorities appointed a trustee as administrator and money collector, and we, the rightful owners, were totally deprived of our income. In spite of this state of affairs, when winter approached, my grandmother claimed that coke had to be bought as fuel for central heating, otherwise the pipes would burst and become irreparable. The German 'Treuhander' refused to buy the coke. My mother, who had no high hopes for the recuperation and re privatization of the house, was not willing to finance the German administration of the house. Let the pipes burst — she said — and who cares... Grandma was adamant and stubborn as a mule. Who was right, what would you say? Who believed that this war would last? Now, of course, we are clever from our perspective. We know that all was lost even after the war, when Poland passed from the German occupation to the communist regime. But wait — surprise, surprise!!! In 1947, mother was able to return for a while, prove ownership, reprivatize the house and... sell it for an absurd sum of 10,000 dollars. So, who was right after all? I have described this incident as an illustration to the strange relationship between mother and daughter, where both could have been right.

Under such circumstances, it is understandable that once in Rabka, grandmother would have to live separately.

When we arrived at Rabka, we found the local picture to be very different and far from rosy. To our great surprise — we discovered in Rabka, a huge boarding school, turned by the Germans into an SS school. It was there, that the Ukrainian and Latvian volunteers to the SS were trained in cruelty...

It was too late to retreat but we decided at least to seek accommodation as far as possible from the SS school and the village center, which was densely populated by Jews. We found a primitive hut, the last hut on the mountain slope. There was nothing above it, only dense forests and the peak of the "Grzebien" mountain. That was the beginning of our pastoral symphony. We thought that we had found paradise. The presence of the SS school was not yet felt in Rabka, not at that stage.

Father and I, who were absolutely nature-crazy, became enchanted with the lush landscape. It was late spring and we passed the great part of the days in the forest. Tipsy with fresh air, we couldn't foresee that this pastoral symphony would turn into a pathetic symphony and finally into a tragic one, one that Beethoven never wrote. Who could have guessed that this war could last five years and nine months, who could have guessed that we shall stay in Rabka over a year, till the autumn of 1942.

At this period, the famous hobby of birdwatching was not yet known or popular. My father seemed to have invented it. He was at his observation post in the forest before twilight. He seemed to know each and every nest and its inhabitants. He gave them names like Ruddy, Cheeky or Coquette. He, who had for two years a dangerous heart-condition, now felt very well. He inhaled this sweet, pure air, as if he knew that in his last breath, he would inhale poison-gases in the gas chamber.

We were not aware at the beginning how dependent we were to become on this forest. We were now like Robinson Crusoe. Our hut with its thatched roof was situated very far from shops, market or any place and point where eatables and first use articles were sold. The itinerant peasants did not sell nor supply their products there, products like butter enveloped in a huge leaf or cheese in its warped cloth. We couldn't obtain wood to make fire for cooking. We couldn't get potatoes, eggs, milk nor vegetables. Nothing reached us, everything became a problem. But there were several things within the reach of our hand, things to be found in the woods. We became experts in mushroom-picking, discerning without failure the poisonous kinds, which often parade in a camouflage, imitating several of the edible kinds. We consumed a mushroom-diet and collected and dried on strings, a safe reserve of dried mushrooms for the winter. We, the three children used to go to the woods at five in the morning and compete between us who would bring a fuller basket. I made marks on trees, where a reproductive colony of mushrooms was hiding under fern, but Rutka and Witek had spotted my marks.

The mushrooms were rich in proteins, the raspberries, blueberries, and wild strawberries provided vitamins. Even fuel was provided by the forest. We brought full laundry-baskets of pinecones that burn as well as coals. We lived literally off the woods.

Once, my aunt Helcia succeeded in buying a hen. The hen wasn't young, meaty or fat, but still it was a hen. The peasant killed it, aunt

Helcia brought it home, plucked and cleaned. Because it was sinewy and tough, my aunt left it hanging on the wooden fence for the night. In the morning... there were only feathers left. A fox must have had quite a feast of it. Still, we liked this Robinsonian life; it was so creative in many ways. When the winter came, it was another story. The little hut was sometimes cut off from the world.

The snow lay so high on the doorstep, that we weren't able to open the door. We couldn't even go to the toilet, which was outside. This privy was a miniature hut, inside was a plank with a round hole in the middle, underneath the plank was a deep ditch. Thus, in winter we were all squeezed in our little hut. It was composed of two rooms and a kitchen. One room was occupied by my parents with Witek, the second by aunt Helcia, Rutka and me. There was in every room a heating stove, and there was one oven in the kitchen.

The fuel was wood. How could we buy wood and have it transported to our hut, so high on the mountain slope? The peasants refused, and with a good reason too; they could sell it easily in the valley, in the center of Rabka. Once I implored a yokel to sell me a cartload of wood, but to no avail, even though I offered a better price. Torn by despair, I took the horse by the bridle, and it complied. "Your horse has already shown some heart and follows me, won't you?" — I said to the man. Thus, we were provided with a cartful of wood. Still, it was uncut, un-chopped and it was wet. It would not burn. Now we had to saw it short, chop it into little pieces, and dry behind the stove till it was ready for use. It was quite a job for women. Father tried his hand at it, but we would not let him. The risk was too high for his heart even though it was good for his morale.

I almost forgot one little detail: there was no electricity in this hut. What did we use for light in these long winter evening? We used kerosene lamps and a carbide-acetylene lamp, which smelled horribly and had to be extinguished outside. Water for tea, we boiled on a primus burner. We wouldn't make fire in the oven for a kettle of boiled water. To go down to the village was quite a trip. Add to our occupations linen-washing, ironing all the laundry, and sock-darning — and you will see that we were busy the whole day long. In spite of all these occupations, I found time to teach Witek. He was now a year and a half out of school. This child was so independent that once he said to me: "Don't you patronize me, I have the books, I can learn by myself. Give me the basics and give me an explanation only when I ask for it". Thus, he became an autodidact at the ripe age of ten. Later, much later, Witek joined a group of children in Rabka, and it became evident that he reached by himself a much higher level.

We lived in total seclusion. It was not so good for our nerves. It was especially hard on my temperamental cousin Rutka. She would rather choose the pulsating life of the ghetto. Uncle Olek sensed it or read it between the lines of her letters. He wanted her and his wife rather to stay in Rabka. That is why he described in his letters all the horrible things happening in the ghetto. I do remember what he wrote, but I got the full picture only after we arrived there. That is why I postpone for the moment the description of the events in the Jewish world of Krakow, till our merger with the stream of life in the ghetto. As for myself, I didn't mind so much this life of seclusion, but I couldn't advance in anything in this constellation. It seems that our days were filled with nothing apart from the very fight for existence.

But to "exist" was quite a feat in the given circumstances. Let me give more examples, some of them make a fascinating story. I never mentioned, so far, the problem of eggs... beyond the fact that they were not obtainable. Once, when we visited grandma, we were told by a neighbor that there was a place, some fifteen kilometers distant, where the eggs of the whole region were bought, checked, packed and distributed. This establishment once belonged to a Jew. Now the country folks were ordered by the German authorities to bring all their eggs to this assembling point. The damaged eggs are being sold there at a symbolic price — we were told. Rutka and I started out at about four in the morning to reach the place at Zabornia at five, so as to stand in queue till seven, when the distribution of damaged eggs would start. We came equipped with cooking pots, one for each of us. Indeed, we each received a full pot of broken eggs. We did it several times.

Once, "shliemazl" that I am, it happened to me that I tripped over a stone and fell down into a pool of eggs. I cried. I cried not over the spilled eggs, but over my clumsiness.

You may think that in the evenings we were able to sit around the table with a petrol lamp, and chat or read, or darn papa's socks. That was not to be, there was still the need for buying milk secretly. We would perhaps willingly give up that luxury if it were not for the child. Witek had to get some milk. Mother eventually found a peasant woman who was willing to sell us milk twice a week, provided we were ready to come for it late after dark. We used to go there, the two of us, Rutka and I, so that it would be less scary. It wasn't. To reach the woman's hut we had to sneak through fields, working our way knee-deep through the snow. Often, we had to fight off dangerous dogs that were let off the chain for the night. We didn't disclose to our family what perils we were exposed to. We even joked about our romantic trips in moonlight. Once, my mother noticed our frayed clothes, after the dogs tried to bite us. That was the end of our Golgotha way.

My health deteriorated that winter of 1941. One day I suddenly discovered an abscess bordering on my groin and this furuncle grew outward — to the size of half an egg. I am not exaggerating. I hoped that it would open up in a hot sitting bath (we had no bathtub of course), but it grew without an outlet. My family called the local physician, a country man from the Goral tribe. "There is nothing else I can do; I have to cut it right here and now" — he said. He used a chloroethyl siphon as local anesthetic. Maybe he should have waited for a while, or perhaps it was not enough for this huge furuncle, anyhow, I felt an excruciating pain during this 'minor' operation. I screamed like an ox in the slaughterhouse. later I asked him to forgive me, I couldn't control it. When this butcher finished his bloody job, he put a dressing on my wound and sat down. Thus, he sat like an Indian on the rock, without uttering a word. I wondered what he might be waiting for.

Then, all of a sudden, I understood. I went into a traumatic shock, almost a coma. After a while everything in me shook in spastic fits. I could hardly catch a breath. Waves of heat alternated with waves of cold, when in convulsive shivers my teeth chattered uncontrollably. The worst was fighting for breath. For days I couldn't speak, let alone eat or go to the toilet, while constantly urinating. This condition lasted for quite a long time. My family didn't know how to cope with it. They left me in the room whispering behind the door. Every now and then they peeped in and said: "Sh… sh… she is sleeping". I wasn't, but I couldn't utter a word. Wherever I had to say two words, I gathered strength for several minutes. Eventually, after two weeks I was able to sit outside in an easy-chair.

My family heard about a Jewish doctor living downtown in Rabka and called him. He was the good Dr.Paster from Krakow. Seeing another boil in state of formation, he decided to inject me with an anti-furunculosis serum. He only forgot this simple precaution of asking if I ever received a serum therapy. It was an anti-diphteric serum with which I was treated in my childhood. Another dose of serum can be fatal, and indeed, I fell gravely ill again. Dr.Paster treated me now with calcium injections. One day, when I was much better and sitting in an easy-chair, Dr.Paster came with his brother-in-law, his wife's young brother. His name was Wilhelm or short Wilek Grunberg. He was twenty-five years old and had a master's degree in economics. I was almost nineteen. He represented this typical Jewish intellectual type, built narrow, with aristocratic hands, bespectacled. From behind his glasses, his dark eyes had a penetrating gaze. He was no Apollo, but he was broadly educated, fascinating and endowed with an analytic mind. He also had a most disarming smile. I was impressed.

He came unexpectedly and here I was sitting in a peasant dress, my long blond hair plaited by my mother into two childish braids. Rutka had curly blond hair, otherwise we were quite similar in the general outline, or so people used to say. Wilek didn't pay attention to either one of us, but he instantly took to my father. The age gap was of no importance, Wilek was very mature for his age.

When I recovered, I still went to Dr.Paster to receive more calcium injections. I had to cut through the woods and fields, go down from the hills to the Jewish quarter of Rabka, where Dr.Paster lived. The doctor's vivacious wife, Wilek's sister, took a liking to me, and we used to chat while I was waiting for Dr.Paster' s return. Wilek didn't pay attention to me, or so it seemed to a shy girl like me. One day, Mrs. Paster suggested that Wilek accompany me. I had a long way to go alone through the forest. From that moment, every time I came for my injection, he used to accompany me, come into the house and talk to my father... Our walks through the woods helped me to unwind and crawl out of my cocoon. When I overcame my inborn shyness, we established a very special relationship. Once, after a vivid discussion, Wilek said to me: "You are very bright, you have a very colorful brand of intellect, it only takes a bit of shaping up..."

"Don't patronize me, you are not my shrink" — I riposted, quite angry. "I don't patronize you my dear, I love you". I was so shaken at this disclosure that I dropped my purse. When we both went down on our knees to search for it in the undergrowth, Wilek caught me, kissed me as one kisses a child, and whispered into my ear: "Lesson number one — never act silly and confused".

Thus, romance was born. It was a double romance, one could say. Wilek had one love affair with me and the second one with my father. There are all sorts of love. One thing is certain; to be lovingly kissed in the woods and groves of pines — is a singular experience that leaves its imprint on the whole romantic life of a young girl.

I quickly befriended the Pasters and the Grunbergs, Wilek's parents. The younger of his two sisters, a pretty spinster, used to manage a fashion house before the war. Thus, she supported her aging parents. Maryla was now willing to teach me the art of sewing and engage me as a helping hand. She still had some clients, mostly among gentiles. And so, I acquired progressively a new skill and trade, which was later to prove a great asset, indeed a life-saving asset.

Whenever I came downtown, I used to visit my grandmother. We all visited granny quite often in her boarding house. Aunt Helcia, unlike my mother, was greatly attached to her in a subservient way. Aunt Helcia never forgot that she was the ugly duckling, having been born after my grandmother was sick with cholera during that pregnancy. It must have been from Helcia that grandmother eventually learned and understood how badly we all fared financially all that time. My mother would never disclose it. Grandma offered her help; she was rich enough to be generous without restricting her own expenses.

We could now afford to move into a better house, one situated closer to the center, but still the last house on a hill slope. Our living conditions greatly improved. The whole style of life underwent a metamorphosis. Who would have guessed that we should miss the former pastoral life of seclusion? Now, we were supplied with provisions, we had contact with people, but from the topographic point of view, we became too close to the "Tereska" building, the school of the SS.

We couldn't have guessed that in this deep ravine, separating us from the "Tereska" building — would repose the body of grandma Felicia Rose, the bodies of Wilek's parents and those of the good uncle Jonas Rose and his wife. All the victims of Rabka were buried in this ravine.

We discovered Uncle Jonas, my mother's paternal uncle, in Rabka, where he had been living for years. Uncle Jonas Rose was a real dove of our family. He was running a tool shop, but his real love was art. Art runs in the Rose family, generation after generation, as became evident from his stories.

His grandmother revealed her artistic inclination by creating and fashioning fabulous women's bonnets, the Jewish 'kupkeh' hats, adorned with intricate, tasteful trimmings. Hers were nicknamed "paradise kupkeh" and were in great demand in the whole area of Loncko, from where the Roses originated.

He himself, Uncle Jonas, neglected his prospering shop to pay tribute to art. One can hardly call him a sculptor. Living among the Goral tribe of mountaineer's, Uncle Jonas became bug bitten by their craft, the craft of whittling in wood and carving intricate ornaments on wooden boxes. After he befriended one such gentile carver, he handed the shop over to his wife. He drew for her on every cardboard box the tool or bicycle part it contained, noting its price. He left the shop; he became free to carve all day long. His teacher was the Goral Wasiek Weislo, who will later play a role in my story.

This family talent of the Roses sometimes skipped a generation, only to reappear in the next one or in a side-branch. From uncle Jonas it passed on to my mother. Though forced as a young girl to play piano, she neglected her musical studies and drew secretly without tuition. I never saw my mother approach a piano. Only as a married woman and mother her of two was she able to attend the Academy of Art. My father supported this venture, becoming quite an expert on art himself. Mother became, eventually, a portrait painter of good reputation, excelling in deft brushwork. But I have already mentioned her sculptures and portraits, especially the one of my grandmother Rachel Sperling. In my mother's case there was no generation gap — I have inherited her talent in a straight line, and with nearly the same characteristics of style. Who knows where this talent will emerge again in the next generations?

At the stage I am speaking of, I was far from art, I started a new career. The skill of typing and my perfect knowledge of German became quite useful. I became the secretary of a very strange personality, Mr.Braun. The man was a Berliner Jew, the former king of paper, rich as Croesus. He was expelled from Germany because it was discovered that he happened to be born in Poland. Like us, he also had the 'good' idea of seeking shelter in the quiet Rabka. Here, having never accepted the loss of his fabulous fortune, he pursued his dream, a crazy utopian idea of trying to exchange his estates in Germany for some native German's estates in South America. Before winter 1941, America was not yet engaged in war with Germany, and he could correspond with U.S.He wrote letters to the whole world (he had such wide connections), and I was his secretary.

Because our upkeep was now financed by my grandmother's jewelry, I decided to offer my whole salary to somebody even needier. I had a bosom friend named Hanka. They had never been well situated because my friend's father, Adam S. was never able to hold a job. What do you expect of him — people used to say — him that had been detained for three years in Siberia during World War I… Is that what people say about us, the Holocaust survivors — I wonder.

Now, the impoverished Adam, Ludvika, Hanka and her little brother, were expelled from Krakow to a village in a very distant region of Poland. Hanka wrote me from there desperate, heart-rending letters. This family was left without means, and the four of them became absolutely emaciated after typhoid. They even lost their teeth, their hair, they were bald.

I sent her my salary every month, and this good deed must have earned me a "ticket" in heaven, because it was repaid later upon our arrival to the ghetto by the help extended to us by Hanka's aunt. I for one never expected a reward.

Witek learned now with a group of children, mother was as usual the ship's navigator, and aunt Helcia was cooking on a miniscule, fuel-saving stove, that was like a child's toy. As my father used to say, she could publish a book entitled "A thousand and one recipes for cooking meals of potatoes". Mother was very astute, taking care of all the major problems.

There was not such a thing as mother was not able to do, cope with or repair. Once, the chimney stalk got blocked and the smoke and soot had no outlet. We couldn't get a chimney sweeper, and you must realize what it means to reach the top of the chimney stalk, climbing on the sloping roof of such a house. What did my valiant mother do? She climbed on the slippery red tiles, she made herself a tow, oakum of rags with a stone inside, she dropped it down the chimney on a long rope and, pulling it up and down, cleaned the passage. She climbed down, blackened with soot like a real chimney sweep, showing a gamut of white strong teeth in her broad smile. That's the way my mother was, a real Cossack as my father used to say. No wonder she ruled over my life.

Rutka and I both had doting mothers, but Rutka knew how to manage hers. "The difference between us" — Rutka used to say — "is that you remonstrate with your mother, you say 'no, no' — and you do exactly what she tells you to do, while I say — 'Yes, yes' to my mother, and then I do what I wish..."

At this point, my father's train of life was to undergo a dramatic change. Gone were the days spent in the forest. Gone were the days of his romantic visits to a she-person called 'Kuaziova'... Who is Kuaziova? We used to ask, but father put on a poker face and wouldn't answer. We discovered eventually that this mysterious woman in his life was a sweet girl aged three, who called herself Kuaziova, unable to pronounce 'Kucharzowa' — meaning the daughter of the cook. My father adored children and had a lot of patience for them. This gentile, 'Kuaziova's' father, worked as a cook in the "Tereska", and he was a distant relative of the common wife of our dear Victor Poraj Chlebovski. That's how this acquaintance started. This cook will play a role twice, later in my story.

Right now, my father had to face a very grave problem. He was to start a new 'romance' if you can call it so, and this a very odd one. I have so far totally refrained from relating about the attitude of the Germans to the local population. You can deduct from it that we, in our hut, lived on another planet. There was no mention of the Germans, their actions and persecutions, because all that didn't concern us in Rabka. All that happened meanwhile in Krakow. We lived for a time like in a cocoon, as on Robinson's island. In this former hut of ours we were cut off from Jews and Germans as well. Now, living closer to the center in the Miskoviec house, we became exposed and were swept with the current. First, we met people and renewed some old acquaintances, tied some new ones.

One day, a very nice man paid us a visit. His name was Naftali Birnzweig or Birnhack, I don't remember. We had never known him in Krakow, but he seemed to know a lot about my father. He asked to speak to my father in private and closed the door. He revealed to my father his plan and quest. His aim was, no less and no more, to recruit my father into the ranks of the local "Judenrat", the Jewish Community Council.

It has to be stressed that Naftali belonged in Krakow to the leftist Zionist Organization, my father to the centralist General Zionists, but here in Rabka, it was of no importance.

My father reacted immediately to his proposal. He explained that never in his life had he coveted a position in the party, a chair or a title. He was always willing to share the burdens, to offer his money, his time, his clerks, but never, never did he accept a position when offered. Why would Naftali think that he would accept it now, here under the German occupation, and in this dubious local constellation?

Birnhack asked my father to sleep on it, to reconsider his plea, and to try to understand its importance. He would be back. Indeed, he came several times.

Here Wilek came into the picture. Wilek and my father had a very special relationship. My father revealed to him all his thoughts and problems. Wilek was of a different opinion. Who, if not an experienced citizen of blameless reputation, a man with clean hands and conscience like my father — should become active in the local "Judenrat"? Birnhack is absolutely right — said Wilek — it is my father's heavy duty to accept this nomination. He can greatly contribute to the way things will be run in the local Community Council. Both, father and Wilek, analyzed the local constellation like in a planetarium and found it composed of many elements. This "Judenrat" was run partly by old members of the Jewish Community Council in Rabka, partly newcomers from Krakow. The main figure, the Judenrat chairman, a mister Sherer, was probably planted by the Germans... It was hard to know if this handsome merchant from Krakow offered his services or was just picked and appointed by the Germans, being loquacious, vibrant with energy and imposing of stature. The old members of the "Judenrat" claimed that, at the very first meeting with the German representatives, Sherer acted as if he were already the chosen chairman, that he was the obvious choice and didn't have to be planted by the Germans. Who will ever know the truth!

For this very reason it became important to Birnhack and other honest members to draw into their circle a man of impeccable reputation, somebody that counts and can unbalance and undermine the growing importance and impertinence of the domineering Sherer. This community needs Henryk Sperling (my father), said Wilek, repeating unknowingly Birnhack's words. There were some more endless discussions, but Wilek won in persuading my father.

History of the Holocaust period has painted the image of the Judenrats as the almighty body, which manipulated everybody and took advantage of their privileges... History ignores many facets of this problem, and mainly the immense burden and responsibility imposed on this body. Lacking regular funds, the "Judenrat" had to maintain the former institution and finance extensive welfare work, taking care of this destitute population. Supporting widows and orphans and running the kitchen for the poor — were still not the hardest…

To supply labor-force in numbers ordered by the Germans, the Judenrat had to balance the burden and support the families of all the men recruited to slave for the SS. The Ukrainians, Ruthenias, Lithuanians and Latvians have quickly learned how to abuse and persecute the Jews. The Germans knew how to milk them. The work squadrons were turned into slaves. Wilek too had to slave at "Tereska" and turned from a refined delicate intellectual into a muscle-bound workman. He had to break and dig out huge rocks or to carry them far away. Whenever a Ukrainian supervisor of slaves saw a man slowing down, he shot him on the spot. They worked from sunrise till sunset but were free to go home. The Judenrat had to support their families.

Soon, the officers were no longer satisfied with the squadrons of men and women turned into slaves. They had developed new appetites. They had discovered that they can stipulate and order from the Judenrat absolutely anything that crossed their minds. Every whim had to be satisfied. Once it was a gramophone, once a watch or a bracelet, once a sewing machine, a motorcycle, a China set, a piano and a violin. Week after week they presented new claims and they passed this message through Sherer. If not delivered… the Jews will suffer the consequences and the Judenrat too. Sherer was their spokesman, and there was absolutely no control over his use of the communal money or the purchase price and the delivery of the different objects. Sherer had his 'minions' to take care of it under his exclusive supervision.

The Jews discovered that the men were extremely well informed about several internal communal matters, and this raised the suspicion that Sherer is an informer. His position grew stronger and stronger. He manipulated the whole Judenrat, claiming that the members' lives are threatened if the Judenrat would not comply. Burdened with all the social problems, the Judenrat turned into a milked cow and a milking cow at the same time. It was extortion on all levels.

One day they asked for a typewriter. It was known in Rabka that the only typewriter in the village is in the possession of Mr.Braun, my boss. All the Judenrat members said that he is rich enough to offer it, he just has to give it. My father took this mission of persuading him upon himself. He addressed Mr.Braun with these words: "Whatever would be done in this matter, you will believe that it was I who informed the Judenrat that you possess a typewriter. The truth is that everybody in the village knows it. Instead of hiding behind somebody's back, I came in person to ask you kindly to offer this object claimed by the Germans, even though I know how important it is to you. Lives are at stake". Braun fumed but he had no choice.

In that year of 1941 moods were oscillating between despair and high hopes. It must be remembered that in June 1941 the Germans fell upon Russia and, almost unopposed, marched into its depth. The population had not yet dried its tears over this new calamity when in the winter of the same year America joined the Allied Forces in the war effort. Now everybody was in seventh heaven, hoping that the war would soon be over, but the Germans became only more vicious. Indeed, at this stage many people had already lost their lives. The sporadic killings were soon to give way to mass-executions.

Whenever a Ukrainian posted to supervise the Jewish slaves noticed a man slowing down in his work — he would shot him on the spot. We, the girls working every other day in "Tereska", were also in constant danger. I shall give a simple example. One day, when we were ordered to clean the wooden parquet of an office, we were told to scrape it, then wash it, lubricate with wax and polish. All that till noontime. Everyone understands that after you have washed a parquet, you cannot wax it, it has to be bone-dry or the wax will not penetrate the boards, it will just glide on them. The woman who supervised our work knew it well. Still, she threatened us with execution if we did not perform in that time limit. Fortunately, there came a God-sent wind from the mountains, and the parquet became dry enough to be induced with wax and polished like a mirror. We were saved, and not yet buried in the ravine bordering on the "Tereska" grounds.

Before this gorge became the ravine of death, it was to play another role in my story. This one a tragicomic one, in the following episode: On the 27th of December 1941, the Germans issued an edict forcing the Jews of all Poland to deliver their furs down to the smallest piece and bring them to a collecting point within a time limit. Now, in that winter the German armies were stuck in the snows of Eastern Poland and Russia. They desperately needed every piece of fur, even a small one to fill the boots.

My mother had sold her magnificent astrakhan lamb fur long time ago, in Krakow, but we still possessed a splendid pelisse fur coat of my grandfather (who was at that time warming his old bones in the sun of Palestine... Separated from Grandma Felicia, he chose to live in Tel-Aviv...). He left his fur coat in our trust and here we were, having no idea what to do with this precious deposit. Pity we didn't sell it. But no, now I remember; it was the other way round; we had simply forgotten its very existence and missed the dead-line date. Now we were stuck with it. We had to find a solution quickly, before a house search would find us red handed (or rather brown handed). Here my father's friendship with the little girl Kuaziova came to our help. We shall ask Kuaziova's father, the goy working as cook in "Tereska", to hide the fur in his house until we decide what to do about it. He was a good man. He took the fur at night to his flat. Some three days later, the cook came at night running to our house, sweating profusely and swearing. He was visibly in deep shock. What happened? As it transpired, or as we learned from gossip, the cook's wife had a lover. The lover was a Polish policeman. While the cook was at work, the policeman paid the man's wife his amorous visits. How could the cook's wife refuse her favors to a policeman? How could the cook dare to throw out a policeman or beat him up? It so happened that during one of the policeman's secret visits, the little Kuaziova said to this 'good uncle': "Mister policeman, guess what are we hiding under the bed? We have a fuuuur coaaat here!!!" Mister policeman pretended to take it for a joke, but the poor wife had to warn her husband. That's why he came with the fur in the middle of the night.

What were we to do, what could we do at this instance? The Germans used to make house search quite often by then. We had to get rid of the fur this very night. Trembling with fear, we took it far away, or so it seemed to us, across the fields and into the ravine. The same ravine, running along the "Tereska" grounds, that was to become the ravine of death. We buried the damned pelisse deep under the snow. Good riddance, we thought. An hour later, having regained our composure, we put on our thinking cap. What will happen when the snow melts? If the Germans spot the fur coat, they will guess that it must have come from the nearest house, our house. We went once more to the same spot, dug the fur out and brought it home. What now? We made a good fire in the stove and started to burn it piece by piece. It wouldn't burn, it was all wet. It took us hours. It stank most horribly, it stank... like the crematoria, as I was to learn much later. When we burn a chicken wing for Pesach every year, it too reminds me of the smell of crematoria.

There was one more problem connected with the danger of house-search. They often stormed the private abodes of the Jews, and searched for jewels, but also for food. Whoever amassed and stored food reserves was executed. Still, one had to look ahead and make provisions. One had to hide them. Where can one hide edibles or even soap? We found a place. We had discovered that in our lavatory (this time one inside the house), certain planks of the wooden floor were loose and removable. Underneath was the mouth of a cave. The opening was so narrow that only Witek could glide into it. Thus, we now stored our provisions under the toilet.

You might wonder how it was possible, at this early stage of single and mass-executions, that life simply went on. Life had to go on — it seems to be a law. Thus, I must tell you some more about our occupations at the time after we had moved into the Miskowiec house. As I implied, we, the girls, worked alternately one day in the "Tereska" SS school and one day in the Jewish kitchen for the poor. Though I was of poor health, my proud and honest father wouldn't take advantage of his position so as to let me be freed from slaving in Tereska. We both hated everything that smelled of favoritism.

I was to acquire at this stage two new skills. They may seem to you almost marginal, but they too played a role in my formation. I have already enumerated proudly, several new skills; now I was to become a champion in potato peeling. Please, don't grin. Working every second day at the folk-kitchen, I had to peel three full pails of potatoes. I invented a system and was always the first to finish my daily contingent, well before old, experienced housewives.

It is such a trifle, but it still makes me proud. Does it indeed? Why was my dear cousin Rutka, who always worked at my side, not so ambitious? Why would she rather chat and do the work at her own pace? It made me think and reach the conclusion that I am too intense a person in whatever I do. Beware of over activity, my dear grandchildren, it ruins nerves and health.

Another talent that I showed in those days was that for organizing a campaign. There came a moment when the Judenrat was unable to find funds for running the folk-kitchen. I was charged with the mission of assembling all the youth and children of Rabka, divide them into groups and send them out for collection. They were to go from house to house and ask for potatoes, lentils, flour, onions, whatever they get, including money. Each group went on its mission, equipped with a list of addresses and with a huge basket drawn on a sledge. Nothing was missing in my planning, not even a tarpaulin cover in case of rainfall, or a reserve rope to draw the sledge.

Twenty years later, when I worked for the Museum of Ethnography and Folklore, I used to plan every move well in advance and down to the slightest detail. Just because I was born so absent minded, I disciplined myself to become a remarkable organizer. It is not vanity that propels me to boast of my achievements. It is just meant for you, my sweethearts, to make you appreciate every slightest skill and ability that you can develop in your personality.

The outcome of that social project was the survival of the folk-kitchen for a couple of days needed to over bridge this impasse. Our Jews, even the poor, were very generous and so were, of course, my parents. This success patted my ego and fed my ambition. How ambitious I can be — proves a recurring dream of that period.

I dreamt several times that I had wings... that I was flying over Krakow. It occurred to me that I might be dead... and return to my beloved city. Sigmund Freud would perhaps know better how to interpret it. I saw myself flying over the rooftops, touching lovingly the belfries and the gothic "gargoyles" on the ramparts of city churches. I touched the crowns of the trees, I felt elated being in seventh heaven. That's the positive part of the dream. But I must admit that the bad part was that I looked upon people from above and they looked up to me. Was I that vain, or was it the need for recognition cherished by a shy girl?

I manifested my inhibitions in many ways. Once, Wilek's little niece said (when he reprimanded her): "Now uncle Wilek, take your fiancée and get out of here". I was so ashamed that I could have crawled under the table. Wilek noticed my perplexity. "Nothing to be ashamed of", he said; "from now on you are my fiancée and let us announce it". Thus, we became officially engaged, but there seemed to be no future for us.

My own family became exposed to annihilation after my father got entangled in a most risky affair, as I shall soon explain. My instinct for survival was not very strong, but this instinct has its own dynamics. I was to discover later that a person in mortal danger thinks or feels that if everybody else dies, he (or she) will somehow survive. "How can the world go on without me?" thinks such a person.

At that stage, semi-normal life continued; we went through the routines, but we behaved like walking ghosts. Let's just see the danger my father ran into. The officers continued to require expensive gifts. Sometimes a gentile courier had to be sent to Krakow to find a rare item. Sherer refused to account for the expenses. He ran the Judenrat like his private enterprise. My father would not tolerate this situation. One day he took Wilek to council and together they tried to elaborate a plan of action. By this time, several of the Judenrat members themselves became victim to the German repressions, among them the honest good Mr.Birnhack who was executed. The average proportion was one Judenrat member among ten victims of reprisals. Thus, my father's life was in great danger, by sheer statistics.

Nevertheless, he was ready to augment the risk to his person and act very boldly. He decided with Wilek to form and shape up a strong opposition, to recruit the majority of the Judenrat members, and to proclaim at the next council meeting... a vote of non-confidence in Sherer.

Wilek believed that Sherer was not aware of being suspected of treason. He wouldn't dare to drop his mask. He would not disclose to them who were the opposition members, because it would be clear then that he was an informer. It is evident — maintained Wilek — that he wants to survive the war without being branded as traitor and be tried afterwards as war criminal. Father "went to work"... He was able to gain the support of many Judenrat councilors. They promised to vote with him against Sherer. The rest of the councilors would follow of suit.

At the next council meeting my father proclaimed, as agreed, the vote of no confidence in Sherer. Sherer was jolted. He had never suspected that somebody will have the guts to act openly against him. When he regained his composure, he saw that he had no choice but to submit this motion to vote. He played it well. What happened was a complete disaster. All the recruited, foresworn opposition members got cold feet and none, absolutely no one, raised his hand to second the motion. My father remained alone on the battlefield.

We cried at home and felt like plague stricken. People avoided us. Father was now in mortal danger and so was all our family. We expected any moment that the door would open, and the men would take my father for execution or round up all of us. Nothing happened. Wilek was right. Sherer was afraid to denounce my father, his declared opponent. His next move as chairman and his only sanction was to suspend my father from his function for the duration of one month. This disciplinary move was Pyrrhic victory, but my father survived.

The executions continued. They were sporadic no more, they turned into mass-executions. Their pattern changed. Several times the whole Jewish population was summoned for a rollcall on the square of "Tereska"' and tens of victims were drawn from the rows to be shot later in the ravine of death and buried there. Thus, eventually, came the turn of my grandmother. Later, Jonas Rose with his wife shared the same lot and so did both of Wilek's parents. Not simultaneously, but in the same period between end 1941 and spring 1942. They not only executed old people, sometimes they picked their victims as their whim dictated. Once they picked at a selection a young woman because she was ginger haired. But she did not die with red hair. We were told by the Jewish slaves of "Tereska" that during the long hours between the selection and the execution her hair turned white... Maybe it is a legend, maybe it was true, as several people testified. I haven't seen it. So, to avoid panic and an eventual revolt, the Germans changed their system. They didn't pick people out during a selection. Now they only checked us all at a roll call, holding a list. They made a mark next to the name of the prospective victim. They had all the addresses on their registration records. They came later for the victim and drew him from his house. That's the way it happened to my grandmother.

Grandma's neighbors told us later, that two officers came for her to her room. They told her quietly to accompany them. She understood. The door remained open. The neighbors saw her straighten up and heard her say in her perfect German: "Gentlemen, you must understand that on this most important day of my life, I cannot accompany you dressed as I am in my dressing gown. I cannot possibly escape from this room. I shall quickly change behind this cupboard, and you may meanwhile take some refreshments from the bottles in this corner. There is liqueur and there is vodka, please be my guests..."

That's the way it was. Later, Wilek and several workmen at "Tereska" saw my grandmother among those concentrated there to be executed. The whole ingathering action lasted from early morning till sunset.

Don't ask me how we cried, how we sat 'Shiva', I don't remember. We must have been in shock, even though you may say that it was expected. Knowing the prognosis and receiving the blow are two different things. I only remember myself shivering and my teeth chattering so loud that I had to take a piece of bread. Afterwards, I started doing the laundry. Every time after a tragic event I was chewing bread or washing linen. It became a pattern.

We were all now in mortal danger. We were all coming nearer and nearer to the valley of death. There was one more incident concerning the death of my grandmother. We were told later that a young Jew, Dattner, working at "Tereska" and suspected of collaboration with the Germans, approached my grandmother some time before the execution. She whispered something into his ear and handed him a small parcel, probably her jewels — to be delivered to us. We didn't dare to ask him, and he made no move to approach us. It didn't matter; we were too heartbroken. Anyhow, it has to be stated that at this dangerous period, when most of the elder people were killed, grandmother managed to pass over to us some very valuable jewels. The story of the jewels and their loss, connected with another tragic death, will be told later.

With my granny's murder the irony of destiny played us a vicious trick. The ravine of executions and burial was so close to our house, that we could almost hear the cries of "Shema Israel" and the shots. Grandma was buried in this valley of death, and thus came closer to my mother than she had ever been in her lifetime.

As I mentioned, shortly after my grandmother, Wilek's parents shared her lot. I still remember Wilek's tiny lively mother and his good, pedantic father. I remember an episode connected with his father's pedantry. Once, when I visited the Grunberg family, Wilek sat on one chair and reposed his aching feet on a bar of another chair. His pedantic father reprimanded him: "Wilek, you are ruining the chair". "Father" — replied Wilek — "it is not your chair; it belongs to the German state..." It was a prophecy, as time has proven.

Between one execution and another there was this feeling that the last execution must have been the final one. Haven't all the old and weak people been killed already? The German beast must be satiated. After all, the beast has never proclaimed that it intends to kill all the Jews. That would be preposterous — or so most people thought at that time, quoting reassurances expressed by Germans of high rank and position.

Not everybody believed or shared this opinion. Single people and families started to flee Rabka. There must be some more secure places — they thought — but most of them went into hiding, even if it was a temporary arrangement with a gentile. The Germans got wind of these attempts at flight. The headquarters of Rabka proclaimed a new strict edict: For every person or family who escapes from Rabka... ten Jewish inhabitants will be shot, among them one Judenrat councilor. It wasn't an empty threat. The next time somebody escaped, they picked out ten people, including one Judenrat member.

We explained this situation to our good friend Victor Poraj Chlebowski on one of his visits. He offered to help us flee, arguing that others would soon expose us to death. He promised to try to find us a hiding place as soon as possible. Before he finished the sentence, we rejected his offer on the spot. We couldn't commit the sin of causing the death of other people. We would never save our skin at that price. There was an absolute consensus on this subject within our family. Nobody objected. "Reconsider my offer once more" — said Victor — "I shall meanwhile look for s solution".

Here I have to stop the flow of my report in order to describe Victor, because he will play a major role in my story later at several points. He was a son of impoverished high aristocracy, an impressive figure of a man, though turning on seventy. He had a crystal pure character and a heart of a dove. He was known to be an art connoisseur. This cosmopolitan served in his good days as Poland's ambassador to Russia. During the Russian revolution, Victor's lovely wife got lost. He never had a proof of her death; he could never remarry. Following his career, he served as ambassador in Turkey, and later, when the Polish Government collapsed, Victor received the title of the Turkish Minister of Posts. How was it possible? Very simply — as Victor explained. The Turkish prime minister, who liked him well, offered this position. "But Your Excellency" — remonstrated the honest Victor — "how can I function as post minister, when I know nothing about post office except the basic fact that recommended letters cannot be simply mailed after pasting on the stamps...". "Excellent" — said the Prime Minister- "that's exactly why you cannot be nominated Deputy Minister, you can only perform as full minister of the Turkish Post..." During the years at Istanbul, Victor, fascinated by the opulence and exoticism of Turkey, painted hundreds of pictures with local colorist. Years later, when he returned to Poland, he was selling his Turkish pictures and acting as art dealer, but he had to live on a skimpy budget. That was when he befriended my father, an art connoisseur himself, and visited him almost daily. Unable to remarry, he lived with his housekeeper, a crafty, shrewd countrywoman. She had a son and Victor adopted him. When Victor was turning seventy, he begot lovely twin girls, who resembled him like a carbon copy. To observe Victor patting his little twins, was like watching him sculpt.

His pictures, painted in "naïve" style, sold less and less. When the war broke out, Victor, the connoisseur of art, became the man of confidence of the Polish aristocracy and of the Jewish art collectors as well. Even monasteries sold their art treasures through Victor. After we left Krakow, he used to sell some of our art objects left in his custody and bring us the money to Rabka. Now, after we had received from Grandma Rose part of her jewels shortly before her death, the faithful Victor was to sell them gradually for us. We wanted to entrust to his keeping all the rest of grandma's diamonds, but he wouldn't hear of it. At last, when we were all in mortal danger, and still refused to escape because of the mutual responsibility, my parents decided that something must be done about the jewels so that Victor would have access to them, in case of our death or partial survival.

We found a solution. The jewels were hidden in a cache dug into the external wall of the Miskowiec house. They were walled in under the window, on ground floor level. Soon it proved to be an excellent solution.

There was still another treasure to hide, this one rather of sentimental value. Its provenance is bizarre. Once, before the war, a country priest came to my father, asked for discretion and offered for sale five thick necklaces of big, irregular red corals. As well known to my father, these were votive offerings of country folk, dedicated to St.Mary's picture so that she would grant a miraculous cure. The priest explained that he had to sell them discreetly so as to finance the urgently needed repairs to his church. Knowing my mother's attraction to folklore, father bought them from the priest, joking privately that the priest had a red nose of a drinking man. Another family joke was that these votive offerings brought about father's cure. My mother didn't want to part with them, even though she could have sold them quite easily to a Goral peasant. We were superstitious in this family, I still am. Now, we had to hide this thick parcel of red-pink corals. I climbed up to the attic and stuck the parcel into the straw filling between the last beam and the roof tiles.

If the Miskowiec house has not been demolished in the last forty-four years, our corals are still there. It is a pity, because corals if not worn on warm neck, turn pale and die. So do people, when lacking affection.

But at this period nobody died of lack of affection. We were all walking corpses. Still, some of the walking corpses didn't want to die in the ravine. Some walking corpses decided that their life is worth ten lives of other walking corpses. That's when a terrible thing happened again and once more. Wilek had a good friend, a young lawyer by the name of Marcel Finster. This Marcel (again a Marcel) was quite often a guest in our house. He was witty and amusing, but he certainly didn't have much character. One day we heard terrifying news. Marcel Finster, his parents and brother disappeared from Rabka. They had escaped. A day or two later ten Jews were executed as reprisal, and one Judenrat member among them. The ranks of the Judenrat shrank to a third. Nobody wanted to fill the 'vacated' places.

I was so outraged that I became speechless. A visitor to our house, an intellectual would do such an abominable thing? It was beyond my comprehension. I hated his smiling smug. I felt a great urge to confront him and to spit in his face. Little did I know that I should have this opportunity two years later.

Soon after Marcel Finster another family escaped, and again ten Jews were murdered by the Germans.

We, the beautiful people with conscience wouldn't escape, it was a taboo. There was still one thing left that we could do. Two months after Marcel's escape there were whispers and rumors about a plan of total liquidation of Rabka Jewry. There was talk of a transport. It didn't seem probable. Why bother? They could finish us off right here. But the cook at Tereska told Victor that he overheard the officers discussing it. His knowledge of German was very limited, still this must have been the gist of that conversation. This grim prospect altered our situation and our attitude. If all the Jews left in Rabka were about to be put on a train and transferred to a camp, the mutual responsibility wouldn't apply any more.

We had to prepare a hiding place for such an eventuality… a place where we could possibly hide at the last moment. We have discovered that a nice younger brother of our landlord, the Goral Miskowiec, owns an empty house on the other side of the hills, quite close to the Polish police station. How can we approach him, what shall we say?

This young Goral liked to chat and joke with my sweet cousin Rutka. Rutka was quite a schemer. She didn't volunteer to speak to younger Miskowiec, she just went about it in her own way. One day, without saying a word, she disappeared in the afternoon and didn't come back after dark. It was summer 1942 and nobody walked in Rabka after dark. Hours passed; we were all in despair. Aunt Helcia was wailing and pulling her hair. Father offered to go to the Polish police, but we wouldn't let him. Eventually, close to eleven, Rutka came home as if nothing had happened. Father was out of his wits. He yelled at Rutka as I had never heard him yell before. But my dear, sweet Rutka didn't say a word. She just extended her little palm and showed a huge key… the key to the empty hut that was to save our lives. How Rutka obtained this key, at what price — we never knew and never asked.

A month had passed since we came into possession of this key (perhaps less), and nothing much happened. All was quiet before the storm. Nobody escaped, and the Germans stopped the executions. As in a Greek tragedy, there seemed to appear a ray of hope before the final calamity. We still rejected Victor's plan, we passed our exam with flying colors. No stain is attached to our name… On the contrary, we have won again a 'good card' to our credit, if the Almighty keeps His accounts. We saved four lives in addition to our own lives and this by means of the magic key. We could save four strangers — we only couldn't save my father. That was our tragedy, and that is the way things happened.

At the crucial moment, when the Germans ordered all the Jews of Rabka to assemble with personal belongings at the railway station (allegedly for transport to a labor camp) — we could make our bold move. The collective responsibility was over. We were free go into hiding in the empty house. There was still time from morning to sunset. We had already drawn into our secret four nice people, offering to save them together with us in our hiding place. I realize now that this noble proposition augmented the peril of discovery, that the four people contributed nothing to the escapade, but we weren't an egoistic sort of people.

When the order of total evacuation of Rabka was published, the four people knew what to do and where to come. Unfortunately, Wilek couldn't do it. He still worked as a slave in Tereska; he was to stay there with the other slaves and he wouldn't endanger his colleagues by escaping. Dr. Paster, his wife and little daughter Anitka, had been killed a long time before, but there was still Wilek's second sister Maryla, the one who taught me to sew. She was left to be saved or to perish. Wilek came for a fleeting moment to our house (cutting through the fields from "Tereska"). He came to take leave of us, and to impose on us the task of persuading his stubborn sister to go into hiding with us. Like the other three outsiders, she was supposed to reach the hiding place separately by herself, but when the day came, she refused to do it. We too, the six members of our family, were to reach this destination each of us separately, so as not to attract attention. For the very same reason of security, we decided to flee without personal effects, carrying absolutely nothing except a toothbrush and a pair of panties in our handbag. Just imagine leaving a house full of all vital objects and possessions and start a new life with a toothbrush.

When we were all ready to shut the door behind us and disperse — there was an unexpected diversion and impediment.

A young man, serving like Wilek in Tereska, but also running errands for the Judenrat, came to ask my father to come down to the Judenrat office, because he was needed there urgently. Father couldn't refuse; he had this inborn sense of duty. Somebody else would say to the young man: "Don't wait, I shall be down there in five minutes" — not my father. He only whispered into mother's ear:" You go, I shall join you later over there". He went down the slope with the youngster. That was the last I saw of my father, but I couldn't have guessed. The tension was enormous.

We all threw a last look at our house and split up, but mother and I had to lose some valuable moments. We went quickly to Wilek's sister Maryla and persuaded her to join us. She was stubborn as a mule. How can she leave their house and possessions just like that, how can she — she wailed. She must pack... she must prepare.

"It is now or never"- said mother quietly — "It is without any personal belongings or not at all. Besides, Wilek asked us to drag you by your hair if you refuse. Still, the decision is yours, and yours only. We have no right to insist". Mother sat down and said no more. Maryla understood. Composed and deathly pale, she took her toothbrush, her few jewels, a change of linen — she was ready.

We separated, but I followed her from a distance. It was a grave responsibility persuading her thus, perhaps we were wrong, perhaps we all should have let ourselves be swept with the tide. Could we guarantee her safety while our plans did not go beyond this temporary shelter? It was a new start, without a foothold. I shall spare you the suspense; she lives today in Canada... That's the way we started a new chapter and that's why I said that if I were to write a book, I would choose as title: "Life with a toothbrush as my only possession".

OUR ESCAPE FROM THE FALSE PARADISE

The empty hut was situated quite close to the Polish police station, and that, in itself, was an advantage, especially since the entrance was from the backside and unseen from the police station. Who would search in its vicinity for hiding Jews?

All of us met at the appointed hour close to the house but hiding in bushes. After we had checked that nobody was observing us, we opened the door with the big key and entered the house. We decided on the spot to move into the storage, where nobody could peep in through the window or hear our whispers. We were nine people, including Maryla and the three acquaintances. We set down on the bundles of straw and waited for father. The outsiders silently checked the arrangements, nobody spoke, no one dared to. We sat thus for hours waiting for father, crying silently, listening for steps, crying some more, and waiting. It was night and it was dawn, and father did not come. We still prayed for a miracle. Perhaps he had lost his way, he is hiding somewhere, he will find the hut in daylight. Nothing happened, all hope was lost.

Here we were — nine people on an island of sorts, not able to leave this temporary abode. We had to organize our life. We had stored in advance some food, two buckets and a washing basin. My mother planned and organized everything with Rutka, who carried these items into the house some time in advance. Our four companions contributed nothing; they were our burden and our responsibility. They were: Maryla, Mrs. Stephanie and her young daughter, and Mr. Wechsler, also a family friend, the only man in this group.

The main problems were: obtaining fresh water, bread and… the toilet.

The privy was outside, facing the police station, we certainly couldn't use it. My parents had foreseen every detail and every problem. We needed a faithful outsider, a gentile, who would supply us with water and food, who would come every second night, bring these provisions, and carry out the bucket of excrements that served as our toilet. There was only one person who could do it… While we lived in the Miskoviec house, we had a country girl, Aniela, coming to us once a month to do the laundry. But she came to us more often than that. Since she was from a distant hamlet and working almost every day in Rabka, she had no place to sleep. Whenever she remained in Rabka overnight, she was invited to stay with us. She shared our supper and slept on a cot. Nobody else did it for her. She grew very fond of us and very grateful. Now, when the time of our escape approached, mother showed her the empty house and asked her to come to it at night, when we would go into hiding. She was to be our only contact with the outer world.

Indeed, the faithful Aniela came on the second night. She was able to tell us only that the train full of Jews left the Rabka station. Its destination was not known. There were different speculations. Coming every second evening, Aniela used to knock three times and once more at the door, imitating the first staves of Beethoven's fifth symphony (unknown to her). She handed us the bread and whatever she bought for us, then she fetched fresh water from a distant well, because ours was too visible. Then she took out the bucket with urine and excrements of nine people. She carried and emptied it far away, so as not to leave traces of our presence in the empty house. The very act of buying bread for us was also dangerous. A grocer in this hamlet knows everybody. Why would a single girl, a laundress, buy bread for nine people? Thus, as precaution, she bought at two different grocery shops, the second one outside Rabka. Though every time she came, she got a fat lump of money for her dangerous services, she was scared to death. Indeed, if caught, she would pay with her life.

How did we pass the long days? At daytime we talked in whispers, at night we cried after father. We, the three of us: mother, Witek and I. Could I imagine my father in a labor camp? Did he stand a chance there? Was it probable that the whole train was taken to an extermination center? Impossible. Having killed so many in Rabka, would they use trains in order to kill the rest? Why bother now that they needed every train for transports to the Russian front. They probably needed these Jews as slaves in

Ukraine. Only my father wouldn't survive it. All such thoughts wandered in circles in our minds.

So as not to become crazy with despair and tension, I used to invent and play games with Witek. One was a simplified scrabble, composed of little cardboard squares with letters. I played a different game with Maryla. I drew for her models of dresses, and this innocent pastime opened new vistas for me. Four years later I was to study in Paris history of costume, as inspired by trends in art, and as a sideline I took fashion drawing. Working as fashion designer, I was able to pay my way through the studies of anthropology.

Once a pedagogue (for twenty-eight years) — always a pedagogue, hence my conclusion: never underestimate a hobby or a pastime.

Here we sat in this cage, suspended between life and death. We had no plans and no options. We just had to wait till the hunt for the Jews would abate in this area. We could then, perhaps, creep out of our shelter at night, split up, take the road, reach a railway station and board a train to Krakow. Very risky, yet not impossible. What next? Could we go to Victor and endanger him and his family? Certainly not. Our companions planned to sneak into the ghetto. That's what we shall try to do. It was like moving from a mud field into a gutter. What else could we plan in this situation? Even that seemed unrealistic, how should we ever cover this distance to the next station, far from Rabka.

If only father were with us. If only Wilek could have joined us. Was he safe over there in the lion's den? Did I miss him? I had no time to grub in my feelings or make an estimate if this separation had an eighty percent impact on my psyche, or less, as compared to the loss of my father.

One night Aniela didn't come when expected. We were left without water and without food. It was end of August 1942, a very hot August, and we were parched. All windows had to remain shut, the roof seemed to be a hot tin roof — the heat was unsupportable. We all had to undress in the presence of Mr. Wechsler and Witek, all women sat in their underwear. There was nothing else we could do. We tried to swallow our saliva, but our mouth became dry. We had shared the last crumbs of bread and the last sip of water three days before. The worst was the problem of the only bucket containing urine and excrements. Something had to be done about it. Mr. Wechsler offered to take the risk and carry it out to the nearby gorge.

He made his way in dark; he was not equipped with a torch. The battery was dead. We didn't even use candles at night for fear of detection.

Mr. Wechsler didn't come back for a long time, and we got worried. When he eventually returned, he was swearing and stinking all over. He had lost his foothold, slipped in the dark, fell with the bucket, and got soaked in urine and excrements. He now kept away from us, sitting on the stairs; he was in the pit of despair. He couldn't get clean. One of us took the risk of going down to the nearest well and drawing water. We washed his clothes as well as we could, we left a sip of water to drink.

On the fourth night Aniela reappeared. She was so scared that we heard her heartbeat, listening from the first floor. She made effusive excuses; she had hardly hoped to find us here. She explained lamely that somebody followed her, it must have been the devil; she noticed his horns in the dark. She didn't dare approach the house (lest the devil take us), she left the provisions in the gorge, she ran away. The Virgin Mary talked to her and persuaded her to try once more the next night. The devil prevented her once more and then again. Gathering all her courage she tried for the last time. She retrieved the bread and margarine from the gorge, Virgin Mary must have kept vigil over it. Seeing now that we were no ghosts but only hungry and thirsty Jews, she went about her task and brought water from the well. The bread that she left in the bushes for three days and four nights was half dried up, half moldy from dew. Mobilizing all our restraint, we cut it into portions and chewed it like grinning apes.

We told Aniela that a merciful Christian that she was doesn't have to be afraid of the devil, he is powerless in her presence. It worked. She promised to come again the night after the next. She did, and we decided not to move out as long as she kept coming. After we had spent two full weeks in hiding, something absolutely unforeseen happened at night. Close to midnight there was a knock at the door. It couldn't have been Aniela, it was not the signal agreed between us: three consecutive knocks, and one more. Who could it be? Nobody else knew of our hiding place. The person knocked again. We all got dressed, we thought that it is the end of us, we have been discovered. But the Germans wouldn't knock and wait, nor would the Polish Police. Perhaps it is an extortionist who has discovered somehow our cache. Perhaps this is Aniela's devil? The person knocked again and again, more nervously now. The game was over, we had to open the door. "Who is it?" — asked our brave Mr. Wechsler. "It's only me, Weislo" — answered the person in a whisper.

You will remember now that Weislo was the young Goral gentile who befriended Uncle Jonas Rose and taught him to carve. Wechsler opened the door. The crafty goy Weislo was trembling all over. Why did he come? How did he know that we were hiding here? He knew but I don't remember from whom. Perhaps from the cook, perhaps from young Miskowiec himself who gave us the key. The whole scene was so charged with emotions and fear that I am confused even now. Weislo told us a terrible story. He himself was concealing in his hut several Jews, a fact of which we knew nothing, not even who it might have been. When he caught his breath and relaxed a little sitting among us on the straw, he told us the rest. He left his Jews in his hut and went to Krakow to make some arrangements for them. When he came back, his cousin waited for him at the station. He approached him for a fleeting moment and warned him in a whisper: "Disappear immediately, your Jews were discovered and taken to the... The whole is after you, run away". Where could poor Weislo run to? No Goral trusts another Goral, besides, who will dare hide him knowing that there is hunting for his head. He became a fugitive like us; he became another hunted Jew of sorts. Contemplate this irony of fate, him asking us to give him shelter in our hiding place...

He stayed for the rest of the night, hiding with us. Nobody slept. We analyzed this new situation, and it became apparent to us that the Jews hiding in Weislo's abode must have known about us and our hiding place. Weislo admitted that much. When interrogated and tortured, these unfortunate Jews will certainly spill what they know about us. We had to do it before dawn. Where to? To the nearest railway station in Zaryte — where no one knows us. We decided to leave the house immediately and separate. Nine Jews cannot walk the roads of a "Judenrein" country. We decided to proceed in pairs. Maryla, who didn't look Jewish, offered to go with Witek, even though mother would rather keep him at her side. Aunt Helcia looked very Jewish but Rutka wouldn't leave her of course. I was to be the forerunner, the spearhead. I was over eighteen, but I could pass for fifteen. A girl with blond braids and blue eyes, a girl aged fifteen doesn't have to carry an identity card.

We put some distance between one pair and another, but I decided to meet once more with mother and Mr. Wechsler so as to adopt a plan improvised on the spot. I was to go ahead and eventually indicate the first stop in some bushes or ravine. Those behind me will stop the next couple and so on, till all are concentrated in a place known to me. I was meanwhile to continue ahead, to reach the railway station of Zaryte, and observe if there is an inspection of identity cards. Then I was to go back to the hiding place of the whole group. It was a long way to the station, but I was lucky to get the desired information almost halfway. When I passed the center of Zaryte, I witnessed a meeting between two Polish policemen. One had a bike. "Where to?" asked the other one. "Oh, there is some nuisance. Some Jews were spotted coming down the road from the direction of Rabka. I am being sent to the station to check every passenger before he boards the train; I shall be stuck there until relived" — said the policeman with the bike.

It was enough for me; it was all I had to know. I turned round on the spot and retraced my steps. I personally was in no danger; I could pass the inspection pretending to be less than fifteen. I had a medallion on my chest, like any good Christian girl. In its oval frame was inserted the picture of Saint Theresa. Actually, it did not represent St. Theresa. It was a photo of me — a cutout of an old snapshot of me in ski outfit. My ski-cap looked like the aureole, the halo around the head of Holy Theresa. I cut out only this head and inserted it into my medallion. I did it well in advance before we went into hiding. Nobody would discover the deception.

There was of course no question of trying to take the train on my own; the idea never crossed my mind. I had to warn quickly all the others before it will be too late. I was now running back. Everything went awry. Somehow my mother and Wechsler were not able to spot and stop all the others, Witek with Maryla, Helcia with Rutka, even Stephanie and her daughter seemed to have disappeared. It was a disaster, or so we thought when I met again mother and Wechsler, hidden in the bushes at the appointed place. What were we to do now, the three of us? We still waited for the others for some time, but it became clear by now that they must have taken another road, perhaps a sideroad, a shortcut. Boarding the train was out of question. We had to let elapse some twenty-four hours. Where shall we hide? Mother wanted to comb the whole area looking for Witek, but Wechsler dissuaded her somehow. We took a lane to the left of the main road, a long lane that seemed to lead to the forest. Having the topography of Zaryte already imprinted in my brain, I knew that the second hill and its forest must be facing the station. We proceeded for about one kilometer or more, and indeed, we reached an ideal observation post. We could now see the station from afar like on the palm of our hand, but it was difficult to spot the policeman. He probably did his checking under the roof of the passage. Anyhow, we decided to wait till noon of the next day.

Once more the forest gave us shelter. We ate some wilted blueberries to assuage our thirst. We must have been very hungry, but I don't remember it. It must have been close to noon. Hours passed, we discussed the situation from every angle, we also noted in our memory the hours when the train used to leave the station. Our watches ticked, birds sang, and we worried. When the evening approached, we didn't feel any more like giving it a try the next day. Being so restless, we changed our plans. Why not try another station? The next one must be Makow. We can start at midnight and reach it in the early morning hours. That's better. Now we have to catch a few hours of sleep. The night grew cold, it was September. We tore heaps of sweet-smelling, purple heather (I adore purple), and made a bed of it, the rest serving as blanket. For a while we felt a little better. Once more the romantic in me enjoyed the bed of heather and the shelter of a forest. We didn't sleep, we wept worrying about our next of kin; perhaps we dozed off for a fleeting moment waiting for midnight. Again, something went awry, and the most unpredictable happened suddenly. We heard voices, they came from below, no more than twenty meters distant from us. The hushed voices seemed to be mixed. Were there two women and two men? It was plausible. Was it a romantic outing of two couples? I strained my eyes. All I could discern in the dim moonlight was that one man wore white trousers. Rather unusual in this region. The two couples seemed to discuss something. The two women argued, then they undressed. That much was visible, and it was plausible too. What happened next was bizarre. The men seemed to approach the two women, but nothing happened. They just talked all the time and the two women dressed again quickly. How could one explain this enigma? Some more whispers and the two couples went back the way they had come.

We were scared as if paralyzed. If the forest is not safe at night, how shall we dare to leave it and expose ourselves at night on the roads? We were shaken by this insignificant episode. Goodbye to Makow, anyhow — we said — it is too late now to follow up this new plan. By force of inertia, we remained in our heather-beds and stayed there till the late morning hours. Weak with hunger we decided to run the risk of taking the train leaving from Zaryte at noon. Shall we first buy some bread at a grocery shop at Zaryte? We were already fasting close to forty hours. We decided against it. Mother insisted that we separate, knowing that alone I stood much better chance. I pretended to comply (at last I learned a lesson from Rutka), but after we descended the hills and reached the station separately, I maneuvered to find myself close to her, at her elbow.

There was a policeman at the station, and for some obscure reason he did not accost the two of us, he let mother and me pass unchecked. Did my St. Theresa medallion protect us after we escaped the embrace of Tereska and the dwelling there? Mr. Wechsler had no such luck. We saw the policeman stop him, but we couldn't tarry, we couldn't help him. We only silently prayed for him, but this time not to St. Theresa.

Here we were seated in the same compartment and who do you think took the last empty seat, hopping in at the last moment? — Mr. Wechsler. How he passed the checkpoint and survived — we couldn't guess. He was to tell us later, when we reached Krakow. Nobody looked at us with suspicion. Slowly, very slowly our pulses returned to normal, or almost normal. We were cold, weakened by the fast and thinking all the time about Witek and the rest of the party. At last, a little miracle happened and a vendor of "begele" passed along the train. Who bought from him in our compartment? Only three passengers, you can guess who. I looked at the fields, all golden in this early autumn, and didn't guess that I would see fields and trees again only two and a half years later.

I felt pangs of remorse that I didn't go with Witek. I should have... it could have facilitated his ploy. At least I would have known what happened to him. Lost in such heavy thoughts we reached Krakow. Now, at the crowded station, Mr. Wechsler could tell us how he outwitted the policeman. Wechsler was about fifty years old, tall and good looking like a diplomat. He had a Tyrolian hat like many Volksdeutsche used to wear. But that was far from enough. What about his documents? He was of Czech origin, he had come to Poland some twenty-five years before, and still preserved his non-valid passport of a Czech citizen. Asked for his documents by the policeman, he made a poker face of a cosmopolitan — and nonchalantly drew from his pocket this old passport. The policeman pretended to understand what it contained, leafed through it scrupulously, saluted, and let this distinguished diplomat pass the checkpoint. It was lucky that I had inspected Mr. Wechsler's suit for traces of the sticking heather and sniffed it for traces of a certain smell. We reached our lovely Krakow with very mixed feelings. Nostalgia, sadness, worry, fear, elation — you name it. We were free as birds, and we were going now voluntarily to let ourselves be trapped in the cage of ghetto. That is if there would be a way to slip in... As I said, we wouldn't bother Victor and impose ourselves on him. If Witek reached him, we would soon know it. We took a tramway to the Podgorze suburb of Krakow and stood in front of the ghetto gate. People wearing the Jewish badge were going in and out. All had a document that they showed at the gate. It was checked by one Jewish policeman and one German of some formation or other. Squadrons of working units waited before the gate to get inside. We approached one person and asked to inform our relatives the Kornhausers or Uncle Olek that we were in front of the gate, and could they smuggle us in. They had their contacts. First, they sent us the Jewish badge to slip it on discreetly somewhere in hiding, and then we were brought in without much ado.

The Kornhauser cousins took us into their arms, we cried, and we laughed. We cried — you know why — and we laughed because Witek had safely arrived, and aunt Helcia and Rutka too. Here are their separate stories. That of Witek and Maryla was very simple. They took a short cut in Zaryte and reached the station well before I returned to warn the others, and before the document inspecting policeman was posted at the station. They arrived there a full day and a half before us. Maryla didn't intend to enter the ghetto, she had another solution. We had a common acquaintance, a German gentile lady who had for the last thirty years been married to a Jew. She was now concealing him in her flat, she was able and willing to accommodate Maryla as well.

As for Helcia and Rutka, we found them happy and reunited with uncle Olek. The story of their escape from Rabka was very strange. They followed a different road, passed through Zaryte, but didn't dare to approach the station. They were looking for me, the forerunner scout, and for the others. They must have moved in circles. It was after sunset that they returned to the main road. They felt that they were being followed. They now decided to go faster to the station, come what may, even if it was too late for the last train. Fearing the followers, aunt Helcia suggested that they separate. Maybe all they want is a flirt with Rutka... She, Helcia, will manage. Rutka wouldn't hear of it. She remained adamant, they quarreled. Shortly before they reached the station they were eventually stopped by their followers, two young, well dressed Polish gentlemen. "Ladies, will you please kindly follow us" — said one of them. Rutka tried to turn it into a joke. "My mother is conservative; she wouldn't let me talk to strangers" — she answered with a pale-smile. "Ladies, let us not pretend, you are not in a position to oppose us, you know it" — said the taller one in a clipped tone. There was nothing they could do now. The two gentiles were leading them far away from the road, taking a narrow lane. There were no more huts on their way, and they reached a forest in the pale light of a half moon.

Here I interrupted Rutka and continued her story; "When you were deep enough in the woods, the two men started to explain something. You tried to discuss it. One of the men was wearing white trousers..." Rutka was beyond herself. "True" — she exclaimed — "but how can you possibly know it? It's amazing." — "I just know" — I continued — "it is very simple. You were brought exactly to the spot where we were hiding. We didn't exactly see you or recognize your voices; all I saw were the white trousers of one of the men. But tell me please, why did you have to undress?" Here followed the full explanation. When they penetrated the forest, the two gentlemen explained that they were active in the Polish underground, and their cell is in desperate need of money. They, the Jewesses, have to give it for the good cause. Rutka tried to appeal to their better feelings, but the men had only one kind of loyalty. Suspecting that Helcia and Rutka have hidden some more money or jewels on their body, the two ordered them to undress and made a thorough search for valuables. Having appropriated all they possessed, the two men changed their tone. They gave Helcia and Rutka enough money for the train tickets and they gave them excellent instructions; what way to take to the Habovka station instead of Zaryte and at what time to take the train in the morning. Helcia and Rutka followed the instructions to the letter and were able to reach Krakow in safety. What became of Stephanie and her daughter — we didn't know and shall never know. They must have been caught and... We have also lost the traces of Mr. Wechsler. It seems all so hectic and hazy now.

It was September 1942, and here we were safely… in the ghetto, all the family. Only one was missing. Now in the arms of our distant relatives we could cry our hearts out and mourn for my father… for a very short while. People who have only a toothbrush in their possession, have no time to cry.

As we learned much later, the train from Rabka (with my father) must have been sent to Treblinka to… It will be a full year and a half later, when we shall meet in the Plaszow Concentration Camp somebody who was the last person to see my father — through a window in the train. This young man, Turek, was the last person to see my father alive. I will tell you more about this meeting in the right context and time.

THE PLANET CALLED "GHETTO"

As you may remember, we left Krakow in March 1941 and returned to it, or rather to the ghetto of Krakow, in September 1942. Many things happened in the meantime while we were in Rabka. Before I tell you how people with a toothbrush start a new life, I must attend to some broader aspects of life in a ghetto.

Though we were constantly informed through Olek's letters what was going on in the ghetto, I got the full picture only after we arrived there. I am not trying to do research work on the history of this ghetto, I can only state here what a girl, eighteen years old, could apprehend, absorb and memorize. Don't forget that we were still in a state of shock, both spiritual and physical. After roaming in the fields and forests, after a night on a pillow of heather, we found ourselves in a pot of boiling elements. The constriction, the noise, the smells, invaded our senses with a strong impact. Worst of all was the feeling of being trapped in a huge cage.

This Jewish quarter in the Podgorze suburb, encircled as it was partly by walls and partly by barbed wire, constituted a sort of autonomic city. The expression 'autonomic' is used here with a certain degree of irony, but it has to be stated that the Germans were seldom seen in the streets of the ghetto, except at the gate and in a certain office. Their massive presence became felt only when an "Aktion" was about to take place. The term "Aktion" is a German euphemism for deportation and murder.

The administration was in the hands of the Judenrat, the order was kept and supervised by the "Ordnungsdienst" (OD), the "Service of Order" — actually the Jewish Police. Here is another transparent euphemism. The president of the first body, the Judenrat, was at the time of our arrival the abominable Gutter, but before him the mantle was (unwillingly) worn by Dr.Arthur Rosenzweig, as it was by Marek Biberstein before him. In order to retrace earlier episodes, I have first to describe these main actors of the drama.

Dr.Rosenzweig was before the war my father's lawyer. Father used to describe him as dry, efficient and uncompromising stickler. He lost nothing of his characteristics when in office as "Judenaltester". Due to his honesty, he had a tragic end.

Symche Spira, the OD commander, a vulgar half illiterate, who used to be a glazier, was a combination of sybarite, megalomaniac, eroto-maniac, psychopath and manipulator. He, who in his past wore a beard and a capote, was now dressed in a splendid uniform with decorations, well-fitting his opulent body. He was directly responsible to the Gestapo with its main office and prison in Montelupich Street. The OD had its own prison in the ghetto.

Talking about the Service of Order (the OD), although I presented previously the complex situations of those who joined the service, I have to stress once more; I am not claiming that there were no informers who volunteered for this ignoble role. There were all grades and shades of informers, yet we shall very soon meet one spy who did his best to save Jewish lives...

As you can perceive now, forcing the hand of the Judenrat, turning the OD into executives and using spies, the Gestapo was perfectly able to rule the Jewry from a certain distance.

All this became known to us only gradually and not at the first contact with the ghetto. We were too busy organizing our new life or rather trying to survive, to take notice of all these circumstances. But bear with me one moment more and let me outline the general internal situation. I am not a chronicler, my only intention is to relate some outstanding and some unusual events, as were described in Olek's letters and were later corroborated by several inhabitants of the ghetto, mainly Dr.Hilfstein.

To describe such events, I have to underpaint the background. The very numbers of Jews varied constantly, but there was also a discrepancy in the numbers provided by the so-called respectable sources. The insiders are rarely aware of the exact numbers. In the official minutes of the trial of Amon Goethe (the commander of Plaszow Concentration Camp) it was stated that the ghetto, when first established in March 1941, was to be inhabited by 68,000 Jews. Another calculation reduced the number to

57,000. How is it possible that in autumn of the same year, 1941, there were no more than 17,000 Jews registered in the same ghetto? The answer is that thousands sought refuge in little villages, the way we did in moving to Rabka. It is true that many were constantly reshuffled, that most perished in massacres of whole villages, and others, streaming in from the provinces reached the ghetto in Krakow.

I shall give here a little example of the first major reshuffle aimed at restricting the ghetto population, which ended in an absurd way due to contradicting orders.

Those who were lucky and worked, received as their only payment, food ration coupons — so as not to let them die of starvation. Those who had no work were depending on the folk kitchen. They were very many and the ghetto being so overpopulated was in danger of epidemics. It so happened in this Autumn of 1941, that the Gestapo imposed on Symche Spira the compiling of a list of non-working people. Some thousand Jews were led to the trains and transported to the region of Lublin. They were set free in the fields and nothing happened. They were told to settle in nearby villages. They had but one desire: to go back to Krakow to their ghetto... On foot or on carts (Jews were forbidden to use trains) most of them came back after many days or even weeks. They glided back into the ghetto, others were caught and perished. Wasn't that absurd?

On the surface, the ghetto of Krakow was vibrant with life. There was even Jewish life and religious life. The entrance gate bore a Yiddish-Hebrew inscription (The Jewish Quarter), the Jewish officials wore a badge malted with Hebrew letters, the ghetto had its own post office and there was even a restaurant and a coffeehouse. Many people went out to work outside the ghetto and returned home in the evening. Crowds roamed the streets. Many people worked in their profession, some traded, others sold their belongings which they brought into the ghetto. Life went on and hopes were high. There was a sense of order and purpose. Now I shall skip the period between end 1941 and June 1942 because I try to concentrate only on certain events. By that time, the Gestapo had taken over the rule of the ghetto from all other factors. It wouldn't tolerate such overpopulation. There were rumors that the German authorities discussed with the Judenrat means of reducing the number of inhabitants. It was said that the "Juden-altester", Dr.Rosenzweig, asked to be left alone and banged his head against the wall.

Indeed, at the end of May 1942, something drastic happened in the ghetto, and that's the order of events as corroborated by several sources.

First, the Gestapo and the "Arbeitsamt" (Work Department) sorted out the whole population of the ghetto. The Gestapo officials checked the documents and gave the BLUE STAMP only to the so-called positive elements, those to be left in the ghetto. Crowds were waiting along the staircase and the whole street, gathered by thousands. There was much confusion. One man in a worker's overall climbed up a ladder straight to the registration office and got the blue stamp on the spot. Another man who was refused the blue stamp at one table, moved to another table and received it there. Some succeeded in bribing the official by slipping into the identity card a diamond ring or a coin of gold. The Germans spread reassuring rumors: those who didn't receive the life-saving blue stamp, will be simply sent to work in the Ukraine, with excellent conditions...

Now the "Aktion" was about to begin. From here on, Symche Spira directed the first steps of this big "Aktion". Between June 1st and 2nd, all those who haven't been granted the permit to stay in the ghetto were called to assemble at the "Plac Zgody" (the Concord Square). Some of them were dragged out from their tenements by the OD-men. They were allowed to take their belongings, as much as they can carry. The combined forces of the Gestapo, the Ukrainians and the Polish Police, which moved into the ghetto at dawn, encircled the square. The ingathered Jews sat now under the full sun for hours on end and begged for water. The Gestapo men started shooting those who got up or moved. The Gestapo ghetto supervisor, Kunde, accidentally shot Dr. Weichert, who was present at the "Aktion" as observer. The bullet stroke up from the pavement and reached his arm by ricochet. More and more Gestapo forces encircled the square which was full of Jews with parcels and suitcases. More and more Jews fainted...

Right then, the Gestapo arranged an almost authentic theater play — German officers bringing water... Jewish doctors and nurses were allowed to distribute medicaments... Several trucks and platforms arrived at the square, and the Jews were cordially invited to climb on them. Women and children were being helped by Gestapo officers to climb up the steps to the truck... They were kindly handed their parcels... Bread was distributed to those on open platforms... Meanwhile, the whole scene was photographed by the Gestapo photographers, from a good vantage point.

This nice scene was thoroughly documented for the purpose of proving to the International Red Cross that the resettlement of Jews was conducted in a most humane and compassionate way... The moment the pictures have been taken, the whole performance was over.

People were brutally dragged off the trucks, beaten and pushed back, back to the square. The trucks departed empty; the Jews were driven to the distant railway station on foot. The Germans played a different sort of game. Grinning and splitting their sides with laughter, they broke the leg of an invalid, pushed a half blind into a ditch, and cracked skulls by bumping them against each other. Eventually squeezed in, pushed and beaten, the Jews were being led to the station. It was hard to carry the bundles over many kilometers. Those who stayed behind were lashed with a whip and dropped their parcels from their bleeding hands. It seemed to be the end of the whole "Aktion".

Still, summing up, the Gestapo was not satisfied with the numbers of deported Jews. From the 4th of June and during the next two days the whole "Aktion" was repeated. Houses and hospitals were searched, almost combed. Thousands more were assembled on the same square. Some of them were dragged out in their pajamas. Several physicians were not spared and were incorporated into the transport. This time it was different — all the parcels were searched, jewels were taken away. Many other uniformed formations had been sent to participate in this renewed "Aktion". All of them were shooting the people on the square, as if they were holding a contest who will shoot more Jews. Some Jews had already been shot before, crawling they have reached the square, and blood was flowing in the streets. The Gestapo was still not satisfied with the numbers of people to be deported. They called for Dr.Rosenzweig, the head of the Judenrat.

Dr.Rosenzweig was accused of sabotage and inefficiency. Because of him, the big "Aktion" failed. He, who never coveted the title of Judenalteste, was now demoted. The shrewd little Gutter was now named in his place. It transpired that Dr.Rosenzweig, who was ordered by the Gestapo to draw up lists of people for deportation, did not deliver. It seemed he didn't voice his protest daringly; he simply dragged his feet and never handed the lists to the Gestapo. He was beaten and was finally incorporated into the transport together with his wife and two children. Unlike Czerniakow in Warsaw, who as head of the Judenrat refused to draw a list of victims and committed suicide, Dr.Rosenzweig became himself a victim.

Rosenzweig is not known to have made a lawyer's speech. There was a Judenalteste in Zdunska-Wola near Lodz, by the name of Dr.Lemberg, who answered in the same situation: "You can only have a list of four people; myself, my wife and our two children". No books have been written about him, and no statue has been erected in his memory. He will remain an unknown hero. Dr.Rosenzweig will remain half-a-hero, and no monuments are erected for half heroes. But who would put himself in his shoes? Who would have been half a hero?

It is now known that the whole transport, including Dr.Rosenzweig with his wife and children, was sent to Belzec to gas chambers. The people were loaded into almost hermetically closed train carriages, where the floor was bedded with quicklime. In consequence many were dead of suffocation before they reached their destination. Several people used tools taken for this purpose, unscrewed or loosened the boards of the train floor, extricated themselves through this opening and escaped. Some were crushed under the train, others were shot in flight. One wounded boy reached the ghetto after several weeks.

That's the general outline of the first big "Aktion" affected between June 1st and 4thof 1942. Still, that's not the end of it. There were more than 5'000 victims, and that, in the eyes of the Gestapo, was not enough. Hardly four days later the whole "Aktion" was renewed on June the 8th. People still did not believe that they were going to die... They still believed the lies about a labor camp. Assembled now on the Optima square, they asked relatives to supply them, through intermediaries, with blankets, medicaments, soap, and money.

Hospitals now became the main target. The chiefs of wards were ordered by the Gestapo to undertake a selection. The doctors didn't comply. Dr.Bornstein, who was in a position to manipulate, didn't even try to save his old sick mother at the expense of somebody else's life. Dr.Alexandrowicz made an astute plan. Forming a convoy of many sick people from his ward, he presented them as being led out for deportation, only to let them quickly disperse around the next corner. Dr.Biberstein, the brother of the former head of the Judenrat, saved many patients and non-patients, guessing right that the Germans would not dare to penetrate and comb his epidemics hospital for fear of contamination.

Altogether, the three 'Aktions' conducted in the first eight days of June ended with 7,000 victims. Now the Gestapo seemed to be satisfied. It quickly started spreading rumors that this has been the last and final "Aktion".

As I already mentioned, the ghetto passed under the jurisdiction of the Gestapo sometime before. I am not going to elaborate here on all the German units roaming the "General Government", and they were quite a constellation. I can only mention some of the more notable formations and uniforms such as: the Gestapo, the Einsatztruppen', the 'SA', the 'SD', "Sonderpolizei", "Organization Toth"... the others I don't remember. The most noticeable on the day-to-day basis was the presence of the Ukrainians (the Ruthenians), the Lithuanians and the Latvians. I have to give a short apercu of the standing of the more numerous, the Ukrainians, because they were closer to us, constituting the routine escort of working groups. The Ukrainians, who in pre-war Poland used to be a persecuted minority, now received from the Germans "autonomy", in double parentheses. They received it only "de nomine" — in name. The only privilege bestowed on them was that of volunteering (forcibly) into the ranks of Ukrainian formations, acting under the aegis of. Haven't I described the training they received at the-school in "Tereska"? Now in the ghetto, they acted as convoy, escorting working groups with their Jewish 'Capo'. They participated also in the "Akions" alongside other formations. When the concentration camp will be established, who will stand on the watchtowers? The Ukrainians will of course be operating the multiple towers in summer and winter, stamping their feet in the Polish frost, swearing and cursing the war, cursing Hitler and their own miserable lot. They found their only solace in drinking.

It is time now to describe the ghetto from the inside. How can I convey to you my reaction to it? Perhaps through the physical impact, harping on the senses: bodies rubbing against bodies in the crowds, total lack of privacy, a sense of bad odor. I was shocked by the smells of dirt, laundry, steam, urine, sweat and unaired rooms. The sounds too seemed to play on my nerves. In this congested habitat, the crossing conversations, the reproaches, the rows — were nothing compared to listening to the heavy steps of the OD or the Germans. The sharp knocks on the door in the middle of the night, which could mean an invitation to death.

But there were also sounds of music. Singing is contagious and, believe it or not, some people did sing or rather hum in the street. It was a sort of self-defense. What would they sing? Some popular songs, some German "schmaltz" songs, which contrasted and clashed with my gloomy mood. These songs persecuted me: I felt an inner fight between attraction, longing and revulsion. That is why I still remember the "Sweet Rosamunde" (mit dem rose munde, meaning "with her rosy mouth") or even better, the "Song of Guitars". It ran like this (translated from German): "I am dreaming of love in the darkness of the night, the guitars play tunes that do my longing ignite"...

These tunes had a long life. A year later they were broadcasted through the loudspeakers of the concentration camp during a selection. They are still with me; I can hear them in my head. There is one that I never even dare to hum to myself, because it pierces me with physical pain. It's the "Star of Rio", sheer saccharine. It was played over and over; it blasted at high amplitude from the speakers on the rollcall square... when my brother Witek was taken. Now, when I am writing these words, sipping coffee, I feel like undressing in public and showing my wounds. But that was later, in Plaszow. Now I have to return to the ghetto.

The children too were singing in the ghetto guts. I still remember a little satirical jingle composed and sung by the ghetto children. It expressed their fear of the terrible fat OD-man, Meir Korner. It ran like this:

Meir Korner the bandit
tadi rissa bom
he doesn't know what he did
tadi rissa bom
when lashing a child wildly with his whip
his trousers he tore from bottom to hip
tadi rissa... tadi rissa ... tadi rissa bom.

The 'tadi rissa' part had of course no meaning. How sweet were the children of the ghetto, having to behave like grownups, hiding, escaping, and still preserving their childish spirit.

All I have to do now is dress these smells and sounds upon the gloomy reality. For us, the pivot of this period became the handle of my toothbrush. All our life seemed to be centered on it and turnaround it. How were we to acquire the most basic articles necessary for everyday life? We possessed less than a caveman. You can pride yourself nowadays how light you travel, but inspect your house and see what it contains disregarding little knickknacks. We had no house, no bed, no sheet, no pillow, no change of wardrobe... nothing.

Olek was somehow able to accommodate Helcia and Rutka. We had nobody left alive to take care of us; we had only distant relatives and some acquaintances. We were helpless women with a child. If only we had father and Wilek with us... and then what? As it was, we were three people, not one, not two, but three.

First of all, we were able to find for Witek one quarter of a bed. What would that mean? I shall explain. My mother's cousin Mala Bluth (the grandmother of Sarah's little Eddie) had also a son, Gershon, who never grew up. Gershon was a bright intellectual with a master's degree in sociology, but he was a head shorter than I.He slept in a child's bed in the ghetto, and now he offered to share it with Witek. That meant one concern less.

We were for a while graciously received by Dr.Hilfstein, the Zionist, the Hebrew school builder whom I mentioned earlier. Dr.Hilfstein had the privilege to live in one room with his wife, and behind the screen of partition was his consultation cubicle, where he treated his patients. In this cubicle stood a white, miniscule doctor's couch, no wider than 65 cm, and a wash basin. On this narrow couch, covered with slippery oil cloth, we had to sleep, mother and I, glued together like sardines. It was like trying to sleep on the back of a dolphin. When we wanted to turn over, we had to do it simultaneously; otherwise, we would fall off the couch. We spent on this "fakir" bed some three weeks. You have to understand, my children, that every situation can have a comic angle to it. We were not allowed to get up before Dr.Hilfstein, so as not to be in his way in this restricted area. Thus, forcibly still reposing on our couch, we had to watch Mrs. Hilfstein do her morning toilette. This huge wife of the tiny Dr.Hilfstein had a system for washing her long, pendant breasts. She would throw one breast over her shoulder, then proceed to wash her second breast in the same way. I could hardly contain my mirth. Mother felt my body shaking with suppressed laughter, and in a moment, I felt hers twitching behind me. When we told Witek about this ceremony, he turned it into a pantomime, and made children guess what it represents. He could now spend his days in the 'kinderheime', a children's center. This concentration of children was dangerous in itself, but we had no better solution for the time being, if we wanted to find work.

We couldn't impose Witek's presence on Dr.Hilfstein. We ourselves couldn't stay in his room any longer; we couldn't abuse his hospitality. We considered applying to the Housing Office, asking to grant us an accommodation in any empty space. There was no such thing as empty space, there was only the possibility of squeezing us into an existing arrangement. Being illegal we didn't dare to apply.

Now I have to explain our legal position. Not being registered, we hardly existed. As I explained earlier, after the June "Aktion" only people with the blue stamp were allowed to reside in the ghetto. We had no work and had no chance to be granted this life-saving stamp. We stood perhaps a chance to receive a job eventually, but what about Witek? Mother had an idea. Many people did their utmost to save their children outside of the ghetto. They placed them with a gentile family, paying sometimes a fortune, to have them hidden. Many children were left on the doorstep of a convent and when their parents perished, nobody knew where they were or where they were shifted to. Books have been written about relatives searching for such lost children after the war.

My mother applied to Victor asking him to visit Olga, Witek's loving nurse. Here she is in Krakow, owning now our apartment as a Volksdeutsche and working at a good salary as a trustee of a shop. Olga's mother, a native German still lived in Silesia, and she had more than fifteen grandchildren dispersed all over Poland. Witek could have been placed with her, and nobody would have known in her village that he was not one of her many grandchildren. She would run no risk at all, especially since Witek didn't look a bit Jewish with his dark blond hair and short nose. Olga, who loved Witek with a jealous, possessive kind of love, Olga who raised him and pampered him — Olga refused.

If there was no way of smuggling Witek out of the ghetto and placing him with Olga's mother or some good Poles, we had to try to arrange something in the ghetto. If only we had the blue stamp. Mother considered applying to some Judenrat members for protection. They should be helpful; they were chosen by the people. There were among them some very noble figures and some people of goodwill. She was told that the idea was absurd. They had absolutely no influence in such matters; they function merely as administrative body. It was all in the hands of the Gestapo. We had no choice but to think of a different option. If only mother could be assigned to work, Witek could be inscribed in her documents and become legal too. But there was still no work available, and how could we get the blue stamp, if we had no job?

Here Bernard Kornhauser enters the picture. Bernard always had some brilliant ideas. He was an artist of sorts. Even working as a dentist, he was an artist in his dental work. He also had a knack for establishing good contacts. He knew of our plight, he heard about it almost daily, because we spent our days with Bernard's mother and his sister Rosie.

Bernard had a bold, crazy idea. It was known that there lived in the ghetto an influential spy and informer, a German Jew by the name of Forster. Having been before the war an international impresario, this spy was easily planted by the Germans in Poland. He must have rendered important services to the German Reich. The Gestapo had much respect for him, and its brass associated with him privately, even shaking his hand in public. That's one side of the coin, but this cosmopolitan was composed of many facets. It was said that he never worked against the Jews; that he had in his heart a weak spot for the Jews. He hated violence, and was willing to help Jews occasionally, using his influence.

Bernard had never met him in person, but he had decided to risk paying him a visit. He intended to tell him the moving story of our escape… and to ask his help in obtaining for us the much-coveted blue stamp. It took a lot of 'hutzpah' to ask such a favor of an omnipotent stranger who happened to be a German spy. There still seemed to be another way of reaching Forster. I heard that a schoolmate of mine, Martha P. was now Forster's concubine. I could have appealed to her, but I felt a strong inhibition. Will she not be ashamed to face me in her new status? I for sure, shall be even more ashamed and uneasy about it. I dropped the idea. Bernard succeeded in his bold mission and Forster kept his promise. We now became the proud holders of the blue stamp.

That story is a lesson in human behavior; never underestimate the complexity of the so-called abominable types. As for Martha, she was not the only girl to associate with spies. Another beautiful girl that I had known before the war turned into an informer. This Stephanie B. had been seen in town riding in a cab with Gestapo officers. Was she acting under coercion, who could guess? It is known that she walked through Krakow and pointed out camouflaged Jews equipped with Arian documents. Speaking of documents, I must stress that we still had no document proving a place of employment, a document that went with the blue stamp.

We had no working papers — but we had a BED. It happened like that. Dr.Hilfstein told us that across the street lived two first cousins of my father: Dorothy Barber with her family and Helen, her unmarried sister. There was also their widowed mother Mrs. Sperling, a Mrs. Sperling like my mother. We had never met them before the war, but they must have known a lot about us. They invited us to stay in their flat, or rather the flat into which they were squeezed by order of the Housing Office. Don't get any ideas. This flat consisted of only one room and a kitchen. Don't ask about bathroom or lavatory. There was none in this habitat of poor people from before the war. It should be remembered that the size of the ghetto was considerably diminished after the June "Aktion" and many people were squeezed now into less space.

The only room was shared by several families. There were the Barbers with two sons, there was Dorothy's mother and sister Helen, and there were the Weisels with two daughters — all together exactly ten people to one room. All we received was a bed in the kitchen. There was enough room under this bed for our personal belongings, but we had none.

Do not see the Barber's invitation extended to us as an act of compassion. If we were not accorded this bed in the kitchen, some strangers would get it. This only proves that we were considered "nice people". So were the Barbers, and we got along quite well. I liked the two sisters, father's cousins.

The flat was so neglected, filthy and infested with bugs, that we decided on the spot to spring a good surprise on its inhabitants and clean the whole place, while everybody was at work. To get rid of the bugs we dismantled all the beds, board by board, and doused them with boiling water. We worked like slaves and were very proud. Do you think that the lodgers were grateful? Forget it. They knew better. They knew that it wouldn't help against the bugs. They must have guessed that the bugs will survive them all — except one Barber boy. There were strange rituals in these lodgings. The lavatory and the water tap were in the staircase one floor below. Instead of a bathroom there was in our kitchen a jug of water, a washbasin and a bucket. Mr. W. who was too lazy to bring water in the jug, performed his washing ritual in the following way: he took water into a glass, rinsed his mouth (without brushing his teeth), spit out the water on his palms, and thus washed his face and even his neck. What we didn't suspect was that all these lodgers were carriers of lice. When I discovered the first lice in the seams of my dress — I cried. I didn't guess that soon would come a time when one of us would search her clothes for lice, while the other munches a piece of bread.

Here I am writing in detail about some trivia while the ghetto was to pass again through a massive tragedy. There were still no news from those 'deported' in June, but the ever-optimistic Poles, endowed with vivid imagination, knew to spin yarns about some secret arms factories where Jewish slaves were allegedly employed, unable to communicate with the outside world. There was a case of a fugitive from the June transport, who allegedly escaped from hell and knew all the details. This Bachner, a dentist, extricated himself from a death camp at the last moment. When his transport arrived at its destination, some camp in a forest, Bachner disappeared into a latrine, jumped through the opening inside the pool of urine, and standing up to his neck in a sea of excrements waited for days (?) till the area was empty and unguarded. When half-crazy he eventually reached Krakow and the ghetto, people didn't believe him, especially since he couldn't tell what happened to the transport from the moment of his escape.

Now, in October, there were new rumors concerning an impending "Aktion". Before I describe its prelude, I have to state that our personal situation was still unbalanced. The blue stamp without an employment card wouldn't defend us in case of a selection. Our only hope was to be informed in time and escape from the ghetto. There was a person who could probably have this information in advance. He was Bernard's older brother. He served as an OD officer, being one of the first volunteers for the Civil Service. He had the good fortune, or the right instinct, to remain blameless. He was well liked by the Gestapo people because having been raised in Berlin he spoke impeccable German, he cut a good figure, had excellent manners and was well disciplined without being subservient. He got only the clean tasks of interpreter and spokesman but was close enough to the high echelons to know where the wind blew from.

Shortly before the "Aktion" he sent his sister Rosie to warn us. It wasn't necessary. By then everybody knew that the "Aktion" would start on the next day. Even Gutter allegedly tried to prevent it, but to no avail. Somehow the secret was out of the bag. People prepared hiding places, one more ingenious than the other. Behind double walls or decorative panels was enough space for two or more people. Many people went around with cyanide poison in their pocket. Many committed suicide. A couple of elderly parents asked their daughter, a physician, to give them poison. She let herself be persuaded. They sat down to a festive supper. It was a very solemn 'Last Supper', one that Leonardo da Vinci never painted. They embraced their daughter for the last time and took the poison.

As for us, on this 26th of October, a day before the "Aktion", the three of us still had to leave the ghetto under some pretext. We slipped off the Jewish badge behind a porch and went to Victor. Where else...? We had some other gentile friends but there was no time to send out feelers. It was of course only for two or three days, but Victor and his wife, with three children, had a small flat. Its walls were so thin that we had to whisper so as not to be overheard by the neighbors. When a neighbor gossiper came allegedly to borrow an onion, Victor changed all his colors and we felt once more how much we endangered him, him who cared for us like a brother. He even brewed, before we came to him, a new plan of salvation, this time for me... Without asking questions, he bought for me forged Arian identity papers and tried to persuade me now not to return to the ghetto. He showed me three advertisements in a newspaper, three vacancies in which good families looked for a well-educated governess, a typist with good knowledge of German, or some similar job. He remonstrated with me that there was no risk with my good (Arian) looks and there is no point in staying in the ghetto. Of course, I wouldn't hear of it. I wouldn't save my skin and leave mother and Witek in the ghetto, even though I couldn't help them — as Victor pointed out to me. I thanked him effusively for his efforts — and never made use of these documents... until... but about that later.

We tried to be useful at Victor's house. Mother made a dress for the quietly hostile Veronka; I made two dresses from the remnants for the sweet baby daughters. As soon as we heard that the "Aktion" was over we returned into the lion's jaws.

What we found in the ghetto was beyond description. Six hundred people had been killed, thousand deported. Everybody checked everybody to find out who was left of the next of kin and friends. When you passed through the streets you heard wailing from all the houses. Here Gershon's mother, the family saint, was torn from him, here Olek's brother with wife and two grownup children, everywhere there was despair. The angel of death passed also through our flat. He took the two sweet women, my father's cousins Dorothy and Helen, but left their old mother who had been hidden in a dustbin. She became manic-depressive and poisoned our lives. The two sisters left a short note: "Fare well and don't cry for us".

Gradually, we could slowly reconstruct the puzzle of this "Aktion". We gathered the many tales of the witnesses. All the people who didn't go out to work were ordered to assemble along Jozefinska Street till ten o'clock. Many took to their shelters. A mother and her fourteen-year-old daughter asked a neighbor with good documents to conceal them in the hiding place which she had prepared for her parents. The neighbor admitted only the daughter and nailed down the concealing panel. The mother sought refuge, at the last moment, under the obscured coil of stairs. An OD man detected her there, and he did his utmost to prevent the Gestapo from discovering her, lying, covering up, misleading them... risking his own neck. A haphazard selection took place in the street, which were now encircled by the "Sonderdienst" the Ruthenians, Lithuanians and Latvians.

The doctors and the Judenrat members, carrying a special protecting badge, moved among the people but were unable to help. They themselves were not efficiently protected by their badge, and some members of the Sanitary Commission were included in the crowd for transport. Some people shoved their excellent protective documents into the hands of the Gestapo official. He took the documents and... tore them to pieces.

Suddenly, the Sturmbahnfuhrer Haase raised his hand, asking for silence. He then declared solemnly: "Now everybody can go home". People cheered, cried and laughed, embracing each other. But no, Haase raised his hand again and added: "Everybody can go home to take his most important personal effects. The ghetto will be cleared of Jews". This too was a trap. Now those returning home for their effects will inform those in hiding that it is no use, nobody can remain hidden in an empty ghetto. Many left their hiding places and joined those marked for transport. Those working outside of the ghetto would never again see their wives, children, parents.

All the people designated for transport were now assembled on the square, squatting, forbidden to rise even for a fleeting moment. Whoever tried to rise was shot at. One young woman, with perfect papers, cut through the cordon of Latvians and entered the square, to willingly join her mother. An SS-man jumped from his place and hauled the fighting woman, pulling her hair. He dragged her back to those permitted to live, for a while.

At noontime, they penetrated the main hospital and shot everybody. Some patients tried to escape. Noticing that the doctors do not try to prevent this escape, the Gestapo shot the doctors. Sixteen physicians fell victim to this purge. At another hospital all the patients, beaten bloody, were thrown down from the staircase.

More and more Jews, flogged mercilessly, joined those squatting on the square. This time the pessimists didn't even take any personal belongings. They guessed that they will not need them. The whole ghetto was thoroughly searched for people in hiding, many more were dragged out. Forster, who arranged for us the blue stamp, was present. He walked among the Gestapo men without any badge. What did he do there? You can guess. He used his influence to extricate a few Jews from the transport. Of all the Jews concentrated on Plac Zgody, only one woman asked for mercy. Only one woman fell to the feet of a Gestapo man, begging him to save her children.

In the late afternoon, the "Aktion" was over. The whole transport brought to the station was loaded on the train about to depart. Not all the trains had left the station. The Jews immediately engaged a gentile railway employee, to follow the tracks. His report was confusing. The trains disappeared in an enclosed area where he had no access. The peasants of the vicinity knew to tell that over there was the slaughterhouse for the Jews... This meager information was passed from mouth to mouth, but it was not believed. When people do not dare to believe they don't believe. Some people even remarked: "A goy is a goy. When he has nothing to say he will fabricate something...".

A few days after the "Aktion" was over, we both received work. It is very hard to reveal, but the cruel truth is that we were able to get this assignment in place of those who were deported. We were recruited to the Madritch factory, a sewing workshop for uniforms. When our relatives heard about our job, they were shocked. "Madritch" — they said — "the firm that most of its employees were deported only a couple of days ago!!! Who wants to work for Madritch, you must be crazy"... Did we have any choice?

Who was Madritch? Julius Madritch, a handsome young Austrian from Vienna, operated this uniform factory so as to get rich on cheap Jewish labor (he paid the German authorities a symbolic price for a day's work of a Jew) and so as not to be sent to the front. Sewing uniforms for various units and formations, he contributed to the war effort and was exempt from military service. So was his lame partner Tutsh. All this sounds very ugly. The truth is that Madritch was a wonderful person who was to turn eventually into the savior of many hundreds of Jews.

When the honest good Madritch discovered that on the "Aktion" almost all the Jews of his factory were taken for transport — he went into a state of shock. He felt personally responsible and guilty of neglect. He swore that from now on, he would quickly learn who of the German top brass was to be bribed, who was to be wined and where to seek protection. From now on he will defend his Jews like a lion. He was as good as his promise, He also found a good teacher in the person of the shrewd Sudeten-German Oscar Schindler, owner of the metal factory "Emalia". From now on the Madritch factory became almost the safest place to work in. Nevertheless, it has to be stressed that Oscar Schindler surpassed Madritch in wheeling and dealing with the authorities.

What was the sort of work expected from us? You will remember that I learned to sew from Maryla, Wilek's sister, but she taught me only the assembling and the finishing work, she wouldn't let me use the machine. To say that I know how to operate a sewing machine was a white lie, but it was swallowed and now I had to live up to it. When I started to sew at Madritch, the wheel was turning backwards. It was not a swift electric machine; it was activated by pedaling. This fact enabled me to master the machine very quickly, indeed so quickly that after a short while I was able to produce seven outfits a day, the required daily contingent. To achieve this quota, I had to pedal intently, furiously, a great physical effort for an unskilled person... If you ask now about my mother and how she managed — there was no problem at all. What didn't mother know to do? Indeed, she was so good at it, that she got special work, different from mine and less intense. She traced pedantically on her sewing machine the outline of collars and pockets of the high officers' uniforms.

I have to stress once more and again, that whatever you learn is yours, whatever you do well raises your shares on the human market scale and in your own eyes (After all, I am recording these memoirs only for your sake...).

Another moral lesson of this kind is the one that I promised to prove later, the one concerning a good deed and its eventual reward... You will remember my good friend Hanka, whose family, evicted from Krakow and planted in some distant region village suffered terribly after typhoid. You will remember that I used to send them my entire salary, earned as Mr. Brandt's secretary. Now here we were in the ghetto, equipped only with a toothbrush and a change of linen, offered by the Kornhausers. We received a bed in the kitchen, a bare bed to sleep on in this late autumn. Who do you think appeared, as a fairy, and covered our bed? Hanka's aunt, Mrs. Lilienthal. She had heard about our flight and arrival, she had made inquiries, she found us. She entered our kitchen, took a look round and said: "Dear Mrs. Sperling, I know exactly what your daughter did for Hanka and my brother's family when they were, poor souls, at the bottom of misery. I see now for myself what you need. Don't say a word. I am bringing it now to you in a moment, and please don't try to thank me". She brought us a sheet, a pillow, a warm blanket, a towel, a cooking pot. It was heaven-sent.

You may ask what we lived on until now. We had some money on us when we escaped, but it ran out very quickly. We didn't want to accept loans; we were too proud and not so sure that we should be able to repay the loan. Happily enough, Victor went eventually to Rabka and retrieved grandma's jewels from the cache walled in under the window. There was one brooch set with several little diamonds. These he sold gradually, one by one, at a very low price. Diamonds sold for a fraction of their value, who would buy diamonds in impoverished Poland. The blackmailers didn't have to buy them; the Germans confiscated and robbed them. Just the same, we had enough to live on modestly. For how long, who knows? Many people who had some money faced a problem; what should they buy — food or poison? Poison was in great demand.

As I have explained, all those who worked didn't get a salary; they got only food coupons that barely covered the basic needs. It was not enough to live on, yet too much to starve. We now entered a phase of a certain routine, but there were people next to us, for whom there was no routine, and every day was a struggle for survival. Next to my sewing machine worked a dear lady, Mrs. Melanie Marmur, who was a saint in my eyes. This brave woman had a child and a newborn baby. When her brother's wife bore a child and died at childbirth, poor Melanie took her brother's newborn and breasted it together with her own baby. You will ask now how she managed to work at Madritch outside of the ghetto and breastfeed two babies. They found a solution; Melanie's husband worked night shifts and took care of the babies at daytime. He fed them some watered milk, some tea, until Melanie, the poor emaciated Melanie came home and gave them her breast to suck. It must have been her blood that they were sucking.

This sunny person with a quick endearing smile used to say: "I worry about being afraid to worry that I worry and may lose my milk in consequence". What were our worries compared to hers?

You can now ask me a question that you already wanted to ask for some time. Was I not worrying about the hard lot of Wilek, my fiancé, what became of him over there at "Tereska"? Did I know? did I care? He managed to transmit to me a short message. He knew from the cook that we had arrived safely in Krakow. He now scribbled this note, stating shortly that he was well, all he cared about was our situation and our well-being. I should contact — he wrote — some of his good friends. He gave the names. It was easy to find them, they were three nice young men who became instantly very friendly and warm to me. It was a great comfort, but no help. I shall mention them soon in the right context.

I wrote a long letter that was mailed by Victor to the cook and handed secretly to Wilek. One day a miracle happened. Wilek showed up in our kitchen, appearing out of the blue.

I am not going to describe this moving meeting and reunion. You can only guess that I cried and trembled. How he managed to come to the ghetto for one day and a night — is a mystery. As he told us, he overheard two men discussing the lack of a certain rare substance (or tool) very essential for a certain project. He dared to cut in and remark that he happened to know how it could be obtained. If the officers are willing to send him for a day or two to Krakow, with a pass and 2 Ukrainian escorts — he will hopefully detect the good source. They agreed. When Wilek's colleagues heard about his good fortune, they asked him, each one, to take something valuable, a watch, a ring, and sell the item for them, so that they could buy some food. They were all constantly hungry.

He took the risk, more so as he had to bribe his Ukrainian escort to let him stay for the night in the ghetto. The Ukrainian was happy to spend the night in Krakow and get drunk. As for us, sitting on the kitchen oven on a blanket, we talked in whispers throughout the whole night. This trick with

Wilek's legal trip to Krakow worked twice in a period of two months.

Has anyone ever spent a romantic night on top of a kitchen oven? I wonder. Speaking of romanticism, I have to mention two romantic affairs that bloomed on the soil of the ghetto. One will concern Bernard and one his sister Rosie. The two separate stories happen to be interwoven. All the Kornhausers were a very romantic breed. So romantic indeed, as their mother remarked, that none of the three children (Herman, Bernard and Rosie) had time to marry, even though they were young no more. Their three-room flat was inhabited of course by very many families. For the time being I have to introduce only one of them, the fiery oriental beauty, Mrs. Fela P., her ugly husband and clumsy daughter. Bernard was in love with Mrs. P. Their romance was a public secret, impossible to hide in the crowded ghetto. Unfortunately, Bernard was not the only man to fall in love with Fela P. He had a strange rival: the fat, ugly little Symche Spira, the Jewish commander of the OD. When Symche Spira got wind of Bernard's romance with this coveted beauty, he went into a rage. When he cooled off, he spun a web of vengeance.

He sent two OD policemen to search the Kornhauser flat and its inhabitants. The two had allegedly found in Fela P.'s handbag a wad of dollars, hidden under the lining. She was taken to the OD prison and from there was sent to Auschwitz. She was not executed; it was said of her later that she had been assigned to work in Auschwitz at the experimental clinic of the war criminal Dr. Mengele. Though she survived and lived in Tel Aviv, she never talked about it, although everyone knew.

But that is not the end of this romantic tragedy. Symche Spira was not satisfied with only one victim, he had to get his hand on Bernard. He fabricated an accusation, according to which Fela had confessed that the providers trafficking in dollars were Bernard Kornhauser and Samek Kempler. Who was Samek? He was Bernard's prospective brother-in-law, Rosie's fiancé. Both men were arrested and brought to the OD prison. You can imagine how Symche Spira croaked with laughter sending the lovers Fela and Bernard on the same transport to Auschwitz...

You may well ask now how it is possible that Bernard's brother, Herman, the OD officer, was not able to intercede, or even implore Symche Spira and save Bernard. It is quite possible that Symche Spira wanted to humiliate the independent Herman, so popular with the Gestapo, that he refused to change his decision.

If I was writing a script for a motion picture, I would let the two lovers notice each other from afar, at the railway station, embrace for the last time and be separated. But that's not the end of the scenario. Now comes the heroic part of it. When Bernard and Samek found themselves in a goods-wagon of the train, carrying them to Auschwitz, they had enough time to break the bars of the little window and jump to freedom. It is easier to say than to execute. Jumping from such a tiny opening is very dangerous, there is no bouncing possibility. Still, the two deft heroes landed unscratched. Hiding by day, moving by night, they reached Krakow... They knew there a "goy" who gave them shelter. Not out of Christian mercy but for a fat lump of money. You may hope now that they remained there sitting quietly on their... and hiding till the end of the war. You are very much mistaken. It is because you didn't know Samek. Samek felt great longing and a great urge to visit his fiancé Rosie, in the ghetto. This darkly handsome man was a country boy, agile, deft and extremely courageous. He left his den at night, approached the ghetto, cut the barbed wire and appeared like a ghost in the Kornhauser flat. He stayed there for three days and nights, endangering everybody. You can imagine how pale was Rosie's mother, when she opened the door for us and revealed the secret. Samek returned to Bernard and their hiding place, but he repeated his romantic exploit once or twice more. By then, the man who was harboring them got cold feet and decided to put an end to his noble mission. He had already discovered where their money was coming from; he could now blackmail the other gentile who passed money. He could also get a nice reward for denouncing two hiding Jews. He decided to kill two ducks (and two Jews) with one shot.

The two heroes were arrested and brought to... the same prison from which they started their Odyssey. It seemed to be the end of them, with a new accusation added to the former one... But no, you don't know the Germans, they like heroes, especially when one of them is their own excellent dentist and the second an apt horse trainer. Bernard and Samek were transferred from the OD prison to the Plaszow concentration camp on the outskirts of Krakow, which was in its first stages of construction. Bernard got there a dental clinic opened exclusively for German forces, and Samek was appointed as the royal horse trainer for the new commander of this new concentration camp, Amon Goethe. Bernard survived and lives today in Tel Aviv. As for Samek, he will be the hero of another romantic story and another heroic exploit.

At about the same period of early winter 1942, I too was involved in an adventure. This one not of a romantic kind. As I mentioned before, I have made new acquaintances, thanks to Wilek. Wilek's introduction and recommendation was a passport into a new society. I participated sometimes in this circle in heated discussions and was courageous in expressing my political opinions. It was known by then that the Jewish underground was very active in many ways. I must have ventured to say, in an abstract way, that anonymous activities of an underground movement are certainly not negligible, even if its achievements seem to be marginal. Their impact on the German forces can undermine the structure of the occupational administration. There was no reaction to my uttering of opinion, nobody else showed his leanings, but it sank in and was to have its repercussions. It could have been a certain person of this group that proposed to recruit me for the underground. On the other hand, it is quite plausible that my links to the old Zionist Dr.Hilfstein, who was the silent patron of the underground leader Dolek Liebeskind, constituted the thin thread that led to me. After all, Dolek Liebeskind remembered me well from the period of my work in the same office. Anyhow, somebody must have sent feelers to recruit me for "Z.O.B." — the Jewish Fighting Organization. These antenna feelers were thin and long, but they reached me in a very unusual way.

One day a young man approached me in the street and asked politely if I am Marysia Sperling. I nodded. "I have to transmit to you some very warm greetings" — he opened — "Still, for reasons that you will soon understand I shall avoid using names. I can play a game with you; I can quote for you a list of many names familiar to you, and make you guess who sends you this greeting, but we better both avoid such a game for very specific reasons. Please don't interrupt me, let me have my say. You have a good reputation as a reliable person. I have to engage you in a very serious conversation and for this reason, because of a delicate matter; I should like to make an appointment with you at your convenience". End of speech.

How would you react to such an opening in the given circumstances? I took a deep breath and said: "That I don't know you doesn't bother me at all, but the moment you use the expression 'a delicate matter', it makes a bell ring. I never engage in 'delicate matter' conversations… it seems quite clear to me that you must be a spy, a provoker... the fact that you could cite many names of my acquaintances only proves this point. If you don't stop pestering me, I shall... I shall in this instant, call the first best OD-man who appears in my eyesight. I shall... I shall tell him...". He stopped me with a wave of hand. "Don't hurry, mademoiselle" — he said slowly — "before you have time to address an OD-man with an accusation, I shall turn the tables and declare that you molested me and tried to recruit me... et cetera, et cetera. It is your word against my word — if I am what you believe me to be. How about that? But don't you worry, it is not going to happen. First and foremost, don't stutter. Don't show that you become tense — that is the first lesson. I shall be around. I shall renew our conversation or rather start it from zero. After all nothing has passed between us. It could be just a story of boy meets girl... Keep well, I shall see you soon." With these words he vanished. I didn't mention this encounter to my mother, but I had to tell somebody for security reasons. If I am arrested, somebody in the family has to know. I told my story to Rutka. She thought for a moment and then believed nothing incriminating happened, that the approach was very cautious and the less I knew about its initiator the better for me.

Indeed, two days later the nice young man waited for me, but seeing me with my mother bowed politely without a word. On the next day he caught me alone. He said nothing beyond one sentence: "Hallo, here I am again, me, your silent partner who will molest you no more until you get used to my presence". I had to smile. He smiled back and disappeared. The next time he made a bolder move. He tried to explain that an agent provocateur would denounce me without much ado. He wouldn't need a tangible proof. I can refuse of course to have any contact with him, and he will not try to persuade me. If I have guessed what it is all about, I can still choose to play a very marginal role. That too will be acceptable.

By that time, I felt involved. You may well ask if he possessed certain magnetism, if he was a charmer, a conqueror of female hearts. He was so handsomely ugly that I couldn't suspect myself of having been drawn into his circle of magnetism. His very speeches to me were concise and pragmatic. I learned about the apolitical, centrist orientation of his group, about the work of a unit, I even guessed that it was composed of five members even though he never mentioned their number. I was given the choice to participate in the discussions of the group or to disengage myself from it. I would, in this case, pass my vote on important issues through his intermediary. I would sign with my cryptonym. All that — once I have passed the initial test. This initial test consisted of the following plan: "You will get a pass to leave the ghetto on a certain errand" — he said — "You will get rid of the Jewish badge in an obscure corner. You will be given the address of a certain house where, in its cellar, you will find a peasant dress and a basket of eggs. You will not check its contents. You will have to pass a section of town and cross a bridge with its checkpoint manned by the German gendarmerie… Whereupon you will find the second address (door number so and so) and you will deliver your basket there".

I had my doubts, as he might have guessed. "And if I am stopped at the checkpoint and ordered to show the contents of the basket?" I asked. "I know of your mimicking talents" — he replied — "I know that you can imitate the clumsy German of a peasant girl. Give it a try. Explain that you know nothing… you were only told to deliver this basket of eggs. Play anxious not to let them break the eggs". I like improvisation games. I gave the performance of a dumb girl stuttering in this style of German gibberish: "Me nothing not know, me only eggs, me spoken take eggs here, me spoken take eggs there". I saw him laugh for the first time. "Excellent" — he said — "the rest is your own risk, but your forged identity card is in order". That seemed to end my questioning.

To make a long story short, I passed all the steps of this plan without any hitch up to a certain point. There arose only one problem. At the given address of delivery there was no answer when I knocked at the door. I started to sweat. What now? I looked once more inspecting helplessly the door and noticed a tiny slip of rolled paper slightly protruding from a slit. There was only one sentence written on it: "Please leave your parcel in the left cellar". I did, and I felt like watching what happens next, but that was not in my orders. The less I know the better — I thought. I retraced my steps, I retrieved my clothes and my Jewish badge, I returned to the ghetto. He was waiting for me, lurking around the corner. I didn't even know his name, I called him Xander (Mr. X). He told me that I was watched by his man, he even knew where I adjusted the laces of my peasant shoes. I asked him if there was anything in the basket under the eggs, something like a pistol or cartridges. "There was nothing" — he said. "And if there was something, what would I do, if searched?" — I dared to ask at last. "You would have been given different orders" — he explained — "If they would really try to search your basket you wouldn't use your parody of peasant gibberish, you would say in your perfect German: Gentlemen, I wouldn't search this basket if I were you. You and I are being watched from both sides of the bridge. If only you do so much as to put your hand into this basket, we shall all be dead, you two, and me with you. Now please smile at me, tap me on the shoulder and let me pass" — he finished his little speech. Now I understood the subtle grades and shades of approach. I had several meetings with him after my test. Several plans were inspected and pushed to a higher stage of development; others were rejected. My false identity papers were to give me a good cover. In one endeavor I was to serve as a decoy, a distraction, so as to enable each of the others to execute his task. I even had a green-light tune and a red-light tune. The object to be destroyed was a huge depot of patrol cars. It was only guarded from the entrance side. It could have been relatively easy to lower the explosives on a string through the narrow window slits. We never got so far. The contacts that were to supply our group with explosives and detonators didn't deliver. Xander said that all had to be stopped for a while.

They probably had enough volunteer girls and hardly any experts of explosives. I was a freelance, an outsider. I didn't even belong to one of the Zionist movements such as 'Akkiba', 'Dror', 'Kadima', 'Emuna', all with a high sense of team loyalty. Who would have guessed that this precious spirit was to become their undoing? My contact with Xander was not renewed. I still don't know who he might have been, or why and how he vanished from the picture.

I now have to speak of other groups, unknown to me, who were activated and executed several most impressive exploits. I just have to, I absolutely have to cover here their activities, at least in a dry and factual manner.

Excuse me my grandchildren, but for this short apercu of the resistance operations I cannot rely on my memory. I have to base it on the research work done by your mother, Sigalit, when she was seventeen. It was her matriculation paper, and it concerned the Jewish resistance in Krakow. She went to great length to unearth the few survivors of this movement, dispersed as they are in Israel, and to interview them one by one. I am extracting from her research work the main points, and also such points as have a bearing on my personal story.

You must have noticed by now how seldom I give names of the important figures who played a role in the events described. I am afraid of scrambling or distorting facts. Even now, this year, at an academy of commemoration of the ghetto heroes, forty years after the liberation, somebody protested that his late brother was not mentioned at the right place on the list of heroes and not in the right context. Who am I to quote names of some forty-six people I haven't known, or of their heroic deeds recorded for history, but not by me? I shall however have to mention Dolek Liebeskind and a few others because he might have played a role in recruiting me anonymously to the underground. How many underground diversions have passed unrecorded because they misfired for some reason or other? How many had to be postponed because the Polish underground did not deliver the promised equipment in time?

The main bulk of the successful actions of the Jewish underground had been ascribed by history to the activity of the Polish underground. The Jewish heroes did not protest at the given time. Why would they? They were not after fame. They fulfilled their not-so-grey missions out of conviction that their deeds were vital in stopping the German machine of extermination of Jews. Most of them lived outside of the ghetto and had their families placed in hideouts. Proclaiming boldly that some glorious exploits were of their doing would only invite cruel reprisals on the Jewish community clustered in the ghetto.

Anonymity became preferable. Some of the heroes of Z.O.B. were not even carriers of arms. Their weapon was the pen. Hiding, changing places and concealing their printing press in indescribable conditions, they continued bravely to publish the Jewish underground paper, "HaHalutz HaLochem" — the "Fighting Pioneer". It doesn't matter that in its last phase it was printed only in forty copies. Passing from hand to hand, it reached many people. The "spiritus movens" of this activity was Szymon Dranger, but there were around him some anonymous couriers that history doesn't even mention. I happen to know one of them, a golden Madonna who rented the flat for Dranger and served as go-between.

It has to be stated here that the Jewish underground of Krakow was one of the earliest Jewish resistance movements in all of Poland. It is also amazing that for the sake of forming a strong resistance, several political organizations melted down into one confederation, in spite of their ideological differences. An innocent technological enterprise "Graffit Granit" served as a convenient facade for various activities. It produced forged identity cards, which were supplied to the underground agents, but were also sold at a high price to Jews hiding on the Aryan side. This source of income financed many operations. In the cellar of this technological enterprise were stocked chemicals and sacks of cement with hidden weapons and explosives. The building was conveniently adjacent to the ghetto. Underground passages and plans of sewers were drawn on maps. Counterfeit passes and official German stamps were produced there by artists of forgery. The archives contained a pool of information supplied to various groups. Even such information as would enable the Jewish partisans to overpower a train of deported Jews. The whole Jewish underground was divided into groups, every independent group of five (to make the vote split uneven) constituted an integral unit with its own weapons, provisions and hideouts.

It was the general policy to plant certain units as partisans in the forests. The first group of five was sent to a forest in September 1942. Abandoned by its peasant guide, in the middle of nowhere, it encountered a police patrol and had to sit tight in the thicket. It returned after five days without achieving its aim. The outing of the second unit, though better prepared, ended not in a fiasco but in a tragedy, with one killed and one wounded. The rest retreated. The plans to send other groups had to be cancelled. Before new contacts were established with the Polish socialist underground several operations were executed without external help. The dismantling of rails that caused the derailment of a train, between Krakow and Bochnia (August 42), was organized without weapons and explosives. Sometime later, one hand grenade was enough to destroy a German officers casino. The burglary of a storeroom of German uniforms supplied the underground with excellent camouflage to be used in further exploits. A huge garage of German cars was set afire in October 1942. A pre-arranged false alarm sent the fire department elsewhere. Meanwhile, the fuel concentrated in this garage added by its bonfire to the success of this endeavor. In the same period several spies and collaborators were killed, in minor individual operations.

The Germans didn't feel safe in Krakow anymore. Often, one single German or two were attacked and shot, the perpetrators disappearing after several shots. By then, the Germans already had a list of many young Jews missing from the ghetto and reported to be engaged in the resistance movement. It became clear that all these operations were not the work of the Poles.

Following the attack and killing of an important Gestapo man in Krakow, the accusation of an informer pointed to the main leader Dolek Liebeskind as the perpetrator. When they came to arrest him, he was able to slip away from the hands of five Gestapo agents. It sounds as if he was a giant, and I have already described him as a pale, delicate and ascetic type. He managed to escape by a simple subterfuge. When the five agents came asking for Dolek Liebeskind, he pointed indifferently to the end of a long corridor. When they proceeded, he jumped, jostled the agent guarding the rear, and escaped.

The next plan of the federation of resistance movements was much bolder. It encompassed several groups that were to activate, in one stroke, forty-six participants on that Christmas of 1942. Each group received its mission to be simultaneously executed at the zero hour. The girls on the fringes of such groups were to distribute leaflets and raise flags on bridges in several points of town. The groups of men were to attack at the same moment three coffee houses, one officers' nightclub and one German cinema. Not everything could be as scrupulously executed as planned (the movie ended later than scheduled), but the greatest success was the grenade attack on Cafe Cyganeria, where eleven Germans were killed and thirteen wounded. Once more Dolek Liebeskind was a main participant in this exploit, which was to become famous all over Poland and kindled many flames of resistance.

Tired, proud and drunk with success, the heroes returned to the main bunker, situated in the empty, abandoned former Jewish hospital, outside the ghetto walls. The exhilarated members of 'Akkiba' and 'Dror' organizations mixed with other groups, forgetting all precautions. It was a cardinal mistake to let most participants of this huge operation gather at one point. As it transpired later, there were two traitors, two insiders who, having been previously caught and tortured, were released to continue their membership as planted informers. It was they who denounced and delivered this whole crowd. They were all arrested in this bunker, and only Antek Zuckerman, who came from Warsaw to participate in this operation, escaped wounded. Soon he was to lead the whole uprising of ghetto Warsaw. Some of the boys hadn't yet reached the bunker. Heshek Bauminger, the only expert in explosives, was hidden elsewhere, and Dolek Libeskind found himself separately in another hide-out. He was not alone on the next day, he was still hiding in his den together with the good, sweet Pole Jan Ropa. The traitors informed on him too. When the Gestapo came to arrest him, Dolek killed two Germans before he fell, or committed suicide according to another version. Jan Ropa was killed together with him.

I remember Jan so well, from the same period that I remember Dolek, from the office of the 'Jewish Social Welfare'. The young Ropa was employed as janitor and messenger. Every morning he came to light fire in the stove of my office and asked the same question: "Miss Marysia, how shall I make fire today, German style or Polish style?" Little did he know that he would die Jewish style... working as contact man for Dolek Liebeskind and keeping company with him in death.

Most of those arrested in the bunker were later executed, but Heshek Bauminger was still at large and free to undertake three more operations before he was betrayed and captured. He too shot himself with the last bullet, but did not die instantly. He died under torture without revealing any secrets. In January 1943, the Germans caught at last Szymon Dranger, the hero with a pen as his weapon — the one who stubbornly published the underground newspaper for one more year.

Women also wrote a glorious chapter in the history of Jewish resistance in Krakow. The Gestapo caught in its net sixteen girls, most of them of various groups and formations of the resistance. They all met in one cell, the cell No. 15 of the Montelupich Gestapo prison. They proudly admitted their participation in partisan activities, they even threatened that somebody would always carry on after their death. How do we know it, how can we believe that it was true? It has all been written down, day by day, on strips of toilet paper by one of the girls — Gusta Davidson (pseudo name Justina). It was saved for posterity by the wife of a Polish jailer who came to like her. This is the diary of Justina which was published in Polish after the war. The sixteen girls were repeatedly tortured so as to make them reveal their contacts. Later, one of the four survivors (out of sixteen) described the medieval tortures. Though I know their minute details down to the fingernails, I shall not enumerate them here. I am afraid of sensationalism whenever I have to describe such atrocities. The girls have decided in their cell that they have nothing more to lose. Their only chance to escape will come when they will be transferred all together before their execution.

And that was indeed the way it happened. Before mounting the truck all sixteen dispersed, as agreed, upon a signal. Only four succeeded in their escape and survived. Gusta, alias Justina, was among them.

This extra-dry report doesn't do justice to the Jewish heroes and heroines of Krakow, but I am not the only one guilty of injustice. The post-war Polish government placed on the now famous Café Cyganeria building a commemorating plaque, ascribing this heroic attack against the German occupiers... to the Polish resistance forces. Israel has repeatedly protested over many years against this injustice, but to no avail. At last, only in 1986 was the honorific tablet finally replaced by one stating that it was the deed of the Jewish underground, acting in concert with the Polish resistance...

As I recorded several minutes ago, I have given an extra-dry report about the heroes among my townsmen. Was I writing an anthropological essay on heroism in a community, I would have to make a classification. I would have to categorize the heroes into super-heroes, compulsive heroes, conditioned heroes, passive heroes, cowards turned heroes and so on. From here to villains, it is a long way. Still, there are some categories that do not fit into any frame of research. After all, I cannot create a compound for a hybrid that could be labelled 'saint-villains', because it sounds utterly absurd. I shall therefore have to prove my point by giving several concrete examples, as I proceed with my story.

Right now, I shall give only one example. I have already painted the portrait of Alex Forster, our savior who procured our 'blue stamp'. This pre-war spy, the friend of Gestapo officers, helped Jews however and whenever he could. He saved them by intervening during a "selection", he sometimes even extricated them at the last moment from a train to Belzec, to the gas chambers. Saving Jews at so many instances, he must have somewhat tarnished his image of a loyal Germany spy.

Forster was free to move everywhere without restrictions, collecting information for the Germans. He had an office at the Gestapo headquarter; he had one three-room flat in the ghetto and one suite in Krakow. He who entertained Gestapo officers in his ghetto flat, giving lavish parties, was one day arrested all of a sudden by the OD and detained in its prison on the order phoned from the Gestapo. Nobody believed it. Jews asked the OD prison jailer if it was true that Forster was under lock and key. It was true, but only for one day. As it was later leaked by a Gestapo man, it was a practical joke played by Forster's good friend, the Gestapo officer Herman Heinrich. Heinrich boasted of his practical joke and let Forster stew in his juice for one day. He then came to the prison, asked the jailer to open Forster's cell, and entered it... splitting his sides with laughter.

As if nothing had happened the two walked out of the cell, clasped in a friendly embrace. Forster continued his mole's work of a spy and in the spring of 1943 was sent to Hungary on a mission. He was arrested upon his return and detained in the Gestapo prison Montelupich, being accused of working for the English spy ring as a double agent.

After many interrogations and torture Forster was clubbed to death in his cell — or so it was reported later by a witness who was set free. His winged legend survived him. He was, allegedly, parachuted over England as an outstanding, astute German spy. In the eyes of some pious Jewish mystics, he must have been a 'Lamed Vovnik', a hidden transvestite saint, even though I have branded him in my research as a "saint villain".

Having thus finished the Forster saga, as seen from the angle of the ghetto, let us penetrate again inside the ghetto. According to the German logic, when the ghetto is overcrowded — several thousand Jews must be "exterminated". At this instance, the size of the ghetto can be reduced because thousands can be relocated to the vacated places. Later, the ghetto becomes overcrowded again. The whole process starts once more. All that, after the Germans have repeatedly given confidential assurances, that in the eyes of Berlin, the last reshuffling achieved its goal and was final...

Every time people are relocated, they take less and less in personal belongings with them. They know that they will be squeezed in into a more restricted living space. Whole cupboards and chests of drawers were thrown away a long time ago. They were chopped to pieces and served as combustibles. After each "Aktion", whenever the ghetto was reduced in size — thousands of people carried their belongings on their back, this way and that. The whole ghetto looked like a beehive.

In our house in Wengierska street, everything changed. After the good cousins, Dorothy and Helen, and the four Weisels were deported in the November "Aktion", new people moved into this one-room flat, into the room adjacent to the little kitchen where we slept. I hardly remember the new arrivals, but the worst of all were still the Beckers, who survived the November "Aktion". Thanks to some mysterious protection, the vulgar, thick-set childless Mrs. Becker didn't have to work. Instead, she opened a business in our little kitchen. She cooked meals for wealthy singles, she ran a restaurant of sorts. You can suppose now that it could have been a commodity for us, that we could perhaps save fuel. No way, not with Mrs. Becker reigning over the huge stove. Whenever we tried to cook a few potatoes on this stove that had to be shared by five families, she would cast off our pot with one fling of her heavy hand, spilling the potatoes and the water. When I tried to protest, she slapped me hard. I had never been slapped, I cried. She was a strong woman, and nobody dared fight her. Dorothy's widower, Mr. Barber and his older son could have managed her, but they took their meals at their workplace. They wouldn't fight for us or all the others. We could only eat uncooked meals, and that means bread.

But cooking was not everything. Ask me questions, ask me how the people who lived in this apartment could undress, wash their bodies, their linen, or even make love when four families lived in one room. Such a room was partitioned into cubicles by sheets or curtains. A family owned only the bed, the space under and over it and the narrow strip of passage along the bed. I have already described how they washed with the jug and bucket in our kitchen. When people washed their clothes and linen, they had to hang it over their bed, they wouldn't hang it in the courtyard or garret, because it would be stolen. Bitter scuffles led to fistfights and blows. The Germans knew how to bring out in the Jews their worst side by dumping them together in subhuman conditions. Under such conditions we had our additional personal problem.

Our poor Witek, aged twelve, was alone all the time when we were at work. We started to take different shifts. One week mother worked the day shift while I worked the night shift, the next week vice versa. Thus, one of us could stay with Witek and find a chance to do some cooking before Mrs. Becker drove us away. The solution had its disadvantage. Mother and I didn't meet at all. There was only one fleeting moment when we could exchange a few words. We took our chance close to the ghetto gate, when one of us returned from the night shift, and the other standing in the rows, going to work at the Madritch factory. Once, at such an instance, I approached mother while a young OD man was already checking her group. He yelled at me: "Beat it". When I tried to catch the last sentence of mother's instructions, he struck me with his club and pushed me savagely. I tripped and fell. The skin of my knees was shorn away, and the bloody pulp was smeared with the thick mud. Dr. Hilfstein cleaned my wounds and gave me an anti-tetanus shot. Though he gave it in three installments, well-spaced between the shots, I had a terrible reaction. It was once more a serum, and as you may remember I am not supposed to be treated with serum. My reaction was quite like tetanus itself. I had huge swellings all over my body, but the worst were the internal swellings. When my kidneys were swelling, I had a kidney attack, when the swellings reached my lungs — I was suffocating. I was gravely ill. To cut a long story short, I was given calcium injections by Dr. Bolek Tilles and gradually recovered. I could go back to work.

As if this were not enough, we had to go through a new calamity, in this harsh winter of 1942. All the pipes burst when water froze in them. As I mentioned before, there was only one toilet for some sixty people. It was situated on the staircase of our floor, the first floor. Water bursting from the broken pipes was streaming along the staircase, but people continued to use the toilet in which the lavatory pan was already covered by a tall cone of ice. The urine, mixed with excrements and water, flowed the whole length of the stairs until the steps disappeared under ice. The ice formed a long slippery slope without a foothold. It was impossible to climb it, not even with the help of the handrail because the rail was broken. We, all the tenants of this house, were cut off from our sleeping corner. A crowd of people returning from work stood helplessly in front of the house. But my mother was never at a loss, never helpless. She engaged somebody to bring an axe and hew footholds in the ice. Then she ordered somebody else to bring a rope and tie it instead of the broken handrail. Now everybody could reach his abode, acting exactly like a mountain climber. Still, we were without a toilet and without water. Nobody was willing to pay for the repair of the pipes. Eventually the sanitary commission of the ghetto solved the problem somehow, but only after many days.

Excuse my describing, again and again, of all the trivia while tragedies struck whole families. But are these indeed mere trivia? Try to live for a couple of days without water and toilet in the whole building, and do not forget that many people suffered from bladder problems. Try to prepare a revolt, a general uprising, when you must cope with daily problems of such "minor" disasters alongside the major calamities.

I am raising this question of a general uprising once more because I still feel that it is in the air and has to be answered, illuminated from all possible angles.

As for us, it was about time — as Wilek pointed out in one of his letters — to look for another abode. We were stuck too long in this abominable constellation. The opportunity arose, coming from most unexpected quarters. You may remember that close to the beginning of my recordings, I mentioned briefly new girlfriends that I met when our high school was merged with another, before all the Jewish girls were expelled from it. One of them was the wonderful Mirka. I happened now to meet Mirka in the ghetto, and we both discovered that our mutual feeling of sympathy remained in this winter of 1942 as warm as it had been in the autumn of 1939.

Mirka offered to accommodate us in the room she shared with her older sister Lola and two other families. There opened a vacancy in this room, because two men were already conscribed to the new concentration camp that was being constructed in Plaszow. We got a bed in this room, we were even able to take my brother Witek with us, at long last. He no longer had to sleep in a child's bed, which he shared with Gershon. The three of us didn't even have to sleep together in one bed because we were working, mother and I, on opposite shifts. The cross section of the society gathered in this three-room apartment was on a much higher social level. Most inhabitants were academic, and the general atmosphere was utterly different. In one of the rooms lived my mother's good friend, Dr.Helena Rosenzweig, a lady with three doctorates: in medicine, history and philosophy. Much later, in Paris, it was she who knitted all the baby outfit for your mother after she was born.

It was like having found a family. There was even some sort of socializing. One of my Wilek's friends, Joseph Abrahamer, kept in touch with me. He also liked well my friend Mirka, and the three of us could sometimes spend a nice hour, chatting amiably in an easy comradeship. The three of us had a good sense of humor. When fuel was lacking for the kitchen stove, Joseph helped us to procure it in a most ingenious way. We climbed to the garret of this big house and discovered that it was partitioned into sections by high-reaching wooden planks. They were fastened to the ceiling boards with several nails, but we found a way of dislodging them. We took the lower extremity of a plank and turned it in circles as many times as was necessary to loosen the fixture on the ceiling. We would calculate jokingly how many Holy Mary prayers it took us to disengage one plank. You can compare it to the Beduin determination of distance and time. A Beduin would say: "It takes seven cigarettes to reach the next camp". After we counted some eleven "Holy Mary's", the plank was free and ours, to be sawed into sections and chopped for fuel. Thus, with Joseph's help the heavy chore turned into a pleasant game. As far as I remember, these were the merriest moments of my life in the ghetto.

I don't know exactly what happened to Joseph, I only know that he didn't survive. I do know what happened to Mirka. She is well, she lives in Tel Aviv with her family and retired after a brilliant career in physics. Whenever I meet her now (Mirka is not her real name) I am always aware of her personal secret from this period in the ghetto. The gist of her story is the following: Mirka and her older sister Lola became half-orphans some time before the war. Their mother was left a widow with a prospering enterprise. It was run by a very efficient young foreman — let us call him Mr. G. The young Mr. G. married the older widow and thus acquired two grownup stepdaughters. The couple had a baby and now the mother perished with her baby in the June "Aktion". Mr. G continued to live with his two stepdaughters, as one very warm family. They addressed him as "uncle". All would have been well, but it so happened that Lola fell in love with "Uncle G." and he, the handsome chap, let himself be loved by this infatuated girl. There is nothing you can conceal in a ghetto, and the situation was very awkward. Hardly five months have elapsed since the mother was killed with her baby and already the older daughter is spinning romance with her belated stepfather. My crafty Mirka was very different from her rosy-cheeked sister Lola. She had a lot of character, common sense and tact. She accepted the situation as it was, she didn't blame them. She did her utmost to conceal the romance, or at least to create a diversion, a camouflage.

When we moved into their room "Uncle G." was already conscribed to the new concentration camp Plaszow, but had the possibility to visit the ghetto about once a week. Whenever he came, Lola, crazy with unbridled love, would throw herself on his neck. She would then shamelessly sit on his lap, cradled in his arms. Mirka played her camouflage game. She just did what Lola did. She made a demonstration of sitting on his other knee, enlacing his neck...

I still remember this awkward picture. Mirka didn't have to confide to me. We all understood her game, and it made us esteem her even more.

As you can see, the romantic life of the ghetto was by no means extinct. Many young couples married in haste. Many girls said that they did not want to die virgins. Many women had abortions; some delivered a baby right there in the ghetto. I shall tell you the story of such a newborn baby, a little later and in another context.

Another friend of mine — let us call her J. because I don't know if she survived — married a most suitable youngster. Both were very intelligent and beautiful people, very much in love. He abandoned her immediately after the post-nuptial night, claiming that she was not a virgin. She was, she swore it to me, he was mistaken, but nothing could change his mind. Such cases of lack of hymen are known to medicine.

As for me, I couldn't marry my dear Wilek. He was too far away and didn't find any more opportunities to visit us in the ghetto. We were in contact through the good offices of Victor and the cook at "Tereska". We exchanged long letters and it was the only comfort we had in our painful separation. Unfortunately, this too couldn't last.

Here I am speaking of love and romance while the ghetto was beset by another disaster. It was now (December 1942) partitioned into section 'A' and section 'B'. All people that had no card of work at an enterprise recognized by authorities, were moved into section 'B'. Those with permit were transferred to section 'A'. Ghetto 'B' was a hell. People were starving there, often frozen to death. I did not see it; we had no access to it, but we knew. Many families were separated and the relatives from 'A' tried to smuggle into section 'B' some food, some clothes, but it was becoming more and more difficult.

Was there nobody able to help? It has to be noted that a Polish "Council of Help to the Jews" did not officially come to life before March 1943, the fatal month of the liquidation of the Krakow ghetto. There were single good souls who helped, as well as they could. There was Tadeusz Pankiewicz, the gentile pharmacist of the ghetto, a true philosemite, always ready to help. There was also a figure of a different mettle, the Viennese Oswald Bosko.

You must have wondered many a time how some people could leave the ghetto without escort or a valid pass. There was a good angel watching over the gate. Some people are born adventurers. If adventurous episodes don't happen to them, they provoke and create them. No matter if they are Jews or Germans, they just cannot pass unnoticed. Into this category enters the enigmatic figure of the German Police Commander, Oswald Bosko, who was mostly seen at the ghetto gate, as if the sentry couldn't manage the gate without him. He had an adventurous past behind him. As a mere boy he escaped from a convent, forswearing Jesus. He became a notorious vagabond, visited most Mediterranean ports, stayed for some time in Turkey and at long last felt a sudden longing for his native Vienna. He decided to be a good boy, entered the police force and joined the young Nazi party. He merely exchanged Jesus for Hitler as the object of his adoration. Soon he became disillusioned with Hitler too, when his beloved Austria was annexed to Germany.

Matured by his experiences, he stuck it out in the police service, hiding his personal feelings. In war time, when he was posted to Krakow as the ghetto overseer, he could at last open his heart and confess to some Jews that he befriended there. one of them was Bernard. Bosko was no fool and knew how to play his personal game. Everybody could hear him yelling at the Jews at the top of his voice and cursing them. He pretended to be a compulsive Jew-hater. Meanwhile, he helped Jews as well as he could. He stole or counterfeited passes, he honored expired passes, he would sometimes even pretend to take a man prisoner and escort him out of the ghetto. When the Poles were no longer allowed to enter the ghetto, Victor approached him one day and asked his help to be able to visit us. Bosko took him by the arm and led him in personally, even though he didn't know him. He refused to accept a gift. Whenever he took bribes, he apologized effusively. He added mysteriously that he had a personal reason for accepting a bribe in a case of profitable smuggling. Indeed, he had a very good reason. When he anticipated that he would be sent to the front, he injected himself with a substance that causes furunculosis. He got festering boils and fever, was hospitalized, but could not play the same game for ever. One day Bosko vanished. He betook himself to a village where he lived with a Polish woman, hiding two Jewish children. He had enough money and valuables to remain in hiding for a long time, but his appetite for adventure dictated to him a wrong move. Why not play it both ways? Why not secure for himself an honorable retreat or a clearing version of his disappearance, that could protect him in the future. He wrote a letter to his superior, in which he stated that he had been kidnapped by partisans, he was in their hands detained in an unknown place, and their only condition to preserve his life was to stop the execution of a group of Poles detained by the Gestapo… His superior smelled the rat. After all, Bosko had quite a reputation for fraternizing with the enemies in spite of his impressive performance as Jew-hater. Bosko felt that he must have made a wrong move. He tried to cross the border in disguise. He was caught and brought to the Montelupich prison. He changed his game. He now played the unbalanced, he played the fool. He fooled nobody. He was sentenced to death and was executed. That was the end of a saint, who played the villain. But that happened already after the ghetto was liquidated. According to a different version, Bosko escaped to join the partisan "people's army" and was betrayed by them.

Our own material situation was very unstable. Victor was no longer able to visit us in the ghetto, but he managed to sneak twice into the Madritch factory. He exchanged a few words with mother, he delivered a letter from Wilek, but he had no money for us; he was unable to sell any piece of grandma's jewelry. Even the kings of the black market wouldn't invest in diamonds, while their value was constantly decreasing. Besides Jews, all the Polish nobility, monasteries and middle class were selling their valuables… Our lack of funds also affected Aunt Helcia, Olek and Rutka with whom we shared, of course, the money supplied by Victor. At long last, Victor delivered. He was not able to penetrate the Madritch factory, but he passed the money through the guard at the gate, the good friend, the notorious ghetto jester Wilek Kranz, of whom I shall say more quite soon.

At that point, we received a good lump of money. We could even buy some meat that we hadn't tasted for a long time. Mother decided to celebrate, and she bought no more and no less than a whole tongue. I pretended to be elated, even though mother forgot that I hate tongue. While we changed shifts, she gave me detailed instructions how to boil the tongue. We had access to an electric cooking plate in our room, it was going to be quite easy. I was after the night shift, I had time. I am skilled and gifted in many ways, but I hate cooking or cooking hates me. Anyhow, this tongue must have hated me even more than I hated it… and it took its revenge on me.

I started the preparations with much trepidation. When I reached an advanced stage, Rutka came running to me. She had sensational news. Uncle Olek stood perhaps a chance to become employed at the public kitchen.

Not as a chef, merely as an underling, still, it was a great opportunity to be close to the pot. The election (I hate the word selection) was to take place in an open courtyard and we could watch it — said Rutka. Here I was, stuck with the tongue, while important things were going to happen, changing the fate of the family. I decided that if I filled the pot with the tongue full of water, nothing much could happen in the next ten minutes, even though it was against mother's instructions. That's what I did, and I felt like a genius. It took more than ten minutes, but Olek won and was engaged to work in the kitchen. We were all elated, we celebrated, and then I started running to take care of the blasted tongue.

Before I reached the house, I saw from afar a crowd amassed under the windows, looking up. A thick cloud of black smoke rose from one of the windows. Had a fire broken out in one of the front flats? When I approached the crowd, several people raised their fists at me."She is the guilty one" — yelled a threatening figure. I still didn't get the connection. What was I guilty of? Then I saw my Witek, his blackened face streaming with tears. As it transpired, the tongue had burned down to coal. The smoke filled the whole flat. When Witek arrived at the scene of my crime, the tenants seized him. "It is your sister who caused it" — they spat at him — "now you go in there, open the window and disconnect the electric plate". He had to do it all on his own, my poor brave little brother. Now it was over. He didn't cry of anguish, he cried and coughed from the thick smoke. The whole room smelled of smoke, even several days later. I became the black sheep of the whole house. I deserved it. Mother uttered only one sentence; "It fits, it is like you". I felt crushed. I never hated myself more in my whole life. My culinary incompetence and inhibitions persecute me to this very day. This incident closed the last chapter of our life in ghetto, or so I seem to remember.

To dramatize the epilogue of the ghetto period I would need a painter and a poet. The world-famous painter of the ghetto, Abraham Neuman, a man of many talents (chiromancy among them) was no more. The poet of the ghetto, Mordechai Geburtig, wrote his scan song some time before he was killed. It was the now famous song of the partisans, "The Shtetl is afire", which he composed (as he admitted) with tears streaming from his eyes. I knew well one of Geburtig's beautiful daughters. None of them survived. His poems survived. The Association of the Jews of Krakow in Israel has a collection of excellent pictures painted by Neuman, and a collection of poems by Geburtig, to be published very soon.

Some strange coincidences were related to the end of the ghetto. On the very same date, March 1943, Szymon Dranger was arrested in Bochnia. He escaped a month later and was reunited with his Gusta-Justina, who escaped in the same month as one of the sixteen girls I described earlier. They continued for a while to publish the 'Fighting Pioneer' until, in November, their traces disappeared.

Another hero of the Jewish underground, a good acquaintance of mine that I failed to mention before, must have been reincarnated after his death. This Henry Wurzel, a man of many travesties, who paraded in German uniforms and seized several weapons from the hands of the Germans, seems to live in Israel. The Israeli actor Yehoram Gaon is the spitting image of Wurzel, down to the kinky hair which the former used to conceal under a German officer's cap.

This seems to close the circle, but I have to connect the last links. The liquidation of the ghetto was executed in one big sweep, but the threads between the ghetto and the Plaszow concentration camp were already drawn and tied. Many men were sent earlier to this camp while it was under construction. They built it. Several OD men were delegated to supervise this work force. The Plaszow camp was within walking distance from the ghetto. Once, quite unexpectedly, a whole detachment of OD men was sent to Plaszow. They returned the same day, pale, shocked and silent. As it was later leaked, they were sent to serve as henchmen. They were ordered to hang several Poles brought to Plaszow from the Gestapo prison in town. The Gestapo took pictures during the execution, which were to serve later as propaganda means, showing that the Jews were executing the Poles... After this incident many OD men started to drink to excess. No wonder.

When the ghetto was totally vacated and empty, some OD men and some work forces were left there to clean the whole area within its enclosure. When the whole ghetto became a ghost-town, several weeks later, there were still some living ghosts crawling out from their hiding places, half dead of starvation. They were executed. The cleaning of the ghetto took some ten months. The last OD men left to live there, including the infamous Symche Spira, were executed in December 1944. That was the end of the high commander, the most loyal collaborator, who believed that he would be the last Jew to survive in Krakow.

MY ODYSSEY THROUGH SEVEN CONCENTRATION CAMPS

In the Islamic beliefs there are seven gates to heaven, but only one to hell. How many sections were there in Dante's hell? I don't remember. I have my seven hells behind me. I emerged from them, half my present weigh, but sane of spirit and coherent.

So, what was the balance of trauma? Let me give you one single example: I don't travel. Not even at short distances. When I try to be valiant — I go through another hell. A long psychotherapy revealed that every time I leave "my nest", I probably feel like being exposed to a deadly danger. Indeed, every transfer from camp to camp signified eighty percent certitude that it led to a gas chamber… So now you know, or do you?

I am leaving out all the other symptoms of my trauma (and they are legion) because I am now going to write the epilogue to the story of life on the planet called ghetto. Then I shall retrace my steps, leading from the ghetto to my first concentration camp.

The Plaszow concentration camp, situated on the barren hill of the Jewish cemetery of Krakow, was for a long time in advanced stages of preparation. We knew that it was being constructed for us, yet we didn't believe that we would ever reach it or be incarcerated in it. Don't ask me why. A miracle will happen, the war will end — I don't know. Hopes, wild hopes, illusions, rumors — you name it.

All that, till the day when the official edict on the total liquidation of the ghetto was made public. Now the sword of Damocles was not hanging over our heads anymore. All became clear. There were solemn assurances given by the Germans that all the ghetto inhabitants would be moved, as they were, to the hygienic, well organized, spacious working camp… This time nobody believed that it will be done without a selection, or that one can survive a concentration camp.

Many families and singles committed suicide. Babies had certainly no chance whatsoever. Wilek Kranz, the ribald ghetto jester with the poker face and the bearing of a Polish nobleman, was the father of a baby. He poisoned him himself, he put him to sleep. He said that he didn't want an SS-man to bash the skull of his baby against the wall — a scene he had once observed. Later he became again the author of the circulating jokes, the jester of the concentration camp. Can you believe it? He was no clown, but once a jester, always a jester. His pale, shy wife seems to have faded away. Was she killed? I don't remember.

After the war Kranz married our cousin's widow, the merry Guscia, who was most receptive to his jokes. A short time before I started these recordings, I tried to find her (by now his widow) so as to gather some of Wilek's excellent jokes. I found her in a home for elderly citizens in Haifa. She didn't recognize me at first. Then she exclaimed: "Ah, so you are Marysia, Rosa's daughter, yes, yes, you are Rosa's daughter". When I eventually broached the subject of her husband's jokes and puns, she looked at me with her child-like round grey eyes and said: "But don't you see, don't you realize that I am absolutely sclerotic?" It was a shock, I admit it. I have missed a golden opportunity to enliven these recordings. Now I only remember two pale samples of his wit. Once he approached the cell for solitary confinement in the camp and whispered into the slit: "Be proud, you are the only man in the whole camp who can pee in privacy..." The second witty utterance that I remember dates from after the war, from the trial of Amon Goth, the commander. Having served in the camp as prison warden, Wilek Kranz was the main witness for the prosecution. Amon Goth pretended not to recognize him. "No wonder" — remarked Wilek in a clipped tone — "When we were at the peak of our ambivalent relationship, the accused was as fat as I am now, and I was as emaciated as he is now..." That's the story of Wilek Kranz, the murderer of his own child.

Before the transfer of the whole population to Plaszow was executed, many chose to seek escape through the sewers, the only outlet from the surrounded ghetto. I know several of those who fled through the sewers. Many were caught immediately or later, a few succeeded. I shall describe here three cases known to me. The first is that of the distant cousin, the dwarfish Gershon, who shared his child's cot with Witek. By then his whole family had been killed, he had nothing to risk but his own diminutive person. Being one of the first to infiltrate the sewers, he emerged safe at the other extremity, on the Aryan side, quite a distance from the ghetto. Where could he go in his state reeking of excrements? The only person he could think of in this dangerous situation was his former university professor, under whose tutelage he had graduated, before the war, "summa cum Laude" with an Academic degree in sociology. The professor held Gershon in great esteem and was ready to help in a way. During their short conversation, Gershon stood firmly on the pallet and refused to budge from it, knowing how he stank from the sewers. Eventually they both remembered that Gershon befriended a fellow student, a catholic priest. Gershon remained standing like a monument hick, while the professor looked up this former student and asked him to hide Gershon in a convent. That's where he spent the rest of the war.

Gershon was raised in a religious family, he was also active in the "Akibba" Zionist movement. Nevertheless, he admitted to me after the war, he admired the serenity of the monks and felt a strong attraction to monastery life. Years later, he still spoke in whispers. The beatitude, the sublimation, the compassion that he observed and acquired there were to accompany him throughout his life after the war, a life that he consecrated to the care of retarded children. But then you have to remember that his is not an objective evaluation of monastery life. Gershon had the problem of a dwarfish figure, topped by a normal head. All his life he was hiding behind a wide scarf that he wound around his neck. Now, at last he could hide behind the high walls of a monastery.

The second case of escape through the sewage-network is that of little Joseph. Here I have to mention my handsome aunt Mania Sperling, the wife of my uncle on paternal side. This uncle and his son fled Krakow with most Jewish men, before the Germans reached the city. Aunt Mania remained alone, but she managed, she had means. She even took care in the ghetto of her orphaned nephew Joziu — little Joseph, her sister's son. Joziu can't have been older than seven or eight when the ghetto was about to be evacuated. He was the most beautiful child I have ever seen. His blue eyes were almost violet under the long, dark lashes. His hair was liquid gold, his dimples most endearing. This clever child guessed right that his aunt would not be able to save him at this crucial moment. Getting some advice from one of his relatives and without saying a word to anyone, Joziu disappeared. Following some grownups, but all on his own, he entered the mouth of the sewers and wading through excrements reached the other extremity of the pipes and ...freedom. He cleaned himself in the Vistula River (in cold March) and found himself in the city. Someone gave him shelter for a few days, a Polish woman who knew his parents helped him — they were all engendered... For the few cents that he had on him, he bought some cigarettes and matches and stood at the corner of a street selling them to passers-by. He soon discovered other boys engaged in this trade, but he decided prudently to keep away from them. He spent his nights sometimes in a garret, sometimes in a cellar. He combed garbage cans in the early mornings, looking for leftovers. Thus, he survived for quite some time still preserving his princely looks. He couldn't pass unnoticed.

One day a lady tried to engage him in a friendly conversation. At long last she asked him the inevitable question; "Confide in me and admit. You are a Jewish orphan"- said the good lady. "Madam, you are mistaken. I happen to be an orphan, the son of a Polish Officer, but I am certainly not Jewish" — answered the cheeky little boy. The lady went away, but returned the next day and found him again several days later. By then she was able to persuade him that if she were an informer, she would have denounced him already. All she wants is to help him. If he is willing to follow her, she will be able to spirit him away, far away to safety. She didn't mention Switzerland but that was where he was finally smuggled to, after a perilous Odyssey with a group of children.

He lives now in Israel where he found again his Aunt Mania, our common aunt. We had lost her traces in Plaszow and were to meet her again in our last concentration camp, the seventh camp. I shall return to that in due time. As for Joziu — he was a good nephew to her until her last days. She died a year ago at the age of ninety-one. The good lady who saved him was a member of the Council of Help to the Jews, but he does not remember her identity, not even her first name.

After this story of escape with a happy ending I have to tell you a tragic story, that of Dr.Berger. At the end of her escape through the sewers her only son was killed, while she herself, unharmed, slipped and broke her leg. Howling with despair and physical pain she crawled back to the ghetto and was hospitalized. Her friend Dr.Blau sat on her bed trying to comfort her, as if one could comfort a mother who just lost her only child. The whole ghetto was already moving out to Plaszow. An SS-man, checking the hospital and shooting whoever he encountered, found the two friends in an empty hospital loom. He pointed to the siting Dr.Katia Blau and commanded: "Doctor, get up and turn around". "I am not afraid to die" — replied Dr.Blau — "You can shoot me while you are facing me". As if it were an order, the SS-man shot her. He must have felt very strange, so strange that he forgot to kill the patient in the bed, the poor Dr.Berger. Maybe he guessed that he didn't have to... because Dr.Berger recovered, was sent to Plaszow, and after some time committed suicide.

Several others were lucky in their escape through the sewage-network, but after the Poles noticed Jews raising the heavy lid of the sewage outlet and emerging to daylight, they notified the German police. It set up an ambush and killed many, the very moment when they seemed to have reached freedom.

So much about the lucky and the tragic escapes through the drainage. Now back to the ghetto. There were still many children living legally as protected children of people who were essential to the German war effort and possessed the blue stamp, as well as a tag identifying the industry which they served. These people had to be reassured. The Germans diligently spread the good news that a whole barrack was being prepared in the Plaszow concentration camp, big enough to house all the children of the working people. All these children will be transferred there in good order and in good time, but first, they must be delivered by their parents to the assigned nursery in the ghetto, allegedly the provisional home for children.

Unfortunately, this order concerned our Witek too. He was twelve years old. Mother saw no other option or solution, but to run to our close relative H., the OD high officer, and beg him on her knees to save Witek, pretending that he was his own child. Who will know at the gate that he is not his son? H. refused shamefacedly. He had already promised somebody else. He had promised his lady lover, the beautiful Mrs. X, to save her two daughters. You can understand that the Mrs. X's handsome husband was quite cooperative and tolerant in the given circumstances... The tragedies of the Holocaust made some strange bedfellows.

Mother never forgave H. to the end of her days. As for me, I had a dilemma of conscience. I understood that he had to keep his former promises. Mother returned to us in total despair. We kept the three of us as if chained together. Mother fought like a lioness, but I was eventually swept by force, unable to resist any more. Mother was clinging to Witek and remained with him at the nursery to the very last moment. Finally, she too was dragged away out of the ghetto and into the concentration camp. We met there and we cried. We didn't even notice what the concentration camp looked like, we just sat and cried. I don't know how many people were killed in the ghetto, how many were deported or how many and who were executed in Plaszow. All this, and the lot of the children, is blurred in my memory. I usually see facts and scenes in pictures, but that day left a lacuna, a grey mist.

We sat like turned to stone, too exhausted to cry any more. I can't say how many hours passed until, until... Witek came running to us safe and sane. After we cried and laughed and crushed him in our embrace, he was able to explain. While he was kept in the nursery with all the children (up to fourteen) he saw suddenly a uniform and a familiar face. It was the young OD man, Mundek Reich who lived in the Kornhauser flat in the ghetto. He had no children of his own and took a liking to our Witek. He was such a remarkable boy.

Witek noticed him entering the nursery, but our Witek wouldn't ask to be taken out of group of children to be saved. He said nothing. Mundek Reich spotted his velvety, big brown eyes attracting him like a magnet. Something prompted him — as he related later. "Witek, what are you doing here" — asked Mundek Reich sheepishly. "As you might have noticed, I am a child" — replied Witek, with bitter sarcasm. Reich took hold of his shirt's collar and pulled him by force in one movement out of the nursery, then through the gate and into the camp. His OD uniform was the best guarantee, no questions asked. Mundek Reich had quite a reputation in the ghetto. He was a notorious glutton, a sybarite, believed to be a cold-blooded bastard, a typical brutal OD man. Indeed, when mother thanked him from the deepest bottom of her heart, he asked her for a reward — a diamond.

He knew we had somebody in town keeping some jewels for us. He couldn't have known how little was left of them. Mother signaled to Victor to bring to the Madritsch factory the most valuable diamond, the center piece of the brooch. She gave it to Mundek Reich without regrets. Didn't he deserve it? Of course, he did. Did we despise him? Not at all. We were so happy and grateful that we would have given all the rest for what he did for us. Aunt Helcia approved the decision with all her heart.

What happened in ghetto 'B' after the transfer of ghetto 'A' to Plaszow — I know only from hearsay and from reliable sources. Some people and a few OD men were left to liquidate the ghetto. Many Jews were dragged out of their houses, cellars and garrets and were driven to Plac Zgody. Some were shot in their hideouts, some were shot later, but some of the elderlies were given a chance to run for their life and thus prove their stamina... Of those who ran well, hundred and fifty were chosen by Amon Goth to work as liquidation squadron. "No", decided Hasse, "too many. Half of them will do"... The others were killed on the spot. Those who were saved, received a new task; to undress the corpses and load them on platforms. When this proved to be too time-consuming, the corpses were loaded by heaps, some of them still alive and stretching their hands out of the pile.

The nursery was liquidated in a very systematic way. Older children were shot at first, not in the presence of the others, but a little further, somewhere around the corner of the street. The middle age children were killed separately, group by group, in a courtyard. At last — the babies were loaded, several on one pram, and shot with one bullet. Then the next batch was put into a pram and...

All in all, some three thousand Jews were brought into the camp, but all these details are not preserved in my memory; I am reconstructing them from other sources. From here on, I can continue to relate the horrors as I remember them. The glorious new life of orderly work in the working camp (as promised by the Germans) started with a blood bath.

The beginnings were marked by the first mass-executions. There was a whole lot of ground preserved for mass-graves. They were dug out in advance by those incarcerated in the camp. Then the victims were brought under a strong convoy, placed naked along the ditches and shot.

There will come a time when the Germans will try to cover up the traces of their crimes. Two years later all the corpses, the thousands of corpses will be dug out by a bagger, out of the several sites of mass-graves distributed over the camp. With the characteristic scrupulosity of the Germans, some of them were mapped. The bagger will prepare the layout, the rest of the exhumation of corpses will be done by Jews — and we shall be among them.

But that will come later.

I myself have opened here too many "mass-graves" and have buried too many corpses under the light weight of my too dry sentences. It is because I try, so desperately, to stick to bare facts. The anonymity of these corpses of mine is frightful. That is why I have now to tell one personal story, one whose main impact can be ascribed to the individuality of its main figure.

It is the story of a very beautiful lady, the owner of a cosmetic institute of high distinction. She was delicate, soft spoken, immaculate and with impeccable manners — she was in my eyes a classic egoist, totally self-centered. Her heroic story disproves my erroneous impression in an incriminating way. She, who never touched earth — jumped into the ground by her own choice. She remained with her baby daughter in the nursery of ghetto to the very end. How did she manage what my valiant mother could not achieve? She was given a white coat of a nurse and was allowed to accompany the children to the last moment. Her child was not shot in the ghetto, but was brought to Plaszow. She could have thought at this stage that she managed to save her daughter, but it was not to be. They were brought to the edge of the mass-grave, and here she was to be separated from her child and assigned to live and work in the camp. But she couldn't and wouldn't take her chance. When she saw her daughter stretching her arms out to her, in an imploring gesture, calling "mummy" — she jumped alive into the ditch holding her child in tight embrace. Was she buried alive or shot — I don't know. That is the story of the "egoistic" beautiful lady and... of my misjudgment.

One can misjudge or misinterpret so easily. Never underestimate the absurd. It has a right to exist under absurd conditions. Let me give you an example; who do you think was most unhappy over the liquidation of the ghetto? The Gestapo. Yes, I am not mistaken. The minor executives of the Gestapo became all of a sudden superfluous. The ghetto was under their jurisdiction and supervision, but the camp was not. They became jobless. They knew that they will be sent to the Russian front because the army is on the verge of mutiny over the exemption of Gestapo from military service. So now you see.

When you will be taught the history of the Holocaust, you had better be prudent and learn to differentiate. Nothing in the Holocaust was monolithic, nothing was absolute, and all the generalizations are dangerous. One period does not resemble another period, one week can be different from the next week, one day is not similar to another day. The life in one section of a camp had nothing in common with the style of life in another section. No status was comparable to another status. It has also to be stated that the Plaszow camp had fourteen dependencies, almost independent little working camps, in the vicinity of Krakow, each with its own conditions and lifestyle. A concentration camp was divided into many sections, one alongside the other or one within the other, each with its designation and function. Sometimes it was a state within a state. What you will learn in general outline does not necessarily apply to the reality, composed of many facets.

To give you some topographic orientation in the camp, I should have attached a map of Plaszow, a camp that was raised on the grounds of the Jewish cemetery. Amon Goth used to quip: "They won't have to go far to get buried". What you will not see on this map is the elevation of this huge, lonely, naked hill. You will not see the Jewish tombstones with Hebrew inscriptions, which paved some streets and served as steps. Many people were stepping on the tombstones of their own ancestors. The rest of the map is hopefully understandable; The gate and the main road, the separation between the enclosure of men's and women's barracks, the huge rollcall square, the tiny Polish camp, the hospital, the kitchen, the public bath, the administration barracks, the southern plots of mass-graves, the quarry, the swamps, the ponds. On the fringes of all this complex were situated the living quarters of the Ukrainians, and separately these of the Germans, with Goth's villa as the main plot. On the higher plateau were concentrated all the workshops in their enclosure, separated as each and every enclosure, with a barbed wire. Still higher, on another plateau, was the hill of executions, so elevated and steep that it was nicknamed 'chujowagorka'- the prick hill. It was topped by an old Austrian fort that concealed the acts of execution.

As I mentioned before, the German commander of the Plaszow camp was the abominable Amon Goth, and the Jewish commander was the cad Chilowicz with his little blond toad of a wife, reigning over the womenfolk, but subservient to the women wardens.

As for the barracks, you might have seen in the pictures taken after the liberation what a barrack — called a block — looked like, with its long rows of bunks in three tiers, divided by the narrow passages. In these barracks people were squeezed like sardines. Over this emporium of a barrack, ruled the 'Blockalteste' — the commander of the barrack. Her power over the inmates was almost unlimited. Her second in command was usually also very nasty. A young, energetic commander of the block felt so elevated in her important function that she could turn to a lady pharmacist, of ripe age, in this tone of speech: "Appel, you'd better stop star-gazing and polish my boots". If she didn't say: "Appel, you bitch, you'd better..." — she must have been in a good mood. The coarse, vulgar vocabulary of these figures could fill a dictionary. Their whims were legend.

During our incarceration in Plaszow we must have changed barracks, or rather have been shifted, some four or five times; I don't exactly remember. Whether the commander was one Franka, Gina, Malka or Helena — there was perhaps a difference of style, but not of the use of power.

Our food rations were "shorn" by Goth (who sold the provisions stolen from us by wagon loads) and by the block commander and her "minions". They were reduced in quantity and in quality. Not only was our bread cut into pieces, so as to leave a margin of 'savings' for the "Blockalteste", not only did the miniature piece of margarine become microscopic and the rare addition of watery jam became a smudge on the bread — the very soup with its low caloric value was even more diluted. The liquid soup was distributed to us, while the thicker dregs were left for the minions.

Of the so-called coffee the "Blockalteste" couldn't possibly make any profit, it was an absolutely non-descript beverage. By what she stole and sold, she could buy the best coffee for herself, as we could guess by the good aroma reaching our nostrils from her personal room.

Not every "Blockalteste" was stealing. Franka wasn't. Though she could be very mean, she was capable of heroic deeds. Once, a Jewish inmate was chased by a man and two Ukrainians. Out of breath, the man turned round the corner, burst into our barrack and took refuge under one of the bunks. It was during working hours, there were only two women present, and they noticed that Franka saw the intruder. She posted herself in the door with crossed arms when the pursuers reached her barrack. "Didn't a man hide in your barrack?" — asked the officer. "How could he?" — replied Franka calmly — "I was standing right here". After we heard about this incident Franka rose in our esteem, but still she remained as nasty as ever. The complexity of such characters never ceased to amaze me.

Franka's barrack was not far from the exterior barbed wire encircling the whole camp. I tried sometimes to approach it and look at the horizon, but there was nothing to be seen. Not a tree, not a house. Here and there was a fuzz of grass. It grew close to the watch towers where nobody dared to tread. I dared to... I had to. I have spotted there a few miserable daisies, which hardly dared raise their heads. I went to the tower and picked them. It must have amused the bored Ukrainian standing on the tower to threaten me with his gun, but I pretended not to notice him. It seems a few daisies were dearer to me than my life.

As long as we worked in the Madritch factory outside of the ghetto and the camp, we went out, we saw the outside world. We passed daily several miles of the main street leading to the factory. When it was moved, on Goth's order, into the camp, we didn't go out anymore. We were going up to the working terrain, on the plateau. One would hope that from this elevation it would be possible to observe the vicinity of the camp and see a tree... there was none on this swampy wasteland. But there was a distant hut, one single little shack, dilapidated and neglected, housing probably a jobless family. How we envied these poor people, the free people... We would climb, my romantic friend and I, to the vantage point from which we could observe them for a short while. We saw from afar the children romping around the shack, and we tried to imagine in the evening what this family were doing at that moment. We made suppositions, we embroidered stories around them.

In the book "Schindler's Ark" by T.Keneally, there is a description of a scrub, a wood that allegedly grew in the proximity of the camp. There was none at our time, and what the author saw must have grown after the war. I missed trees. I am crazy about trees and the barren vicinity of the camp was most depressing. Here I am, describing my Werther's suffering, as if inspired by Goethe, while other people suffer Gehenna caused by another German, caused by Goth. Isn't it a morbid coincidence?

Shortly after our arrival at the camp I saw Melanie Mariam, or rather her ghost. She lost all her three children, including her brother's infant, that she breastfed together with her newborn. She hardly recognized me. She was not depressed, she was devastated, she was ruined. She looked at me with empty eyes, she didn't even wipe her running nose. She didn't even have to be killed, she simply disintegrated. Next to my sewing machine worked now Bronka, a merry wench. During the passage to Plaszow she lost her baby daughter. Whenever something funny was going on, Bronka would explode in her horse's laugh, and immediately a terrible grimace would twist her plain features and her laugh would turn into loud howling, bemoaning her lost Rutusia. Then she would beat her breasts, accusing them of having fed a condemned child. Here you have two bereaved mothers mourning their children, each in her personal style.

On the highest plateau, the "Chujowa gorka"- the prick hill, an execution took place almost daily. We hardly knew who was shot there. Sometimes it was a group of Poles brought from the prison in town, sometimes a group of Jews. Jews from villages, Jews from the prison who were caught hiding or were apprehended with Arian papers. Sometimes camp inmates were executed for the slightest transgression or for no reason at all. Often whole details were murdered so as to reduce the number of camp inmates. Once we saw a group of inmates led through the camp to the prick hill. Among them was Sophie, Dr.Hilfstein's niece with her husband and son. I don't remember why they were executed, all the three together. You should have seen how proudly they marched to their death with heads held high and a serene expression on their faces. Would I sculp her thus in all her beauty with her high cheekbones and neck of Nofretete — critics would say that it is a glorified kitsch.

From the work-camp enclosure, we could often hear the shots. After a year in this camp, we got so used to the executions that we hardly paid attention to them. We had to get used to them actually from the very start, the very beginning. Hardly two days after our arrival at Plaszow (March 13, 1943) ten people were executed by hanging. We didn't have to watch it, but everybody knew. Hardly a week later over two hundred Jews were executed on the prick hill, Jews who were caught hiding in the empty ghetto. Two days later the whole camp was searched for valuables. Again, a mass execution followed.

A year later we were so used to the executions, that I had a strange incident during one of them. I was detained in the barrack for some duty or other while everybody was at work. There were only new arrivals in the barrack, a transport of Hungarian Jewesses brought from Auschwitz with shaved heads. Though our food rations were limited to no more than some twelve grams of bread, I was munching a crust of bread, even though I knew that an execution was taking place far away at the second end of the camp, right at that very moment. Maybe I was munching this crust because I was nervous about it, I always munch when I am upset. A young Hungarian approached me with hatred in her eyes. "How can you eat bread when you know that human beings are being murdered over there on the hill?" she spat at me. I took it calmly and sadly. "When you are here for as long as I have been, you will perhaps understand, I don't blame you now".

But let us return once more to the beginning. In this early period, we were still going to work outside the camp. Wearing shabby civilian clothes and not the striped ones (they were scarce in this camp), always wearing a white kerchief on our head, we were marched daily to work after the long rollcall and counting of heads which took place at five thirty. We started at dusk and returned after dusk to the same rollcall square. While we worked at the Madritch factory, Victor Chlebowski was sometimes able to sneak in with the few Poles that also worked there. He came, exchanged a few words with my mother in a dark corridor and sneaked out. As I mentioned before, after Wilek visited us twice in the ghetto, we had some contact with him through Victor, but he didn't come to the ghetto anymore. Now, several months had elapsed and there was no letter from him, no sign of life. There could be no sign of life; Wilek was not among the living anymore. As Victor learned from the cook at "Tereska", Wilek succeeded once more in obtaining a mission sending him to Krakow, and once more, as before, took some watches or whatever it was from his colleagues, to sell them in town and to bribe the Ukrainian serving as his escort. Somebody must have known; somebody must have denounced him... he was searched bodily and shot on the spot or later. The cook didn't know the details.

Can you imagine what it meant to me? My private world, my hopes for the future collapsed. The pain was purely physical. I felt dead, buried with him. I felt the taste of earth in my mouth... I felt his slim body with fingernails growing and growing after death. I was constantly shivering. I wanted to cry but I couldn't. I felt guilty that I didn't cry after father's death because we were in the middle of our escape. How could I now bemoan Wilek's death? Finding no outlet for my deep grief I withdrew into myself; I became depressive. Rutka tried to cheer me up, she brought some gossip, but she didn't have the right approach. Who helped me? My so sweet brother, Witek. He knew me so well, he found for me a medicine of sorts. He knew my craving for creativity. He was working in the paper workshop and he brought me some sheets of paper. He persuaded me to write together with him a story for children. It was a sheer escape from the glum reality, but it worked. Sitting on my bunk in the evenings, we put our heads together and composed the story. I remember parts of it. There was an adventure of children constructing a raft and floating on it along the river. We never finished the story, but these were precious moments. What was the source of our strength for this bizarre occupation in the middle of a concentration camp? I don't know.

After all, don't forget that we were getting up before five o'clock. For almost one hour we had to stand in rows during the endless rollcall, shivering in winter and in summer. Then we were marched, often in rain, to the factory where I was riding on my sewing machine, till five. Then the way back and again the rollcall. Returning to the barrack we were queueing up for the daily distribution of bread and the so-called coffee beverage. Only then did we catch an hour for ourselves, till the sounds of the night bugle drove everyone to his barrack. Witek too went then to the men's camp to his barrack. That was the daily routine. I shall later dress on this skeleton the painful details.

We had some old and some new friends in our block. Between washing our linen and body in the washing compound, going to the distant latrine and finally undressing and performing the evening ritual of hunting for lice in our garments — we could chat for a while before the lights went out. Mother was always in the center of things, not so much in socializing (she was not so eloquent) but in organizing our communal life.

When my mother decided that our whole quarter of bunks had to go to the shower so as to enable the delousing disinfection to be done, she herself stood in queue until she obtained the admission tickets, for the whole group of some thirty women. Thanks to our contact with uncle Olek, mother was sometimes able to obtain from the kitchen a mess-tin full of hot soup. Olek passed it discreetly through the barbed wire, at his own and mother's risk. It was the usual thin soup, but one more portion in the evening was a blessing. Mother would then distribute it among our friends, leaving for us equal portions. My tiny mother had that kind of personality.

I won for myself a new friend that will accompany us through all the camps, and who is my bosom friend to this very day, even though she lives in Australia. Her name is Janka (pronounce Yanka — equivalent to Jane) and our friendship started in a most peculiar way. I noticed on the bunk facing our cot an unfamiliar, quiet, beautiful young woman, so clean aesthetic and well-bred that she caught my attention. She was actually seven years older than me, but she was so virginal that you wouldn't suspect it. One evening, as I observed her preparing for the night and combing her freshly washed black hair, something disgusting happened to her.

The incident itself was not so unusual but the circumstances were different. We all suffered from bladder inflammation due to the exposure to biting cold during the endless rollcalls. Try to run at night, with a sick bladder, to the latrine that is situated at some three hundred meters distance. You will never make it. Some of the sufferers found a solution. They bought for a piece of bread an empty can from preserves and kept it on their bunk, to be used as a chamber pot of sorts. It happened not once and not twice that the one on the upper bunk, trembling from cold and urge, overturned her "chamber pot" and spilled its contents on the bunk underneath. Such cases ended invariably in vulgar abuses, fisticuffs and face slapping.

Janka possessed, exceptionally, a sheet and a nice nightgown. She was sitting like a princess on her clean bed, and as I observed her with eyes full of admiration — it happened to her. The woman on the cot above her used her narrow can in such a clumsy way that it fell down and a shower of urine dripped on Janka's hair and bed. Everybody else would beat the perpetrator black and blue — not Janka. She raised her innocent eyes to the woman above her and said in a quiet complaint: "How could you do such a thing to me, how could you". That was all her reaction, nothing more happened. I was speechless, it was unique. I saw for the first time in this camp, a person that remained a gentle human being. I felt an urge to express my admiration, but I didn't know how. The next day we worked the night shift, I didn't meet her, but in the morning, instead of going to sleep, I went under the watch tower and gathered a few dreary daisies. This time I didn't creep under the tower, I kept within the eyesight of the sentry, showed him the daisies, and he even smiled. I added a leaf or two. I tied the posy with a thread, and deposed it on Janka's bunk with a note:

For the one who doesn't let off her steam —
with my whole admiration and esteem!

Your vis a via, Marysia Sperling

When we met after my night shift, Janka said: "I waited so impatiently to meet you, I waited like for a lover. I see that I have found a friend after my own heart". This incident cemented a friendship that was to last for a whole lifetime. We became inseparable even though we were so different, the two of us. Janka's younger sister who lived in another block was much closer to me in temperament and in age, yet there was never a click between us. As the French say — "les extremes se touchent".

Mother adopted Janka and took her under her protective wing like a second daughter. Janka had this helpless passive attitude to life that simply invited protection. When she suffered stomach cramps caused by this bread of ours baked with addition of sawdust and horse-chestnut flour — mother bought somewhere a cup of barley and cooked it secretly at night on the block commander's stove.

Were it not for the shower of urine that besprinkled Janka — this friendship would perhaps never have been born. Speaking of urine reminds me that I have not yet explained the problem of latrines. The first time I entered a latrine in Plaszow, was a shocking experience to me. There was a long board with round holes, and in order to get your bowel movement you had to sit down next to another woman, a stranger. It so happened that the first time I entered a latrine all the holes were occupied except one, and this one was next to Dr.Maria Pechner, a good friend of my parents. I blushed. How should I behave, should I pretend that I didn't notice her? Impossible. Should I bow and ask politely: Excuse me, Dr.Pechner, do you mind if I shit next to you...? She solved the problem for me by greeting me first. Eventually we quickly adapted ourselves to this new style of chatting during the performance of physiological functions.

In this early period, when we still went out of the camp to work in the Podgorze suburb, we smuggled some food into the camp. Having this rare opportunity, we just had to. People were daydreaming about food and most conversations turned around "what would I cook now if..." We smuggled not only for Witek and our relatives, but often for some needy people. The mother of my old friend, Lula Bieberstein, suffered from stomach cramps. I often brought her a piece of white bread. Smuggling was very dangerous. We were sometimes stopped at the camp gate and searched bodily. In such cases whoever carried some food on his person would drop it and grind it into the mud that always accumulated close to the gate. That too was dangerous. Once, a whole group, of forty-nine heads, was killed for smuggling food... If spotted, one endangered the whole group. Of course, the real smugglers operated in different ways, mostly through incoming trucks.

Anyone who still had means, could buy, even eggs. There was in our group returning from the Madritch factory, a solitary egoist woman with pale eyes of an owl. She took great care of her person. Once she smuggled a whole omelet for herself into the camp. An omelet on its pan. When we were searched, she dropped it into the mud. She admitted to us that it was for herself. Once an egoist, always an egoist... Several of those who smuggled food into the camp were executed. Some took the risk — life had a low price. What didn't one do for relatives or out of friendship?

My mother discovered in our barrack a schoolmate of hers, the serious, intelligent, just, noble of soul — Sophie. The renewed old friendship bloomed for about half a year. Like the French 'vous' and 'tu', there are two forms of 'you' in Polish; the formal 'pani' and the informal 'ty'. The formal disappeared in the camps, and I now addressed Sophie or other ladies of mother's age with the informal 'ty'. Informality reigned. But Sophie's march to her death was very formal. When her number was called up at the roll-call, the tiny Sophie straightened up, seemed to grow in stature, bowed her head to us in a formal heartbreaking adieu, stepped out of our ranks and marched like a queen to the group of the selected ones, to be sent to the gas chambers in Auschwitz.

Among my own new friends there was one that I have to mention under an assumed name, because of her amorous adventure, and because she lives now in the ultra-religious suburb of Bney-Brak in Israel. Let us call her Leica Berger. She was raised in a religious, tradition observing family, but it didn't leave an imprint on her. She became very dear to my heart, she was so romantic and poetic that she created for me a new realm in this vulgar inferno. She would sometime say to me: "Look how blessed we are, the two of us, being aware and happy that the sky is blue". It was with her that we embroidered fantastic stories about the jobless plain family in the shanty. But Leica became herself a heroine of a romantic story that was so strange, considering her background.

She, who came from a rich family, was before the war married off at a tender age to a religious man. It was considered an honor for such a family. She never complained about it, good daughter that she was, but we could guess that the man was a total stranger to her. Anyhow, it was a short episode because he disappeared from the scene in the first day of the war, escaping with most young Jews eastwards. Leica lost all her family in the ghetto and now she had only us, her new friends. There was also someone else, a man of importance, the manager of a workshop, who sought her friendship. There was even an affinity of names between them; while hers was Berger, his was Bergman (both pseudonyms). This joke of fate united them, their friendship turned into love and into romance.

It was evident that she was very much in love with this sensuous man in his prime. Leica had a splendid body, but she moved as if she were ashamed of it. She must have been too modest, shy and unearthly for him. The romance had short legs, he seemed to grow tired of her, more and more distant. We worried for her, because she still believed that he was too busy to see her more often.

It so happened, that Leica became sick with rheumatic fever and was hospitalized in the camp's sick ward. We, her friends, visited her daily, often out of doors after the sunset. Once during our visit, we spotted her lover, quite close to us, but visiting another she-person. We, the devoted friends, exchanged glances and as if by accord tried to create a diversion so that his voice would not reach Leica's ears. The couple was behind her back. The four of us began to talk in a pitched voice, to blabber unisono, no matter what. "What happened to you"- asked Leica — "I may be sick, but I am not deaf". Soon after she recovered the cat was out of the bag and she knew that she had been jilted. She grew pale, distant, lost interest in life and seemed to attract ill fortune. When we were, much later, sent to Birkenau, she was the only one of our transport to have her head shaved. She only said: "It fits, it is an appropriate punishment for a sinner". She avoided us as well as she could, saying that ill fortune is contagious. We tried all we could, but to no avail. Soon she disappeared from our horizon, she was sent to some other camp.

Many, many years later, some twenty years ago, my mother met Leica in Tel Aviv. Mother was overjoyed. She said: "When Marysia learns that you are alive and here, she will jump sky high. She mentions you quite often wondering what became of you". Leica took it calmly, hiding her emotions behind a screen of tears. "Dear Rosa" — she said — "I am living on another planet now. I rejoined the religious circles, my husband returned from

Russia, I would be like a stranger to you. I don't want Marysia to see me in my reincarnation. I want her rather to preserve the sweet memories of our friendship, as I shall cherish my memories of her. We couldn't bridge the present gap". With these words she took leave of my mother in a final way.

Mixing romance or friendship with horrors seems to be my trademark. I am not guilty. Life mixed them for the sake of my story. So now back to horrors. The worst were the public executions by hanging. I am not allowed to omit them. I must describe such a scene. Not the very choking to death of the victim, but the reaction of the spectators. These hangings are noted by history. We were forced to watch them several times.

One of them was the case of the young Haubenstock, a mere boy, who was hanged for a very serious transgression: He was allegedly caught by a German singing or rather humming 'Volga, Volga' while working in a construction detail. According to the accusation he, a communist, tried in this way to detect among the Ukrainian watchmen, a brother communist who would respond to this appeal. Another culprit to be hanged together with Haubenstock was engineer Krautwirt, who tried to smuggle some letters to friends in Krakow. Goth decided to arrange a fiesta of public hanging. The participation of all the camp inmates was to serve as a warning. I saw the gallows with their innocent bare poles, and they reminded me of a swing for children in a park. Years later the sight of a swing aroused in me this glum association.

When the boy Haubenstock was already hanging by his neck, a miracle happened and the rope broke. Was this an accident engineered by the Jewish hangmen — who will ever know? It is a custom, in the whole world, that in such a case the victim is to be set free. Evidently this old custom of amnesty did not apply to Goth. He drew his pistol and shot the boy. I lost all sense of time; seconds seemed to draw into hours. Finally, Krautwirt who had time to cut his wrists was hanged in the deadly silence reigning over the huge crowd amassed on the "Appelplatz", the rollcall square. Though our group was placed quite close to this terrifying scene, I did not watch it, as you can well understand. I cannot tell you if the body twitched, if the neck snapped. But I can tell you that I felt a unique peculiar sensation tingling in the tips of my nerves and travelling through my whole system.

Several SS men stood very close to me. One stood holding a huge Dalmatian dog on a leash. There is no research work stating how dogs react to hanging, but this one was smacking its lips and slowly, so slowly wagging its long tail. The SS man was slowly, very slowly wagging his long whip in the same rhythm. I was looking at the dog's tail and at the SS beast's whip as if I were mesmerized, as hypnotized. All of a sudden, I felt a strong impulse, an urge to seize this whip and to apply it mercilessly to the man's back. It was a physical urge to whip and to flog somebody. I wouldn't believe I had it in me, even though I experienced it only this once in my whole lifetime.

All the hangings and mass-executions performed on the order of Amon Goth, did not have to be authorized by his superiors as long as Plaszow was "de nomine" an "Arbeitslager" — a Forced Labor Camp. Goth grew so omnipotent and was in the eyes of his superiors so efficient, that he was promoted by two ranks, from "Untersturmfuhrer" to "Hauptsturmfuhrer". After all he extended the camp's absorption capacity, from seven thousand to the number of thirty-five thousand inmates, including the special Polish compound, numbering no more than twelve hundred souls. Comparatively, the Madritch work force inside the camp constituted an important feature employing close to three thousand prisoners, if this number is reliable. I was not aware of all these numbers at the given time, I learned them later.

I was well aware of the fact that in the general outline, the numbers of the incarcerated prisoners were controlled in the following way: The firing squads of SS Horst Pilarzik performed smaller mass-executions, while the huge transports of those to be culled from the camp were sent to the Auschwitz gas chambers. I have to stress however the most incredible fact, that at the given time, we did not know or did not believe that these transports were destined for annihilation. It didn't make sense. What prevented Goth from executing them on the "prick hill"? Didn't we all know how vital were the trains for the extended German front lines?

The changes in the German official policy were hardly understandable to us. From January 1944, the Plaszow camp was declared a concentration camp, now under the direct orders from Oranianburg headquarters. Little did we know that under the new orders, even flogging had to be reported. The permission of hanging a culprit for sabotage had to be granted by Oranianburg on base of a formal application, supported by formal testimonies.

The German logic created a series of absurdities. As long as Plaszow was noted as a Forced Labor Camp, it was in reality a concentration camp; when it became a concentration camp, it was an extermination camp of well-regulated and calculated annihilation. When Oranianburg authorities asked Goth if he would be able to "accommodate" thousands of Hungarian Jews, Goth obligingly complied, asking for permission to "reduce" the actual population of inmates, so as to make room for the new arrivals. Reducing had only one meaning... as you can guess by now.

In the official documents, the euphemistic term for the word "killing" was — "applying special measures"... Goth made the selection by a very simple strategy. Every "capo" of a hard-labor detail had to submit a list of those falling behind in work. If he left a "shlimazl" in his unit, his own head was in jeopardy. An election in workshops was a different matter. Older men of high experience had to be protected. Goth would enter a workshop and order its head to form his people in two equal files: one of highly qualified craftsmen, the second of auxiliary forces. These, being expendable, were sent to a transport. All this rarely applied to the Madritsh factory, which was under its own authority. Still, there were cases when Goth played a trick on Madritsch so as to prove him his clout and thus to extricate from him more substantial bribes.

Skilled craftsmen had their value in this camp. It still had to be productive, to supply its products to the German war effort and to Goth's private pocket. Everything was recyclable: eyeglasses, teeth, protheses, clutches. Even the tattered and blood-stained clothes were recycled, often spun and woven afresh with the addition of nettle. From these fabrics the Madritsch factory made uniforms of many patterns. Human hair was recycled in socks manufactured for the crews of submarines, but I wonder if it was true that a pair of gloves for Goth's mistress Mayola was made of human skin.

All Jewish skills were put to good use. From engineering, construction and machinery repairs, through metal, upholstery, brush workshops and paper industry, down to jewelry. Not only did the jewelers repair valuable pieces that landed mostly in Goth's safe, they also melted teeth and caps of gold, extricated from the corpses.

All these prisoners, from skilled craftsmen down to construction and quarry laborers, working from seven to six or even longer, were kept alive on a ration of seven hundred to eleven hundred caloric value, including one loaf of bread for a week. The official rations were evaluated at twenty-five hundred calories. Our main meal, the mid-day soup was cooked of cabbage, turnips, carrots, beets and... sago. What was sago? Have you ever seen it? It is shaped like lentils, but it is absolutely transparent like glass, has no taste, no consistency, no nutritious value. Sometimes the soup tasted of meat scraps or bones, but it happened only when an inspection was expected at the camp. As for the rest of our diet, I have already explained who profited from it and what it consisted of. Once, during an inspection, a baker was asked how much bread a prisoner receives as his weekly ration. Goth, hiding behind the inspector's back, showed two fingers, and the baker said two loaves. Dr.Hilfstein, who worked at the camp's hospital, wrote a research work on hunger. He described how it burns the body's fats, destroys irreparably vital cells, and finally affects the brain.

We were less hungry than the other prisoners because the good Madritsch was smuggling bread into the camp to be distributed among his working teams, as a reward for keeping the production rate as high as possible. Schindler, whose "Emalia" factory was never integrated in the camp, did likewise. It doesn't mean that we weren't hungry, but we were able to exchange sometimes a loaf of bread or two (I don't remember the price) for a cake of soap. In order to economize on a loaf of bread, we had to share one portion between the two us for several days. Hunger gnawing at the stomach and intestines of the prisoners produced a strange effect. Everybody was incessantly speaking of food. This mental onanism was so much part of our daily life that I should insert after every half an hour of my report one and the same sentence: "...and then we spoke of what we would cook and eat if we were free". Whatever the subject of conversation, we would eventually always return to food.

Meanwhile Amon Goth lived in his villa like a king and grew fatter and fatter until he became immense. After a hanging or a shooting performance, he would spend some time listening to classical music. He was well cultured, the son of a book publisher. An evening orgy with participation of several male guests and a matching number of Polish women of easy virtue, was also enlivened by music, the excellent music played by the Rosner brothers. I was a great admirer of the younger one, Poldi, who was married to Janka's sister. These two artists knew well when to play serious compositions, and when to switch to light music or 'schmalz', according to the mood in the room and to the quantity of alcohol imbibed by the orgiastic guests and mainly by Goth himself, who was a heavy drinker. Oskar Schindler was often one of the guests, our own Madritsch avoided it as well as he could.

Goth's official mistress, the lovely Mayola, had a special status. This working girl, a secretary employed in Krakow, never participated in the orgies. Her amorous relationship with Amon restored to him the little self-respect that he so badly needed, being debauched and bisexual on top of everything else.

This sadist remained dangerous in any mood, drunk or not. He was quite sober when he let his dogs Rolf and Ralf bite off the breast of a woman or the groin of a man. He was quite sober when in the morning hours, he would observe through binoculars a group of slaves working in the nearby quarry, and take his aim at one that slowed down for a while... He often killed men wearing long coats, knowing that they must be religious. Once he shot a urinating man, pointing his gun from the lavatory window of his villa. He easily shot two women who were slow in potato peeling or a man who did not march in step with his column. He shot people so often and so unexpectedly that working in our workshop, my back to the window, I constantly had the terrible feeling that any moment, if I stopped for a second pedaling on my sewing machine, he would shoot me from behind, through the open window.

He constantly maltreated his personal cook Lena, slapped and pulled her by the hair. He did it for the slightest alleged negligence in the performance of her many duties, even though she was a perfectionist, a real pearl.

He hated skilled and intelligent Jews, just because they disproved the Nazi theory that Jews are "Untermenschen" — an inferior race. In the early stage of the barrack construction in Plaszow, there worked a young architect, Diana Reiter. She must have been quite cocky because a woman architect had a hard time competing in this male dominated world. One of her competitors told me that before the war, when Diana tried to show her clout, she would climb to the top of the construction and yell from there, at the top of her squeaky voice: "Enforce the sideboards. What do you think you are pouring here, concrete or shit!"

Now, in her Plaszow camp career, Diana Reiter remarked to Goth that a certain foundation of a barrack was started in a wrong way, because of contradicting instructions given by the SS Hujar commanding the squad. Goth seemed to listen, he even called Hujar to him. Diana was certain that Goth would reprimand the man. She didn't guess that Goth couldn't stand her superiority over a man and a German. He told Hujar coldly to shoot her.

Hujar hesitated... he thought for a moment that this must be a joke... after all, the woman was excellent at her job. Goth repeated the order and Diana Reiter was shot, shot from behind. Perhaps Hujar couldn't face her.

While I try so desperately to paint for you the portrait of Goth, the monster, I feel very depressed. Not by the enormity of his crimes — I have already passed through this emotional stage a long time ago — but by the problem of my personal shortcomings. Here I am, speaking for hours into this silly microphone, and I haven't even revealed one tiniest segment of the man's crimes. The grapevine functioned so well in this camp that one hour after "an incident" (read 'murder') everybody was informed about it. They left their imprint. Every incident was witnessed by several survivors. Let me just tell you that the minutiae of testimonies at Goth's trial after the war filled five hundred and nine printed pages... Instead of reconstructing and passing my memories to you, shouldn't I rather translate from Polish these 509 pages? But would you read them?

To hash fragments of memories or rather to establish a whole list of Goth's main crimes — would be a crime in itself. I shall not commit it. I am so afraid of cheap sensationalism that I shall spare you this torment. Haven't you heard enough about the German atrocities? If I tell you that he flogged people over the eyes, if I tell you that he took a baby out of its mother's arms, smashed its skull in her presence and then shot it from great distance as a shooting target — shall I better fulfill my duty to you? If I tell you that he once ordered two Jews to club each other to death (promising life to the survivor), and then shot both of them for merely pretending to club each other — shall I then accomplish painting Goth's portrait? So, let us leave it at that.

As for his henchmen, the SS officers, what does it matter to you if John was more dangerous and feared around the camp than Willie or Hujar. What does it matter to you that Scherner, Goth's superior, worked hand in glove with Goth, or that one of the wardens over women, Alice Ostrowski, was probably a man accidentally born as a woman. Several other women wardens looked just like stupid cows, who volunteered for this job out of ignorance. I wish I could tell you more about the SS forces, because I felt fascinated with them as individuals hiding behind a uniform. "Know thy enemy" would be a motive behind this fascination, but I never came close to them and that was my luck. Mother was of course more in the devil's way.

She once fetched hot water for linen washing from the bath-instillation and found herself face to face with Alice Ostrowski...

"What are you carrying here in your can?" — asked this horse of a woman. "Hot water"- answered my mother. The she-devil was so disappointed that she struck my mother across her face from right and from left, and she had a heavy hand. Her nickname was 'Pelerinka' because she was said to strangle little children under her cape.

These were Goth's executives running the camp for him because he was drunk most of the time. Otherwise, Amon Goth was no fool. He was quite ingenious in amassing a fortune. The wagonloads of food provisions, which he stole by robbing the inmates of their rations, were quickly sold in town by his man for all seasons — Wilek Chilowicz, the Jewish commander of the camp in Plaszow. All this was only a trifle compared to the jewels detected in the seams of dead people's garments by the minions of Chilowicz, and delivered to Goth. Still, Goth was not above accepting bribes from Schindler and Madritsch.

The vulgar ruffian, the thug Chilowicz, who never walked but seemed to jump, served Goth as a third dog. Chilowicz ruled over the camp through terror, like his predecessor Symche Spira. His coarse language was imitated by other OD men and by his own bedbug of a wife, who ruled over us womenfolk. "You regiment of whores" — she would address us — "You are dispersing like a fart in pants". Other OD men invented similar epithets.

An exception to this style was the soft-spoken Schnitzer, who happened to be the brother-in-law of Chilowicz, the husband of his sister. Schnitzer was our direct boss at the Madritsch factory, one of several workshop bosses. This excellent tailor and good manager was severe, efficient, demanding but just. He used to say: "I didn't climb to my position through the protection of my brother-in-law Chilowicz, I have climbed the ladder by my own capacity". Though he had nothing in common with his brother-in-law, he shared his lot in death. Here they were reunited.

You may now ask how did we manage, under this constellation, living on the meagre rations shorn by Goth? With the little sums of money provided by Victor we could smuggle some food into the camp — but was it enough? Food was not the only problem. The bowl for soup and the tin mug for coffee were all we had beside the toothbrush. Mother was never helpless. Once, we found a basin with a hole in it. We paid with bread to have it repaired.

We acquired a jug and a pot in the same way. With a basin and a jug, we could wash our garments. We couldn't carry them with us, where could we conceal them? The bunks were often inspected, so the deputy of the block commander would throw them away. Didn't mother find a solution? Of course, she did. She pried loose two boards under the head of this lowest bunk where we lived, and made beneath it a cache, a safe of sorts formed of a wooden box. There we could now preserve our treasures; it was perfectly undiscernible. Possessing a cooking pot, we were sometimes able to cook some barley on the block commander's stove, paying with half of it to her deputy. That too only if she was in a good mood.

Hardly a couple of months after we landed in the Plaszow camp, our material situation — and consequently our physical condition — deteriorated so suddenly and so drastically that one day we found ourselves at the bottom of poverty and misery. Before I relate how it came about, I have to mention someone who tried desperately to assure his or rather her material situation at our expense.

You must remember Olga, Witek's loving German nurse who raised him, the same Olga who eventually refused to take him from the ghetto to her mother and to save his life. Now the situation had changed. Now it was Olga who needed a favor from my mother. It was in that early period before the Madritsch factory was moved into the camp. We still worked outside the camp and Olga was able to visit us there. Yet she never did. Now she had to. She was afraid of this conversation and very nervous when she stood in front of the Madritsch factory gate and asked kindly to be allowed to speak to Mrs. Sperling. Wilek Kranz, the gate keeper, facilitated for her the meeting with my mother.

Olga was trembling all over. She didn't ask how we were faring. She was in great haste to present her case. "Mrs. Sperling" — she said — "you probably know that your former flat in Krakow with all its contents is now mine. It belongs to me as a "Volksdeutsche", but unfortunately, I have nothing to prove it, no document. If asked, I have to produce something. I need a fictitious contract, date retroactively, in which you confirm, with your signature that some three years ago you sold me your flat with all its contents, like furniture, carpets and paintings" (you will remember that we had to leave behind some such items).

Mother looked at Olga with her intense blue eyes and became almost speechless. Then she said, after a moment of reflection: "You must need this document very badly if you dared to come to me after you refused to save your beloved Witek. You must be in conflict with a genuine German claiming the possession of this flat against you, who are merely a "Volksdeutsche", just a German born in Poland...". Mother must have guessed well because Olga changed all her colors. Mother now set a trap for her. Thinking quickly, she challenged Olga: "This gives me an idea. I still have a certain chance of extricating Witek from this terrible camp. Never mind how. What do you say, will you now take him under your protective wing and place him with your mother, provided that I sign for you this fictitious contract?" Olga shifted her weight from one foot to the other. She had nothing to say, she lowered her head.

"Never mind" — said mother — "I was merely testing you. I have no such possibility. It is too late. Witek is probably doomed. But I have learned one more lesson. I have learned who lived under our roof for almost ten years. That's worth my signature. You will now live with your own abominable self, for the rest of your life..." She quietly put her signature to the contract submitted by Olga and returned to her work without a word of goodbye.

The worry for Witek never left us, by day or night. He was not one of the protected children of people in high position, and even these were not secure. While we were working outside of the camp, Witek was employed in the paper workshop inside the camp. He was working, he was loved and protected in his workshop — but was it enough? This skinny boy of thirteen was so noble of character and bearing, with his intelligent and aristocratic features, that he was nicknamed "The little Lord Fauntleroy". Everybody cared for him. When a German was approaching his workshop, our Witek was spirited away by good people, and hidden under the roof between piles of paper. As long as Victor provided for us small lumps of money, we were able to smuggle for Witek some nourishing food, but it was apparently not enough, and this growing boy remained pale and lanky. Don't forget that we also had to smuggle this food for aunt Helcia, Olek and Rutka. Olek, though working in the kitchen compound, had access only to the thin camp soup. Victor delivered this money, sneaking from time to time into the Madritsch factory. Sometimes he used the good offices of the gentile Pole Sliwinski, who was, long ago, mother's fellow student at the Academy of Art. Madritsch employed some Polish freemen too and

Sliwinski was one of them. The few provisions that we dared to smuggle into the camp were bought by Sliwinski with the money handed to him by Victor. Had we disposed over more money, we could have avoided the heavy risk of smuggling by buying these provisions at exorbitant prices inside the camp. Indeed, Witek, Helcia and Rutka beseeched not to risk our lives for their sake. If only we had the premonition what tragedy was to befall us and how destitute we would become — we would have used all the reserves left in Victor's custody. What happened was so unexpected that nobody could have foreseen it. Here is how it came about.

At one time Victor promised to bring a considerable sum of money the following week. He didn't show up or pass it through Sliwinski. It wasn't like him. He knew that we were penniless. One day Wilek Kranz asked mother: "The distinguished Polish gentleman who comes sometimes to visit you here, isn't his name Victor Poraj Chlebowski?" When mother confirmed it, Wilek Kranz looked sadly at her and informed her gently, that on the wall facing the Madritsch gate there was a death notice in black frame, announcing his sudden death. We could hardly believe it, so Wilek pointed it out to us. I can hardly describe the shock that the terrible news caused us. As I have explained earlier, Victor, the art and antique expert and dealer, was the man of confidence of people from different backgrounds. Even monasteries and Polish noblemen remitted to his custody valuable objects of art or jewels. Somebody must have known that in this modest flat were sometimes concentrated real treasures. This somebody must have even been familiar to Victor because Victor opened the door for him. He didn't have to break in. Veronka, Victor's spouse and their three children were away, vacationing in her family's hamlet. Victor was alone, and the intruder knew it.

The beast killed Victor with seven blows of a mallet. Poor Victor was found sprawled on the floor in a pool of blood. The whole little flat was turned upside down in search for valuables.

Several days later, a lady shrouded in black asked at the gate to see my mother. It was Veronka, the statusless widow, primitive, greedy, shrewd — and probably antisemitic. She came to cry on my mother's shoulder and tell the story of Victor's death. She cried some more, and only then did she tell my mother that she came to inform her that everything was lost, their own saving, valuables, and our jewels as well. They searched the whole flat, they searched under mattresses, carpets, cupboards, leaving no stone unturned.

She will have nothing to live on and of course nothing to return to us.

How could mother comfort her and at the same time reveal the truth. She didn't have much time, but she managed to explain to Veronka: "I know that you must be in a terrible state of shock. No wonder that you have lost your balance and your senses. When you recover a little, you will remember, as I do, about the cache, the cubby in the wall. Dear Victor of blessed memory informed me some time ago that for security reasons, he had hidden his own well reserves for the future together with the rest of our diamonds. He concealed it in the wall under the gas-shelf, and the wall was repainted". After these words Veronka squinted and reacted immediately: "No, no, forget it, they broke the wall too, they found it there, everything is lost, yours, mine, everything". Mother knew that it wasn't true (as she would be able to prove two years after the war), but what could she do under the circumstances?

Thus, we found ourselves, all of a sudden, in a tragic situation a few months after we were transferred to Plaszow. The tragedy was twofold: the loss of the best and most faithful of friends, and at the same time the loss of the last resources which could help us survive.

Ill fortune never travels alone. There is even a rule of series. If only we were offered at least a respite, an interval, so as to absorb this double tragedy. But it was not to be. The very same day, when we returned to the camp broken-hearted, but decided to conceal the tragic news from the sensitive Helcia — the same day another tragedy was to strike us.

When we crossed the entrance gate to the camp, we spotted Witek expecting us. This in itself was unusual. We were only able to meet after the roll call. Witek approached us slowly, very pale, and asked how our day had been. "What are you doing here at this hour? How did you get free?" — we interrupted him. "Oh, there is nothing to it, I only wanted to tell you — but don't get upset — that I am not so well, so I got a sick-leave from work" — he prepared his approach carefully. "What's wrong with you" — we exclaimed both simultaneously. "Somebody has decided that I have scarlet fever, but don't fret, I already have the admission to the epidemic ward of the hospital. I slipped out of there because I wanted to tell you myself, now I must return, they will miss me, and it will screw up the whole rollcall for everybody." That was the way we learned about this additional calamity.

Witek was gravely ill, it took him a long time to recover, and it was a miracle that he wasn't finished off at the hospital with a lethal benzine injection. His defenses were so low that he actually didn't recover at all, he remained pale and emaciated. He was now over thirteen, but he looked no more than eleven. The worst was that there was nothing we could do to help him. We were left without means, there was nothing nourishing that we could afford to buy for him. We belonged now to the lowest stratum of the camp society. We have fallen to the bottom so suddenly, so cruelly. So did Helcia, Olek and Rutka.

The best we could do under the circumstances was to earn some bread and exchange it for some sugar or egg for Witek. How could one earn bread in this camp? There were a few instances when every prisoner had to be, once a week, on duty besides his regular work. One of them was the compulsory cleaning of the barrack at night, when everybody was on his bunk. The second was the night watch duty at the entrance to the barrack. A person of means could provide a replacement, a poor soul who for half a loaf of bread was willing to undertake this additional duty. We became now the poor souls asking for such a replacement job.

Everybody who saw us working at night as a replacement was wondering. We were known as persons of means. Before the war, my father was considered in Krakow a rich man — which he wasn't, as I have explained. Most of our acquaintances knew that we had in those days a gentile friend in Krakow who took care of us. People didn't believe their eyes seeing us scrubbing the wooden floors after lights out or sitting on watch throughout the night. It was a queer feeling to scrub the floor under the bunk of a lady who paid us as replacement and now lifted her feet to enable me to clean the floor under her bunk. Some people didn't believe that it was true, that we had fallen so low so suddenly.

There was even more to it and something rather absurd was happening to us. As you know we had this cache, this "safe" under our bunk. Many acquaintances knew about it. The fact that we had an excellent reputation goes without saying. It then so happened, quite often, that some lady acquaintance who was warned that all the inmates of her barrack were going that night to disinfection, would come to us and ask to conceal her possessions in our cache. There was often a diamond or two and several coins of gold or just money in her possession. It was very risky for us, but we couldn't refuse. Sometimes, even two persons entrusted to our safekeeping their treasures on one and the same night. Thus, penniless, hungry, and desperate, we slept upon diamonds and gold. There was no end to absurd situations.

You may well ask why we didn't turn to such a person for help. I have no explanation that would make sense to you. Were we indeed so proud? In view of Witek's deteriorating condition, did we have any right to remain so proud, so obstinate, so enclosed in our cocoon? Today I see it as criminal lunacy. But today I am looking at things from a different perspective.

Gradually the word got round that we were left without resources. The good cousin Bernard tried to help. We refused. Seeing how stubborn we had become, he did it in his own humoristic personal style. He would sometimes drop in at our block, in great haste, carrying a whole loaf of bread and say to me: "Marysia dear, hold it for me for a while... I am on an errand". Before I could utter a word, he would disappear and didn't come back. He did it shortly before lights out, so that I wouldn't be able to cross over to the male living quarters and return the bread to him. That's what I call style. He would ride high on the scale of benefactors, as established by Maimonides in the 12th century.

Someone else got wind of our hard situation. Some people of influence, the noble Stern brothers. They were both active Zionists in pre-war Krakow, and they knew my family well. Father was always a generous contributor to such causes. Now, under the occupation, in the early stages of Oskar Schindler's career as German industrial promoter, Isaac Stern became very close to Schindler. He became his confidant. We didn't know about it, but I shall soon explain the implication.

One day, both Stern brothers approached my mother, and one of them opened his speech in this way: "Dear Mrs. Sperling, we have learned about your present situation and Witek's sickness. We have heard how valiantly you and Marysia try to cope with it. We think that we can help you. Being old family friends, we can give you a substantial loan on excellent terms." "What loan?" — exclaimed my mother, stretching proudly her diminutive figure. "Don't get alarmed, don't worry, you can pay it back after the war, no strings attached", said Natan Stern. Did my mother reflect? Not even for a moment. "How can I be sure that I shall be able to repay it after the war. How can I accept it from you, knowing that you are not rich, have never been. How could I cause you so much privation?"

Isaac Stern shifted his weight from one foot to the other. He was not in a position to disclose that it wasn't their money. It was a carefully guarded secret. They wondered how to handle this difficult situation, unable to disclose that it isn't a loan, it is a donation.

For three consecutive days the Stern brothers accosted my mother again and again, trying to persuade her, but to no avail. All their arguments didn't affect her. I simply don't understand today how we could refuse, and why we didn't accept the loan for the sake of Witek.

The money that was so generously offered to us by the impecunious Stern brothers, had a history of its own, as post-war research would later prove. It was smuggled from the Zionist organization in Hungary (with links to Turkey and Palestine) by the good services of a gentile dentist from Budapest. It was handed over in Krakow to the savior of Jews Oskar Schindler, the owner of the "Emalia" factory, to be passed on to a trustworthy Zionist in the Plaszow camp. He would then distribute it to the needy at his discretion. One honest Zionist by name of Mandel refused to accept, being afraid of a trap. When reassured by Isaac Stern that it was safe, he came once more to Oskar Schindler for the money, but by then it had been already handed to another Zionist. The prudent Stern brothers acted behind the scenes, and we are the best witnesses that they were involved in the distribution. How the money was distributed, and what part of it was transferred to be used by the Jewish underground — I don't know. Many secrets had to be kept not only from the Germans but also from the spies of the OD police, run by Chilowicz.

About the OD police forces and individuals, I have much more to say. I was constantly amazed that they were Jews like the rest of us, and yet could become so distant, so cruel and debased. But I often caught glimpses of a human spar in them. Several of them tried to help, or at least not to interfere too much. Some played a game, pretending to be severe and harsh. Once, the OD man Liebling noticed that one of the two corpses of Jews shot by Goth was still alive. He took the risk and taking a side trek, carried him to the hospital.

The OD officer H. preserved his good name throughout the period of the ghetto and the Plaszow camp. He was now appointed to supervise the little Polish compound, numbering sometimes less than 500 gentile prisoners, sometimes 1,200. He behaved so correctly, justly and tactfully, that the

Poles who were set free returned to Krakow and had only words of praise for him.

You may now ask how was the OD policeman Mundek Reich faring? He was the one who extricated our Witek from the ghetto. He was far from popular. Known to be cruel, arrogant, vulgar and... getting fat. Yet he was about to disclose his other self, at least once more, and I have to describe this incident which took place much later, when we already worked inside the camp. It so happened that one evening, one head was missing from the prisoners group returning from the "Neues Gelande" (the section of workshop). The whole detail was stopped and kept waiting for endless hours, in a narrow passage between two electrified fences. Several details were stopped in this passage, leading down to the "Appelplatz", and it became blocked like a bottle neck. It lasted a long time till things were sorted out and in the meantime a tragedy happened. One prisoner was accidentally pushed and caught by the current of the electrified wire. His whole body shook in spasms, but the current was not strong enough to kill him on the spot. People gasped, cried and pushed each other, afraid to get close to him and become caught with him. Nobody knew what to do. Mundek Reich was leading a group, waiting as we did, not far away. When he heard the cries for help and spotted the incident, he made a swift decision. He cut for himself a passage through the crowd, took off his jacket, reversed it, inserted his hands halfway into the sleeves, and creating thus an isolation — caught the poor man. He shook him and detached him from the wire. Reich was risking a lot by his bravery. If the man with one liberated hand should clasp his neck, Reich would be electrocuted together with him. Everybody admired this swift rescue action and the courage of Mundek Reich. People said: "Who would have believed him capable of such heroism, him the sybarite, the glutton greedy for bribes".

Is there a scale to measure heroism? There are so many grades and shades of it. Sometimes it seems to me that it takes a hero to become a villain, and it takes a hero to become a victim. Is this absurdity plausible? I shall soon explain this queer philosophy. Let me present a certain situation, a specific incident, and judge its actors according to their reactions. It happened at a later period when the Madritsch factory had already been transferred to the working compound inside the camp. The Madritsch people were not always protected, not in all situations. One day we were quietly sewing, riding and pedaling as usual on our sewing machines. In order to produce seven uniforms a day, each of us constituted her own uninterrupted conveyor belt. I would first sew in one line seven left side-seams of a pair of trousers, then seven right side-seams, then seven insteps… and so on. It was a race against time. Mother worked as usual on the unusual, the finery of the elite uniforms, their pockets, flaps and collars. We worked intently and silently. From time to time, mother tried to overcome the noise of some twenty-six machines and call for some more threads. She would call out in her thin weak voice: "nici" (threads) and Bronka would imitate her high-pitched squeaking like a reinforced echo. Everybody laughed, even Bronka herself, who never stopped bemoaning the loss of her baby daughter.

We were so concentrated on our work — as if our life depends on it… so we didn't notice the entry of a young OD man. He looked so insignificant, so innocent in his immaculate uniform, as if he were a boy parading on Purim in a travesty. He tried to overcome the noise of our machines and asked: "Which one among you is Wdowinska (pronounced Vdovinska)?" Our boss Schnitzer indicated the woman in question, who was quietly sewing buttons, sitting in her corner. She must have been over fifty because her daughter was over thirty. "Wdowinska, follow me please" — said the young OD man, quietly approaching her without haste. "What for?" — asked Wdowinska, turning deathly pale. "I have here a list of people that I have to accompany to my headquarters. Your name is on it. Get up, take off this silly apron, and come with me" — he said now in a stronger voice that became audible over the clatter of our machines. We all interrupted our work and heard Wdowinska stammering: "Why me… what for? Look, I am young, I am working here at Madritsch… I am productive… I, I…" — she stuttered. The OD man now insisted more forcibly. Her daughter tried to intervene. The 0D man ignored her. He came closer to Wdowinska in a menacing manner, then thought better of it and didn't touch her. "Look" — he said — "You are on the list; I have to deliver you. It is my responsibility. What do you want me to do? Do you want me perhaps to take this young woman working outside with her spade? to take her, instead of you? Look at her, will you? Answer me!!"

Wdowinska only shook her head, choked by tears. Her daughter once more interrupted these strange negotiations. "It must be a mistake; you'd better check it" — she said with dramatized certitude. "Could be" — the OD man nodded, playing her game. "You too are Wdowinska, aren't you?" — he looked shrewdly at the daughter. "Yes, yes, you are, of course. So, I can take you instead of her, I don't mind which Wdowinska I deliver as long as I do not jeopardize my own lot. So, you better come with me" — he challenged her. He moved over to the daughter, became aggressive, and took hold of her arm. She retreated step by step, he advanced step by step. "That's enough" — said the mother, weeping no more -"You let her go, I am coming with you". She didn't embrace her daughter; she didn't utter another word. Chalk-white, shrinking in front of our eyes, dragging her feet, she seemed to become suddenly a very old woman. She meekly followed the young OD man. Like a real gentleman that he was, he let her walk ahead and followed her out of the workshop.

Nobody was noble, nobody was a hero in this story, because it is not easy to be a hero facing death or making someone face death. I still see this scene as if it had happened yesterday. I see all its actors as if I had filmed the whole episode and carried the reel in my head for forty-two years. There is in this incident, a sketch, a draught of a lesser figure of the OD forces, one that tried clumsily to negotiate and persuade an oldish woman to go willingly to her death. How about the top figures, the high officers of the OD? How did they rule over us? You may now ask how Marcel Goldberg, the one who because of me was shamed in public and fired from the Jewish Social Self-Help, was behaving. He was now very powerful in the camp. He was so elevated and high of rank, being pampered with bribes for protecting endangered people from death. Sometimes he delivered, sometimes he didn't.

Marcel Goldberg, working at the registry office, gained access to the "Schindler list", the list of applicants asking to be employed at the factory of Oskar Schindler, this good Sudeten-German who knew how to protect his Jews. Goldberg manipulated this precious list, slipping bribes into his pocket. Schindler put many names on his list without expecting any reward, just to save many worthy people. Most of them were absolutely impecunious.

Marcel Goldberg was also associating with the shrewd OD officer Finkelstein. I saw Finkelstein daily because he became the lover of Frieda, the younger of the Tanzer daughters, who lived in our barrack. They were my schoolmates, Frieda one grade below me, Karola one above me (pay close attention to this family, because later on they will play an important role throughout our concentration camp 'career'. Our fates will be entwined several times by peculiar coincidences).

Now Frieda was the mistress of the smart Finkelstein of the pouting lips. They went about their lovemaking in a most ostentatious way. In the early night hours Finkelstein used to creep into Frieda's bunk, a bunk above her own mother's cot, and they copulated furiously before the eyes of the whole barrack, and over the head of mother. Frieda became so shameless that she gave herself airs and demanded special privileges. It exploded once in an incident.

While we were queueing up for the evening coffee surrogate, Frieda pushed aside Gusta (our cousin, later to become the second wife of Wilek Kranz). Frieda demanded to be served her coffee without waiting. Gusta was not one to be pushed and hold her tongue. "Do you think that because you are sleeping with Finkelstein you don't have to wait for your turn?" — Gusta reprimanded her in her sarcastic way.

Frieda tossed her head disdainfully and hissed at her like a snake, but that was not the end of the incident. The next morning, while we were all standing in rows on the "Appelplatz", Finkelstein approached us, walking with Marcel Goldberg. "Show me the shrew Gusta Beckmann" — he ordered the "Blockalteste". She was pointed out and I was standing next to her. Finkelstein came at her in one leap and slapped her hard once, and twice. "It is to teach you, you bitch, not to give moral lessons to people" — he spat at Gusta.

That would have been the end of the incident if it weren't for the presence of Marcel Goldberg. All the time in the ghetto and in Plaszow, I was avoiding Marcel Goldberg as well as I could. I had heard that he hadn't forgotten the humiliation I caused him and was looking for me in the ghetto, but by that time I was already in Rabka. Now I stood facing him and couldn't move from the spot. He could now take his revenge. What saved me was my white kerchief. I pulled and pulled at it to hide my face. I avoided him so well that our paths never crossed until after the war, when he emerged in Paris and was denounced as a war criminal to the French authorities. That story I shall relate to, in due time.

You may now ask what became of Samek Kempler, the fiancé of Rosie K., the same Samek who sneaked to her into the ghetto, cutting the barbed wires. As you may remember, it was after he had jumped with Bernard from the train to Auschwitz. This handsome country boy served now in Plaszow as the personal horse-riding instructor to Goth's mistress Mayola. He was free to ride with her outside the camp, romping in the fields. She must have enjoyed the lessons so much that she fell in love with him. She was hardly able to conceal her infatuation. Samek found himself in a very precarious position. Would he yield to her amorous advances, Goth's spies would soon discover the liaison. Would he reject her, she might accuse him before Goth of trying to seduce her. That would be her revenge. He didn't confide in Rosie, he made his own plans of salvation. He must have somehow established contacts with the Polish partisans, and he fled to join them. But he picked the wrong formation of partisans, the rightist nationalist anti-Semitic "Armia Krajowa".

Samek had a dark complexion and raven-black hair. Was he too conspicuous to be kept in the ranks of these partisans, or was it reason enough that he was Jewish? They didn't denounce him to the Germans because he knew their hiding places... They got rid of him: they killed him (or so it was reported to us). That was the end of this succulent personage.

Speaking of heroes, half-heroes or anti-heroes, I have to tell you the strange story of the foxy-eyed Scheindlinger. Goth collected and ordered enough furniture to fill a palace, which he would have possessed after the war, if his good luck hadn't run out. Scheindlinger was such an excellent carpenter that Goth appointed him his personal wood artist. This craftsman had his whims and demands. When he had to select a special kind of rare wood, Goth had to send him to Krakow under the escort of a Ukrainian. Once on such an errand he told the Ukrainian that he had to buy, at the Alexandrowicz shop, special graphic tracers. He moved over this huge shop, peeping here, peeping there. The bored Ukrainian eyed women. Scheindlinger said: "There is none of the stuff here on the shelves; I have to look for it in their storerooms". He knew that the Alexandrowicz shop had a second entrance, he planned everything in advance. He disappeared before the Ukrainian noticed his prolonged absence.

There were relatively few cases of escape from Plaszow, because of the mutual responsibility. For one fugitive out of a group, ten were executed in reprisal, including the 'capo'. Scheindlinger didn't make part of a group and there were no reprisals, only the vile Ukrainian was punished in this case. Each escape caused us to be kept, the whole night, at the "Appelplatz". In the case of Scheindlinger, his style of escape provoked much hilarity in the camp. We didn't mind the lost night. Scheindlinger did well among the gentiles, having already prepared for himself an Aryan identity paper and a hideout among fellow carpenters. He was moving around town as a gentile workman. One day, a long time after his flight, his luck ran out. There was in the streets of Krakow an "ambush" intended to trap Poles who were on the blacklist for evading conscripted forced labor in Germany. Scheindlinger was caught in the net and brought with other (genuine) gentile Poles to... Plaszow. Soon the news and the sensation were all over the camp. "Scheindlinger was caught, he is in the Polish compound" — tingled the whispered grapevine. People were shaking with laughter.

Believe it or not, there was in the whole camp not one informer who would denounce him. He passed several weeks in the Polish compound, parading to the general mirth as a Polish gentile, with Jews winking discreetly from a distance. He was set free for lack of incriminating evidence. He spent the rest of the war hiding in Krakow, working as carpenter. After the war he landed in Israel, running a good carpentry workshop. He died of throat cancer. When he was reduced to whispering, he told me all the missing details of his story over a cup of coffee.

Dr.Hilfstein was also one of the survivors to reach Tel Aviv. He worked in Plaszow in the camp hospital. Sometimes, when uncle Olek was not able to pass to us directly the additional portion of soup, Dr.Hilfstein brought it out to mother. They both managed it over a short period, later it became too dangerous, and we refused to expose Olek to danger.

One day, when mother was waiting for Dr.Hilfstein and his messtin of soup, she was all of a sudden surrounded and caught for transport. As I mentioned before, Goth promised to his superiors to 'reduce' the camp population so as to make room for the transports of Hungarian Jews. When Goth didn't have enough Jews selected for the death-transport, he sent his hunters to catch some more, picked at random. Now mother was among them. She signaled to me that she was trapped, somebody passed on the message. What could I do now? Madritsch would certainly claim her back, he defended his employees, but all this happened in the early evening hours, and Madritsch or his partner Tutsch were not reachable. Our boss Schnitzer was helpless, so were the other bosses. I ran in circles in utter despair, there was nothing more I could do. But then, you don't know my mother. She didn't remonstrate that she was from Madritsch and had to be set free, she didn't implore. She crawled between the feet of the others, dug out some earth under the wire of this temporary detention compound (the wire was not electrified) and slipped out to freedom… the freedom of being alive in a concentration camp. Somehow, she reached the central camp before the women's compound was closed for the night. I was sitting with Witek, Helcia, Olek and Rutka, sitting and crying. We had already given her up after we tried everything possible. Now we were crying the tears of joy and relief. The 'Blockalteste' was not yet informed that mother was missing from the barrack, so the numbers checked well in the morning and the incident passed unnoticed. Only we, the family, were emotional wrecks.

Soon several transports of the Hungarian Jews were brought to Plaszow. They came almost straight from freedom. They "only" passed a selection at Auschwitz; the women's hair was shorn off, they were dressed in striped garments and they were in deep shock. They weren't used to the skimpy food rations distributed in this camp. One has to adapt to hunger very gradually. We had already passed through all these stages. Besides, currently we were getting at Madritsch an additional portion of bread, as bonus for overproduction.

I took pity on the Hungarian girls, they looked so forlorn with their bare skulls under the kerchiefs. I gave them sometimes a piece of bread, if I could afford it. I was once accosted by one of them who looked very different from the rest. Her black eyes pierced me. Her dark hands caught my hand and arrested it in a commanding grip. She said to me in fairly understandable German, "I am not begging of you to give me a piece of bread, I can give you something in exchange. I am a Gypsy, I am a fortune-teller. Please let me tell you your fortune, and if you decide that my 'speak' of your past and 'now' (present) fits your truth (reality), I shall look into your future, and only then will you give me a slice of bread". I was fascinated. It is true that I was born ingenuous, naive as a simpleton. I still like mysteries, spiritualism, telepathic experiences and all the stuff about extrasensory perceptions. Still, tell me please how she could have known so much about me, me — one of the crowds?

Because a friend of mine tried to tear me away, to extricate me from her grip, the Gypsy begged me to give her a chance to give me a free sample. "You still have your mother" — she said after a moment of concentration — "You also have a child, no, a brother, a brother close to you. You also have a double, your second you, she is right here, she looks very much like you (you may well guess that she was describing Rutka), she is not your sister, but like a sister to you. You are going to see her now" — she added, and she was right, I was on my way to Rutka's barrack.

Wasn't that enough to convince me, to whet my appetite to hear some more? My friend ceased to pull me away, and the Gypsy woman became pensive, concentrating in a visible effort. She said that she was not going to speak about my tragic personal losses, there were too many. She will concentrate now on my future. "It would be too easy to paint for you a rosy picture "- she said, looking at me intently — "but I see in your palm and in the circles of your eyes that you will survive, yet you are not going to have it easy at first. But I see you climbing a mountain, I see you higher and higher, I see you on top of this mountain. You are very visible now, and you are almost twice your actual age. I see you speaking to very many people. No, the picture is changing... I see you now speaking to thousands, no, what am I saying... to thousands of thousands. Wait... they are not together, but they all listen to you intensely, they all look straight at you, all of them. Wait... you speak to them, you look at them, and yet you do not see them. Wait... it is impossible because you are not blind and yet you see none of them. I don't understand it... no... no... forget it. I swear that this is what I see, I do see it clearly, but I don't know what it means..." The Gypsy shook her head and would say no more. When prodded by me, she refused to continue, she felt spent.

What was she speaking of? What she saw so distinctly was actually, no more and no less, but her prophecy of my appearance on TV, in Jerusalem, broadcast to all Israel at the peak hour. That's why in the Gypsy's vision I spoke to millions but didn't see them. Isn't that sensational?

Do you now remember the prophecy of the wandering rabbi who predicted my survival? As for my TV appearance, it was in 1964. I was invited to give a lecture on the symbolic meaning of certain features of Jewish ethnic costumes. It was the fruit of my research work on Jewish customs and symbols, which I conducted as curator of the Museum of Ethnography and Folklore in Tel Aviv. If it is of any interest to you, I can give you here a few examples of such symbols, because the material is so fascinating to me that I want to share some of it with you, even if it is out of context in this frame. Here are a few scraps of information.

The headgear of a Jewish woman in 19th-century Poland was composed of seven parts, so as to symbolize the seven species of the harvest, as mentioned in the Bible. On her other bonnet, the festive bonnet, one pearl was missing from the ornament, because the joy is not complete for the Jews, as long as the fallen Temple has not been rebuilt... So as to stress the mourning for the lost Temple, a Yemenite bride had one single row of back beads embroidered on her huge tower-like head-dress, shining with filigree silver ornaments and coins all over. She wore bracelets decorated with alternating motifs of two shapes of tombs; one tom ball shape commemorated the fall of the First Temple, the other protruding shape symbolized the fall of the Second Temple. A Jewess of Kurdistan had tiny bells sewn to her head-dress, so that by tossing her head she could give a warning to her men who were secretly studying the forbidden Torah.

Since then, I have written a book in five volumes on Jewish customs and beliefs, on all these Jewish exotica (the title of the book is 'Jewish Exotica') — but all this does not belong to my story, recorded here on the tape. I must return to my subject. This was merely a refreshing digression.

Do you believe now that the fortune-telling Gypsy had a prophetic vision of my appearance on TV? This mystic genius did it for the price of a slice of bread. You may wonder now, what was the value of "a slice of bread" in this camp. Sometimes an egg was worth half a loaf of bread, sometimes a whole loaf. Though all the jewels, valuables and money denominations were confiscated, two weeks after we were transferred to Plaszow, some people still had money, and in the camp you could buy, eggs, butter, sugar, sausage, soap, cigarettes — if only you had the means. We had no money, no means, and we could only pay with our ration of bread.

More than two hundred years ago, when captain Cook came in contact with the primitive islanders of New Zealand, he noted in his diary: "They are content to be naked but ambitious to be fine". That could have applied to us. Mother and I, though dressed in tatters and constantly hungry, could stand all the privations except being deprived of soap. As far as I can remember, we had to pay for a cake of soap (at a certain period) with eight rations of bread. Practically, it meant that we had to share between the two of us one daily portion of bread for eight days in order to pay off the debt with the second portion.

Imagine now that after such a self-sacrifice purchase of a cake of soap — you enter proudly the wash installation barrack with this treasure in your hand, and an acquaintance at the next tap turns to you innocently: "Buddy, please lend me your soap, I have forgotten mine in the bunk". That's what we called "the height of chutzpah".

You may now ask how does one live without soap. When we had no soap and no means to buy it, we would take from a barrel in the latrine a handful of chlorine and wash our body and our linen with it. Washing your body and face with chlorine causes blisters that with time change into a thick layer of crust. After the liberation, our faces were still covered with this crust for some time, until it peeled off.

There are all sorts of hardships and you wouldn't believe what some pampered egoists can perceive as the peak of hardship. At the time when we still worked outside the camp, I still remember the long way we made under sun or rain to the Podgorze suburb. There was a lady among us, a certain Mrs. Standig — and if I say a lady, I mean it — who must have been very beautiful and spoiled by her husband. She also had some literary pretensions or so it was said. Once, I found myself marching next to her when going from the camp to work. This Madonna-like lady, who was close to fifty, aroused my interest. I took this opportunity to engage her in conversation. We spoke about some trivia and later about the peculiarities of the life in a camp. "Yes, yes" — said the lady — "If I survive this terrible camp, I shall certainly write a book". I admitted that I found it an excellent idea (I had no such ambition). Then I ventured to ask her: "And tell me pray, what will be the crucial moment, the strongest experience related in this book of yours?" She became pensive for a moment and then replied: "Do you remember the day when we marched like now to the Madritsch factory, and it rained and poured from the skies by bucketsful? We could not disperse and seek shelter, there was nothing we could do about it; we had to go on and on, soaked to the skin. We reached the factory dripping wet, unable to change our clothes, and we had to work in our soaked rags…". I remained gaping at her with open mouth. At a time when naked people had to stand over a ditch to be shot from the back, at a time when we saw corpses in a pool of blood — this lady's hardest experience was being forced to march under rain. Nothing else affected her, she had no children, she was pampered, healthy and… alive.

Poor Mrs. Standig didn't know that there was worse to come. After half a year of such marches to Podgorze, the Madritsch factory was forcibly moved into the camp, in spite of Madritsch's protests. We were not to see the outside world for a long, long time. As long as we were marched to work, we had to be back for the evening rollcalls, consequently we didn't have to work night shifts. Now, inside the camp, we had to work one weekday shift and one weeknight shift. My brave little brother wanted to share our timetable, otherwise he would hardly be able to see us. He now worked in his workshop the same shifts as we did.

One night, despite the peril (and it was even dangerous to visit a latrine), he sneaked out of his workshop at midnight, crossed the empty space, and at the risk of being shot came over to our workshop. He brought with him... steaming hot goulash. How did he cook goulash? We received, on this day exceptionally, a slice of 'Blutwurst' — a blood sausage, because a commission was expected for inspection. I hate it, I wasn't able to swallow it when it was distributed in the evening. Witek asked me to give him my slice. Then, without telling us, he pinched some potatoes and one onion, passing his slim hand through the dense wire of the kitchen compound. At night he cooked from these three ingredients an unusual goulash, heating it on the stove next to the pot of glue. Very proud of himself he brought it to us after midnight. Mother scolded him for this dangerous exploit, but she had tears in her eyes.

The night shifts were a nightmare for us. It happened quite often that one of us, becoming drowsy with fatigue, would doze off sitting with her back to the window, which was of course on the ground floor. If Goth, Willie or Hujar were to peep in, he would shoot this person without hesitation, as it already happened in other workshops. Since that time and even nowadays, I never sit in a strange place with my back to the entrance or to the window. I was not aware of it until my husband took notice of this strange habit of mine.

At the night shift it quite often happened that one of us, drunk with exertion after pedaling for hours on her machine, let the needle go through her finger. The needle passed through the cushion of my index finger and broke on it. Happily enough, one end was protruding. I asked for pillars and extricated the broken needle pulling it myself from the second extremity. Happily enough, it healed well.

When the same thing happened to my mother, sometime later, she was less lucky. Her finger became so infected that it had to be operated on twice in the hospital compound. Her tendon was so damaged that the finger remained thin, crooked and inarticulate for the rest of her life.

As I said, the night shifts were a curse. If somebody thinks that after eleven hours of nightwork, we were able to sleep it off at daytime — he is mistaken. First, there was the interminable rollcall. Then the barrack was being cleaned for an hour of two, and during that time everybody had to leave it, be it rain or sunshine. Only then could one hypothetically turn in and catch some sleep. But could one? There were whole long periods when a sanitary team of "leaches" would comb the housing camp for available people to catch them at random and take their Jewish blood for the wounded German soldiers. Emaciated as we were, they used to take from such a victim, no less than two pints of blood. The only salvation was escape. If they entered the barrack through the door, we escaped through the window. They would wait there too. We feared this blood-sucking so much that we didn't go to sleep at all. Anyhow it was no use trying to sleep.

If it was daytime or night, the bugs wouldn't let us sleep. These densely populated wooden barracks were a paradise for them. Working the day shift, after we performed the permanent evening ceremony of whisking the lice out of the seams of our garments, we would go to sleep and... a shower of bugs would fall upon us. I could write an essay on the pattern of behavior of bugs. One summer night, we tossed on our bunks and couldn't stand the bug-bites anymore. A whole group of us left the barrack and walked out with the blankets into the night. We couldn't sleep on the ground; it was all wet from the dew and the fog of the swamps. We saw a stack of wooden panels of a dismantled barrack and thought for a while to have found paradise. Drunk with sleeplessness, we fell on these panels and took cover from the fog under our thin blankets. What we didn't guess was that these abandoned panels were still infested with bugs, now resurrected. Bugs can lie low without blood for quite some time. The place was their paradise not ours. Deadly exhausted we crept back into our barrack.

You would think that now, at least, we had free access to the latrines and to the barrack serving as washroom. Don't take it for granted. Both were situated at a considerable distance from the living quarters or rather on their outskirts. Both were often inaccessible being locked for hours. How is it possible? Very simple. The women in charge of these two "temples" had their policy. After they had cleaned the place they would wait for the inspection, locking it up for several hours. In the washroom the water was turned off for hours on end. There was nothing we could do about it, we were impotent. A complaint would serve no purpose. These women in charge were protected by their inspectors who feared a high-level inspection, which would eventually decide that the place had to be permanently clean — no matter at what price.

Many books have been written on atrocities, high policies, conferences etc. I deal in trivia because I feel that they have been overlooked. And those were the trivial obstacles that sapped our strength, no less than the crucial atrocious events.

Not only Witek was undernourished. My strength was sapped as well. I too was showing signs of deterioration of health. I was suffering from lack of vitamins to such a degree that wherever I scratched myself, pus was soon showing on this innocent scratch. It wouldn't heal. My dear cousin Rutka had a talent for asking the right questions. She brought me a cure culled from folk medicine; if you grate a raw potato into pulp, apply it to your festering wound and tie it with a strip of fabric... the potato sucks out the pus and leaves the wound clean. It did indeed, but it wasn't a radical treatment. Somebody told Rutka that consuming a lot of onions can save me from avitaminosis. I revolted, but Rutka had her ways of persuasion. "Do you want to walk around in a repelling state?" — she asked me. That did it. I hated onions; I could not stand even their smell on somebody close to me. Now I had to devour onions.

I found a way to provide me with this treasure. Someone who was working in sorting vegetables was willing to throw me one onion over the fence, almost every day. Now I ate on my dry bread thick slices of onion. The body must have had its claims. It claimed these vitamin-rich onions and I came to love their taste. Onions probably saved my life. It was an experiment in medicine that doctors could never conduct, not in normal conditions. They would have to reduce the patient to a diet of thin soup, coffee-substitute, black dry bread of poor-quality and... a lot of onions. My experience proves the efficacity of such a cure of avitaminosis.

Here I am at it again, dabbing in unsavory things, in excrements, bugs and festering wounds. Was there indeed no sunshine, no smell of grass, no consolation apart from family bonds and much treasured friendships? I had one consolation, a very private one, and it was like a rose on a dung-heap.

I had... books. Would you believe it? I had a friend, an old pal, or rather an undemanding platonic lover. He worked in the 'Effektenkammer' stores where various objects were segregated. There was a shelf of English books and my friend, afraid of stealing anything of value, did sometimes negligently throw a book out of the window and over the fence. He would later pick it up and bring it to me. It wasn't without danger, but he took the risk willingly. I shouldn't have exposed him to this risk, but he understood what it meant to me to have books. It drove me crazy; it was food. You will correct me now that it was food for the soul, but I shall claim persistently that it tasted to me like real food.

I used to read at night, in the dim light of a weak bulb affixed to the high ceiling. Mother was furious. She said: "You are wasting the best hours of sleep; it saps your last strength". I was adamant. "On the contrary" — I objected — "it gives me the strength to bear it all, it is an escape from the gloomy reality". And indeed, it let me forget the corpses we saw in pools of blood and the shots on the 'chujowagorka'. I still remember several of the books I had there, especially the book "Oil for the Lamps of China". It was a flight into an exotic world, I felt like finding myself on another planet. It was not an island of bliss, it described the hard lot of the Chinese people, but it transplanted me somewhere else. I loved this book so much that some twenty years later I read it again in Tel Aviv. It lost its impact; it didn't taste the same.

Nothing was permanent in life in the camp. One day we were moved from one barrack to another. Gone was the hidden cache under our bunk. By then it was so full of other people's objects that I didn't keep my books there anymore. I kept them now under my thin pallet of straw. I used to ask my friend and supplier of books jokingly to pick them evenly thick so as to be able to sleep on them. Now, one day when we came back from work, they were all gone. It is a shame to admit, that I dropped a tear. Just imagine... a tear over a lost book.

You must understand — the books were my salvation. Did I share them with somebody? No, nobody was crazy enough to read books instead of catching the opportunity to sleep.

Now I had no consolation, and I couldn't drown my sorrows in the wine of books. Our Witek was in constant danger. However well he was protected by the good people at his workshop, he was visible at the rollcall square and his age was noted in the files of the registration office. Somehow in this winter of the end of 1943 there were no selections for some time, so the main danger in my mother's eyes was the registration file. Here, out of the blue appeared a prospective savior, or so my mother thought. But what a savior and at what price...

Let me start this new development from the beginning. Who would appear, all of a sudden in Plaszow? A most unexpected figure from the past...? the young lawyer, Marcel Finster. Do you remember him, this friend of Wilek, this witty visitor who was a frequent guest in our house in Rabka? Do you remember that some time before the total liquidation of Rabka Jewry, when the whole population was paralyzed by mutual responsibility and nobody dared to flee — Marcel Finster, his brother and his parents escaped from Rabka? Ten people were executed as reprisal (my father could have been among them) and I came to hate this amiable former friend. Now he emerged in Plaszow. As it transpired, this family had spent half a year hiding in the woods, probably with the help of some gentile Goral. They were apprehended and only Marcel saved his hide by who knows what means. I don't remember where he was hiding for the rest of the time but having been discovered (and handed over to the Germans) by the Polish police, he was not executed. He was simply transferred to the Plaszow concentration camp. Sometimes the German bureaucracy could be quite enigmatic.

What was he doing now at the camp? There were so many experienced lawyers working now with a spade, and yet Marcel Finster was placed to work conveniently at the main registry office, where the files of prisoners were kept. This in itself was a mystery, but there were so many mysteries on this planet.

We had heard about his arrival; we knew that we should sooner or later have to face him. The very idea was abhorrent to me. It never crossed my mind that he would dare to face us, to seek us out. I said to mother: "If I come across him in this camp I shall spit in his face. I feel this compulsion, I just have to do it". Mother became pensive. She said: "Stop it, keep your horses and let me explain something to you. As you have heard he is working at the registry office. He has free access to the files. Witek's age must be noted there. It must be marked in his file that he is 13 years old. Marcel can draw out his file and with a slight correction of two tiny strokes of pen turn the number 13 into 18. Isn't it a fantastic idea? Don't ruin it. I beseech you now, this can be our only chance to save Witek". I was shocked, I didn't know what to say. I swallowed very hard and reflected. I knew what I knew but couldn't divulge my thoughts to mother. I couldn't have guessed that he would look for us, that he would dare to come nonchalantly, like an old friend, to pay his respects and continue socializing with us. He did it as if nothing had happened, as if he didn't have ten lives on his conscience. He possessed this kind of 'hutzpah'. He did even more. As I was to perceive gradually, he had the gumption to presume that he could become the natural heir of my dead fiancé Wilek… that he could eventually inherit me and become my fiancé. He considered himself the natural candidate.

Now I felt like spitting twice in his face. If mother guessed what was brewing, she never mentioned it. She just asked of me to show him for the time being some civil courtesy and to ask him as soon as possible to play his role, ergo, to draw out the file with Witek's name and to change the mark of age 13 into 18.

I went through hell. As you must have guessed by now, I realized perfectly, from the very beginning of this affair, that age noted in files must be written as the date of birth and not as the actual age. I couldn't disclose it to my mother, I didn't dare to rob her of her only hope to save Witek from the constant danger. When Marcel heard for the first time about this crazy plan, he must have realized, as I did, that there is only the date of birth in the files. Yet he didn't bat an eyelid, he didn't point out how absurd it was. Seeing that he didn't react, I thought for some time that mother could be right after all. I could have asked him this simple question, yet I didn't.

Maybe I myself instinctively desired to preserve this illusion, or didn't guess that Marcel did everything to ingratiate himself with us. He was obviously playing for time. He explained how difficult it is for him, how dangerous, how he is being watched — in short, he postponed it from day to day. He came every day with a different version, a new excuse. "How can he penetrate the room of certain files" — he asked — explaining that he must wait for the right moment; he played a whole drama while it was clear to us that he was pretending. He left mother in suspense and forced me to play along, to play his game. Meanwhile he was showing more and more clearly his intentions toward me. His courtship was now almost aggressive, he dared to pat my arm, to hold my hand. I kept distant and aloof, but for mother's sake I had to comply to a certain degree. I too was playing for time.

Whenever somebody speaks nowadays of a problem of conscience — it makes me laugh. I had here a real problem of conscience. I felt worse than a prostitute. I had to play my act like an actress. Here reappears again the eternal problem of this period; what is better? empty hopes or cruel reality? I hesitated. Should I keep on going so as not destroy mother's hope? should I reveal the truth about the file, as I suspected it? Out of inertia I continued to believe in this crazy plan.

A new opening came to my rescue. We were informed that the Madritsch factory was starting a new list of applications for the admission of additional employees. Madritsch, exactly like Oskar Schindler, knew how to bribe Goth and could ask for anybody he wanted in his factory, and Madritsch was a good man. Mother addressed several prominent bosses in the factory, all these tailors running the department, who knew us well by now. Witek could be placed on this list an errand boy. It was plausible. They didn't refuse, they didn't promise: That they couldn't deliver was quite understandable to me, but not to my persevering mother.

At long last mother said to me: "Why couldn't you go yourself to the head, to Julius Madritsch himself. He must remember you, he has still this lovely mascot of yours in his car". Indeed, a year before, when the factory was still in Podgorze, I created for Madritsch an exquisite mascot. It represented an artist-tailor. He was wearing a dress coat with long, flying, pointed tails, and he had in his hand a huge pair of scissors. Shy as I am, I didn't hand the mascot directly to Madritsch. I slipped it during a work intermission into his shiny car and hung it on a thin rubber-band, close to the back window. The tailor seemed to dance and swing there, and was an appropriate symbol for Madritsch, a manufacturer of clothes. Madritsch was delighted, he had not enough words of praise. He investigated who prepared for him such a lovely surprise. He insisted on thanking me in person. I was called to his office, he shook my hand and placed a kiss on my forehead. A kiss on the forehead of a Jewess... Unable to pronounce my name as it was spelled to him, he decided to call me Marielka.

All that happened a year ago and Madritsch hasn't seen or noticed me for a whole year. Now, the poor shy girl that I was, I had to approach him, him the big boss ruling over some three thousand workers. I dragged my feet. How am I going to do it? Nothing is now as it used to be at the factory outside of the camp. I have to slip out of the workshop, endanger myself, cut my way to Madritsch's car, wait, find the right moment to approach him and... will he remember me? Why should he put the name of a mere boy on his list of specialists claimed by him for the benefit of his factory?

What prodded me eventually to act and to dare approach Madritsch was this miserable, odious drama with Marcel Finster. Anything rather than this. One day I did it. I spotted the car after sneaking out of the workshop, and I waited around the corner, risking to be shot. The mascot was still hanging in the car. Eventually Madritsch reached his car unaccompanied. That was my luck. I approached him timidly and made my plea. Trembling all over, I tried as quickly as possible to present my case. Madritsch looked at me intently and exclaimed: "But you are Marielka, the same Marielka who created for me this enchanting mascot which became my trademark. Do you know that it was copied at my order by a graphic artist to serve as the symbol of my firm? Of course, Marielka, I shall do it for you most willingly, be reassured my dear, your young brother will be appointed a courier, an errand boy in my factory".

Thus, the very same day Witek's name appeared on the Madritsch list, and not at its bottom but among the first names on the precious list. Now it had to be submitted to Goth for his signature, but Madritsch knew how to handle Goth. Can you imagine the sensation that it created in the Madritsch circles? All the heads of departments now saw Witek's name at the head of the new list. What did they do? One by one they came to my mother and each of them assured her that this achievement was of his doing and thanks to his intervention... One of them even whispered to mother: "Rosa, I have excellent news for you. Don't mention it to anybody, it is a secret, but I managed to persuade Madritsch to put your Witek's name on the new list". If mother thanked him effusively or told him the truth — I don't remember. Mother smiled at me with a sad smile and remarked: "That's people for you. One learns the lesson over and over".

The list was like a balloon. It became too inflated, it exploded into our faces. It was rejected in total, the time for expansion was over — explained Goth to Madritsch. Before that happened, I became at last free to disclose to mother the impossibility of her astute plan of changing the age 13 into 18. I disclosed to her the truth about Marcel's false game, his real intentions and my sad collaboration in this stratagem. Mother was very upset, she was shocked. She never realized the full implications. She now admitted that I must have been right, she told me boldly to get rid of this false pretender. I wanted to do it in style, but I had no plan how to proceed. Fortunately, Marcel himself provided me with an opportunity. Though I never encouraged his courtship and behaved in a distant and cool way, he thought that time had come to take me by storm. He encircled my waist in an intimate gesture. That clinched it, my chance had come. I said slowly and distinctly: "I owe you something. I owe you something from the moment you appeared in this camp. I delayed it because for the sake of my mother I played your false game of pretending. But I never gave you hope to become Wilek's heir. Now I owe you something, on two accounts. I owe you a spit in your face". I was crying and laughing and blabbering, I don't remember what. At last I added that my curse will follow him to his grave. The shy, innocent naive Marysia is dead — from now on my name is Nemesis. He fled, and I never saw him again.

As you may have noticed by now, my story often turns in circles. Certain people fade out of the picture, only to return to focus much later. Marcel Finster disappeared, but I wasn't through with Rabka. Three years ago, I met in Haifa a nice, well groomed, beautiful woman about my age. She looked at me and asked: "Don't you remember me, Marysia? I am from Rabka. Don't you remember how we scrubbed together the floors in 'Tereska'? My brother Mark used to play together with your brother Witek".

Now I remembered her, this tall girl from Rabka. Then, as an afterthought, I asked her when they escaped from Rabka, because I still didn't get the full connection. She answered simply that it was some three months before the total liquidation of Rabka Jewry. It gave me a shock. Now I realized that this must have been the second family after the Finsters, which in spite of the mutual responsibility, caused by its flight the execution of another ten people. Didn't she know? Didn't she realize their crime? Or did she think that under the circumstances it was justifiable because the Jewry of Rabka was doomed anyhow. Doomed it was, but the truth is that at the given time we couldn't have known it yet. That was why my family didn't go into hiding until the very last moment, when the collective responsibility was no more applicable.

I looked at this nice lady and... didn't spit in her face. I kept silent. I cannot be God's whip all my life. It has to be noted that as far as I know, besides the Jews hidden by Weislo, only two more couples escaped from Rabka, as we did, at the very last moment. They live in Israel and I have met them here.

You can now hope that I am through with the reminiscences from Rabka. That was not to be. There was still another ghost, there was somebody else from Rabka who drifted into Plaszow after Marcel Finster. Almost two years after father's death, this shadow from Rabka was driven into Plaszow after several other camps. It was a poor man in tatters, the former messenger of the Rabka Judenrat, the young Turek.

Do you remember that he came for my father in the last moment, exactly when we were about to leave our abode and seek refuge in the empty house? It was because of this last call for duty that my father didn't join us in flight and... had to perish.

Turek loved and admired my father as if he were his own. Because he was a slave at Tereska, like my fiancé Wilek, he was not to be sent with the death transport, he was to be left to continue to slave there for some time. But for some reason or other Turek was present at the railway station before the train left. He was the last person in Rabka to speak to my father and to know his last thoughts. He noticed my father's head in the little close window of this cattle train and came running to him. Father asked him to approach closer... (I have probably told this story already, but this meeting was very dear to me).

My father whispered to Turek: "Turek my boy, do me a favor, I know that I am going to my death. Don't interrupt me, just listen. I shall need nothing more. Take these items..."

My father took out his thick signet ring, his wedding ring, his watch and some money. He handed them quickly to Turek. "Listen, Turek" — he continued — "If you ever encounter my family — hand these things to them; but if not — feel free to use and sell them, they may save your life at a critical moment. I could have fled and joined my family an hour ago, but I had the feeling that someone was watching me... I was afraid that I may betray their hiding place. That's why I let myself be swept with the crowd and into this train. It is better this way. Farewell, Turek".

These were father's last words reported to us, two years later. They had a terrible impact on us, I still try to visualize this scene, it never left me, it never will. Soon after this last encounter with my father and well before the execution of Wilek, Turek was sent to some other places and camps. He eventually sold gradually father's last possessions and bought with the money some food that kept him alive for quite some time. All that happened long before he was sent to Plaszow. He felt now an obligation to tell us frankly all the details, and we felt grateful to him, even though it hurt. It still hurts after all these years, forty-four years later.

Turek, the honest man had a feeling that he owed us something, and all he had to offer were his warm feelings and small services. He just begged to be of some service. He would sometimes fetch hot water from the bathhouse, so that we could wash our linen, and he would come with Witek in the evening from the male camp, as if he were a second son. One day he disappeared. He was sent with a transport elsewhere.

I must now once more return to my father. If you listen to my story carefully, you will notice in retrospective and in the following tragic events, that all my nearest and dearest went to their death knowingly and without the slightest illusion. It hurts. It hurts terribly. If only they would have had a straw of illusion to cling to and to sustain them to their last moment. How happy were, comparatively, all those people shot by Goth most unexpectedly, with only a second to realize their lot. Didn't our loved ones deserve the same lot?

Soon after Turek's departure from the scene somebody else tried to care for us and offer some little services, but they were of a different kind and were dictated by a very different motivation. As you will remember, my bosom friend Janka had a sister, married to the musician Poldi Rosner, who played with his brother for Goth and at the rollcall square during selections. Janka also had a younger brother by name of Kuba (Jacob), a dentist by profession. He now served as "Blockaleste" in the Plaszow camp. The barrack under his command was run ship shape, and his people seemed to be grateful to him. Kuba, on the other hand, was grateful to my mother for taking care of Janka like her second daughter. Mother sometimes cooked for her at night a pot of barley, which Kuba tried to deliver because Janka had a weak stomach. He also admired my friendship with Janka. That's how he started to pay attention to me.

This no-nonsense good administrator and disciplinarian was a real romantic, at the bottom of his heart. He started his courtship in a delicate and heart winning manner. He came to visit Janka but paid more and more attention to me. I behaved in a guarded way. After all he was a block commander and as such was not a candidate to become my friend, let alone my boyfriend. I had the daring to put it in a blunt way and told him once: "Kuba, you are losing your time. Between me and you there is no place for friendship because you are what you are. It is said of you that you are very harsh on your people. It is even said that you sometimes hit them. Is it true?"

Kuba reacted instantly: "I am very happy that you have raised this subject. It gives me an opportunity to explain to you a certain policy of mine, which you wouldn't understand without my elaborating... Look, I have a secret to share with you". He took me aside and drew from his inside pocket a little sheet of paper, much used and carefully wrapped in a piece of celluloid. "Look at it" — he said — "this will be my passport to freedom and to exoneration. I shall be able to answer the same question raised by you now. As you may have heard from Janka, I reached before the war the rank of officer in the Polish Army. I finished the Officers' Academy, to which I was conscripted, with high distinction, an achievement very rare for a Jew in pre-war Poland. I know the military drill and the expectations of the Germans who love discipline and drill. This enables me to preserve the lives of the people of my barrack. All I am doing as block commander is keeping my people alive. How do I do it? I keep my barrack spotlessly clean. When my people march to the "Appelplatz" square and one of them steps out of line, I leap to him and strike him with my rod, so that the Germans may see it from afar. If I wouldn't do this, a German would draw his pistol and shoot the man. My people know it. I have to be harsh with them, and they understand. What do I achieve? Here is the answer on this tiny slip of paper. These are the statistics of death cases noted in every barrack, month after month. The numbers speak for themselves because the cases of death (by execution) in my barrack are permanently much lower than in any other barrack in the male camp. So now you see and can judge".

Impressive as these apologetical were to my ears, I checked them thoroughly. It was true and it was known in his block. I was told moreover that Kuba didn't take bribes, didn't accept presents because to him justice was justice, according to his own code, and there was no place for favoritism of any kind, except for the sick that had to be protected. His people who went out to work outside used to buy for him, with his money, a few victuals, smuggled conveniently among utensils. Seeing how badly we fared he wanted to share them with us as well as with Janka. I wouldn't accept; I was that proud, as you know by now. What did Kuba do? He asked one of his men to bring him flowers from outside and offered them to me. Can you imagine this chivalrous kind of courtship in a concentration camp? Imagine me pedaling on my machine, on which stood a can with real flowers. Many people from Madritsch circles came to see the flowers...

Sometimes Kuba found a subtle subterfuge to feed me: He invited me on some pretext, with his sisters Janka and Hela, to come to the cubicle in his barrack and we had a chat and a snack. He would then point to the few remaining victuals and ask innocently why we shouldn't take them for my mother and Witek. I saw through this subterfuge and refused to come again for a visit. We even had a row on this subject. He reproached me, quite rightly, that I was exaggerating in my obstinacy. He claimed that he was not trying to win me over by food. Janka was tactful enough never to intervene on his behalf.

Kuba also had some other winning approaches. He would say something like this: "I know that you don't accept me as I am today. But the time will come, after the war, when seeing my loyalty and devotion and my total exoneration — your heart will mellow. We shall pass our lives hand in hand. Then at last as a couple of very old people we shall sit on a bench, holding hands, exchanging reminiscences — and then you will admit that I was a jolly good fellow to walk with through life. I know that I have it in me to make you happy". Only one part of it was to become true; he survived the war without blame and blemish.

Much later, when the Plaszow camp was in the first stages of liquidation, Kuba said to me once: "Nothing is permanent in this camp. When the day comes, on which we shall be forcibly separated, I want to make sure that we shall be reunited after the war, if we survive." After these words he handed me a small, strange object. It was a tiny disk set on a pivot that was attached to a half-ring. On both sides of the disk were grooved illegible hieroglyphs. When you set the disk spinning on its pivot, the hieroglyphs of both sides merged into an inscription. I could then read in German: "Kehrewieder"- meaning "Come back".

For some reason I grew so attached to this little life-preserving talisman that it passed with me through seven concentration camps, and the liberation found me clutching it in my palm. It evidently served its purpose but only to a certain degree. But that isn't the end of its story, and I shall relate it at the proper moment — if I ever reach the end of my recordings.

This romantic story of mine must sound absurd against the background of life shared with ghosts, bugs and lice, with hunger constantly gnawing and harping at your stomach. We still lived on the same meagre rations, but now there was something swimming in our soup. It was the so-called 'sago', a sort of lentils but devoid of any nutritious value. They were transparent and had no taste whatsoever. We used to joke that Goth has improved our diet by adding... glass to our soup.

We never stopped the masochistic fantasizing about food, inventing a menu of Lucullan, sybaritic dinners. It was very harmful to the system, it made our stomachs overflow with digestive juices, digesting nothing and ruining the stomach with acids. These manic improvisations were to obsess us to the very last moment.

The lack of sleep took its toll. We were getting up at four o'clock, sipping coffee and marching till six when it was time for the morning rollcall. Now add to this list of afflictions a very trivial one — the lack of toilet paper, or any paper at all. Try to imagine a revolt of people afflicted by diarrhea and unable to take care of their physiological functions. There was even no way of stealing paper from the paper workshop; its employees were searched for the tiniest slip of paper. There was not even a leaf in this camp that you could use instead of paper. The tiny fabric cuts and offals had their price on the camp market, but we had no access to them, we were too far from the cutting workshop of Madritsch. One of my friends possessed a tiny strip of linen, with which she used to wipe her private parts. She washed it, dried it, used it again, and washed and dried, and...

You may now ask if there were no newspapers in this whole camp. A prisoner was not allowed to carry a newspaper, but sometimes one of those still working outside would risk smuggling a newspaper. He had a whole following group of "sub-subscribers". People would queue up next to the person's bunk and wait for their turn to read this official German newspaper. My mother had of course to be there. She stood like a soldier until her turn came. She would then read and absorb the German lies about the situation or rather try to read between the lines, as father had taught us. Nothing had changed. Like three years before, a sentence like "our forces moved into better positions" still meant a retreat.

Now, to step out of trivia, I must make you pay a visit to the camp hospital. It has to be stated that Dr. Weichert, acting from outside, managed to send into the camp the basic medical equipment and essential medicines. Goth knew of it, but being afraid of an outbreak of epidemic in his camp, he tolerated this secret help from outside. Thus, he didn't have to finance the hospital from his budget.

The Jewish doctors were very dedicated, very efficient, but they had to face the gravest problem of their professional ethics. Dr. Blancke, the German supervisor of the hospital gave order that cases of grave illnesses had to receive a special treatment. 'Sonderbehandlung' — the "special treatment" had only one meaning in the German lexicon: it meant killing! The oath of Hippocrates did not apply to the race of gods, and Dr. Blancke gave terminally ill patients injections of benzine with his own hands. It was not euthanasia; it was the most terrible torture. Dr. Blancke had a partner in murder. He also made Dr. Gross, the Jewish director of the hospital, give benzine injections. It is believed today that Dr. Gross was the only one among the Jewish doctors who gave such lethal injections. He was put on trial and hanged after the war. But I know somebody who maintains that Dr. Gross was not the only one to do it, and that somebody very respectable was another accomplice. I had to mention this rumor because I always point out the complexity of such phenomena. The other Jewish physicians were now facing a dilemma; knowing that an almost terminal case would be exposed to the 'treatment' with benzine to be applied by Dr. Blancke or Dr. Gross, shouldn't they rather take the initiative and facilitate the patient's passage to another world by giving him an injection, an overdose of morphine? There had never been such a problem presented in the history of medicine. Sticking to the old routine, couldn't a Concilium of three physicians make such a decision, and execute it as well? It is alleged today that this policy was applied in few cases, but nobody would confirm it. The seal of silence hasn't been broken.

Knowing about these murderous practices, the young medics at the hospital had to develop a strong psychical armor, and what is a better armor than cynicism? Out of cynicism they prodded each other to macabre excentricities. Being on guard on a night of lesser pressure, three of them would play a game of bridge. And who would be the fourth partner? A corpse. Yes, a corpse seated against the wall. Many years later, the person who reported to me these macabre practices denied the story peremptorily. Yet, here it is exactly as I remember it, and I would have never invented such an episode, that must sound like taken out of a Hitchcock scenario.

You may now ask what was my personal experience with the hospital? I was once hospitalized for a very short time. I had been running a high temperature, probably sick with flu or angina. In spite of mother's protests, I was forcibly taken to the hospital, which in itself was dangerous enough. Any selection would often start with the hospital. I was put into a bed, together with another girl, a very sick one. I escaped the next day, I chose to work in spite of fever and shivering.

About this time, I was to have a very dramatic contact with the hospital, which ended in a tragedy. In order to relate it, I have to make a statement. As I feared from the beginning of these recordings, I must have committed injustice to many near and dear people. Because of the immensity of the material accumulated for these recordings, I have missed many an opportunity to depict figures that played a dominant role in my life. I have hardly mentioned my dear cousin Rutka, or did so in a very superficial manner. The fact is that we grew up not as cousins or sisters, but rather like twins. Why? Since my father partly supported the Klein family before the war, my mother used to buy for both of us, Rutka and me, identical coats and even dresses. It went certainly against her grain and taste, but she did it for sake of equality. Thus, we walked the town like twins, being almost of the same age and the same figure. We were also both platinum blonde, but here the general similarities end. She had different features and beer-brown merry eyes. Still, many people didn't distinguish between us, and we grew used to it. Rutka was all smiles, I was reticent. Grandma Rose liked my poise, grandpa adored Rutka's exuberance and ingratiating chatting. I think in retrospective that we actually complemented each other.

After we had spent a year and a half together in Rabka, here in Plaszow we worked separately and lived separately, but the natural bond remained the same, it was biological, I would say.

One day Rutka was hospitalized. I don't remember the symptoms, it was nothing palpable, and I don't remember the diagnosis of her ailment. But something very strange must have happened to her. When I visited her in the hospital ward, she gripped my hand and pressed it so hard that I felt her fingernails digging into my hand. She started to talk in a hoarse whisper. She talked quickly, as if afraid that her time was running out. She said that we must flee that camp as soon as possible. Just the two of us. We are young — she said — we must live, our lot is intertwined like twins... It was so absurd that I didn't dare interrupt her. Anyhow, she wouldn't let me. What followed made sense up to a certain stage, but was on the whole utterly preposterous.

Carts and trucks are entering and leaving the camp — she said — they are loaded with crates, sacks, furniture, mattrasses. They are escorted by the Ukrainians. She, Rutka, will try to persuade a Ukrainian to help us hide in a truck. She didn't mention bribing him because we had no means, but she will promise him a fat reward, payable after the war. We shall succeed... she was positive.

She was now blabbering and repeating herself, embroidering on other variants of this escape — she was talking as if possessed. Was she hallucinating? I touched her forehead, but it was close to normal. I was at a loss, how was I to react? I asked her why only the two of us. I tried to explain how impossible it was, and were we to succeed in this escapade, where could we go, what would we do? My logic was lost on her. She only hardened her grip on my hand, and her fingernails dug deeper into my flesh. I left with very mixed feelings.

Rutka was released from the hospital a day or two later. The very same night the German conducted a big hunt for forbidden possessions. I may have mentioned that a year before, hardly two weeks after we had been transplanted from the ghetto, the same scenario took place. Curfew has been imposed on the whole camp, and nobody has been permitted to leave his barrack or to budge from his bunk. Throughout this whole night a group of SS-men, headed by Goth and Chilowicz, had been passing from barrack to barrack, ordering all the inmates to throw into a basket all their jewels, watches, gold, silver, fountainpens, foreign currency and local denominations such as Zlotys and Reichsmarks. Like the previous time, when several people were shot by Goth, the Ukrainians searched the bunks and examined bodily prisoners picked at random. Like the first time, most of the treasures amassed by the German forces eventually filled Goth's private coffers. Only this time it had been a meagre 'crop', and Goth was furious.

Trapped in our barrack, we had no idea what had been happening in the other blocks. We couldn't have known that Rutka had got a splitting headache, vomiting again and again. Helcia implored the block commander to let her go out and seek medical help at her own risk, but she wouldn't let her out. Before the morning hours Rutka was unconscious and comatose.

It was only after the curfew had been lifted that Olek could carry her in his arms to the hospital. Dr.Hilfstein was at the hospital and took care of her. Unfortunately, for an incomprehensible reason, Dr.Hilfstein had deduced and decided that Rutka must have taken poison!!! He proceeded, therefore, in accord with this theory and kept on pumping her stomach... Our poor, dear Rutka expired without regaining consciousness. I cannot state here that this was what had caused her death, but the post-mortem revealed meningitis as the cause of her collapse. In retrospective it was concluded that her hospitalization had already been the prelude to an undiagnosed meningitis. Is it not tragic to die so young, in this terrible camp, because of meningitis?

For as far as I can remember, the self-effacing aunt Helcia had been absolutely crazy as mother of an only child. She looked at her Rutka as at the picture of the Holy Madonna. Helcia lived only for Rutka; she, Helcia, was only a shadow of a person, demanding nothing of life except the happiness of Rutka. Now for Helcia life ended with Rutka's death.

It affected me in a very peculiar way. It was not only as if my second half had been torn away from me. I could stand it, we had already been hardened by our many tragedies. But to feel Helcia's eyes watching me, gave me the creeps. I felt guilty and ashamed of being alive, while Rutka was reposing in her grave. I couldn't face Helcia anymore, it was beyond me. I admit that I started to avoid her. Whenever I spotted her entering our barrack, laboriously making her way along the crowded passage between the rows of bunks — I fled. As it was, Helcia developed a new attitude. She decided that her life had become utterly superfluous (which it had indeed become), that she lives now merely as a number, a prisoner number so and so, who receives a daily ration. She now intended to starve herself gradually to death and bring her whole ration to us, for as long as she lived. That was her only aim. She explained it to my mother. She said that if she doesn't cut her wrists, it is because she can still serve us as a purveyor of her daily ration; her bread, and once a week a tiny cube of margarine and a spoonful of watery jam. She will live for some time on soup and coffee-substitute.

There were bitter rifts between my aunt and my mother. We refused to accept her ration, we rejected it, and she threatened suicide. She said that my mother had no right to refuse, she should accept this food for Witek's sake.

Try to understand our problem of conscience. Should we accept her self-sacrifice or drive her to suicide? Both solutions were equally cruel. We could only try to avoid her by keeping constantly far from our bunk, hiding elsewhere. And that was no less cruel. To punish us, she still used to leave her ration, there on the bunk, persistently day after day. Let it be stolen — she said. Instead of hugging and comforting her, we kept avoiding her. Uncle Olek, formerly a merry egoist, also became a shadow of his own self. He too turned old before our eyes.

We were, the three of us — mother, Witek and I, engulfed in gloom. Was there no comfort, no ray of sunshine for us, in this dark period? We had to find something, something to cheer us up, and then cling to it desperately. There was one tiny comfort which I incidentally discovered. Not far from our bunk lived a nice lady, visited daily by her son, Michael Goldwasser. Mrs. Goldwasser told her son about our plight and problem. He did a simple childish thing: he offered to sing for us, arias from operas. He was not a professional singer, but he carried the tunes well, and he knew to choose the sweetest of operettas. Until this very day I remember the melody and the libretto of "La Mattinata" by Leon Cavallo, as sung by him. The song offered promise of a new morning when nature comes to life. It was sheer poetry. It was about dawn and the first ray of sunshine. It was about lilies and roses awakening, shrouded in dew and trembling with the expectation of sun's love. It is such an elated and soothing song that one can 'use' it instead of valium. Whenever I am distressed and agitated, I sing this song to myself. (Here the song is recorded on tape.)

My mother didn't seek consolation in operas. Being less romantic or having suppressed such feelings, she always tried to come to grips with life's problems. She had to, she still had her two children, she had us, and one of us was in constant danger. I was much less of a fighter, I had less stamina, less resistance, but then I was not the mother of two children, I was the child to be protected and pampered by mother. Soon, unfortunately very soon, I was to remain her only child.

Meanwhile, there came, as usual, an unexpected ray of hope, piercing the nebulous line of the horizon. The Russian bear was moving, moving slowly and persistently, preparing to break through the German lines. Sometimes we felt like telling Helcia to wait and not to starve herself to death, because the war could be soon over, there were signs pointing to such a possibility. We knew now that the beginning of the Russian offensive was imminent.

The Germans knew it before us. It must have been decided on the high level to undertake the necessary steps to wipe off and erase all traces of the German crimes. The big camps posed no problem. All had been envisaged there, all had been planned in advance. The great "advantage" of the crematoria had been the fact that they left no traces of the crimes perpetrated there. Once the crematoria would be blown up, nothing would be left, and ashes would go to ashes — the ashes of the buildings enveloping the last ashes of the human bodies. Not so in Plaszow. Goth had been so careless in his murderous euphoria that he had let the bodies be buried haphazardly in many scattered places, some inside the camp, some around it, no matter where. Only in the later period had the bodies been burned on pyres on the 'Chujowa Gorka' right after each execution. Goth has now been reprimanded for his earlier carelessness and has been ordered to detect all the dispersed burial sites. He has been ordered to exhume all the cadavers.

The German administration scanned its maps in the effort of pinpointing all common graves. Only some of them had been marked. On these main sites, the belly of earth was now opened up by this monster — the mechanical shovel, known to us as "bagger". The "bagger" did only the preparatory work, the rest was done by the prisoners. They had to shovel the soil, fill pails and lift them from the pit, fill the wheel bars till heavily loaded, and push them up on long trails of planks. Only then did the corpses gradually emerge, stashed on the bottom of the trenches.

These cadavers, having remained for a year in the womb of earth, emitted now a terrifying stench, which spread all over the camp. The Germans used to hold handkerchiefs to their noses, we had none. I remember a day when we stood on the "Appelplatz" inhaling this deadly stench of putrefaction of carcasses, and the warden, Alice Ostrowsky (nicknamed 'Pelerinka') missing her handkerchief exclaimed: "I would give a kingdom for a hanky". An SS-man was overheard mumbling: "It couldn't stink more on the Russian front". The Germans were instructed to accelerate all this operation. Work was continued during the night, in the light of torches. As soon as a mass-grave was located and opened up, the corpses were extricated from the pit and carried by prisoners, one by one, to the funeral pyre (Goth became afraid of epidemics).

The prisoners had to construct the pyres in the following way: First they laid out a broad base of dry wood, with a second layer spread across the first. They sprinkled both with benzine. Then they laid out a layer of corpses. They now piled up on them again two layers of wood and again, one of cadavers. Then fire was kindled at the bottom of the whole pyramid. The corpses emitted now a most terrible stench, one of a different kind. Not of putrefaction but of burning human flesh. Stiff, quiet corpses behaved like in Armageddon. As if raised to life by Messiah, they twisted in the flames and tried to sit up.

The whole camp seemed to disappear under a cloud of soft soot, ashes, smoke and stench. Soot covered our faces, heads and shoulders. It was floating in our soup and coffee. The excavating process had been started simultaneously in so many places that not hundreds, but thousands of prisoners had to be engaged in it. The slaves of "Barrackenbau" construction and quarry were not able to carry it out, their numbers were limited. Many people were taken forcibly out of their working compounds and sent to the excavation sites. Whenever I see an archeological excavation site — I shudder, and you will understand why. Because we, we too, had been engaged to participate in this scenario of horror. Madritsch was helpless. He too had to contribute part of his employees as working force. Fortunately, we were sent to excavations in their initial stage. Thus, we didn't have to look at the cadavers or to carry them. We were loading the earth on wheelbarrows or carrying the planks serving to lay out the long trails, so that the heavy wheelbarrows would not get stuck in earth and mud. Sometimes the trails of planks were laid out perched so close to the precipice that we were afraid to fall into the pit and find ourselves among cadavers.

The bonfires were burning day and night. We were chocking on the smells, vomiting. Our eyes constantly running. Do you remember smells? I always do. I could tell the story of my life by smells or by tunes. And this smell was unforgettable. Nowadays, whenever I have to burn a wing of chicken for the Seder Pesach plate — I suffer agonies. Every Seder Pesach reminds me of you know what, and it was around the Pesach period that these proceedings had started. They were to continue well into the summer.

You may now ask how many cadavers had to be exhumed or rather, extricated from the earth. There is no official record, but we, the inmates estimate the numbers as oscillation between eight thousand and twelve thousand. The ever-exaggerating Poles set the numbers much higher. If you try to establish the total numbers of victims executed in Plaszow, it has to be remembered that in the latent period the corpses were annihilated immediately after the execution, right there next to the old Austrian fortifications, dating from World War I. Their count adds to the statistics. The groups of Poles brought to the 'Chujowa Gorka' numbered sometimes five, sometimes twenty people. Not having mapped all the mass-graves and single graves, Goth has left many corpses undiscovered, and they still haunt the Plaszow hill, emerging forty and two years later.

You may now think that with the Russian offensive approaching in giant strides, the story of the Plaszow camp comes to its end. Far from it. The Russian offensive was stopped for a long, long time. The murderous German beast, having washed its hands from its crimes, proceeded to run the camp as efficiently as ever. It even had to make room for more Hungarian prisoners. Making room could only have one meaning: Reducing the actual camp population by sending a death transport. Afraid of a riot during the assembling prisoners, for such a mass transport, Goth prepared the ground carefully by a volley of false rumors and encouraging lies.

The whole action started almost innocently. It has been astutely "divulged" by somebody close to Goth and has been spread by the camp grapevine, claiming that the International Red Cross wants to check the physical condition of the prisoners. They probably want to see if the food rations are in accord with the Geneva Convention — added a "clever" man... From here the allegations went much further. The rumor claimed that the International Red Cross is seemingly ready to supply an addition of fortifying food rations but being unable to distribute them to all camp inmates, it needs a list of undernourished prisoners. For this purpose, the delegation of the Red Cross commission desired, allegedly, to arrange an inspection. Feeling that the end of the war may be close now, Goth will have to comply — explained those "knowledgeable" people. It was believed for a while.

When the so-called inspection eventually took place, it didn't look like being conducted by a civilian commission. Still, it didn't resemble a selection. A physician and some civilians were seated at a table, but one of them was Dr.Gross, the head of the camp hospital, which in itself seemed to be reassuring, because we didn't know at this time that he was giving benzine injections to the fatally ill...

Men were inspected separately from women. We all had to parade naked, running quickly back and forth in front of the commission. Thus, we passed, the inmates of one barrack after another. We noticed that several women of our barrack had been stopped for a while, their name and number checked on the registration files. So, after all, the registration files were used now, as mother had foreseen, but not the way she imagined it. The whole proceedings were highly suspect. Something had been marked on the files, we didn't know what. Had it been a selection, people would have been divided and sent to right and left, on the spot and without delay.

When we met later with all our family, it transpired that Helcia and Olek had been stopped and marked on the list. And our Witek too!!! We were highly alarmed, but the reassuring rumors persisted. It has been explained again and again that these people are simply going to receive an additional ration, and that the Germans must be eager to make some improvements, now before the end of the war.

Time passed and nothing happened. When we started to breathe again — the thunder stroke!

On May 14, 1944, exactly one week after the inspection, the "Appelplatz" was encircled by strong forces. Heavy silence reigned on the square. Then it started. Gradually names and numbers were called out in front of the waiting ranks. People were being dragged out from amidst us. Mother mumbled with blue lips: "Now they are taking Witek... Helcia and Olek". All hell broke loose. Cries of despair mingled with the saccharine tunes broadcast from the loudspeakers, which were now set at the highest pitch and volume. The sweeter the tunes, the more piercing the pain. I am not exaggerating or groping for a literary onomatopoeia. You must believe me that what I shall describe now, I felt and experienced right there, as I still feel it now. The tune of "Star from Rio" stabbed us as if the word 'Riooo' was a sword. The cries of pain that sounded like 'Iyooo' mingled with 'Riooo' like a parody of this song. The lullaby "Mamatschi, schenk mir ein Pferdchen..." — meaning "Mummy, buy me a pony, with a pony I shall feel in Paradise" — constituted a peak of irony because the children of this camp were just being sent to "Paradise"... And our Witek was among them. We knew it for certain, even though we could only see what was happening in our vicinity. Our hearts went out to him. A human heart can ache as if a hand would grab and squeeze it. This time mother was utterly helpless.

Goth observed the seething and swaying crowds, people breaking the ranks, people tearing their hair or writhing on the ground. He sensed that the whole camp was on the verge of mutiny. He had sent for reinforcements and they approached us threateningly, separating one group of prisoners from another. But Goth made one mistake; Instead of mixing the children with the elderly and the weak and spiriting them all quickly away, he let the children be abducted to the area behind the barracks while the railway was on the opposite side. He now had to move them to the station on trucks that had to pass alongside the "Appelplatz", in sight of the parents. The children cried and waved their hands, the parents screamed like demented. A real riot broke out.

Goth would probably have started to shoot into the crowd if it had not been for his auxiliary forces that were now almost mingled with these undulating massed. We didn't see the trucks, we were standing too far away. I would dare to say, from my present perspective, that we were spared this sight.

As it is known today, one thousand and four hundred adults and two hundred and sixty-eight children were sent that day to the gas chambers of Auschwitz. Nobody dared to mention to us that several children remained hidden in the latrine pit or elsewhere. Did their parents know that it would happen on that day? We didn't. Have we failed? Could we have prevented it? After all, my mother was not one of the prominent parents that could count on somebody to protect their child if saved after the May action. And then — for how long? It is tragic to think that my brother had to die when the Russian offensive had already reached Eastern Poland and was stopped there.

It is tragic to think that my brother had to die four days before his fourteenth birthday. He too, like our father, had to go to his death knowingly, knowing without doubt, that these were his last hours on earth. These thoughts drove us crazy.

It was clear to all Plaszow inmates that the May transport went to its death. Only my mother never accepted defeat, and to her that had been one, as if it was her personal one. She, the realist, the pragmatist now lived clinging to a nebulous, fantastic conception. According to it, this transport has after all been left alive and integrated into the Auschwitz camp. How could an intelligent person have believed it? It has an explanation. Mother was running all around the camp, running hither and thither. She was trying to gather a scrap of information, and eventually there was more than one. The cook Meyer, allegedly, received a letter from his wife and child that had been in that transport. Mother was not shown this letter, but she spoke to a person, who knew a person who had seen that letter with his own eyes... People, eager to reassure their friends who had lost somebody, were spreading such rumors. It is believed today that there has been such a letter... and that Goth, afraid of a mutiny, gave an order to procure such an authentic letter by forcing Meyer's wife to write one before her death. There has been even a second source of information, no less fantastic; A load of wood boards was, allegedly, sent from Auschwitz to Plaszow, and upon them were scribbled with coal several greetings from the deported ones. Mother hadn't seen the boards, but she knew a person, who knew a person, who was able to read these inscriptions with his own eyes...

Thus, she kept running in circles, and I had to face again the same dilemma: Am I to let her believe that Witek could be alive or should I ruin all her illusions. She seemed so despondent by now and I had no way of comforting her. We were both ashamed to be alive. This time I have decided to let her nourish these crazy illusions, hopefully they will keep her going.

How did I react or act? I retreated into my shell and the echoes inside the coils of my shell kept boring into my skull the schmaltzy tunes of 'Rosamunde' and 'Star of Riooo' and that tragic lullaby. I can still hear them whenever I think of that period.

Sometimes I sought refuge in work. I was pedaling furiously, like crazy, hoping that the noise of my machine would kill these tunes in my ears. I shook myself into reality and decided to take care of my mother. This time I invented a white lie, one with a good dose of probability. There were for some time no executions, and I was able to build my wild theory on the assumption that the Germans, aware of the approaching Russian front, had to change their policy. They were now (allegedly) most eager to preserve and concentrate in one point many children and elderly or weak people. This "show case" had been astutely prepared for their future exoneration. Plaszow was too close to the approaching front, it had to be Auschwitz. The Germans simply needed some proof that they took care of the weak...

so far it seemed almost plausible. Such a crazy concocted theory could not come from me — I had to put it in the mouth of Wilek Kranz, stating that he had overheard it, eavesdropping on a conversation between two men. I knew that mother would check such sensational news, so I asked Wilek to corroborate this version, and he did it with some embellishments. Serving now in Plaszow as the prison warden, he was close enough to the Germans.

Mother seemed to swallow the story; she became less despondent. Nevertheless, she once confessed to me, admitting heavy, deep remorse that she had all the time always been closer to me than to Witek. She hadn't been proud of having begotten a son; she didn't know how to play with him. She doted on me, she dressed me like a doll. It had been mostly father who paid attention to Witek, father had a wonderful way with children. Unfortunately, it had partly been true, I had been her doll and Witek belonged to men's world.

There is no love stronger than that of a mother for her child. After this love there are only grades and shades of a durable infatuation or some mixed feelings, composed of many facets. Close to the period I am speaking of, I have encountered a case of a strange love. Since I am portraying here unusual figures, I must describe the heroine of this case.

She was the commander of our block. She was blonde, good looking, impressive, dynamic and efficient. There was even a masculine trait in her, which seemed preposterously to add to her force of attraction. It was not apparent in her face or body but rather in her carriage and authority. She was not from Krakow; she must have come to Plaszow from somewhere else, and she arrived with her husband. He was a physician, but not employed as one in Plaszow.

The contrast between the two was amazing. They were poles apart in physical appearance and in character. He was delicate, soft spoken, a modest intellectual, almost a boy. He used to come to her every evening and they seemed so engrossed in each other, forming so harmonious a couple that we could almost forgive her harshness. As soon as he left, after the lights-out signal sounded by a bugle, strange things were happening in her cubicle, her private room in the barrack. In those late hours she was changing from the sweet loving wife into a harlot. Even her voice underwent a change from soft cooing into a coarse speech and laughter. The men who visited her in her cubicle were a regiment. There were OD officers, block commanders, capos of groups and other prominent figures. Sometimes two men came on one and the same night. After the first left close to eleven, another came close to midnight. They were free to move between the men's and the women's camp. Several of them returned many a time, others gave a one-night performance. Did she receive presents and food from them, or was it rather her sexual appetite that drove her to promiscuity on such a scale?

One day there was a selection on the "Appelplatz" among those slaving in construction works, where her emaciated husband was employed. An OD man moving between the rows brought her the information that her husband's name and number had been called out. It had only one meaning: death. It so happened that she was standing in front of me, actually one step in front of all of us, the inmates of her barrack. She fainted in my arms. Then she woke up, roared like a wounded bull and fainted once more. The selection and checking of numbers lasted for hours. Once she cried like a baby, once she fainted, once the screamed and writhed in pain. I took care of her, cradling her as well as I could. Then I had an idea. Why not give her a psychological shock? Why not spur her, why not whip her with a bold accusation. I forgot for a moment that she was my almighty barrack commander. I gripped her shoulders, shook her and asked: "tell me pray, but tell me the truth. Your style of life is known to all of us, there are no secrets. How could it fit with your deep real pain and despair over the lot of your husband. How could it be compatible with your true love for him?"

She could have slapped me, she could have tortured me in many cruel ways, but I didn't mind; I was that curious. She stopped wailing, took a deep breath and then belched her answer in an agonizing voice: "Nobody can understand, nobody could. Between my dear husband and this riffraff that visit my room — there is no connection whatsoever. To me he means everything. He is my child, he is my father, he is a saint. I could kneel and pray to him. He is all I have in my miserable life. He is not a security for the future, he is the only aim of my survival. The filth I am carrying on me couldn't rub on to him. He is a saint that married a woman born to be a whore. I love him much more than myself. I am willing to offer my life in exchange for his life, but who wants my life?"

She now cried silently, spent and relieved.

As for me, I learned a new lesson. She didn't take revenge on me, nothing happened. She carried on and automatically, absently continued to run the barrack. She was not her own self anymore. She lived like a nun for quite a long time. There were rumors and whispers that she tried to take her life and her deputy saved her. Then I was transferred and lost her from my sight. I don't even remember her name, which in itself is strange.

I am reaching now in my story the summer of 1944. There were other barracks, other people and friends, but Janka was still clinging to us. She admitted to us that after we lost our Witek, she didn't know how to behave or how to comfort us. She, with her treasury of wise sayings and clever quotations, was at a loss and lost her grip. She became self-effacing in this period. Now I was again basking in her affection. Kuba was also a great comfort but of a very different kind. He acted with the same tact and knew how to keep his distance, proving constantly his discreet loyalty. He was well informed on the political situation but had to admit that the Russian front had come to a standstill. Nevertheless, the Germans were very nervous, afraid of being sent to the front. The constantly drunk Goth also had his apprehensions. He must have known the Plaszow camp was going to be gradually liquidated. What would happen if Chilowicz would be transferred, all of a sudden, to another camp? Trying to save his skin, he might spill out his, Goth's secrets... giving away details about the amassed fortune, stocked in several places. He must get rid of him, the sooner the better. That's what we know now. But at the given time we heard a very different version.

In August 1944, after Chilowicz had served for over a year as the Jewish commander of the camp, some SS officers had the good idea of betting that he was not as faithful and devoted to Goth as he pretended to be. Can he be tempted? They set a trap for him. They instructed a Ukrainian of high rank, to befriend Chilowicz and to gain his confidence. He had to insinuate to Chilowicz gradually, that his position is not as secure as it appears to be. Any day he can become the victim of Goth's black moods... There were already some hints pointing in this direction. Wouldn't Chilowicz better prepare for himself a way of escape while still at the peak of his career and power? Shouldn't he better be armed? He, the good friend, could try to provide for him a gun, just in case. Chilowicz listened silently. He must have had similar thoughts, a kind of premonition. He realized that he already knew too many of Goth's secrets. He decided to take the risk — he let himself be caught in the net. It is presumed today, that Goth himself instigated this scenario so as to get rid of Chilowicz before he would spill his many secrets.

Chilowicz realized that even though free in his movements over the city of Krakow, he couldn't walk out with his wife, as if going on a shopping spree. Were he to escape somehow with his wife, hidden in a truck under a load of upholstery, his sister and brother-in-law Schnitzer would certainly be killed in reprisal. He had to include them in his plans. Schnitzer tried to remonstrate with him, arguing that he didn't want to participate in this elopement, being secure due to his high position in the Madritsch factory. Chilowicz probably convinced him finally that he and his wife will be the victims of Goth's rage. That must have been the scenario, otherwise it is hard to understand why our prudent Schnitzer would walk into the trap.

When all was ripe for the escapade, the Ukrainian 'Friend' denounced Chilowicz to his superiors. This was the hilarious clique that was to win its bet. You can now well imagine Goth's reaction when he learned of this treason. He took his vengeance slowly, letting them stew in their juices. The truck with the four hidden fugitives was not immediately detained at the gate. It was inspected superficially along with the other trucks; it seemed to have passed the gate — but then it made a reverse movement and was greeted by Goth...

Not all the pieces of the puzzle were leaked to the camp inmates. If Chilowicz made his last plea, if he cried, if he threatened with written inside information deposed in reliable hands (which a clever man would do) — we didn't know. He was killed together with his wife, his sister and our good Schnitzer. As we know now, Goth reported to his superiors that he had to kill Chilowicz instantly because he was the head of a dangerous uprising, about to explode any moment. After the execution, the four bodies were exhibited on the main square, and all the camp inmates had to parade past them, reading the inscription "Thus are punished the traitors"... Impressive figures reduced to corpses are very unimpressive. They look like dolls reposing in beatitude with all their muscles relaxed. Some people took their primitive pleasure spitting on Chilowicz and his wife. We passed the bodies with very mixed feelings. Here at our feet was spread the dreadful Chilowicz, without his well-fitted uniform, an impassive citizen of Krakow. Next to him, like an abandoned doll, was laid out his tiny cruel wife with her intact blonde curls, smart dress and shiny boots of soft red leather.

We should have felt satisfied; she inflicted so many scourges on use, but we felt only mildly interested. Next to them was quietly reposing our agile, honest boss Scnitzer with his insignificant wife. Everything was so familiar to me about Schnitzer. I still remember his gesticulating hands, now in serene repose, I remember the very shape of his fingernails (I always remember people's hands). I even saw the glimmer of his one golden tooth on the side of his mouth as if he was going to smile soon. Everything was in place, only our lively Schnitzer was dead.

The secrets of Goth didn't die with Chilowicz, only a part of them did. There were people of various segments and different backgrounds that "collected" the evidence of Goth's crimes. If we single out three of them, each one represents a special category of collectors. One was a Jew, one a Sudeten-German, and one an Austrian. The first two memorized the evidence, the Austrian took hundreds of pictures.

The Krakow Jew, Mietek Pemper, a scholar endowed with an exceptional memory, got access to most secret documents thanks to his secretarial skills. He was recommended to Goth, and though he only took dictation on innocent matters, he actually managed to sieve and check top secret documents. He ingratiated himself with the German secretary of Goth to such a point, that she never noticed how he, the gentleman, changed for her and snatched the carbon copies of letters typed by her. He reconstructed the text from these carbon copies, and memorized them word by word, as proven by his testimony during Goth's trial after the war. In his collector's craze he even risked peeping into the registers of incoming documents, memorizing them with the same zeal. He could calculate, in his research-work, the exact quantities of provisions supplied to Goth for the maintenance of prisoners, comparing them to the quantities actually distributed. He could, in this way, calculate exactly the illegal profits made by Goth by robbing the camp population of its meagre rations. Chilowicz, who sold the margin profit wares and tons of food, would have never been able to memorize their extent. Pemper was also able to topple Goth's defense arguments at the trial, namely that all the executions were performed under exact orders from above. He was able to prove that Goth was a compulsive murderer.

The Sudeten-German, Oskar Schindler, remembered all Goth's German contact-men and those who participated in the orgies. He also remembered the names of the Germans in highest positions who took bribes and lived like kings. Schindler didn't testify in Goth's trial because by then he lived in South America.

The third collector of evidence was the benevolent Tutsch, the partner of our Madritsch, a compulsive amateur photographer. Running the Madritsch factory, situated inside the camp, he was free to move around and take pictures at will. Who would suspect this Austrian industrialist of subversive intentions? Yet, he was quite a spy. I saw him once, shooting a picture from one of our windows. I don't know what his camera perceived, I only know that somebody screamed out there. It couldn't have been one of those stubborn pious Jews who refused to work on Shabbat; they were all dead by then. Tutsch was seen taking pictures of construction workers and they probably proved that the heavy loads had to be carried running. Whoever fell under the load of the sacks of cement was, in certain cases, buried alive in cement. Hujar would see to it. If a prisoner fainted, he was flung alive into the foundations being cast, and liquid cement was poured over his body. To "perish in concrete" — was not a mere threatening figure of speech.

I don't know what was the extent of the evidence which was photographed by Tutsch. It must have been such dynamite that poor Tutsch never dared to develop his pictures... He kept them buried in solid containers for more than thirty years. Even by then, the political climate in Austria was not propitious for such revelations. Tutsch was afraid of the ever-present Neo-Nazis, and with good reason too. Shortly before his death, he reached the conclusion that his documentation should belong to the State of Israel. I haven't seen this treasure yet and I don't know what it contains. But the forty-six witnesses who testified at Goth's trial after the war, corroborated every detail of Goth's crimes. The hundreds of pages of these protocols should be translated and sent to the authors of books who claimed that the Holocaust was the fruit of Jewish imagination!

As I have mentioned earlier, from the moment when Plaszow became a concentration camp there were, paradoxically, no sporadic killings without a verdict, because Goth had been ordered to report each case of sabotage or escape before an execution and to receive a written order from Kaltenbrunner himself, in order to perform an execution. Goth even had to camouflage the execution of Chilowicz and company, as a case of a riot that had to be killed in embryo. There were still executions going on the 'Prick Hill', but only of people brought from the Montelupich prison and sentenced to death. Some were Poles, some were Jews caught with forged papers.

Otherwise, the situation seemed to become steadier shortly before the gradual liquidation of the Plaszow camp, which was geographically too close to the Russian front.

There was another factor rendering the conditions more balanced. This factor was the appointment of Erich as the commander of prisoners and the replacement for Chilowicz. Who was Erich? He was a gentile and a genuine German. What did he do there in the camps, he who was not even a political prisoner?

Erich's personal story could constitute a subject for a thrilling biography. He became a legend in his lifetime. He could even have acted in a film depicting his own life and adventures. He had a body of a gladiator and a well-shaped head of a hero. He carried proudly his blond head. He had a profile of an eagle with a fine chiseled sharp nose and a strong jawline. His blue eyes, set like an eagle's close to the nose, had an intense expression of force and concentration.

As he liked to boast in front of his few friends, he had been a notorious gentleman-gangster, operating for a long time in America. I had the details from Kuba, whom Erich chose to befriend before he became the camp commander of the prisoners.

Chatting with Kuba, he once implied that he had an indirect connection with the kidnapping of Lindbergh's child. As you may know (or not?), Lindbergh was the first pilot to cross the Atlantic Ocean. Shortly after this exploit, his son was kidnapped and murdered, and the kidnapper later proved to be a German. So far it is the only connection linking Erich to this affair. But his allusion was so vague that it must not be taken in seriousness.

About his other exploits, he was much more outspoken. It seems that over there, in America, he lived like a cosmopolitan gentleman, performing his gangsterism in gloves. In one of his thriller stories he described a burglary of a bank, in which he was the main figure. He, the perfect gentleman, moving in high society circles, brought a refined lady to a restaurant and night club. When the lady reached the last course, Erich made his excuses, pretending that he had to make some urgent phone calls. He sneaked off the booth to the toilets and into the back yard. He now passed through the breach in the wall (prepared by his partners) into the bank close by. In a couple of minutes, he overcame the safe combination, took off his gloves and returned quietly to his table and his companion. He spent the rest of the night dancing with her — he had a perfect alibi. The police was certain that the break-in must have been his work, like many other jobs similar in style, but was unable to prove it then or ever. Then somebody remembered that Erich was a German citizen. He was deported to Germany, where he was promptly incarcerated in a concentration camp. He found himself there well before the war and having passed through several camps, became immune to the conditions and well attuned to the system. In Plaszow he was appointed to serve as "kapo" of the men slaving in the quarry.

That would be one version of his official biography, but there was a second one. According to it, he had never been to America. He was sentenced to forced labor for the murder of his parents and two sisters. Indeed, if he perpetrated his crime in Germany, how and why would he land in America? If he did it in America, why was he sent to Germany? Why would he boast of his gangster connections and activities? Was he arrested for gangsterism or patricide? His cruelty to prisoners as the foreman of a quarry detail was notorious. His elegant performance after he became the camp commander, was remarkable too. Once more I am fascinated by the psychological dualism of such figures.

Whichever version was true, one thing was certain. Erich became a typical German disciplinarian and knew how to rule a camp with a strong hand, wearing fine kid gloves. As a commander he was a perfect gentleman, demanding yet just. A different tone of speech was now heard in the camp. Gone was the vulgar vocabulary of Chilowicz, his wife and his minions.

In order to put the finishing touches to Erich's portrait I have to add two anecdotes. The first incident is related to the period when he was still a Kapo. Once, Kuba was not at his post when his barrack was being inspected. He was sentenced for his absence to receive a punishment of twenty-five lashes. And who was appointed as the executor of this punishment? — his good friend Erich. Erich used his whip mercilessly and counted exactly twenty-five lashes. Then he helped Kuba to rise. After Kuba drew up his pants Erich shook his hand and said: "Excuse me bod, but friendship is friendship, and duty is duty".

After Erich became the camp commander, we were given more sanitary facilities. The washroom barrack had to be open at all hours. The showers became more often accessible. One evening, when we were marched to the showers, Erich stood at the entrance dressed in immaculate uniform and wearing white gloves. He was beaming with benevolence. He addressed us most formally: "Good evening, ladies. I wish you a pleasant bath. Take your time, there is no rush". That was now for a while the new tone ruling in the camp. Erich, the gangster, was a capable administrator and knew how to introduce normalization. But there was more than normalization in this period.

Breathing more easily, people regained their sense of humor, often a macabre humor. Let me give an example. In the barrack of showers, the only one in this huge camp, was employed a youngster, Janek Dresdner — today Dr.J.Dresdner in Tel Aviv. All the women of Krakow knew the Dresdner family who owned a big shop of textile and knew young Janek from his childhood. He was now operating in the showers the faucets of hot and cold water. He did it facing some fifty naked women. At first we were very much ashamed in front of him, then we got used to his presence to such a degree that sometimes a naked lady, who could have been his mother, called out: "Janek, would you please scrub my back". Everybody laughed. Humor is nourishing, please believe me.

In this apparently more stable period, everything seemed to develop like in a Greek tragedy. The Greek tragedies, as you have learnt, are constructed with a psychological insight into the reactions of the spectators. It was believed that the spectators cannot stand too much suspense. They need a respite. It was being provided by opening new vistas of hope, and prospects for a happy solution. Only then did the thunder strike and the final tragedy occur... We too were offered by fate such a period of respite and of new hopes connected partly with the Russian offensive. We were offered even more than that. The monster of the camp, Amon Goth, vanished from our horizon. He was arrested on September 13th, 1944.

The camp was buzzing with rumors. The reality exceeded the wildest hopes, fantasies and conjectures. But the whole truth was to emerge only after the war, namely at Goth's trial. The investigation of Goth's wrongdoing started quite innocently — as Kuba learned from Erich. According to this version, some petty SS officials of Plaszow came under suspicion squandering too much money. When interrogated, they laughed. "Our expenses here are but a trifle compared to the cost of the upkeep of Mister Rolf and Mister Ralf" — they quipped. And who are Mister Rolf and Ralf, asked the inspector. "The two dogs of Herr Commandant Goth" — was the answer.

The investigator was not amused. He passed on the information to his superiors. Now the inquest took a new direction. It was not to be handled by small fry. An inquiry commission composed of top brass SS investigators was now sent to Krakow and to Plaszow. Meanwhile Goth was arrested, while on a visit to his father, a publisher in Vienna.

As it transpired, Goth had acted from the beginning like a squirrel, storing food for winter. He had so many storage points and hideouts that he could hardly remember them. 'Only' four have been discovered, one in Plaszow, one in Krakow, one in Vienna and one in Moravia. Like a squirrel he stocked his goods, mixing very valuable items with furniture and junk. The rest of space he filled with cigarettes till they reached the ceiling. He never dared to store the stolen treasures in his father's flat, good son that he was. He must have placed great confidence in Oskar Schindler, because when the latter moved his "Emalia" factory from Krakow to the Brinlitz village in Moravia, there was a whole room (permanently locked) filled with Goth's treasures, discovered after Goth had already been arrested. His loyal mistress Mayola was flabbergasted when she was shown this room, shortly before Goth's trial after the war. She even expressed her sorrow that poor Amon, rotting in prison, was deprived of the basics, while a roomful of goods, that could fill a palace awaited him over there in Moravia. It is questionable if Schindler was that much dedicated to his pal Amon, or rather uncertain of the outcome of the investigation, and afraid that after all, Goth may be set free and come back to claim his possessions. Schindler played it safe. So did the Jewish prisoners questioned as witnesses in the Plaszow camp. They didn't dare to incriminate Goth, afraid of his revenge — if he would be somehow exonerated and set free. Goth's confidants and close associates behaved very much in the same way, remaining cautious. But the fame of his origins and of the treasures amassed by him was so widely spread by some envious Germans, that the incriminating evidence was sufficient for the prosecution.

Days before the end of the war, Goth was released or escaped. After the war he was soon captured and brought to Krakow to trial. By then, the testimonies were flowing in and corroborated from all angles. During his trial, Goth still believed that he could pedantically abolish one or another accusation. In vain, everything was pinpointed by the knowledgeable witnesses, and only Chilowicz was missing from this gallery. It is of little consolation for us that the monster has been brought to the gallows.

Even before the arrest of Goth, it had already been known that Plaszow would be liquidated soon. The camp was gradually shrinking, huge transports of prisoners being sent out. This fate was about to strike us too. One day, in September, we were encircled and caught into the net, our whole group of friends within many women. We were separated from all the camp inmates. We didn't have to wait; we were marched straight to the railway station of the camp.

We had by then other new friends, because people were often shifted and separated in this camp. One of our new friends was the clumsy Reginka, a living portrait of Miss Piggy, well before that one was created. She had a perky nose and a porcupine mouth. People were wondering how we could befriend such a strange creature. But they didn't know Reginka. They didn't know her dry wit or her doggish loyalty. We got so used to her that we didn't even notice her physical appearance. "Shlimazl" that she was, she once tripped on something, fell and broke her leg. This was when she came to visit us in our block. It happened two days before we were caught.

Now we were trapped, and Reginka amidst us, marching with a brand-new, heavy plaster-cast on her broken leg. Our whole transport was being loaded on to the train. We were whipped like cattle and made to progress in the direction of the wagons. All of a sudden, we had an idea. Was it Janka who mentioned it first or did we do it by instinct? We decided to "take care" of the laboriously hopping Reginka, to cling to her, to support her and... to progress more slowly than the rest of the transport. This trick was quite dangerous for Reginka and perhaps for the rest of us too. We asked her if she would be willing to play this game and risk being shot. "I am willing to die for you, but will you please take care of my dear leg after my death"- was Reginka's answer (we laughed only later). We stopped, we pretended to check her cast, we dilly-dallied as well as we could... and see!!! The trick paid off. The train was by then filled to its maximum capacity, the marching column was stopped two rows before us, and we and a few others were left on the platform and marched back to the camp.

As we were to learn after the war, this transport for which we were designated, was eventually sent far to the north of Germany, to Stutthof. There, these unfortunate women were driven by shots into the sea, where they all drowned and perished. Were it not for the clever trick, it could have been our lot.

To return to the terrible but familiar Plaszow camp, was like coming back home. In this gossamer of absurdities this is only one more... We flew back as if we had grown wings. Kuba, his face streaming with tears, clasped his sister Janka in a bear's hug, enveloping me and my mother with his second arm. Now we were all of us shedding the tears of joy. We were well aware that it would be a short-lived joy. Live while you can — was the motto of this period.

"To live on" meant to struggle. You had to seize every opportunity. Gradually, as the transports of inmates were leaving the camp, their blankets remained on the bunks. Winter was approaching, and people needed coats. They turned to us, mother and me, the Madritsch seamstresses, to cut and sew these coats for a modest price. We didn't have to learn cutting, we just knew how to cut a coat out of a blanket. We now worked like crazy during the nightshifts, delivering our daily contingent for Madritsch and working on the coats, at the risk of getting caught red-handed. In this way we earned some bread, butter, sugar, eggs and sausage. We cried over this food, tears dripping over sugar or sausage. We cried that we didn't earn them while Witek was alive. We didn't devour these hard-earned victuals. We shared them with friends, and we preserved part of them for the doubtful near future. We should have guessed that we would have no opportunity to consume them, that we would lose them in Auschwitz.

The camp was now in advanced stages of liquidation. Madritsch was helpless. Was he indeed? Didn't Oskar Schindler, the genius, have a solution for both enterprises? Didn't he by then put into high gear the plan of moving his whole factory to Brinlitz in Moravia? Hadn't he proposed to Madritsch and Tutsch to join him in this venture?

But Madritsch was tired of protecting his Jews and bribing the SS officials to the right and left. He was also afraid of a partnership with an adventurer like Schindler.

He also correctly foresaw that it would be a short-term solution. The war would soon be lost for the Germans. He decided to avoid any farther implication. Meanwhile the Schindler list was being compiled. Tutsch fought the last-minute battle, adding from memory to Schindler's list many names of Madritsch employees as he knew them from his Jewish mistress, a girl about my age. But there was someone else who tampered with the Schindler list. Trying to reach this person the camp became like a beehive. It became known that one could buy a place on this life-saving list by paying with diamonds. And who cashed them, who became the "deus ex machine"? — Marcel Goldberg, the cad, my old enemy from the pre-ghetto period. Who will ever know how many diamonds "glided" into Goldberg's pocket, and how many were passed on to Schindler, who needed them to bribe the German top brass officials for the final ratification of his list. Schindler placed on his list many people who didn't have a cent to their name and none of them was skilled in metal and enamel work. He just wanted to save some Jews that he had come to know and like. Among them were the Stern brothers who were his confidants, the two Rosner brothers (including Poldek's wife Hela, Janka's sister) and others. He even included my buddy, Joseph Bau, the skilled graphic artist, but without his newly wed-in-camp wife Rebecca. Joseph was sick with grief, he couldn't foresee that they would eventually survive separately. Our cousins, the three Kornhauser siblings were also on the list, their parents having been killed in the October action in the ghetto. I am mentioning all these names because they will play a role later on in my story.

As for us, we didn't stand the slightest chance to be encompassed by the Schindler list, and didn't give it a thought. We were almost certain that we would perish in the next camp. Thus, it came to pass that in October we were once more rounded up and taken again to the railway station. This time we didn't play tricks. It was amazing to discover that our transport included also all the women marked on the Schindler list. Had they been duped? It is true that the list of women designated to be sent to the Brinlitz factory of Schindler accompanied this group wherever it was moved, but they were just the same incorporated into our transport. All that had probably no bearing on our personal lot.

We were now forcibly hoisted into the almost hermetically sealed carriages of the train. We were stashed like sardines, some hundred and twenty women loaded on one wagon and unable to sit down. Reginka still had her plaster cast on her leg. There was no time to remove it before boarding the train. She was stopped by an SS man who said: "Break it, remove it. If you can march you will live". A cast can be broken but not removed without a cutter. We had to shred it with a stone. Reginka got up and walked straight — into life. She was saved. Once inside the train, we cut the cast patiently with a knife.

The train took us to Auschwitz, or rather to its dependency, to Birkenau. Here some details are foggy and blurry in my memory. I don't see us on the platform of the station. I see us sitting naked for hours on end, hundreds of naked women, clustered in a big hall. We were stripped of everything. The precious victuals, the hard-earned bread and sugar saved and preserved for this unknown future — were taken away. We were left once more with a toothbrush as our only possession. We were expressly allowed to keep it.

SOME ILLUSTRATIONS DRAWN FROM MY MEMORY

Horrible density in a cattle wagon

The scarecrow

Red puppies on a snow carpet

Who will be the first to collapse?

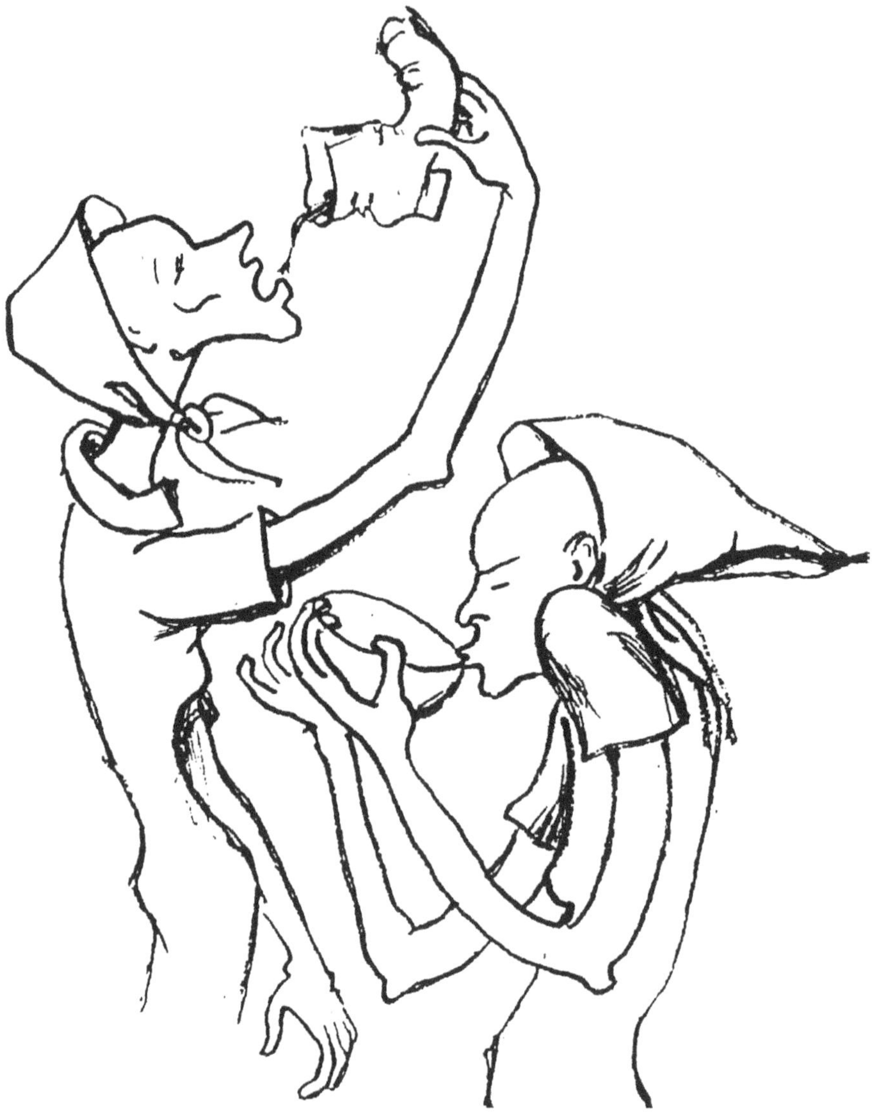

When a prisoner's bowl was stolen...
she had to drink soup from her boot

“The March of Death” during the
evacuation of Auschwitz

200 women enclosed in one class-room

HOW MANY MORE "GOLGOTHAS" ARE THERE BETWEEN *BIRKENAU* AND *AUSCHWITZ*?

A drop of an old lipstick...

I had only one thought; is there an afterlife? Are we going to meet our nearest and dearest? We were almost certain that the moment we enter the showers, gas will be diffused from the pipes, disguised as showers. Here my memory is fragmented; I was probably in a state of shock. I am not even able to remember if the selection took place shortly before the showers or earlier. But I do remember one scene, and I see it. As we thus sat naked for long hours, a door opened once, and a young man in a prisoner's striped suit entered the hall. He carried in his arms several loaves of bread. In the same instant many naked women fell upon him like wild beasts. We didn't even move. We stood with Janka and our group of five, with arms crossed on our breasts. The man fought and chased away the naked hyenas, made a passage for himself, reached us laboriously and handed to us a loaf of bread. He must have chosen us because we had enough pride not to beg for bread while naked. We shared the bread with friends. Other details escape my memory.

I now have to relate the drama of the selection. One of my friends seems to remember that we passed two selections. I remember only one. That's a picture which I see very clearly. We were gradually chased into a second hall, a smaller one. One of the prisoners who pushed us into this hall, batch after batch, said in the passage: "Behave yourselves in front of Dr.Mengele, don't make him angry". Thus, I am certain that it was Dr.Mengele himself who conducted our selection. He was standing behind a small table, guarded from both sides. We had to pass running in front of this table. We were segregated to the right and left; those directed to the left were designated for the gas chambers...

This is the moment to tell a little story. One day I found somewhere a drop of an old lipstick and a little more blush remained at the bottom. I scraped off what was left from the bottom and wrapped it in a little piece of celluloid. Mom and I have used it before selections, to look "more alive"... We took the blush with us, even when we went to the shower, keeping it between our fingers. It was so small that no one could see it.

Coming back to Dr. Mengele and the selection. Mengele was looking intently at the walking, half fainting, women and from time to time stopped a woman who didn't seem to be in good shape. It has to be stressed that in this transport there were certainly no women over forty-three. My dear mother was no more than forty, yet she was so thin and emaciated that she became a real 'Muselman', if you know what this term meant in the camps.

When Mengele stopped her, my heart stopped beating. She was so young in my eyes, I didn't realize that she may be in danger. He made a sign with his finger and asked her an odd question: "What is your profession?" He didn't ask about trade or occupation. There must have been something about my mother, she projected a certain aura. Her blue eyes shone in her thin bony face. She had prominent cheekbones and her teeth were like pearls. He must have noticed it when she opened her mouth to answer. A woman who had been stopped earlier pretended that he didn't mean her. Not my mother. She looked straight at him without hesitation. And what was she going to answer at this crucial moment? She said the simple truth. She said: "I am an artist, a painter". It was risky, in fact it was most dangerous, but it worked. The Germans are cultured people, and Dr. Mengele must have certainly been a lover of fine arts. "Also los" (beat it) — he said. He let my mother pass the selection with a wave of hand.

I was so much in a state of shock, that I don't remember what followed next. I don't remember who were the victims of Mengele's selection, but I do remember one case. It was the peculiar story of Mrs. Thieberger and her sweet daughter Friedka. It was a case rare like ours, where a mother and daughter survived so far together, never separated. Now, during the selection Dr. Mengele looked Mrs. Thieberger over and sent her to the left side, even though she was not underfed. She had but one blemish: a red scar on her breast, left after a phlegmonia from which she had suffered some time before. Her sweet, beautiful daughter Friedka didn't say a word. She just slipped to the left so as to join her mother in death. I didn't notice it. I was still in shock. But I know from their report what happened next. When they were later marched to the hair-shearing before entering the gas chamber, one of the supervisors stopped Friedka and asked what she was doing there. She answered that she was joining her mother. "There is nothing wrong with my mother" — she said — "she just has this old scar". Was he struck by the absurdity of these proceedings or by Friedka's blossoming beauty? Anyhow, he sent them both quickly back to join the women who were to survive, to join us.

We passed together with this mother and daughter through Birkenau and Auschwitz, then I lost track of them and didn't know what happened to them. After the war Mrs. Thieberger emerged in Tel Aviv, but without Friedka. This lovely girl died a few days after the liberation. She had to die of typhoid, after the end of the war, in a liberated camp. That's the irony of fate.

We found ourselves in Birkenau under the chimneys of its crematoria. We entered the showers clasping in our palm our only possession — the toothbrush. But I was holding one more item: the amulet offered to me by Kuba, the amulet spelling "come back". My anthropological bend was already showing by then; I was and still am superstitious. We were naked like Eve but still dressed in our hair. There was probably no time to shave off the hair of those mass-transports of that late period. All that was shaved was the hair of our armpits and pubic hair. For me it was enough of a shock, even though nowadays every woman has to pass through this ordeal before giving childbirth. The showers were real showers, but I can't say that we enjoyed them. Still, we were alive. There was even a mark of life imprinted on us — the tattoo number. Mine was (and still is) A-26551. When you admire sailors carrying tattoo drawings, you consider them real heroes. There is nothing heroic in receiving a tattoo mark. It is only painful, but one can bear it rather easily. None of us screamed, none whined. It is done with a fountainpen of sorts. The pricking doesn't reach the blood vessels, it only leaves the ink dots under the skin.

Now besides the toothbrush we had a number, but we were still naked. When we came to Birkenau, we even had a coat. It bore a red-painted stripe running along its back, to mark a prisoner and prevent his escape. Now we were handed a pair of panties and a rag that pretended to be a dress. Nobody cared if it fitted. It was October, and we were given summer dresses. The huge Mrs. Hilfstein received a skimpy, narrow dress of fine thin georgette, that she could hardly squeeze herself into. A tiny person was given a loose sack. Believe it or not, but when we saw this travesty, when we saw each other in these queer rags — we exploded in laughter. We laughed so drunkenly that tears were streaming from our eyes. Then we cried. Then we laughed some more. Weak people do that, and we were not only weak but in a state of shock too. Dressed in these rags, sticking to our bodies still wet from the showers, we were driven through the dark streets and into the barracks. We were used to barracks, but these were different. It was permanently dark inside. There were only small windows under the ceiling. The air was stifling, the stench permeated the whole barrack, hanging there for years as if the barrack had never been aired. You would never believe that living human bodies could smell so foul. And there was even worse. The air outside the barracks was permanently permeated with the stench of burnt flesh from the crematoria. Add to it the foul air of swamps, and thus you could never get a whiff of fresh air into your nostrils.

Birkenau was a town of many streets and many rows of barracks, gray from the outside and graphite gray inside. Even the planks and the faces were gray. The "Blockateste" of Birkenau, ruling over us inmates, were a special breed. They were young Slovak girls, who after some time spent in Birkenau had been so brain-washed that they became like wild beasts. They never spoke, they yelled on top of their hoarse voices. They never walked, they jumped like big apes. When we had to get up in the morning and were all drowsy from lack of air and from hunger, the block commander jumped from bunk to bunk, from the lowest bunk to the top bunk. She pulled our hair, slapped our faces, pinched our chins with her claws. There were some women who didn't get up even when beaten blue. They didn't rise because they were dead. There were others who got up, swayed and collapsed. Most women of Birkenau were already 'muselmans'. You could learn anatomy on these living corpses; the bones were hardly dressed with skin over the protruding joints of these walking skeletons.

In Plaszow a sick person had a chance to recover and a dispensary to turn to, even if it was highly dangerous to be hospitalized. Here the dispensary was a legend. Whoever fell ill, whoever fainted — his fate was sealed. The corpses were quietly carried away without much ado.

We heard from some old-timers (there were hardly any left) the well-known story of a woman who arrived pregnant at Birkenau. Dr.Mengele had set his eye on her. In this case he didn't send the woman to the gas chambers. He had a brilliant idea. He decided to conduct an experiment on her. He gave the block commander strict orders to inform him when the woman delivered. He was absolutely certain that this pregnant walking cadaver would have no milk in her breasts. He didn't suspect that the poor mother moistened her kerchief and gave it to the baby to suck, and Mengele was curious to find out for how long a human newborn can survive unfed. As it was, the baby survived three days and three nights. On the fourth day, the woman was secretly visited by a doctor. This good lady explained to the unhappy mother that having sworn the oath of Hippocrates she was not allowed to kill, but would the mother wish to spare her baby this terrible agony, she as the physician, would provide her with a lethal injection. The desperate mother gave her baby the fatal injection with her own hand — and the baby went quietly to sleep. When Mengele came for his daily inspection, he was shown the little corpse. He never learned the truth and must have noted that the lifespan of an unfed newborn is no more than three days. That was the story related to us.

We wondered now what would become of us. We were utterly superfluous here in Birkenau. There was no work for us, and we were constantly astonished to be still alive. Day after day, we had to leave the barrack at dawn and were unable to return to it after the rollcall. The barrack had to be clean and empty, ready for inspection. To walk through the streets of the Birkenau camp was dangerous, to hide impossible. But somebody "cared" for us, we were eventually employed. Birkenau was situated on swamps. The streets were covered with a thick layer of mud. It reached our ankles. We were given spades and pails to gather the thick mud, and to carry it out beyond the barracks. That it plowed back and returned to the same places — was of no importance. On other days we were ordered to carry long boards from one heap to another. Then we were ordered to carry them back to the same heap. It reminded us of the myth about the toils of Sisyphus.

The humid cold was penetrating and chilling us to the bones. The worst were the rollcalls. We were already experienced from Plaszow how to protect ourselves from cold, how to stomp our feet and flap our arms, but over there we were clothed in summer dresses in October, November. Now, during the rollcalls we had to cling to each other — all five of us — one entwining the body of the other in front of her. The fifth, the last one, suffered the most not being protected from behind. We took turns. We had no watches, but we developed a perfect sense of timing. All these maneuvers were, of course, possible only when we were unobserved.

In the evening hours, after the rollcall, we were at last free to move on our own. Once, after the distribution of bread, I decided to visit Leica. Leica has been not just separated from us, she has been — I would say — castrated. She was one of the few in our transport whose head was shaved. The vicious Slovaks must have done it to her because she had such a perfect body. Leica was as if paralyzed with shame. She shunned us, her best friends, she became depressive. I wanted to visit, to comfort her and to share my bread with her. When I passed through the muddy, dark streets, clutching my portion of bread under my armpit, I was suddenly seized by strong arms, and dragged into a side-street behind a barrack. My bread was snatched from me, my arms were raised, and my dress lifted. I was attacked by the Gypsies and was being undressed by them. Passing the thin fabric of my dress through their greedy fingers, they decided that it wasn't worthy while, this dress couldn't be sold for bread. It saved me. Because I screamed, they had probably no time to take my wooden solid shoes, which were not so bad at all and were to carry me into freedom, through two marches of death. A coarse claw-like hand clamped my mouth, while the other Gypsies fled with my bread. Witches are but rosebuds compared to them. They have been systematically "exterminated" by the thousands in Birkenau and the wild beasts, my assailants, were the last specimens of their breed. Despite the part-time work, this absurd slavery, it was clear to us that even though we had been given a number — our days were numbered. We shall soon be sent elsewhere, or we shall perish in the gas chambers on a day (any day) when not enough transports will be supplied to fill the crematoria to maximum capacity. Here I have to explain a technicality. The crematoria had to work around the clock. If the permanent high temperature were to drop, it would cost much fuel to let it rise again. If not enough corpses from the incoming transports were fed to the crematoria, the contingent had to be filled by catching the local inmates and feeding them to the Moloch. There was even a 'block of death', where the potential victims were "stored" until needed.

We would be the best candidates. The number tattooed on the inside of our forearm and also printed on a strip of white cotton and sewn to our dresses — had only one meaning: that we had passed through Birkenau and had been registered there. It was not a guarantee of survival.

It came to pass one day that we were caught, mother and I. We were encircled and driven into the block of death. Not our whole group, just the two of us. That it was the block of death we knew, we had been informed by the veteran inmates. If I am not mistaken it was block number 23. It was empty of bunks and almost hermetically sealed. It was pitch dark inside, the air and light slipping only through small apertures under the high ceiling. We had been told that we constituted the reserve for the crematoria, it was no secret, the old-timers enlightened us. It was only the question of a rational timetable. After all, the incinerators worked at a rate of some 4,700 corpses, turned to ashes day by day.

We all sat on the concrete floor, some women wailing, some pulling their hair, others swaying like in trance. Here again I have a black hole in my memory. I have lost the count of time — I don't remember if we spent there twenty-four hours or perhaps only eight hours. But I do remember exactly the scraps of our conversation, which was so typical for mother and me. Mother wouldn't give up, never. She said: "Look around you, concentrate and think. There must be a way". I explained patiently that thousands must have passed through this block of death and none was known to have escaped. I pointed to the concrete floor, to the high ceiling and the few windows below the ceiling.

Mother said accentuating every word: "Stop thinking in the negative, think positive. A human ladder could reach one of the narrow windows beneath the ceiling. A human ladder could also reach this narrow shelf of sorts, formed between the top of the wall and the ceiling. One cannot hide there, but the Germans would never think of looking up, being so busy with supervising this crowd." For a moment she ran out of further ideas. What was I to answer? I explained patiently that these women were not trained for circus performances, neither were we. We could never reach the top of the human pyramid. And what about the bottom? Who would volunteer to be at the bottom of the pyramid? After all — I added — I was born a fatalist. Ergo, why should we survive, if our nearest and dearest didn't.

"Our nearest and dearest" — said mother mimicking me cruelly — "must have chosen you to survive. That must have been their last wish". I objected in the same sarcastic tone, replying: "That couldn't be true. In our patronymic society a female is of no importance, she couldn't carry on the proud family name". Mother kept doggedly on, insisting: "You have to fight, you haven't lived yet". I kept my ground. The eternal fatalist in me prodded me to prove to mother that I have lived after all. I have known a home, a warm family, I have received basic education, I have been skiing and dancing and laughing. I have known friendship and I have tasted love. I haven't known the marital bliss, and I haven't brought a child into this cruel world. I have had a short-condensed life, and what of it. End of speech. I have used up all my arguments. All of a sudden, I felt like embracing my mother and telling her that I love her. But I didn't and I felt ashamed of it.

Mother was hardly listening. She was already brewing a new scheme. She will provoke and organize a general uprising in this fatal block 23. The moment the wide door will open, all the women will burst out, disperse and run for their life, run in all directions. Half of them will be shot, but the other half will mix with the inmates of Birkenau and never be found out. We are not even registered in this barrack, there will be no evidence. I let her spin this plan, there was some logic in it.

I let her try. She rose from the ground, she started to strike her tin bowl with her spoon so as to overcome the noise made by all the weeping and wailing women and to attract their attention. She even opened her speech asking for a moment of concentration. Right then, in the general silence that followed… the door opened, and an SS warden entered. She posted herself in the empty space close to the door, empty because everybody kept away from this door to death. She said simply: "You are free to get out… you can now all return to your barracks". That was all. We were ostensibly free, but nobody moved. We all thought that it must be a trap, a trick to make us get out quietly and then be driven to the gas chambers. The door remained ajar and there was nobody in sight. Unbelievable as it was, we were indeed free to remain incarcerated in Birkenau and survive for a while. As we were explained later, a whole train from Belgium had arrived at the station just in time to save us, the victims taking our place in the gas chambers. I was to befriend later one of the girls from this transport, a girl my age, who lost her parents and siblings, being the only one of her whole family to pass the selection.

A researcher of psychological traumas would like to know what the aftermath and the impact of such an experience is. I can only state that I felt a masochistic satisfaction. I was probably glad that we went through the same hell through which had gone father and Witek. We were spared the last crucial moments before the death — that is true — but we had at least passed a part of this corridor to extinction.

I have to confess that in certain situations, I had not much desire to survive. I was too tired of life. If it weren't for my mother, I probably wouldn't have survived.

We had spent in Birkenau no more than some three weeks, but every minute there must have been equal in intensity of sensations to one hour of life or more. It was November, and the cold and hunger seemed to become unbearable. Little did we know what more fate had in store for us. I had some regrets that we didn't die after all. But then, all of a sudden, in an instant shift of mood I would catch myself laughing. It took but a trifle to make us cry or to make us laugh. But you will certainly laugh at that one: once at a rollcall a warden appeared in front of us. She passed along the lines calling in German in a loud voice: "Werspielt Geige?" (Who plays the violin?). She repeated it several times, but nobody reacted. A woman in front of me turned to her friend and asked her in Yiddish: "Vus is a Geige?" (What is 'Geige'?). Her friend looked at her with disdain and replied haughtily: "Die veisst night vus is 'Geige'? Geige is a 'Piane'" (Don't you know what is a 'Geige'? A violin is a Piano). We laughed so hilariously that even now, whenever I tell this anecdote, I shake with laughter every time.

At the rollcalls in Birkenau we were always in the company of these Plaszow women included in the Schindler list and designated to be sent to Brinlitz in Moravia. They were by then worried to death. Did Schindler abandon them? Was the list that still accompanied them valid no more and disregarded here in Birkenau? Had they been duped, and would they have to share our most precarious lot? As for us, we were much less agitated, we had no hopes and nothing to lose — except life.

One day, as we are standing at the rollcall, something strange happens in a matter of minutes. An SS man of high rank, elderly, tall and dry, walks along our lines, calling out in German: "Gibt es da irgendwelche Kunstmalerinen and Kunstgewerlerinen?" (Are there among you any painters or art craftsmen?). It is a very strange question when asked in Birkenau.

What are we, the artists, to do? It may be an invitation to gas chamber because artists are certainly superfluous people in this constellation. But Rosie Kornhauser, who was on the Schindler list and stood behind my mother, whispered quickly to us: "You'd better volunteer, both of you, it must be something real, whatever it may mean". We looked at each other, we had only seconds to decide — and we stepped out. After us, some twenty women volunteered too, none of them an arts and crafts worker, let alone an artist. And who would be among them? the Tenzer women... of course. Mama Tenzer, Karola and the wicked Frieda, the one who was Finkelstein's mistress.

The SS man noted down the names and the personal numbers on his list. As it will later transpire, he didn't put down the name of mama Tenzer. We were now informed that we shall be moved this very instant. We had no time to say goodbye to all the other women, we were spirited away. Janka was of course with us, though we still didn't know if it was for life or for death.

We were marching out of Birkenau, rushed in an unknown direction. We speculated if the gas chambers were also situated outside of Birkenau. After a couple of kilometers, we were stopped in front of a gate. It was made of twisted iron and it bore the enigmatic inscription "Arbeit macht frei" (Work liberates). We were kept waiting for some time. We consoled Janka who had been separated from her sister. Hela was on the Schindler list, and it was not clear what will become of her... or of us. We had now time to speculate. One of the elected women had a theory: If this SS man who picked us over there is serious in his endeavor — he can only need us for one purpose. He will make us decorate with ornaments the lampshades made of human skin... By that time, it was no secret that the Germans are producing soap made of human fat, and that they place orders for lampshades made of tanned human skin. That would be the secret of our employment, this theory made sense, nothing else did... In those days whenever friends parted, they used to say: "See you soon, we shall probably meet as two cakes of soap on a shelf..." This cynical, macabre joke was very much in the spirit of the ancient greeting of Roman soldiers to Caesar: "Ave Caesar, morituri te salutant" — "Farewell Caesar, those about to die are greeting you".

As I said, we were now waiting in front of the famous gate with the famous inscription. Seen against the evening sky, this black inscription was still visible. Where were we? We wondered. We were counted. The total number of women in our group didn't tally with the list. There was one more. It was mama Tenzer, who had not been included and had clandestinely joined her two daughters... The SS men at the gate were impatient, after all we were only passing from one camp to another. One more was no problem; it would be clarified the next day. We were let in.

Wonder of wonders, we found ourselves in a regular town. There were in front of us clean streets and solid buildings of red brick. Prisoners in clean striped suits were walking in the street. "Where are we?" — we whispered to a passing man. "Don't you really know? You are in Auschwitz" — he answered. So now we knew...

As we were marched slowly along the main street, I raised my head. I noticed two brightly illuminated windows, and inside the room what did I see? I saw a whole assortment of musical instruments hanging on the wall. I pinched myself to make sure that I am not dreaming, but the picture did not fade away. I couldn't know that there was an orchestra in Auschwitz, nobody told us about it in Birkenau.

We entered now deeper and deeper into this camp of men, and we were stopped in front of a building bearing the inscription 'Badeanstalt' (bathhouse). A bathhouse is fine with us, we like that, but unfortunately it had a chimney. If it has a chimney, it could prove to be a crematorium. There can be a gas chamber disguised as shower room and annexed to a crematorium. We had been told in Birkenau that one crematorium was destroyed by the underground, but we knew that there were others, and this could be one of them, situated in the heart of Auschwitz.

We entered with much trepidation. We were not the only group, there were others. We were ordered to disrobe, and we were allowed to keep... the toothbrush. The scenario was familiar, but there was a new lament to it. This time we were given, each of us, a cake of soap. It had been used before. We were told that we shall have to return it after the shower. Was it reassuring? not very much. We tried to bolster our courage by making fun of it. We shook hands with friends, uttering this macabre sentence: "We shall soon meet as cakes of soap on a shelf". We were now in the shower room and... real warm water besprinkled us from above. We were in euphoria. We soaped our bodies, we played with water, we were saved once more. When we emerged from the showers, I kept in my hand the eternal toothbrush and the amulet from Kuba, the amulet which will accompany me to the liberation and to Paris. We came out naked and wet, and what did we see? A free passage in the middle, and on both sides of the passage stood young gentlemen in striped suits, each holding a towel in his hand. Each of us was greeted by a smiling gentleman, handing to her politely a clean towel... The gentlemen were French, and they said to us in the local mixed lingo composed of three languages: "Mademoiselle, panienka, bitteschon, nehmen Serviette, proszebardzo". If reduced to the basic it meant: "Miss, take a towel please". We dried ourselves at leisure, we could hardly believe that it was happening to us.

This exhilarating scenario had an explanation, which I can provide now, being much more knowledgeable. This bathhouse was run by a team of Frenchmen, political prisoners. Being granted this secure position, they were in good health and had preserved their natural French sense of humor. They seemed to enjoy this performance, and that was the background of this unusual reception that we received in Auschwitz.

Here again I have to stress that it was not typical for the entire camp of Auschwitz. This was Auschwitz One, the model camp, a golden cage, a cocoon. It was kept spotless, and run by healthy, good-looking prisoners. This for a very special important reason. Would a commission of the International Red Cross ask permission to visit a concentration camp, it will see this exemplary model camp and find it run in best order, peopled by healthy prisoners, kept in good, humane conditions... We, of course, did not know it then, we were to learn about Dr. Mengele later.

We passed on to the next hall. Here we were once more given summer dresses, but not tatters. They were not adapted in size, but what does it matter. We laughed again, like we did the first time in Birkenau, when we saw each other in travesty clothes. This time we did not laugh and cry, we only laughed.

We were now back in 'town', and this town was composed of many compounds, separated by barbed wire. We were being handed over from one compound to another, this one a women's camp. We entered a building, a block, we did not know yet that this was a temporary abode. The young block commander received our group, accompanied by the list drawn up by the SS man who engaged us. We learnt that his name was Deutscher, and that he will expect us tomorrow to show up for work. There was, however, a problem. There was in our group one woman more than noted on the list, and as you remember, it was mama Tenzer. But rely on the Tenzer women, they could always manage. They entered into conversation with the block commander, they asked her politely where she came from… they whispered something into her ear. They were now invited into her private room, they were making a deal with her. What the deal was about would become easy to guess. Indeed, the next morning at the rollcall the list of Deutscher's employees was handed by the block commander to the SS warden, and when she read it, it became evident that mama Tenzer is in and my mother, who was the first one on the list, is out…! The trick was transparent, the block commander must have manipulated and doctored the list.

My mother had now nothing to lose. We approached the SS warden and mother tried to explain that her name must be missing by mistake, this fact can be easily checked on the Obersturmfuhrer's original list — she added. But the warden wouldn't listen. "Tau ab" (get lost) — she yelled and stroke my mother with her whip. Mother disappeared for a while and then, when the warden wasn't looking, she sneaked back into the lines. Nothing happened. Our group was now kept waiting and freezing for a long time after everybody else had left.

At long last, Obersturmfuhrer Deutscher came to receive his flock. He threw one glance at us, turned purple and exclaimed: "So these are the clothes that they have been given?!!! Didn't I expressly ask for decent clothing suitable for work in the model camp?" The SS woman smiled a conspirator smile and said: "You give orders and the scum at the bathhouse disregard them. You better give them hell". That he will do, prodded by her. There was now no question of the list. We were simply driven back to the same compound and the same unit in the bathhouse, which distributed the dresses. We shall eventually be outfitted with slightly better… summer dresses. But not yet. These people over there were not afraid of Deutscher, he had no authority over them. They dragged their feet, kept us waiting. We were standing naked inside an enclosure, separated only by a rope from the rest of the hall. Some men in striped suits were passing to and fro. Mama Tenzer pressed her overflowing naked body to the rope, she tried to catch the eye of two men. She tried to enmesh them in a conversation in this way: "Do I not know you? You seem familiar. If you don't remember me, you must remember my two lovely daughters (she extends two fingers in a 'V' sign). Karola, Frieda, come here, come quickly to meet these gentlemen" — she prodded the daughters, still holding her fingers in the 'V' sign.

The two prominent prisoners were amused. They smiled at Karola and Frieda, they invited them to step over the rope. They took them to a side room; the two couples disappeared. We waited and waited. We even amused ourselves by adopting for the Tenzer women the 'V' sign, as made by mama Tenzer. From then on, we shall never mention their names, we shall just make the 'V' sign with two fingers.

Karola and Frieda returned. The two men gave a sign to the women behind the counter, and we were all given other dresses. They were hardly better or more fitting, but what did I care when I was still so concerned with the damn problem of the list and my mother's missing name. This time I decided to make a clear breast of it. I approached the Tenzer daughters and said: "I have seen through your trick with the list, but it is not going to work, I promise you. I only regret that I felt pity for you when your mother was rejected by Deutscher. The way I feel now I am ready to take my revenge. I am ready to unmask your maneuver, and I shall spill it to Deutscher at the first opportunity". I have had my say.

We were now sent to the other compound. Sometime elapsed, we waited in front of our block, shivering in our summer dresses. At last, Deutscher came to take us over. The block commander rushed to him in one leap. She pushed the doctored phony list under his nose. He waved her off, he had his own list. Here my mother's name was first, and mama Tenzer was not mentioned. The Tenzer daughters remonstrated with Deutscher; they begged him to add their mother to the group. Their argument was that she had taught them arts and crafts and all their skills (as if they had any). He was not a bad man, he gave in and added her name to his list. Thus ended our first day in Auschwitz, a very long day.

THE SMOKESCREEN OF A MODEL CAMP IN *AUSCHWITZ*

On the next morning we were transferred to another compound and another block of this model camp, namely the women's compound in the men's camp. We were to remain there till the end of our 'career' in Auschwitz.

I can state without exaggeration that our new block was resplendent (being situated in a model camp). The three tiers of bunks were arranged and decorated according to a color scheme; all the first-floor bunks were covered solely with pink blankets, the second-floor bunks only with blue blankets, and the third only with flowery ones. Can you believe it? Yet it was true. The soft blankets had to be stretched as precisely as if straightened with a ruler, but we were used already from Plaszow to this precision. The commander — we were informed by the old-timers — was demanding, but just.

The spotlessly clean washing block was decorated with two huge fresco paintings on the wall. The first painting represented a dressed girl washing her neck with her fingertips, the second a naked girl scrubbing her body thoroughly. The respective inscriptions under the two paintings read: "Not this way — but this way". The model camp prided itself of being lice-free. The latrine was also nonplus ultra. Only the food remained scarce and nondescript. One day we were fed a good solid soup. The knowledgeable ones knew to explain that an inspection commission was due to arrive on that day, which explained it.

On the next day the tragicomedy of the list was to plague and endanger us once more. The list doctored by our former commander reappeared. Once more mother had to explain and base her claim on Deutscher's authority.

This time it worked because a different SS warden checked our ranks. The subterfuge of the Tenzers was not mentioned. I gave up my revenge; I must have been born like "The good soul of Setshouan".

We were now eventually delivered to Deutscher and our situation became clear at last. We were sent to work in the camp's printing workshop, run by Obersturmfuhrer Deutscher. This printing house (serving the entire huge Auschwitz camp) occupied two floors of a solid brick building. From the moment we entered the premises, Deutscher must have been eager to test and sift his stable of new acquisitions and segregate the women according to their ability and skill. We were brought to one huge room. Deutscher appeared accompanied by his deputy, SS Unterscharfuhrer Bodnerash. This Bodnerash was a Rumanian Volksdeutscher, who was fortunate enough to get this convenient position. From now on he will be our supervisor and report to Deutscher on all our activities.

Not knowing what was expected of her, mother decided to draw a portrait of a woman sitting opposite, and to paint a watercolor landscape too. As for me, I knew that I was good at drawing but did not know how to use oils. I couldn't pretend to be a painter. I made a plan for myself. I decided to make for the new boss a letterbox of cardboard, to be used for sorting of the incoming post.

I drew and cut out the figure of Hermes, the messenger of Gods (the Germans like mythology), carrying a huge portfolio of many compartments. I prepared captions for every compartment, big or small, but I didn't yet paste them, leaving the final decision to Deutscher. I supposed that a rational division for the incoming post would have to be the following: "General matters", "Special Departments", "Urgent matters", "Private letters", "Reminders", "Plans for Future" and "Miscellaneous". It took me less than three hours, and here was my model in front of me. Everybody admired it. None of the women and girls were capable of producing anything approaching my model, they had no skills whatever.

I quickly helped Janka to make a prestigious book cover, others tried to imitate her work. The Tenzer women produced nothing at all. Mama Tenzer pretended to be in command and distributed the utensils, as if anybody needed her services.

Minutes after the deadline, Deutscher returned to the premises. He had hardly entered the room when something unexpected happened this very moment. The shrewd Frieda snatched and took hold of my model, rushed with it quickly across the room, and presented it to Deutscher, asking innocently: "Herr Chef, gefallt es ihnen?" (Boss, do you like it?). He admired my model, he was full of praise — and I felt as if I had a primus burner in my chest. I was so aghast that I lost my power of speech. And indeed, what could I say in these circumstances?

Meanwhile Deutscher moved over to the three artists. They sat together in one corner, next to the paints. He passed slowly from one to another, he checked thoroughly their work, he rubbed his hands, he asked many questions. As it will later transpire, Deutscher had need only for the real artists, the rest of us would constitute auxiliary forces in printing, and... a camouflage for his real plans. I was to fit in between the two categories. You must now be curious what were his real secret plans for the artist painters, but he was not going to reveal them yet.

He returned to my model, now placed again in front of me. "Who made it?" — he asked. "I did" — I replied, noticing that Frieda had disappeared. "But it isn't true, it isn't yours" — said Deutscher piercing me with his cold grey eyes. Here Bodnerash looked over his shoulder and remarked: "It is hers all right, I saw her work on it". Deutscher said nothing because a German doesn't apologize to a Jewess. He carefully inspected the model, listened to my explanations, opened the compartments, made one suggestion, but was in general very pleased with my idea and its execution. He ordered me to write his rank and name on the top of the portfolio, to put the finishing touches and hand the model to Bodnerash. "That's fine" — he said — "As from tomorrow you will work in the special department of prestigious book-covers, you will work under Kertesh, the Hungarian. Your additional task will be to teach Kertesh German. I have to be able to communicate with him". Thus, I was given a double assignment.

Before I am going to describe the pattern of my collaboration with Kertesh, I have to reveal and explain Deutscher's main game, the game of exploiting the artistic talents of his three women-painters. Deutscher was not stupid, in fact he was a genius of sorts. His plan was based on a careful scrutiny of books on Polish art. Most of the national paintings had been plundered by the Germans. Deutscher had no such opportunities, so he decided to procure for himself forgeries... He chose from the books not the most famous paintings, but the second best. He gave the chosen reproductions to his three painters, ordering them to execute "authentic" copies, exact to the minutest detail, down to the size as noted in the books. The copies had to be so perfect that nobody would detect the hoax of forgery. I can presume that he planned to "sit" on the forgeries for some time, and then — after the war — sell his treasures as originals bought (or rather pillaged) in Poland. The books with the reproductions would prove how valuable and prestigious were the paintings in his possession. Under the circumstances nobody would have any reason to doubt their authenticity.

He provided his artists (including my mother) with the best materials and equipment. He was, however, aware that if German officials would enter the premises and detect the employment of the artists — his secret would be out of the bag. He therefore prepared for them a clever subterfuge. He took them to his office, swore them to secrecy and explained that they were to work close to a table with a double top. They had to watch the door (situated at the far end of this huge room). At the first sight of an intruder they would have to fold the easel in one movement and slip it quickly into the compartment of the double table. They would then pretend to be occupied with other works, spread on the top of the table. He mumbled something about the copies being a surprise for the high commander, but he knew that they knew that he knew that they knew — that it wasn't true.

I had the opportunity to watch my mother working on such a forgery. The reproduction was divided on transparent paper into a net of squares, each and every square to be reproduced in drawing and then painted with oils. During her "career" in Auschwitz mother executed three major art-forgery works, the other two painters did likewise, as far as I remember. The last work was not finished when we were evacuated from Auschwitz and started the march of death.

The artists were aware that their secret constituted a danger. Wouldn't Deutscher have to "liquidate" them so as not to leave witnesses to his forgeries? Janka was delegated to work on the printing press. Many secret orders and circulars were printed there and she too considered herself endangered. The situation was becoming ambivalent; this paradise of clean, light work could turn into the ante chamber of death. As for me, my personal paradise had also several pitfalls and shady corners, even though Kertesh proved to be a very sympathetic boss to work with. He was a small bald man with innocent blue eyes, dumb as an ox, but an excellent bookbinder. He was too dumb to learn German. There was no other way, I had to learn some Hungarian, so as to translate between him and Deutscher. I have forgotten it in the last forty-two years, but I still remember a few words and this strange accent on the first syllable. Counting to ten is quite melodious, especially the "nyols, kilens, tiz" — the eight, nine ten. I still remember how to say "nokom van keveshkenyer" (I have a little bread), because this was the main topic of our conversations.

To work with Kertesh was quite thrilling, but he had two assistants who were not my cup of tea. They were two gentile Poles from Silesia, both by name of Joseph, both arrogant and vulgar. Their style of speech in Polish was constantly interwoven with "pioruna, piorunska, piorunowata" refuting constantly to thunder (may the thunder strike you). Out of boredom, they started to pay too much attention to me. They would ogle me, smacking their lips and exchanging some vulgar remarks. The big Joseph would ask the little Joseph: "How about this snippet of a woman Marysia, how do you think she would be in bed?" Little Joseph took my measure and answered slowly: "Hm, hm, not bad at all after you have fed her for a while. She would know how to wiggle her tail... but brother, you would lose a lot of time searching for her under a fluffy eiderdown". A passing Polish gentleman saved my reputation by saying: "She wouldn't know much about sex, but being so skilled in taking exact measure, she would know where to kick you". I could hardly mind, I had grown a thick skin.

The two Josephs were nagging and mocking Kertesh too. One of them said: "Kurva this Kertesh". 'Kurva' means 'whore' in Polish. They didn't suspect that it might be the same word in Hungarian. Hearing this, pithed Kertesh raised his innocent blue eyes to the ceiling and asked, this time in perfect German: "Warum is Kertesh Kurva?" — (why is Kertesh a whore?) — without punishing them.

Not everybody was vulgar in our surroundings. There was also place for some nobler feelings. There was even a pathetic, platonic love blooming in Auschwitz. The inmates came from many countries and diverse social strata, but they all seemed to need an outlet for bottled up emotions, because "people need people" and they need love. It often came to pass that a girl met once, and only once, a boy, a total stranger, and they felt such an instant mutual attraction that, unable to meet again, they started to write letters to each other. Some of such couples didn't even have any language in common and each wrote in his or her mother tongue, both using the services of a translator. They also needed a postman, a go-between, who had opportunities to deliver the letters from one compound to another. The epistolary art was blooming. People who had never been great letter-writers, now poured out their hearts on paper.

There was even a name to the game. Polish, French, Hungarian or German prisoners fancied the Polish word "Kochany" — the beloved one — and used it. A Belgian girl in my block would ask me in French: "Do you have a 'Kochany'?". It became an institution, an escape from the brutal actual world into a world of romanticism. In a way it helped to survive. Just imagine romances in the shadow of crematoria.

We, the women employed in the printing workshop, were the main suppliers of paper to the 'litterati', the letter-writers. Stealing paper was not very dangerous, we were not searched when leaving the premises. We willingly undertook this little service. The effusive, poetic letters clashed with the gloomy reality. The crematoria were still operated at full speed, and those people wrote perhaps their dream about a rose garden while inhaling the stench of burning flesh.

There were also other smells in these sterile, clean surroundings. Next to me worked a pale, thin, silent Jewish girl, Ilse. She smelled constantly of pus or putrefaction. She was sitting there, hardly able to work, rotting and eaten up from inside by some mysterious infection. As I was to learn eventually, she had been the victim of Dr. Mengele's medical experiments. I don't know what had been done to her womb. After all the experiments, a good soul must have arranged for her to be sent to work in our workshop. It was hard to stand her stench, it raised a wall of silence around her. Nobody asked questions and she spoke to nobody. I didn't dare to break the seal of her secret, and to what purpose, if I couldn't help. She must have died quietly, she just disappeared from our horizon.

Following the revelations on the Mengele experiments, we were struck with ricochet of another information. We were told that Dr. Mengele also kept a "stable" of children to experiment on. My mother jumped. She thought at once of whom? My brother Witek, of course. Perhaps he has been taken out of the transport. Being so unusual, perhaps he was picked by somebody and chosen to survive. If there are any children in Auschwitz, there is still a chance that he is among them — thought my tormented mother. She started once more to spin plans and build hopes. She had to send out feelers, she said. There worked in our storage room a certain Meir, a man for all seasons. Mother thought that he would make a good scout, he could sniffle around. Karola was flirting with him. Sometimes they disappeared in the storage room, for obvious reasons. Mother planned to approach him. She would offer him her bread ration for several days — she said to me — if he could come up with some specific information concerning the children in Auschwitz. Should I or could I restrain her? Before she found the opportunity to start on this new venture, we received the desired information from other quarters. According to this source there remained in the children compound only small children, and they were mostly twins, because Dr.Mengele was curious and speculating if one could transplant their organs from one to another, or if one could change brown eyes into blue eyes. Thus, we didn't need Meir's help after all, and mother's wild hopes collapsed once more.

This Meir had wide connections. He even had a special relationship with Deutscher's deputy, the Rumanian SS man Bodnerash. Bodnerash, uncertain of his lot, was drinking heavily. One day, when Deutscher was away, having gone to Berlin, Bodnerash took the Jew Meir aside and being half plastered made a confession to him."I promised my wife"- he said —"that I shall not go on solitary drinking. So, I declare you my partner". They were drinking for a while in the storeroom, then Bodnerash, drunk as Lot, felt a compulsion to spill his secret. His position was quite precarious; he could be sent any moment to the Russian front — he blubbered — it was driving him crazy. Not being much of a specialist in printing, he was vulnerable. However, would Deutscher refuse to shelter and protect him, or would he drag his feet — he, Bodnerash, could divulge and spill Deutscher's secret, ergo his forgery studio. That was his trump card, but how was he going to play it, how could he blackmail Deutscher without straining the mistrustful relationship? All these thoughts he disclosed to Meir, who repeated them to Karola, who told it to our group.

In this big house of red brick were situated two more workshops besides the camp's printing shop, which occupied the basement and the ground floor. The building was kept immaculately clean. We had to take turns in cleaning the premises. I was once sent to take care of the staircase. While I was polishing the windowpanes, a good-looking young man from another workshop was washing the stairs. He started a light conversation with me, which was to turn eventually into something much more serious.

How shall I describe him? His name was Ulrique. He was a Jew brought up in Vienna, who escaped with his family from Austria after its annexation to Germany. He was quite a Parisian before the war. He became also quite an "Auschwitzian" by the time I am speaking of. Having been of non-French origin, he was among the first Jews to be sent from Paris to Auschwitz. Being an old-timer, he had the early opportunity to learn some Polish in the camp. He picked it up first from the University professors, who had been the first victims deported by the Germans to Auschwitz, in the hope that breaking the spirit of "intelligentsia" would prevent an uprising (They were all invited to a conference, encircled and swept straight to the camp). Later Ulrique learned some more Polish from a wave of proletarians and scum. He distinguished between the two kinds of Polish, but in order to amuse me he addressed me in a mixture of both. We soon discovered that we both knew French and German, and we had no problem of communicating during this half hour of our first encounter, or later.

He was my senior by some six years. He had Slavic cheekbones and a snub nose, but a dark Mediterranean coloring matched with coffee black eyes. He was pale and slim, but his eyes projected the internal dynamism. That his manners were perfect came to expression in this very first encounter. Before we had to part and return to our respective working places, he said to me: "You have to forgive me that after such an unexpected short acquaintance, I shall dare propose to you to correspond with me. We can exchange letters slipping them from hand to hand every morning on the staircase, when both groups enter the premises. If we don't meet, you can slip the letter to any one of my team, he will deliver it to me. I shall do likewise". I have agreed with un-lady-like speed, and thus I acquired myself a "Kochany" too.

Our correspondence was composed of many facets, uncovering, layer by layer, our innermost feelings. But there was never in our letters a syrupy sentence like: "I love you, I am longing for you, I wish I could embrace you". There was never the slightest romantic innuendo. Ulrique knew how to console me like one consoles a little child. When I sounded pessimistic, he reminded me of the well-known fable about a frog drowning in a jug full of milk. The frog kept swimming until the milk turned into butter and it was able to climb out of the jug. The moral of the story is understandable, and it was well applied to the circumstances. We exchanged such letters almost daily. When did I have time to write? In the evening, sitting on our uppermost bunk, with the worm lamp on the ceiling next to my head. This lamp was like a friend. At this period I was to acquire another new friend. One day I was accosted near my bunk by an unknown lovely girl. "Excuse me, are you employed in the printing workshop?" — she asked. When I nodded, she wanted to know if I understood French. Then she added with a disarming smile that she had picked me at the first glance from among the others, because I simply looked friendly. Her name was Ruth and she was from Frankfurt-am Main. After this introduction she explained her plea. She had a "Kochany", working in our building, close to our workshop. She had met him only once and they had been exchanging letters for several months, never having met again. Rene was a French gentile, while she, Ruth, was raised in a Jewish religious home. But here it didn't matter, and Rene was sympathetic to Jews — she quickly added, knowing that her parents must turn over in their graves. "Fortunately" they had no graves... they had been cremated in Auschwitz, among the victims of the early period. She asked me to become her postman. And that was not all. I was asked to translate for her Rene's French letters into German, while Ulrique was to translate Ruth's German letters into French for Rene. I have made the acquaintance of Rene in a fleeting moment on the staircase and thus we, the two couples, became good friends, learning many an intimate detail from the exchange of letters.

By a strange coincidence, both Ruth and Rene had rosy cheeks. Were they that healthy? Now, from my present perspective, I can presume that they were both flushed from consumption. It must be stressed, however, that Ruth, being an old-timer and a prominent figure in her task, had perhaps good connections and sources of some additional food. The old-timers had a good organization. Ruth being employed at the camp's laundry had certain special privileges, as will be understood from my forthcoming example.

As I have already mentioned, there was an orchestra in Auschwitz, and I don't mean the Gypsy band that played on the platform for the incoming transports before they underwent the selection. I mean the orchestra of fine musicians, playing excellent classical music. From time to time it gave a concert for the prisoners. To get a ticket you had to be a very important figure in the camp. Ruth was now fighting not for one but for two tickets, the second intended for Rene. It took her two weeks to pull the strings, and she spoke of nothing else. It was to be her only chance to meet Rene and sit next to him, hand in hand. I was very happy for her when she at last received this second ticket, passed it on to me, and I handed it triumphantly to Rene.

You must he wondering by now, my grandchildren, why my relation from Auschwitz is interwoven with such schmaltzy stories? But 'schmaltz' means fat, and under the circumstances it was quite nourishing. We are hardly aware how 'schmaltz' and 'kitsch' penetrate our lives. Weren't people happier as long as they didn't distinguish between 'kitsch' and art? Weren't they happier dying of overeating, unaware of the discipline of a diet? After this philosophical tractate, I have to add to 'schmaltz' a pinch of melodrama for good measure.

The evening after the concert I went to Ruth's block to hear her relation and share her elation. I found her in tears. Rene didn't come to the concert. As he explained later his commander didn't grant him permission to leave the block. Moreover, he took the ticket from Rene's hand and... went instead of him. Thus was shattered the modest dream of this lovely couple.

As for me, I was able to meet my 'Kochany' for one second almost every day. One day Ulrique whispered to me: "Try to get out to the staircase at ten o'clock sharp, just for a couple of minutes". I did as requested, and who was my 'chaperon', who was standing guard to warn us in time? My faithful friend Janka. She was that kind of understanding and broad-minded friend. Otherwise, we had no contact with Ulrique beyond the letter exchange and the one second of crossing each other in the staircase.

Getting used to the style of life in the model camp Auschwitz I, I started to look around me and explore my surroundings. I was and am an avid collector of observations, but I am foremost a collector of people. I have inherited this quality from my father, who did it in his own very peculiar way. Father was capable of placing on a bench in his office a gentile university professor next to a pious Jew with a long beard and side curls. There, the two discussed the points in common between the teachings of Confucius and the precepts of Judaism.

Studying people in Auschwitz, I have to sketch a few portraits of some unusual types. One of them was a glazier sent to the room we were working in. He must have been an academic in his "former incarnation", or so he looked to us. Being a glazier in a concentration camp was not a bad occupation. It gave one opportunity to move in the camp from one compound to another. He could pass information, render services, he could take advantage of his freedom of movement. He made the impression of a very likable and well-informed man.

When such a man (and not one of the vulgar Josephs or Meir) appears in the midst of working girls, he arouses general curiosity. Janka tried to engage him in conversation. She didn't do it in aggressive way, she just asked questions concerning certain rumors circulating in the camp. He answered in monosyllables with a yes or a no. He was intensely concentrating on his job, never looking at us, working briskly with pursed lips. It was odd, it was almost hostile. At last Janka asked him straightforward if he had something against us. "Yes — he said — "I have a lot against your whole lot, you women. When I was a child, my mother divorced my father. She abandoned me, she went to live with her lover. My beloved fiancée flirted behind my back, turning me into a laughingstock. I had to drop her. Later my beloved wife eloped with a lover. What do you expect of me? Do you still wonder why I hate women?"

The communists constituted a special brand in the camp. Like all of us they were branded. All the prisoners wore a tag with a triangle and the personal number. The triangle marking a Jew was yellow, the color designating a political prisoner was red, purple was for clergy, brown for Gypsies, and pink was the color of homosexuals and prostitutes. The gays, constituting an obvious target for the molesting strong men, stole sometimes a red triangle from a cadaver and wore it instead of the discriminating pink one. To parade as a political prisoner was, of course, more honorable.

Most of the communists were incarcerated years before WWII. Many of them perished. Those who survived must have been endowed with exceptional strength of character or stamina. One such communist that I came to know was an honest man of iron-clad principles. One day a prominent woman prisoner, who had her sources and resources, offered him a slice of bread. He declined politely. "Look" — she said — " I am not doing it out of pity, I simply happen to have more bread than I need, and can share it with you, you who must be starved for years, being such an old-timer". He reflected for a moment, then answered philosophically: "Excuse me, comrade, but it is not out of pride or arrogance that I refuse your offer. It took me years to train my body and my mind to live on the daily ration of calories supplied here. Woe to me if I disturb this balance. Were I to accept today the slice of bread offered by you, I Should miss it doubly tomorrow, and my whole self-discipline would be shattered. Try to understand, and pardon me".

I have also met a different kind of communist. One evening, as I was sitting on my bunk and writing a letter to Ulrique, an unkempt tousled head from the bunk adjoining ours moved close to me and asked: "Are you writing a diary, perhaps?" I replied that I was only writing a letter. "That's a pity" — said the ugly, dwarfish person — "because if you were writing a diary, I could have some material for you. So, you, you letter-writer have a 'Kochany', but I, I have a page in history. I made history. The question is, who is going to write it?".

"How come that you have made history?" — I asked, suddenly very curious. "I may not live to tell it, therefore I feel an urge to pass it on to somebody who could record it for posterity. You can denounce me, I don't care, I just have to tell you", she said. "My secret is that I have actively participated in the plot for blowing up one of the crematoria. I am a member of a communist cell, and it was my cell which was responsible for the famous destruction of the main crematorium. My part of the job was to carry every time two satchels of explosives hidden under my dress and deliver them to a certain point, and then to carry back two satchels of earth from the dig under the crematorium. The satchels dangling between my knees were attached by bands to my waist, thus, even during a search they could pass undiscovered. It took us a long time to carry out the earth from the sap, leading to the undermined spot".

I remember the girl and her story, I recorded it faithfully, unfortunately I don't remember her name — and that is criminal.

When I heard this heroic story, it didn't occur to me that I would myself become the heroine of a story concerning sabotage. That I would be accused of sabotage not once but twice, that I would be accused of having offended the Fuhrer Hitler himself.

I can see your sarcastic smile. You don't believe me. You better do, because I shall give you all the details of this affair; but first, a prologue. You see, in the background of my story will figure the conflict between the boss, Obersturmfuhrer Deutscher, and his deputy Bodnerash. They were now linked by their secret like Siamese twins. Deutscher was afraid that Bodnerash might spill the secret of the forged paintings, Bodnerash was afraid that Deutscher might use his influence to expedite him promptly to the Russian front. The story of my personal misadventures with Bodnerash developed gradually.

There came a time when I was too hungry and weak to work in the book-binding workshop while standing. Kertesh noticed it and tried to help me. He adapted for me a kind of work that could be executed sitting and took my part of work upon himself. What was the work adjusted to my capacities? We had received a batch of real leather skins for the prestigious covers of Hitler's 'Mein Kampf' book. When you make book-covers of leather, the edges have to be paper-thin if you want to paste and press them properly. Kertesh gave me a special scalpel knife, with which to shave thin the margins of leather.

One day Bodnerash entered our room, visibly in bad mood and probably drunk. "Why do you work sitting, Maria?" — he yelled at me. I tried to explain that this is a precision work which can be only executed sitting. "You have a lot of cheek, you Jewish philosopher" — Bodnerash scolded me. Kertesh understood somehow what was going on. He tried to defend me. He could afford it, being such an exceptional master in his craft. He repeated by gesticulation and in broken German what I had said. He mumbled: "Messer scharf, Maria mussen sitzen..." Thus, once more my skin was saved. I passed the evenings with Ulrique's letters, but not all of them were comforting. In one of the letters Ulrique provided for me historical information: He wrote:

"...I had the opportunity to speak to a certain team of men working in the gas chambers and in crematoria of Birkenau. It took me some time to make them open up to me. What they revealed is a new field of specialization, never heard of in the modern world. Every gas chamber and crematorium has its crew and there were five of them. This is one of the teams. The moment the gas chamber has been opened and aired, these men must empty it of bodies and clean it very quickly, so as to make room for the next batch of victims.

From the very beginning, the men of this team have to brace and steal themselves against the horror of the sight that met their eyes. The moment the door is opened — the bodies spill out. It is because, by instinct of survival, the people about to die cling to the door, up to their last moment. The center of the room, where the gas can was thrown, through an aperture — is empty of people. The Cyclone gas, being heavy, concentrates in the low level of the room. It takes some time before it rises. That is why the victims make a tremendous effort to climb… Climb they can, in this empty room, only upon the bodies of others. Thus the children, the old and the weak are trampled on to the bottom of the gas chamber. The stronger individuals are on the top when death reaches them. That's the way the teams find them, all dead, in this chamber. These are the technicalities of the victims at their last battle for survival.

As for the team, these men had to develop skills and systems. If they didn't they would be executed. There are among them specialists in speedy transfer of bodies from the gas chamber to the trucks. There are specialists in loading the cadavers on the truck, and there is a team skilled like bakers in filling the furnace of a crematorium. The first group told me that at first, two of them carried one cadaver to the truck. It was a time-consuming physical effort. They asked permission to try more effective method. After several experiments they have found the best system. One man can now drag two corpses at one time. Pulling them by their hands, he drugs them gliding upon a sheet of tarpaulin. There is no lifting, no carrying, just dragging. Thus the weight of the corpses is reduced by some sixty percent and the whole operation is speeded up.

Loading the corpses on a truck takes two skilled men. Were the corpses loaded and deposed across the floor of the truck — they would tend to spill, the moment the back flap is opened, or even before it was shut. If stashed lengthwise, with heads in the same direction — they would slip from the heap. That is why they should be deposed by layers, each layer with the heads in opposite direction, for good balance. Isn't it ingenious? There is a horrible logic in these technical proceedings…

The team of some fifteen barbers has to shear off the hairs of the victims while they are still alive, but already naked. While they were still dressed, the hair stuck to their clothes. It was no good. The clothes had to remain clean. After the victims are dead, there is blood oozing from their noses and their ears. There are excrements and urine in the gas chamber, soiling the precious hair. That is why the hair has to be cropped from the living but naked people. It also has a reassuring psychological effect, because the prospective victims now believe that with their cropped hair they are designated to work and live in the camp. They go meekly to the showers.

Their hair, clean and neat, is needed for the manufacture of socks for the crews of the submarines, because hair is, allegedly, less sweat provocative than wool or cotton... One couldn't let the crew suffocate in its own stench.

The dentists have to check the teeth of the dead and extract gold crowns. This has to be executed while the cadavers are still warm, before the "rigor mortis" clamps their jaws, so that they would have to be pried open by force. Thus the team of dentists has to be squeezed in before the last team would take over the bodies.

The last crew, the one filling the furnace of the crematorium, has to stash the bodies most economically. It is best done before the corpses become rigid and twisted in fantastic positions, with protruding limbs.

As you see, never have people acquired such high skills as these teams, slaving in the gas chamber and crematorium... The life spam of these teams is short, many of the men go mad. They know that sooner or later they will be killed because they know too much. When they see in a transport of prospective victims their next of kin or a friend, they are not able to warn him... and to what purpose? Could they save him?

Once, a member of this team saw a friend's wife. He warned her and the whole group of women rebelled. Beaten bloody they were pushed immediately into the gas chamber, but she was extricated by the SS guards. Under torture, she revealed who was her informant. The man was torn to pieces before the eyes of his team. I have some more to tell you about them, but not in this letter..."

With these words (as I remember) ended Ulrique's letter. The next day, when we met for few seconds in the staircase, he whispered quickly into my ear: "What I couldn't add in my letter was that they seemed to be members of the underground preparing an uprising. This underground seems to have grown long tentacles." That was all, he had no time to say more, or no more information. To organize underground organization in a country under occupation is one thing, but to build it up in a concentration camp is quite different. Here emerges once more a new specialty, a new skill.

Speaking of skills, I shall soon have to develop not one, but two new skills and techniques.

Coming back to the art restoration room — Bodnerash knew that Deutscher liked my work. That in itself was reason enough for him to torture me. He now turned to Kertesh and said slowly in German: "Maria is no good, she will be kicked out. She will be sent… you know where". He pointed to the window and to the visible chimney of crematorium. Then he pointed to the pile of the "Mein Kampf" books still waiting for their leather covers and said to Kertesh: "If Maria is good, you are no good. I happen to know that Obersturmfuhrer Deutscher is already looking for a younger book-binder". This time Kertesh understood. He turned white as a sheet. Defending me, he became himself a prospective victim. It was now my turn to defend Kertesh. "It is strange" — I mumbled as if speaking to myself — "because only yesterday the Obersturmfuhrer was very pleased with the achievements of Kertesh". Bodnerash raised his whip in my direction. I tried to hide my head between my shoulders, but he thought better of it, and only added his last threat: "You just wait and see, you will both walk out of here through the chimney, you scum".

From this moment Bodnerash was snooping around, and just waiting for the next opportunity to catch us at a bad moment. He eventually caught me pausing for a minute. He jumped at me and yelled: "Now you see for yourself that you are finished off". What did I have to lose…? I risked answering back. I said: "the opposite is true; I am right now ordered to plan and create a new model of a leather cover for 'Mein Kampf' books". It was as risky a reply as none. "A new model?" — repeated Bodnerash — "You have till tomorrow morning to produce it. In fact, you have one hour from now" — he added with a crooked smile on his pouting lips. He must have believed that I had been ordered by Deutscher to create such a new model. What have I done? I invented a white lie. I shall pay for it with my life. But then… I have always been a constructive pessimist. What does a constructive pessimist do in such a situation? He at least tries to deliver…

What can one do in one hour before the workshop is closed? I had to mobilize all my reserves of adrenaline and put on my thinking cap… Thinking of the fires of crematoria inspired me with a fiery idea. Things can be done with fire. I remembered how mother used to create shapes in embossed leather, when she taught my aunt to make artificial flowers. But mother had tools; I had none, only the scalpel knife in my hand. I heated its blunt edge over the flame of the alcohol burner. When it was red-hot, I started to trace lines on bits of leather waste. The brown pattern was quite interesting. There was a potential in this technique.

I also found among the tools a ruined screwdriver with curled edges (that for the sake of control of tools had not been thrown away). This one, when heated over the flame, marked wide, band-like impressions on the leather. But they still lacked depth. In order to achieve deeper impressions, I would have to underlay linoleum — I remembered. Instead of linoleum I took a heap of soft leather-cuts as padding and… it worked. The markings became now deeper, creating a fascinating pattern in relief. I have quickly produced several samples with floral patterns, executed in this nick of time before the zero hour — the end of our working day. I felt hopefully saved.

I took the samples with me to show mother. I didn't mention to her the incident with Bodnerash, but the grapevine had already reported it to her. She made several further suggestions and I felt that I have discovered a new technique to present to Deutscher. Here came the crucial day in which I had to prove my capacity. In the morning, when Deutscher entered the building, I didn't give Bodnerash the opportunity to check with him if he had indeed ordered new models from me, I waited for the boss close to the entrance with the samples in my hand. He followed me to the workshop and inspected my experiments carefully. He was excited like a boy who has received a new toy. He saw instantly the potential of the new techniques. I explained that there is more to come if I am provided with appropriate tools. At this instance Deutscher sent for Bodnerash. "Repeat to Unterscharfuhrer Bodnerash what you need for the execution of these ornaments imprinted on leather" — he said. I explained how screwdrivers could be filed off to produce blunt edges, or how a blunt skewer could trace intricate patterns. "Bodnerash, go to the metal works and order it done, every tool provided with a wooden handle. What else do you need?" — said Deutscher. I explained about ball-shaped tools for embossing. "Bodnerash, get her such tools" — yelled Deutscher, visibly excited. What else? — he asked once more. I mentioned the linoleum paddings and satchels with sand. "Bodnerash, get her these too, and whatever else she needs. And do it promptly!!" — orders Deutscher. Thus, Bodnerash turned into an errand boy to serve me, me the humble prisoner, now in command. How he must have hated this situation, how he would take his revenge — I could only guess.

Bodnerash delivered promptly almost everything. Now arose the question of what would constitute the most appropriate ornaments for the leather-covers of 'Mein Kampf', Hitler's famous gospel book. Bodnerash immediately suggested the imprint of several swastikas. Deutscher could hardly oppose such a suggestion; it would be considered unpatriotic. He couldn't risk it. I guessed his thoughts and suggested floral designs proving that the book is blooming... Yes, nodded Deutscher, overlooking the irony in my suggestion. "Yes, let us try both patterns and even the third option with the embossed flowers, cut out and affixed later in appliqué. That is it; now proceed with the work, starting with the easier techniques". It was evident that he was charmed with the whole project, sure of its success. Bodnerash tried to have the last word in the whole enterprise. He implicated that the swastika pattern is the most important of all the suggestions. Deutscher pretended not to hear.

I executed several book-covers, variating the approach to the new techniques. I even executed one cover with swastika emblems dispersed over the surface in various sizes. Bodnerash was watching my progress, entering our room once too often. He didn't scold me for working seated, not anymore. Once, engrossed in my work, I suddenly heard him yelling over my head: "What is THIS!!! Is THIS a swastika? It is totally askew, it is broken!!!" What could I answer? could I say that a swastika is, after all, a broken cross?... Now Bodnerash whipped himself into total frenzy; "You did it on purpose, you Jewish swine!!! You did it deliberately with the intention of defiling the swastika. You will hang on the gallows for this offence to the Fuhrer's emblem!!!" — he yelled at the top of his voice, happy to find against me the heaviest accusation.

I was doomed. Even Deutscher wouldn't be able to defend me. Bodnerash himself stopped screaming. He took a sheet of paper with a double copy and started to write a protocol. After a repeated scrutiny of the swastikas he counted and noted in how many points I had deliberately twisted the line. Nothing could save me. I gathered my courage and addressed him most formally; "Herr Unterscharfuhrer, please try to understand. I couldn't and wouldn't be that stupid to do it deliberately for the sake of a bad joke. You must believe me." Bodnerash went on with his protocol. I ventured an additional explanation: "You can see for yourself that I have to draw the lines very quickly so as not to burn the leather, and that is when my hand slips.

I cannot use a ruler because the red-hot tool would burn it..." As I said these words, I felt somebody's presence behind my back. Who could it be? Obersturmfuhrer Deutscher, of course. Deutscher had his spies on the precinct, just as Bodnerash had his faithful spies. Deutscher must have heard of the incident. He reacted swiftly: "Of course, that's the way it happened, that explains this mishap. It is a risky technique, after all. She needs more time to master it. Besides, how can she properly execute her work while you stand behind her and breath down her neck..." And that was the end of the incident. I was saved once more.

When I say that I saw myself already on the gallows with a rope around my neck, I am not exaggerating. Hardly a week before this incident we were forced to attend an execution by hanging. The victim was a fugitive, a man who had already escaped to freedom, and was caught in the marshes. As in Plaszow, this time too I didn't watch this horrible scene, I kept my eyes closed. But I remember that before he was brought to the gallows he was marched along the lines of thousands of prisoners and accompanied by the orchestra ordered to play, ironically, that nostalgic tune about awaiting the lover's return. I still remember this song in its original French version, as I knew it before the war.

"J'attendrai, le jour et la nuit, j'attendrai toujour ton retour. J'attendrai, car l'oiseau qui s'enfuit vien te chercher, l'oubli dans son nid..."

Would Bodnerash have his way? Was I going to hang on the gallows — what would the orchestra play in my honor? This time I was saved, but what would come next? Twice humiliated, Bodnerash didn't give up; he was already sniffling around and brewing his vengeance.

Enjoying a tremendous success with the leather-bound, embossed covers of 'Mein Kampf', Deutscher was supplied with the finest kinds of leather. He came beaming to our room. He said, indicating the newly delivered skins: "Take the greatest care of these skins, they are unique". After he left, we all gathered around the precious skins, and I felt a sensuous pleasure passing my palm over the soft velvety surface.

One of the Josephs looked like transfixed on the skins spread out on the huge table. Suddenly he exclaimed: "Oh God: Pioruna, may thunder strike me if this isn't HUMAN skin!!! Look, just look and consider its elongated shape and size. Don't you have eyes?" — I must have been hypnotized or under a spell. I screamed like a wounded animal. "Pioruna, look now at the second skin" — continued Joseph — "This must be the skin of an embryo!!! The belly of the woman was cut, the embryo was extricated and skinned. Its hide was tanned to the softest kid leather. Pioruna, don't you believe me? Don't you people know that the SS order lampshades made of human skin? Why not the covers of the glorious 'Mein Kampf'? Didn't you see Deutscher's cunning smile when he mentioned the 'unique' leather, you bunch of idiots!!!" His words were hardly audible over my screams. I screamed like possessed. I felt like cutting off my hand that stroked the fine leather only minutes before.

Kertesh took hold of me. He gripped my shoulders with his strong hands, he shook me like an apple tree. He yelled in Hungarian. When Kertesh was upset he could only speak Hungarian. I almost fainted. Kertesh clutched at his head, swayed, then composed himself, and started to explain in his brand of German: "Das Leder Schwein... das Leder gross Schwein, and das Leder klein Schwein. Ich wissen, ich Schwein arbeiten". Meaning more or less: "This leather pig... this big pig and this baby pig. Me know... me work pig..."

I understood, but I was still shaking like a leaf. Before I was able to compose myself, Bodnerash was already here, towering over me. Did he hear me screaming or did a spy report to him? He didn't lose time: "What's going on here? Nobody is working, what's the commotion?!! Didn't I hear your voice, Maria?" — he pierced me with his beefy eyes. I couldn't deny it. What was I to answer, to explain? Certainly not the truth. I mumbled that I had been scared by the sight of a cockroach. "A cockroach here, in the printing shop? Here in this immaculate place? It couldn't be. Yet, if you are not lying, the people, the cleaners, will get each fifty lashes".

What have I done. I cannot take back my words, and I cannot let innocent Jews receive fifty lashes for my sheer fantasy. Once more I had to improvise. While everybody was diligently searching for the imaginary cockroach, I tore a piece of black paper, rolled it quickly between my fingers, and dropped it behind the table. The little Joseph spotted it and exclaimed: "Here is her cockroach, that's what she saw". Everybody laughed, including Bodnerash. That was the end of the episode.

I didn't mention the incident to my mother, but there was somebody who spilled it to her. Who? Of course, one of the Tenzer daughters, Karola did. Mother was trembling out of fear for my fate. She, the former elegant lady, dressed in the best of tastes, ascribed my misfortunes and continuous incidents with Bodnerash to... my shabby dress. "If only you could be better attired and more presentable — Bodnerash wouldn't treat you like dirt", she concluded, and when my mother gave a verdict — it had to stick. She decided to do something about it, and you know by now that she would deliver. There was an opportunity to earn something. It was close to Christmas time and the Germans were joyously preparing for the feast under the Christmas tree. Longing for family and friends, the female SS wardens were sending beautiful Christmas cards. They have somehow heard from our block commander about the women-painters, and after one has ordered from my mother hand-painted Christmas cards, several others ordered some more exquisite greetings. They even paid graciously with bread. Mother executed her artistic side-job on her bunk, so that the spies would not begrudge and denounce her.

We had now a problem with this well-earned bread; Undernourished as we were, should we fill our bellies or rather "dress my belly" with a new dress? Mother was adamant. She decided that a good dress would save me from constant dangers. I had nothing to say in the matter. That we lived and subsisted on some 120 calories daily, that the soup contained only cabbage — didn't matter to my mother. That we haven't seen for ages a raw vegetable or fruit, an egg or sugar — was of no importance. The dress for me was now mother's main objective. "Why not for you, who are older and emaciated?" — I ventured to ask. "Because my dress is better than yours, so diaphanous and in tatters, and because I am protected by Deutscher who needs me" — were her arguments.

The dress that she bought for me from one of the well-placed prisoners was splendid. It was of dark-blue wool, it fitted the waist and extended into a bell-shaped skirt. It even had an embroidered pattern on its upper part. It must have been bought in one of the best shops in Budapest, a city nicknamed "The second Vienna". Mother beamed with pleasure when Janka said that I now looked like a princess. My new friend Erica from Saloniki, who had a Viennese mother, was certain that this dress was a creation of the Viennese "haute couture". Erica grew up in a villa in the outskirts of Saloniki. She used to say that in her parents' villa on the seashore, the windowpanes were covered with dots of salt from the sea, while now her cheeks were covered with salt from her tears, after she had lost all her family in

Auschwitz. As for me, I thought of the person to whom this dress belonged. Was she alive? Shall I meet her?

Erica brought us the latest news, some contradictory rumors, hard to interpret. It was said that the mass-transports from Hungary had stopped. There were still many transports from Holland, from Belgium, but not from Hungary. What did it mean? We didn't know. Nowadays historians have all the answers — we had no means of analyzing this phenomenon. The other news concerned the mass-liquidation of "Muselmanns". The population of the numerous dependencies, the camps situated in the vicinity of Auschwitz was sifted, selected and reduced to a minimum by gassing and cremation. Was it a prelude to total liquidation? Will this process reach Auschwitz I, the model camp? — we asked ourselves, finding no answers.

How can you define a "Muselmann"? It is a former person, whose skeleton remained dressed only with skin. His ankles are swollen from hunger. He is too weak to wipe his running nose with his sleeve. The last symptom was decisive in my eyes.

There was a third rumor in the camp, this one concerning the beginning of a Russian offensive. We hardly believed it, but it has to be stated that the SS men and the Ruthenians and Latvians were becoming jumpy and less boisterous. Bodnerash revealed to Meir that the Allies bombed the German centers so thoroughly that most cities were in ruins. We had been fed with false 'good' rumors for so many years that we wore an armor of protection. We didn't lap them up, we were apathetic.

To break the gloom, we sought any kind of mind-bogging distraction. One day my new friend Erica informs us that on Sunday afternoon there will be an entertainment of sorts in the block inhabited mainly by the German Jewesses. They are going to give a theater performance. I was very curious what it might be. Theater in Auschwitz? Were they going to recite excerpts from famous plays? We shall go and see. We — meant of course Janka, and perhaps Ruth as well. When we arrived, there was already some audience and several young women from Berlin were starting their performance. If there were some good ideas, they were spoiled by this cheap vaudeville approach. The whole affair smelled of a night-club atmosphere. Somebody's good ideas had been ruined. A Muselmanns' party or a parody of "The last Supper" were basically good macabre ideas for sketches. As I have stated many a time, macabre ideas and utterances served as a vent, an outlet for accumulated pressures. The climax was a sketch ending with this famous sentence ever so slightly adapted to the local circumstances: "To be or not to be... that is HERE the question". Never did this sentence make that much sense. It ridiculed Hamlet's silly turbulences, it grew in dimension beyond Shakespeare's wildest expectations. It is a pity that it was followed by some stupid sketch. With my elephant's memory, I remember its idiotic refrain: "Ziehtaus die Strump fewieeine Nymphe, und das tralallalallahlallah, lallah la lalah...". I just have to translate it to show you what idiocies were sung in Auschwitz: "...like a nymph showing off, she took her stockings off, and also her tralallah, Iallahlah..." Now you know that there was not only orchestra and cinema in Auschwitz, there was also a cabaret performance...

This disappointing recreation had an adverse effect on us. If this is culture — it was in its worst presentation. We had to do something about it, we owed it to ourselves. Our minds were trained for better things. It is about time to use them for a certain purpose, a project of importance. What better modest project than to collect and register some personal experiences, stories and episodes from this Holocaust period, from the people surrounding us. Perhaps somebody will survive to pass them on to humanity (if humanity is not a dirty word).

We appointed a team of "scouts" to find people with exceptional tales. We also appointed a secretary, who wrote the relations down. We had no great illusions that we would be able to preserve this material, even if we dig a cache under the wall of our block. We had therefore to rely mainly on our memory. I have stored in my mind many astounding relations, some of them hardly believable. If I shall have enough strength and time left after I finish my personal recollections, I shall return to these observations and register them for posterity.

There were such pearls like the story of a family who concealed the father's cadaver so as to continue to receive his food ration. The same person related that in the same ghetto in Lodz, bonuses granted for overproduction were paid in form of... potato peels. There was in our collection the story of a child hidden somewhere in a tomb and leaving it only at night. His frozen fingers fell off. Another child was placed with a gentile family and provided with forged identity papers of a girl, and never guessed that he was really a boy. The child only knew that he had to conceal his private parts from strangers. But no, why wait and postpone what is so relevant right here. I have already missed and rejected so many episodes, sacrificed for the sake of brevity and concise rendering of my tale. I shall try and place here at least a few pictures, rounding up the landscape of Birkenau and Auschwitz, while they still constitute the pivot of our story.

Birkenau and Auschwitz were constructed on a vast marshy, empty terrain, avoided by the former inhabitants of the town Oswiecim (the real Polish name of Auschwitz in Silesia). This fact explains why so many exotic diseases thrived in Birkenau. We were informed by the old-timers that the situation had been much worse before we arrived there. Because in the hospital people were given poisonous injections, many women went sick to work, with blood and excrements trickling along their legs. Whoever was admitted to the hospital was put four into one bed. When the patients were given 'fresh' sheets, these sheets were not disinfected, they still carried the stains of blood, urine and excrements. The rats were gnawing at the patients' toes and hands or biting off their noses. The latrines too were the source of mass-infections. People aware of the danger didn't dare to sit on the openings, others were hardly able to reach them, leaving the droppings wherever they stood.

The various ethnic groups were not treated on the same level and the attitudes were shifting. Most of the Gypsies were kept in Birkenau till July 1944. They even lived in families in separate blocks. Dr.Mengele was fascinated by this race. He endeavored to try if they could be changed into Aryan types. The Gypsy orchestra played for the incoming transports right in front of the gas chambers. In July most of the Gypsies were 'exterminated', including the orchestra. When it played no more, the camp understood that this was the end of the Gypsies. Still, we encountered many Gypsies in October when we came to Birkenau. Maybe there were just a few, but their presence was bitterly felt, as I have already related.

The bad traits were thriving in this atmosphere, robbing brother prisoners of a slice of bread, the only pair of shoes, the only dress. When I described the colors of the identification tags, I forgot to mention the green for notorious criminals and the black for prostitutes. The recidivist criminals and murderers had also a discreet black tattoo spot on one cheek, by which they identified each other and formed gangs. They also collaborated with the SS and denounced brother prisoners. The term 'to organize' was known in all the camps, as if there existed a camp jargon. It meant to "steal" but not from fellow prisoners. To pinch from "Canada" or other storerooms didn't mean stealing, it meant organizing... Who were the most impudent thieves, stealing on a large scale? — the Germans themselves.

The "Lager Alteste", the commander in chief, ruling over Birkenau was Maria Imola, a German convicted murderer, now living like a queen. She participated, in her far past, in a gang skirmish with the police and even killed a policeman with her own hand. But let us start with the leading head, let us start with Hess, Rudolf Hess.

He launched his glorious career as a murderer years before the war. He was convicted to ten years imprisonment. He was granted amnesty five years later and promptly joined the Nazi party. He advanced so quickly in his career that he was immediately nominated commander of the Auschwitz camp and all the camps in its vicinity. Soon he became the main executor of the "Final Solution". After the first clumsy stages of gassing people with the exhaust fumes of a car, the Cyclon B containing the Prussian acid was applied with success (it took "only" ten minutes for a victim to die). It is estimated that almost one half of the Holocaust victims perished in Auschwitz under the efficient supervision of Hess.

Hess was such a talented organizer that ten thousand victims were gassed every day, their bodies being cremated in five crematoria, each with a maximum capacity of two thousand bodies, if activated day and night.

Hess left Auschwitz in December 1943, but he returned so often that his figure was familiar to the newcomers too, as I can prove. I don't know the details of his financial wizardry, but he and his family fared very well. Aufseherin Franz, responsible for his camp's bookkeeping, knew how to "cook" the ledgers: When a truck with six hundred kilograms of meat entered the camp, she registered its contents, but she immediately disposed of it in another column, noted down as if supplied to the kitchen. In reality the same driver took the meat back, to sell it on the black market and share the profit with Aufseherin Franz. She was selling in the same manner sacks full of sugar, margarine and flour. Just like Goth did in Plaszow. All this commerce was carried out at the expense of the meager rations allotted to the prisoners.

The Polish women were allowed to receive food-parcels from their families. If they wanted to cook something, they had to bribe the commander's deputy and they gained access to the stove only after two o'clock at night.

The Blockalteste was supposed to divide every loaf of bread into four portions. Her deputy managed to cut it into six portions. Thus they gained some six hundred portions, and not in slides but in whole loaves, ready for sale. Thus, everybody in a key position got rich in the camps. Meanwhile some poor prisoners walked around the kitchen, searching frantically for some bones from the SS kitchen, or for some rotten potatoes.

The possession of a personal soup bowl posed the problem "to be or not to be". Those who had no bowl got no soup. The orders were changing every once in a while. There were long periods when the soup was distributed only in the evening hours. Hence the prohibition of carrying the bowl to work, while formerly this bowl was pierced close to its brim and attached by a string to the belt. Now it had to be left in the barrack, without any guarantee that it would be retreated. The unhappy prisoners risked taking their bowls with them to work. When there was a guard at the gate, they had to detach the bowls quickly and throw them aside. Later, the cleaners gathered the rejected bowls and sold them for a slice of bread. As I said, if you didn't have a bowl, you didn't get soup.

There were even times when the soup bowls were turned into chamber pots, just as they were occasions when the chamber pots had to be turned into soup bowls... It was either that or no soup at all. Needless to mention, that the same bowl served also as a coffee-mug. Sometimes a whole group was simply stripped of its bowls, which were distributed to a new transport. At the period when the whole distribution of daily rations took place in the evening, a prisoner was given at the same time his portion of bread with a teaspoonful of margarine, his soup, and immediately after the soup he got his coffee, into the same bowl that was not even rinsed. If you tried to run to the washing block to rinse your bowl — you lost your coffee.

The SS officers had orders from above to keep the camp clean, so as to prevent the spread of epidemics. In a frenzy of cleanliness, they sometimes ordered the whole camp simultaneously disinfected in all its compounds. It was a "mission Impossible" and it was a drama for all the inmates. When the whole camp was being turned upside down and disinfected, you couldn't run to your good friend and entrust to her your meager possession, because she was in the same situation. Some prisoners were seen digging a hole under the barrack or a heap of stones and hiding there a soup bowl, a spoon, a knife, a piece of cloth serving as towel, a toothbrush. The Gypsies had eyes all over their heads. Before the prisoner returned from the disinfecting bath, these treasures disappeared from their hiding places.

Needless to mention that the whole comedy of pretending to disinfect was a wasted effort. All the pallets filled with straw passed the delousing process in such low temperatures that the lice got only more nervous and vicious. Meanwhile the naked prisoners waited the whole night outside, before being admitted to the showers. After the shower, naked and wet, they had to wait for their deloused clothes. Eventually many cases of pneumonia devastated the population of the camp and took the place of a selection.

The Polish prisoners had it better, they still received some parcels from home and still had some hope to be eventually released. These girls even menstruated. We hadn't menstruated any more for many months. We all lost our period from malnutrition, because thus nature defends its last reserves. Some of us lost their menstruation after a shock.

There was a flower of sorts on this heap of dung. There was in Auschwitz a block for prostitutes, a brothel for German soldiers or rather for the low rank SS squadrons. These healthy wenches weren't (God forbid) Jewish, they had to be of a purer race. They were better clad and better fed. They had a hairdresser, and they had a lot of make-up at their disposition. Forced to exercise the oldest profession, they were not known to have put up a heroic resistance.

Speaking of heroism, we have to mention that there were some heroic deeds of certain prisoners, which became a legend in the camp. There was this case of a Jewish artist, a woman who observing an SS man torturing a prisoner, jumped up, snatched his pistol from the holster and shot him on the spot. She died under torture. There was a Jewess, Mala Zimmermann, who serving as an errand boy for Oberaufseherin Drexler, had a certain freedom of movement. She escaped from Birkenau with a Polish boy, Edek. They paused for a while near the town of Bielsko in Silesia and were apprehended there. They were brought back and sentenced to the gallows. He, Edek, dared to exclaim before the rope strangled him: "Long live Poland". She, Mala, managed to cut her wrists, and with a hand dripping with blood, slapped her block commander.

There were many glorious heroic exploits and there were some heroics on a lesser scale. Here is the place to mention the whole group of "Effinger girls", who worked in the Effektenkammer storerooms. They were nicknamed "Effinger girls" because Effinger was their boss. They used to steal some dresses and throw them from the window over the barbed wire fence. There was someone waiting to pick them up during the general commotion preceding the rollcall. They themselves were not supposed to leave the storerooms for the rollcall. They were counted inside the building (The kitchen staff enjoyed the same privilege). This gave them time to go into some mischief. Their nimble fingers knew how to search for hidden diamonds, sewn into the seams of clothes that were confiscated from the incoming transports. Finding a diamond, they didn't dare to carry it out of the building. They were searched very thoroughly, sometimes even gynecologically. All they could do was to throw the diamond into the latrine.

They also busied themselves with lesser sabotage. They couldn't carry out the splendid furs stored in the fur compartment, but they could tear and cut the furs into pieces. They used to cut from the pieces some plastrons to warm the breasts, and some fur inlays for shoes — these being much in demand for German soldiers on the Russian front. The girls had a problem how to dispose of them and how to smuggle them out for their friends. The storerooms of the SS officer Effinger were so full with all kinds of precious goods (sequestered from the transports, which brought their very best), that Effinger himself filled every week several suitcases with the best of the best and took them home to Germany. This went on for a long time. Effinger was a type composed of many contradicting characteristics. He was apt to be very cruel or very lenient. When he was in a bad mood, he punished his girls for the slightest real or imagined transgression. He made them crawl through a long pipe. When they emerged from the other side, they were ordered to jump like frogs to the fence and back. He laughed like possessed. The Effinger girls didn't get any better food. Their soup, like ours, was cooked of vegetables good for fodder, and their bread, like ours, contained a high percentage of horse-chestnut flour and sawdust.

Effinger himself came to a tragic end. One day he returned from Germany a broken-hearted man. His house was bombed, his wife was killed, and all the riches amassed to make her happy were gone too. He started to drink. It was understandable and at first even tolerated. But then he drank openly in daytime. Once he was found in his office stark naked laying in a pool of his vomit. When he was eventually brought to his senses and apparently coherent, he started to curse: "I shit on Germany, shit on

Fuhrer and on the crematoria too". He even added a local jingle, an astute parody of the inscription on the Auschwitz gate. It was allegedly known only to the prisoners, but Effinger knew to quote it: "Work makes free — through crematorium three". He was arrested and turned from the almighty boss into a forced labor slave in the nearby camp Buna. Here his trace seems to disappear.

Birkenau had never been a camp that could be shown to an inspecting commission. Auschwitz 1, the model camp, had to become even more immaculate before the arrival of such a commission. The preparations were like the production of a performance. There existed even one latrine and one wash-installation block that had never been used and were permanently locked. They were constructed solely as a "museum piece" for the sake of prospective inspection. Before the commission entered Auschwitz 1, all the pale-faced inmates were spirited away, and only a few good-looking specimens were sent to walk in the streets of the camp. There were even flower beds in the center of Auschwitz 1, and lovely girls in clean aprons tended the flowers. A pastoral picture... There was also a model stemmatological clinic and a roentgen unit, both merely showpieces. As the end approached, whole populations were shifted and sent into the depth of Germany because Birkenau and Auschwitz were bursting at their seams and situated too close to the front. All the incoming and not gassed transports after summer 1944 received serial numbers starting with the letter 'A'. My tattooed number is A-26551. Allegedly, the total number of the 'A' series reached 130,000.

As the end was approaching, the Allied Air Forces penetrated the depth of Germany. Several times an alert siren was sounded in Auschwitz. Needless to state, how we rejoiced at it, ready to die under the ruins of Auschwitz. Sometimes the Germans camouflaged the camp by spreading artificial clouds over its surface. But let it not be said that the Allies were not able to bomb and destroy the crematoria, had they had such intention.

The knowledgeable historians claim that there has never been such a plan because Auschwitz was too far. Was it indeed? Didn't the planes penetrate that deep?

Here is perhaps the place to add some finishing touches to the relation of the communist girl, who allegedly participated in the destruction of one crematorium. This other relation seems to change their whole version. I am no historian, and I am not going to check the facts. Here is what I heard in

December 1944. In November of that year a group of Jews employed in the "Sonderkommando", serving in the crematoria — dared to rebel. They must have known that they would not be left alive as dangerous witnesses. The uprising was not properly organized, it was almost spontaneous. It started too early, it started in the afternoon and not at night as planned. Just the same, one crematorium burnt down. Some of these Jews succeeded to escape, cutting the barbed wire during the upheaval. They sneaked, allegedly, through the less guarded women's camp. There were several cases of escape in that period, and whenever it happens the rollcall lasted for hours on end, though we hardly knew the reason.

In this late period, when the Ruthenium Ukrainians and Latvians sensed the approaching end, one could even buy arms and uniforms of this or another formation. Who dared, knowing that it could be a trap…

In this inserted puzzle of relations, I didn't pick episodes, I merely gave the finishing touches to the depiction of the conditions in Birkenau and Auschwitz in their various periods. Here ends the insert of gathered information, and I am returning to my personal observations.

I have described the performance by the girls from Berlin, with their stupid sketches and "Can-Can" imitation. This reminds me of a only other instance when I saw prisoners… dance. As I have mentioned, the alert sirens were sounded in Auschwitz several times. Once, it caught us in our block. The commander chased us quickly to another building, one that had a basement of sorts, which could serve as shelter. We found ourselves in the presence of a very mixed company from several other blocks. Many nationalities were represented there, but mainly Jewesses from many countries. I was always eager to observe such groups and find a common denominator for the pattern of behavior of each and every group and nationality. This was an excellent opportunity. All generalizations are dangerous, but I have to note my observations as gathered on the spot. I asked myself if I was not prejudiced a priori, because I have already had certain apprehensions concerning the Hungarian Jewesses, back in the Plaszow period. It is not that I hold my Polish Jewesses in high esteem, but the Hungarian Jewesses, here in Auschwitz were not my favorites. Here too, stuck in this basement for several hours during alert, instead of exalting in this unexpected relaxation, they mostly quarreled and even pinched each other. The Polish Jewesses were pacing the room, back and forth, never relaxing. I had the opportunity to observe the Greek Jewesses squatting next to them. What were they doing? In contrast to all the other groups, they were not only chatting and laughing; they even mounted a performance. And what was its subject? A pantomime mimicking the performance of a Greek Gypsy with his dancing bear, held on a chain. One of the girls impersonated the Gypsy. In a nick of time she made a headscarf of her panties, and painted over her lips a thin moustache, traced with soot. The second girl impersonated the bear. A kerchief filled with paper formed a huge square head of a bear, and I understood from her gestures that her tattered dress was similar enough to a bear's fur. Instead of a chain they tied a rope around her neck and the Gypsy was holding the other end of the rope. The bear advanced with heavy steps, swaying from one foot to another, his upper paws kept rigidly in the air. Then the 'bear' danced. Whenever it advanced too close to the spectators, the girls screamed and the 'Gypsy' pulled the rope. When the bear stopped, the 'Gypsy' prodded it to dance using the whip. All this provoked great hilarity and hand clapping. The Greek spectators were not passive. Once a girl took the risk and tried to feed the bear. Another one dared to pinch it. A tiny girl pretended to be the bear's cub. Every time they exploded with laughter.

I pretended not to understand and asked one of the Greek girls what could be the meaning of this performance. "Don't you guess" — she whispered — "the bear represents Germany when it will be defeated". Thus, this childish performance was not so innocent after all. The sense of humor of these persecuted Greek Jewesses was admirable. It is believed nowadays that ninety percent of them perished in Auschwitz (or rather in Birkennau). How is it possible that I came across them in this late period in quite considerable numbers? They must have been the last remnants.

With this performance I have not yet finished with the alert. There was somebody else who, allegedly, gave a very different performance. The next day when we came to work, Bodnerash knew to relate to his pal Meir that our boss, Obersturmfuhrer Deutscher, hearing the siren snatched his helmet, put it on his head and crept under his bed, where he remained for hours till the all-clear signal. Poor Deutscher had seen enough bombings in Germany, and in retrospect his behavior becomes understandable.

We too behaved sometimes in a strange manner. Let me give you an innocent example. There was among us a young woman, a naive, simple country wench, still healthy and merry. Her name was Tova. One morning, as we got up, we heard her screaming and wailing: "They have stolen my shoes!!! My shoes have been stolen; can you understand it? Oh, my shoes, my shoes!!!" We deeply sympathized with her. To find oneself without shoes in December, was a calamity. What can one do? Report to the block commander? Report to the Kapo of her group? Would it help, would she bring her another pair of shoes? She, Tova, could even be accused of having lost German property. We empathized with her profoundly. She continued to wail and repeat the same sentences all over. Then she added bursting in a new fit of wailing: "Not only the shoes, my shoooees, my garters toooo!!!" Whereupon we all burst out laughing. Out of tension or perhaps to break the tension, we laughed to tears, because in one breath she bemoaned the valuable shoes and the shabby garters. Today I understand that the much used, loose bands of rubber were holding her skeletal stockings, full of holes. It wasn't absurd. We were just cruel or perhaps it was simply a laughter of weakness. Weakness can affect one in this way; it erases the borderline between laughter and weeping.

On the other hand, there were certain phenomena and occurrences which seem to us very funny now, but were not funny at the given time. The episodes of my conflict with Bodnerash belong in this category. I had by that time a group of assistants whom I taught how to emboss leather and how to trace ornaments on it (copied from my patterns).

One day the wicked Unterscharfuhrer Bodnerash approached me very formally: "Maria, do you know how to use paints?" What was I to say, I tried to gain time. I said: "It depends what paints and to what purpose?" He explained: "that's the problem. We have received from Berlin a huge photo portrait of our Fuhrer Adolf Hitler. Unfortunately, it is all gray. We plan to enliven it, to paint it over, to change it into a painted portrait. You volunteered here as an artist, hopefully not under false pretenses. You must therefore be able to do it".

What could I say — that I volunteered as expert in artistic crafts? Would it help? I could only argue about technicalities. If the photo-portrait is mat, I can enliven it (as any kitch) with pastels. If it is shiny — there is nothing to be done. But no, Bodnerash wants me to use oil paints. "One doesn't paint with oils on paper" — I quickly protested. "But that's exactly what the commander-in-chief desires — oil paints and nothing else". I was still on defense: "He may desire oil paints, but not from me. He doesn't even know that I exist". Bodnerash now used the biggest cannon: "On the contrary, you have been warmly recommended to him... by me. You cannot disappoint him... or me. It could cost you twenty centimeters — the twenty centimeters of your head..." Here his voluptuous lips opened in a broad smile. Checkmate. If only I could gain a little time without commitment. I was positive that Deutscher wouldn't let me undertake this new task. He must understand that it couldn't be done on photo-paper...

The next day I felt that Deutscher was very uneasy. He pretended to inspect the work of my assistants, then he ventured standing on the threshold of our room and announced: "Maria, you will be delegated to other work..." Saying that he vanished like a wet rat. No help from this quarter. Deutscher was afraid for his own hide, he was not going to argue with the commander-in-chief, even if he realizes that technically it is "mission impossible". Obviously Bodnerash was in charge of the project, and Deutscher would only be happy if he were compromised.

Hardly has Deutscher disappeared and Bodnerash danced in like a marionette. He took me to the office; he was all smiles and explained patiently: "The photo is not glossy. It has a lining of thin linen; it is stretched conveniently on a wooden frame. It will be framed later. The Big Boss says that you will have to paint the Fuhrer's face in rosy, healthy natural colors, and the rest in hues corresponding to the color of the uniform. You will be given samples of the buttons too". Did I detect a sneer on his lips? He wouldn't discuss it any further, he will supply me with all the necessary utensils — he said- "the best of the best". The rest will be my responsibility. Because it is also his responsibility since he recommended me. If I fail, if I try to sabotage this work on the Fuhrer's portrait — it will be my end. That was the gist of the interview. There was no retreat, no salvation.

I ran to the three women-painters to take their advice. "I am telling you to apply the oil paints very thick" — said the Hungarian — "it will be most impressionable". Mother took me aside and explained: "If you follow her advice, the paints will peel off as soon as they dry. Paper rejects oil paints. You will have to dilute them with turpentine and rub them in quickly. The oils will stain the paper, you will have to be very careful not to let them spread. You will have to cover the background of Hitler's head as well". I was sure that mother was right, and that the Hungarian painter didn't wish me so well in giving this risky advice.

Why didn't Bodnerash pass the job on to one of the three painters? He probably didn't want to risk enraging Deutscher. That must be the answer. He knew that I would be guided by my mother.

Bodnerash delivered what he promised. He even gave me as assistant one of the two vulgar Josephs. It didn't comfort me.

Here we start on this new venture. Bodnerash hands all the utensils to Joseph, ordering him to accompany us. He leads the way through the whole camp, compound after compound. It could be a good opportunity to learn more about Auschwitz, but I was not curious. What would it matter if I took more information to my grave...? We passed several gates until we reached an empty playground. There was a net for playing handball and implements for basketball. There was also a little building with showers and W.C. This playground was certainly used for sports by the SS men or Ruthenians. There was no one in sight, only the three of us. But there was a fourth person... a very dominant one — Fuhrer Adolf Hitler himself. His huge portrait was standing against the wall of the building. Bodnerash ordered Joseph to spread all the utensils close to the portrait. He also told him to carry the portrait into the building, every day after work.

"You have limited time, Maria" — said Bodnerash — "the portrait has to be painted, dried and framed before Hitler's birthday". I thought quickly and exclaimed: "But this will be only in April, on the 20th of April" — I added. "How do you know?" — asked Bodnerash. "I know, because it is also my mother's birthday". Bodnerash slapped me hard for this historical impertinence. I swayed, I checked my teeth with my tongue, but Bodnerash said with a mellow sardonic smile: "You better recover quickly because you have a lot of work awaiting you. I wish you much success". He even bowed and went away. I thought quickly and ran after him: "Herr Unterscharfuhrer, I shall also need cotton swabs and a lot of soft rags". He interrupted me: "you can send Joseph for whatever you need". I was now speaking to Joseph. Happily enough he was the milder of the two Josephs. In fact, I was speaking to myself: "I shall have to do a lot of experimenting before I dare to touch the portrait... I can only do my experiments on the margin of this portrait, the margins that would eventually disappear under the final beautiful frame". Joseph looked at me and at Adolf Hitler, as if to seek his advice. He must have been given one — "you can ask for scraps of similar photographic paper, or even some photos executed in the same technique" — he ventured. I thanked him for this wonderful idea, I thanked him from the bottom of my heart.

I started immediately with experiments after the delivery of the requested materials. Bodnerash suggested that Joseph could paint in the huge portions of the portrait and I could thus take care of the details. It was wrong. One cannot proceed in the usual way by preparing an all over background layer of paint. Hitler's face and uniform would disappear underneath. I had better follow my instructions. "Take it easy" — I whispered to myself — "don't rush it".

I shall spare you now all the technicalities of my preparatory research, and they were not like passing the seven gates to hell, but rather like passing seventy-seven such gates. I shall only add that next to each sample were noted all the relevant details of its execution. I proceeded by elimination until I found the right approaches. Bodnerash was not breathing down my neck, not this time. But when he came two days later and saw nothing, absolutely nothing on the Fuhrer's portrait — he exploded.

My grandchildren, do you know the story about the emperor of China who ordered a painting of a cock from a painter who was rising in fame? Month after month the emperor sent his envoy to inquire about the progress of the painting, but there was nothing to be shown. Eventually the emperor came himself to the painter's studio, puffing with rage. "Where is my cock"- he asked threateningly. No problem, your majesty" — said the painter. He took a brush and painted a splendid cock in five minutes. "What?" — exploded the emperor — "you can do it in five minutes, and you kept me waiting for several months? This is preposterous, you will pay with your life". The painter didn't answer. He merely opened the door to a room, and there were hundreds upon hundreds of paintings representing a cock...

Almost the same happened here. When Bodnerash was shown all the samples with meticulously noted details of technique — he was appeased. But Bodnerash was Bodnerash; he had to show his clout. "From what I see, I reach the conclusion that you don't need the services of Joseph" — and he took Joseph away. He only added that a Ukrainian will come every morning and evening to carry the heavy picture out and back into the building.

Night after night I discussed my problems with mother, bringing the samples with me. We were sure that if I was going to work on the vertically posed picture, the turpentine will drip down. It may run from Hitler's face down to the collar of his shirt. It was most advisable to depose the picture on the floor. Without help I couldn't bring the portrait to a horizontal position. In the morning I asked the Ukrainian to help me lay it down. "That's your problem" — barked this huge beast and left me alone. I didn't feel the biting cold, I was sweating profusely, not only from the effort of lifting the huge contraption, but mainly from fear that I could drop and damage it. It was now in a horizontal position and I started to work on it. I started with the left sleeve and the results were positive. The sleeve came to life. So far so good, But I could not endlessly postpone taking care of the face of the monster. I knew I shall give it a basic warm tonality. I knew that I shall then add the highlights and eventually paint the shadows in blue and green hues, so as to give my work some artistic value and not turn it into kitsch. Deutscher will know the difference.

But this inapproachable face was physically inapproachable to me — being situated far off, in the center of the picture. The picture was two meters high and a meter and a half wide. Try to bend your body, to advance its upper part far from your feet, and to paint with delicate strokes without the slightest support for your hand. No painter would work in such conditions without mastery over his movements. Was I to lose my balance, my hand would pierce a hole in the picture... My back could take it only for a couple of minutes at a time, which meant it would take weeks to fulfil my task.

I tried to place my body in all possible positions. To no avail. I remembered that Michelangelo worked for four years on the ceiling of the Sixteen Chapel, lying on his back on a plank of the huge scaffolding, his arms numb, the paint dripping into his eyes, his lungs lacking air. But I am not Michelangelo, I am merely Maria, prisoner number A –26551.

I prayed for an enlightening idea, and I found one. I placed two blocks of concrete at the two sides of the picture, and a plank upon them. I could lean on it but not too much, it could cave in. This solution must suffice for the basic touches of color. The rest had to be done with almost dry patches, using a cotton swab. This could be done while the picture stands upright. That was now my plan.

The Ukrainian came every morning and placed the picture upright. After he left, I dragged it and put it down. Every evening he came to carry it inside into the wardrobe of the shower room. We never exchanged a word.

Bodnerash must have guessed my excruciating pains and efforts, but I never complained. I was too proud. "What if the rain would surprise me in the middle of the day?" — I asked. "That would be your problem" was my boss's answer. What else did I expect? If I could change the position of the picture every day, I must be like the mythical German heroine Valkyria and I could manage — thought probably Bodnerash.

One day I had an accident, and it was a disaster. In spite of all my precautions, a fat drop of paint fell on Hitler's collar. I tried quickly to cover it up, but the paint was fresh and the new layer translucent. To my unfortunate luck, Bodnerash arrived at this very moment. Now he had something to holler about. He used the juiciest epithets of his vocabulary, cursing me to the tenth generation (as if I had a chance to produce a new generation). I was even astonished that he didn't slap my face. He didn't dare to. It could really ruin the portrait at this advanced stage. He looked at me as if he saw me for the first time. Indeed, I must have presented quite a sight. I was enveloped all over in wrapping paper, fastened with ropes to my body. I did it to protect my precious dress, but also to keep me warm because I was working in windy open space. "You bitch" — yelled Bodnerash — "you know how to protect your fancy dress, but you are unable to protect the Fuhrer's shirt!" O.K. he had his say, but he could not deny that I have made excellent progress so far. Hitler's face was glowing and alive. The coronation of my efforts was Deutscher's appreciation. He sneaked in, asked me to keep his visit a secret and observed: "It is an artist's free conception, but let me advise you to dim the blues down, nobody would understand them". I was elated.

One Sunday afternoon (a day free of work), we were formed into rows of five, we didn't know what for. Would it be a delousing? But no, we were told that we are cordially invited to the movies. Is it true? Probably yes. That is when my mother slips out. She would not be dragged to the movies... she takes a beating but she persists and hides in the block. I am swept along with the crowd. But I do not resist, I am curious of everything, I have to taste this experience too.

We are marched into another compound and stand in front of a building. There are a few steps and a platform. An SS officer, visibly of the highest rank, stands there visible to all. "It is Hess, commander Hess himself" — whispered the old-timers. And what is he doing there? He holds his sides and is laughing in cascades. He is visibly happy that the movies are such a success. To him it seems highly amusing.

We enter and sit in the dark cinema like in the good old times. I pinch myself; I can hardly believe that it happens to me in Auschwitz. This room is a microcosm, a capsule detached from the gaging and hanging going on outside of this cocoon. I don't remember the title of this pre-war film. The main actress was Magda Schneider, the mother of the later so famous Romy Schneider, who also belongs to the past generation, and I mean MY generation. I don't remember the plot of the film, and it is hardly relevant to my story. I only remember one innocent scene that left the greatest impact on me. Magda Schneider walks through the fields of ripe corn. She hardly walks, she floats through the high ears of corn, pushing them aside like a swimmer. Here I started to cry. This simple scene was so pathetic in my eyes. It symbolized freedom.

A woman who can walk through fields was to me the personification of Freedom. I cried and I sobbed, and Janka could well guess why. But one of the 'V' sisters, Frieda Tenzer, who sat in a row in front of me, turned back and whispered "You poor idiot, why are you crying? Don't you know that there will be a happy end?"

Next day after Sunday — back to work and to my problems. I was now reaching high above Hitler's head, painting in the cloudy background. My arms were numb, I felt as if I was going to faint. I must have been working all those weeks by sheer force of will. To reach that high I took a chair and I now worked standing on it. My head was protected from the wind by my kerchief. Thus, I didn't feel the first drops of rain. When I felt them eventually, the rain gained force and started whipping the portrait. I hopped down from the chair, took the heavy picture, trying to drag it quickly to the other side of the building, to the entrance to the showers, where the Ukrainian stored it every evening. It was too far, I thought to myself — "I shall never reach it. I must drag it to the nearest door, for the moment any shelter would do. There is a back entrance, a low door..." Finally I managed to push the picture, slightly slanted, past the door. It was inside, it was safe!

I remembered that all the paints in many hues were spread outside and were becoming diluted by the rain. I rushed outside, gathered the paints, the utensils, the oils, the turpentine, the cotton, the rags. I ran in and out. I was drenched.

But I was not totally abandoned and forgotten. When Bodnerash noticed the rain he came running, completely out of breath. He came through the main entrance and saw no one. He called from the other side of the building: "Maria, where are you? Where is the portrait?"

I answered from my end: "I am here on the other side and the picture is safe". When he reached me, I noticed how upset he was, he must have run for his life. Now he understood how wrong it was to leave me all alone. He looked at the picture, he checked it for any damage, then he lifted his eyes, and what did he see? Exactly above the picture and over Hitler's head he saw two innocent letters: 00. Yes sir, the portrait of Adolf Hitler was standing under the sign of the toilet. It even spelled that Hitler is twice zero...

It dawned on me what I have done and what is in store for me. I had an automatic, instant reaction; I hide my face with one hand and protected my head with the other. But Bodnerash didn't strike me, not yet. He said: "Now you have done it, you saboteur. It is worse than sabotage, it is an insult to majesty. You have deliberately put our Fuhrer Adolf Hitler into the shithouse". He extends his two huge hands, he gripped my neck. I was so close to him that I smelled his breath. Soon, very soon, I shall choke, be strangled, and feel and smell nothing. But his grip on my neck loosened. I felt him shaking as our bodies touched, I felt him shaking uncontrollably with... laughter. The more he laughed, the more he pressed my body to his breast, so that I could not see his face contorted by laughter. As we stood thus, embracing like a pair of lovers, I knew that this would become the best joke of his life to tell his friends (after the war) over a mug of beer.

I should stop here lest I spoil this episode, but I have to remind you that Bodnerash was half German and half Romanian. He was an opportunist who rode the right horse, but he had certainly no love for Hitler.

We still stood enlaced like a pair of lovers, and laughter being contagious, I felt myself swept along and shaking all over. Right then we heard the voice of an SS man coming from the other end of the playground. Thanks heaven he hasn't caught us in this compromising position with quasi sexual overtones. "Bodnerash" — he hollered — "where are you?" Bodnerash dropped me instantly. He emerged from the 00, the loo, he even lifted his trousers. The two SS men met in the shelter of the main entrance. They now talk Romanian, being both of the same origin. They wouldn't do it in an ordinary situation. They were so excited that they didn't even take precautions.

They argued, they must have been in a state of shock. They left the playground, forgetting me and the portrait. I was left alone with Adolf Hitler in the toilet.

Now, in retrospective, I can guess what it was all about. The second SS man must have brought to Bodnerash the news of the disaster; the Russian offensive approaching Auschwitz, and the perspective of the total liquidation of Auschwitz. Did I mention that Bodnerash promised me fifty lashes on my buttocks? Yet, it was not my destiny to finish the portrait or to receive the fifty lashes. Everything happened now at an accelerated rhythm. Hardly a couple of days after the "Hitler in the loo" incident, we returned to our block and were given a most unexpected order. It was January 18th 1945 (who doesn't remember), we were given one hour to get ready and to leave the block, leave Auschwitz. The whole camp will be evacuated. Where to? We could not even guess. The camp was like a beehive. What was there to prepare? We could not even carry water with us, we had no receptacle.

Somebody signaled to me that I am wanted at the compound's barbed wire. It could only be Ulrique. Indeed, he managed to approach the fence to take leave of me. We knew that we have only minutes or seconds for this conversation, so we spoke in broken sentences. "First of all, try to memorize my address in Paris, so as to stay in touch if we survive". He tried to spell it, but I interrupted him: "I know it by heart, it is 156 rue St.Maur, Paris XIX-th". He was happy. He tried to pass me an object, to slip it between the barbed wires. It was a little bottle. "It's spirit" — he said — "when you will feel very weak and cold, it will give you a boost. Please try to keep alive... I wish so much to meet you after the war. I wish I could pass on to you some of my inner strength, you are so frail, so delicate". At this instance we heard shrill whistles and commotion. I only heard his last words "Farewell, my dear" — and we were separated.

In the block everything was topsy-turvy. How should women dressed in summer dresses prepare for an evacuation in mid-January. Should they cut their soft, fluffy blankets of the model camp into pieces and fill their dresses with them? Or rather, how could one get hold of an ordinary grey thin blanket, which could serve as a cape enveloping one all over. Suddenly we heard the air raid sirens. It meant "lights off", but who cares. Why not get bombed right here, together with the bloody Germans. Wouldn't it be better than to starve in a long march on foot? We heard an SS man yelling from downstairs, admonishing us to turn the lights off this very moment. We didn't pay attention. He was so outraged that he shot straight into our window. The bullet broke the glass and entered into... the buttock of Tova, kneeling on her upper floor bunk. Tova yelled, the bullet was stuck deep in her buttock. A minute ago, Tova was perfectly capable of participating in the long march because she had been given a pair of shoes. Now she had shoes, but she had also a bullet in her bottom. She was finished. Who could take care of a wounded heavy woman, who among all these walking shadows...? All her friends turned away, deeply ashamed... But hear, hear. A hardly known woman, quite boring, keeping to herself and generally considered an egoist, approached Tova and offered to take care of her: "I shall not let you down, I shall support you and hold you, just rely on me, lean on me" — said this woman by the name of Netta. How unexpected, coming from that quarter. How we had misjudged this Netta. Once more, it was a lesson never to form an opinion, based on misinterpreted symptoms. We all felt ashamed.

One cynic among us observed: "She will not have to support her for a long distance. Don't you all guess that this is a German trick? Would they try to finish us off right here in Auschwitz, these tens of thousands of us — there would be a general uprising. But if they lead us out of here, group after group, they can take each group into the woods and shoot it there". Nobody answered, these speculations made sense. The interest of the SS people was to disperse and disappear as quickly as possible. Why drag and convoy us to nowhere or to some overcrowded camps? We are now given one more order. We were being marched to the "Brotkammer"- the nearest bread storeroom. Bread will be distributed to every prisoner for the long march. The conclusion is that the Germans have been planning this evacuation for some time and prepared enough bread for distribution to prevent the outbreak of a revolt. The Russian offensive must have made tremendous progress.

Here we are, forming a long queue in front of the "Brotkammer". There is also one of the women wardens with a key, ready to open the storeroom of bread. At this instant there happens something that we haven't foreseen. The Russian women broke the ranks. They seem to split into formations; the "storming troops" beat up everybody right and left, meanwhile the "porter troops" are already inside, loading the loaves by armfuls. The storming troops guard their passage. The single SS woman yells and strikes with her whip. She is blocked by one single Russian giant of a girl. The SS warden whips her mercilessly, but to no avail. This giant doesn't budge or bat an eyelid. The SS woman tires of whipping. The giant still blocks her way while the Russians quickly distribute the bread between the comrades of their cells (I mean the communist cells). The giant one shrugs her shoulders and says: "She whips as if godmother would besprinkle me". What could seem a spontaneous conquest of the "Brotkammer" was in reality a well-rehearsed and orchestrated blunt attack. I was to learn about the Russian tactics only gradually.

As for us, we didn't even get one crumb of bread. But you can rely on the 'V' team, the ever-victorious Tenzer women. They took advantage of the Russian trick, and riding on the backs of the Russian invaders they got hold of many loaves of bread. We saw in the streets of Auschwitz that every prisoner was given a loaf of bread for the road, distributed at his respective Brotkammer. Only we, some fifty women, have been duped and overcome by the Russians. We were to start this long march without a reserve, without a slice of bread.

Our whole permanent group is destitute, all the five of us: mother, Janka, me, and the two Liebgold sisters, Rysia and Fela. Rysia is as beautiful as Fela is ugly. Both are good partners. There are also not far from us the lovely sisters Stenia and Dzidka, and right in front of us mama Tenzer and the 'V' sisters, carrying armfuls of bread. Ruth is not far away, but I don't see Erica. Thus, we are being formed into hundreds, a long serpent of women assembled from several blocks, soon to leave Auschwitz through the famous gate. The SS women count us and check us back and forth. Suddenly, somehow, there are six of us in our line instead of five. My mother is torn away from us, she is pushed down the rows and transferred to another formation of hundred prisoners. Mother takes a beating, but she sneaks back to us. Thus, we are now hundred and one. The SS women would lash at us the moment they discover this irregularity. Mother is admonished by the Tenzers to draw back, to return over there. She doesn't budge.

A solution is found. One woman who got trapped among us volunteers to move back instead of my mother. She wants to join her friends.

All this happens in the pitch-dark evening of January 18th, 1945, before we leave Auschwitz. One woman knows to inform us that we are 60,000 prisoners here about to be evacuated. The historians claim nowadays that it was much less, that in Auschwitz itself there were at that moment no more than 20,000 prisoners left. Still, the large number could be plausible if you count all of Auschwitz appendixes, the large and small camps around it. Some were huge like Birkenau, some were formed around one factory. Some were for the commandos draining the marshes and one camp, Buna, was an agricultural farm, where the prisoners could feed themselves a little better, as we shall soon see.

BEYOND THE CHIMNEYS OF *AUSCHWITZ*: THE FIRST "MARCH OF DEATH"

It is a cloudy, dark night and the wind whips us without mercy. Hardly have we passed the Auschwitz gate and on the wide road there are already several bottlenecks. We march and we stop, we advance several yards more and we are stopped again. Do you realize that along this road — if you measure it across — marches not one group of prisoners, but some three or four groups of males and females, simultaneously driven and whipped by the SS wardens, the Ruthenians, the Lithuanians and the Latvians. Thousands upon thousands are concentrated on one road.

That is when a miracle happens right in front of me. In this moonless, pitch-dark night, Ruth spots Rene among these crowds of thousands. She calls out his name, they both leave their ranks, jump at each other and fall into each other's arms. The crowds continue to flow and they stand like a dark sculpture of lovers. What the concert couldn't do for them — the evacuation did. Had I read it in a book — I would say: what a cheap, schmaltzy melodrama. But reality can be that romantic and syrupy.

The men are now advancing, we are stopped. Eventually when we resume the march, we are stopped less often. The tactics of the Germans must be to let the men — who are a more dangerous species- pass first. This achieved, our tempo is accelerated, as if the Germans were determined to leave behind the greatest part of the road on this first night. Our arms-carrying escorts seem to be in a hurry lest they be overtaken by the enemy. Perhaps they were given such orders from above. Anyhow, they whip us to make us progress faster. As if we could.

The elements play havoc. A snowstorm breaks. The snow and wind beat our faces. We pull the thin kerchiefs almost over our eyes. Anyhow, the fog and the snow are so thick, the night is so dark, that I can hardly see the back of the one marching in front of me, sometimes I even collide with her.

Soon we become very tired. When you are so weak you are apt to cry or to laugh without reason. I laugh. One of the Tenzers who march in front of us remarks: "There is one who has already lost her wits". Janka throws me a glance with a question mark. I explain: "I just remembered the damn portrait that will never be finished, and the fifty lashes promised me by Bodnerash. But I also remember Bodnerash cuddling me in his arms, and that's the most preposterous situation, seen from our present perspective". Janka joins me in laughter and some people look outraged. In reality, in the last few days there developed a new chemistry between Bodnerash and me. He was elated that the portrait looked like a work of art, but he was also amused by the funny secret we shared. Perhaps he was mellowed by the imminent danger. He even mumbled something about expressing his thanks to me. What a pity that it had to happen in the "Last days of Pompei".

The snowstorm doesn't lose its impact. The masses of fresh snow turn into mud under the feet of tens of thousands marching on the road. Our shoes with wooden soles are not so bad, but I have seen many prisoners taking to the road with shoes enveloped in paper or rags and tied with a string. Soon they can hardly lift their heavy feet from the thick mud. All of us have wet feet, our shoes getting heavier and heavier. We try to ignore it; we are treading along like somnambulists.

When we are permitted to stop for a while we cannot sit down, not even for a second, how could one sit on mud? What time is it? Is it close to dawn? We have lost the sense of time in this transcendental nightmare. We are now walking and sleeping "schlepping" our feet like robots. Would you believe that one can walk and sleep at the same time? Yet we do, or rather we do on and off. When you sleep — you relax, but the moment you wake up, it grips your heart with an iron fist. The heart flutters like a trapped bird. Parching asleep we are from time to time whipped to accelerate our progress. We make a febrile effort, then fall asleep again.

From time to time we are shaken by the sound of a shot. In the darkness and in our somnambulist state we do not yet notice the first bodies of the victims on the margin of the road.

You may now ask what we do with our physiological needs. Whoever feels nature's call steps aside on the edge of the road, and regardless of the presence of the male escorts — does her thing. Shame doesn't exist anymore. She does it squatting quickly lest she be taken for a fainting person and be shot at. Then she hastens to join her advancing group. When my mother steps out for a pee, she returns exclaiming: "I almost tripped over a cadaver, do you believe it". Indeed, now in the light of dawn we see from time to time a body thrown on the ramparts of the road. It becomes evident that whoever tripped or fainted was shot and dragged to the side. There is some untrampled snow on the margin of the road, and such a cadaver, sprawled on its white backdrop looks like a rejected doll of rags. Cadavers are much less impressive than you expect them to be. The red poppies of blood forming next to the body are quite decorative. What you perceive is a picture in white, black and red. Please excuse this metaphor, I just happen to think in such terms. Only after a moment does it dawn on you that the next victim could be your friend or even yourself, and that is when you become emotionally involved in this picture. It ceases to be abstract.

It is a queer process, but I must register our reactions faithfully. Without such explanation, the historic term "March of Death" would be an empty term. So far, I have only described to you the first night. How shall I now be able to relate the events of two more days and two more nights of this nightmare, so more that there is no passage from night to day except in the nature. We just go on and on.

We have in front of us the 'V' team, the Tenzer women. We travel light — they have a problem. They have stolen so many loaves of bread that they can hardly carry them. The mother could find her death under the load of bread. This reminds me of this moral fable about the greedy man lost in the desert and dying of hunger. Upon finding a satchel in the sand, and checking it feverishly, the man exclaims: "I thought it would contain barley, but unfortunately these are diamonds..."

Mama Tenzer, though she carries only two loaves, cannot bear their weight. She trips ever so often, every time supported and saved by her daughters. The danger becomes imminent. The daughters whisper, quarrel, agree on something, and turn to us. They propose us a deal. If we, the five friends, would be willing to carry one loaf of bread — then upon the arrival at a camp (but only then) half of it would be ours to share, the other half would be returned to them. We agree. Do we have a choice? Your generation would say: "why not rob them of this bread which they have robbed at your expense?" I don't know now why we didn't. Some character we had, the five of us... It is not easy to walk with bread on an empty stomach. Anyhow, all these emaciated women around us can hardly walk, let alone march. When we rest for a while (without sitting down on mud) I find a tree and cling to it like a drunkard. Then I jump away from it. An SS man may think that I am fainting and shoot me. I cannot even have the consolation of embracing a tree.

As the evening approaches I exchange a few words with mother. We feel that we shall not be able to continue. Should we not try to escape after dark? Though we don't wear striped dresses, we are easily recognizable as prisoners being so emaciated. We couldn't hide in the woods in this harsh winter. Anyhow the Russian front doesn't seem to be approaching. We couldn't knock at the door of a hut and ask for shelter. We are deep in Silesia, where most of the population is German. Could we say to such a German family in a hut; "if you give us shelter, the moment the Russians arrive, we shall testify on your behalf and protect you". Would it work? Wouldn't they quickly denounce us to the local authorities? We drop the idea.

In order to describe that day, I would have to say one sentence repeated ad infinitum: "We see cadavers, and we go on and on..." This long day and the previous night means, altogether, marching and fasting for twenty-seven hours.

Late at night, at about ten, we reach the outskirts of the village Pless, which used to be on Polish territory and was called Pszczyna. The Germans responsible for our convoy know that enough is enough. They place us, group by group, in the barns of the local peasants for the night. We can lie down on hay, and we drop like stones, but not my mother. She finds the strength to enter the hut and speak to the woman of the house. I don't know what she says and how she charms this stone-faced woman, but a miracle happens. Mother brings me a glass of fresh milk. She says, of course, that she was given a glass of milk over there in the hut, and this one is for me. I am too weak to check it or to quarrel with her. Never in my whole life has milk tasted like this.

If she is so good, this country woman, could we not hide here deep in the hay of her barn, and just stay dug in? It is fortunate that we don't risk it, because in the morning come our oppressors, the SS wardens with the Ukrainians, chase us out and check the barn. They take the huge fork used for hay-lifting and stick it deep into the stacks of hay to check if no one is hiding there.

Some women who took off their shoes for the night are now unable to put them on. The wet leather has shrunk and lost all shape. Others have torn a strip of their dress and bandaged the blisters on their feet. Eventually many prisoners will die because of their well sore feet.

We take again to the road and among them the five of us and some fifty other women who have been fasting already for more than thirty-five hours. The bodies spread out on the roadsides look so quiet, content and reposing that we envy their eternal bliss. Is there no salvation for us? Why don't we simply eat the bread taken into custody from the Tenzers, or at least our half of it? What could they do to us? Indeed, afraid of being attacked they have made a similar deal with other partners, they are less loaded now.

None of us is the first to suggest devouring our half of the bread, so we don't. The beautiful Rysia asks her sister Fela: "Were I to faint from hunger and be shot here on the spot, what would become of you, my sister?" Somebody answers: "The good friends would embrace her, comfort her, and continue with her further and further to… the gas chambers". All the five of us laugh to tears. Somebody remarks: "Is it possible that all the five of them have gone out of their minds?" Thus, we continue. The thirst is worse than the hunger. From time to time, an SS man lets a girl jump to the fields and fill her soup bowl with snow. At first, we feel warm, it burns our stomachs, then we feel even colder. Anyhow, the snow quenches the thirst, and fills the stomach for a while, engaging the juices that gnaw at it. One of the escorting Ukrainians, attached to our group, walks dragging his rifle and his knapsack. From time to time he curses openly in his bad German — "Verfluchte Deutsche, verfluchte Fluhrer, verfluchte ich…" meaning: "Damn Germans, damn Fluhrer, damn me (for having joined them)". After some reflection, he adds: "But it won't help you. I shall shoot you if you sway or step out of line". As if to confirm it he uses again his whip on us.

We hear shots, we see more and more cadavers, even though not all the tens of thousands march along the same road. We must have been split up on the first night and taken to different roads. Many women have lost their shoes in the mud or dropped their shoes that had deeply wounded their feet. The upper bodies move forward, but the feet and the legs refuse to follow suit. Some collapse, get shot, their bodies are dragged out of the lines. The road must be kept free.

Thus, we reach the third night and the town Loslau (Wodzislaw in Polish). There is a big military camp, now empty of soldiers. In its huge stables, now horseless, we shall be able to sleep. We are even given from the cantina a glass of tea and a slice of bread, our first after forty-eight hours of fasting. We are now ordered to climb up the ladder in the stable and lie down on straw. What a bliss!

It is dark up there and quite warm on the straw under the roof. Before we lie down, we hear masculine voices very close to us. Who is it? — we ask. "It is us, a group of guys evacuated from the Buna camp". There is access to this elevated platform from the second side too and there is also a ladder. We hear them climbing and moving closer and closer. They sound like being in a better shape than the average prisoners.

My mother says: "I had better lie down on this side of you girls". What is she speaking about? Does she intend to defend her four virgins? We are too exhausted to pay attention. Minutes later it is silent and everybody is falling fast asleep. In this total silence we hear my mother's voice loud and clear: "Mister, if there was any light in here, you would take your hand away". General laughter follows her words. No comment is necessary except one: these men from Buna probably haven't seen a woman for months or years. Working on a farm they managed to be less undernourished.

In the morning, our watchdogs come to wake us. We are even given coffee, but nothing else. Here we decide that enough is enough. The Tenzer women are nowhere in sight, we have probably been separated. It is high time to consume the first half of the loaf of bread, the one belonging to the five of us. Who knows how many more kilometers we shall have to walk? Thus, slightly refreshed after the long fast we take to the road. Hardly have we passed several kilometers when we reach the railway station of this town Loslau, which used to be Wodzislaw before the German occupation annexed Silesia to the 'Reich'. There is a train ready for us. It is not what you imagine, it is a train of open carriages used for transporting coal. We are loaded, hundred and twenty of us on one carriage. We have to sit down on the fine, black coal dust covering the floor. What else can we do, remain standing? We cannot sweep it. Each of us feels as if she had too many body parts. The legs are superfluous, there is not enough space for them even in an embryonic position, or doubled up like a penknife.

The train moves, then it stops in the middle of nowhere, then it moves and so on. It is not a regular train with fixed schedule, it can move only when the field is free. I can hardly remember how much time it took for this train to reach its destination (if there is a clear destination?). Two days, three days?

At night we are smitten by cold winds mixed with wet snow. If we spread our kerchiefs over the head as protection — our heads are still exposed to the cold wind. If we tie the wet kerchief — it acts like a cold, wet compress. I have no idea how we survived it. Soon there are many cases of pneumonia. Many women, unable to restrain themselves, urinate where they sit. Eventually, when the train stops for some time, the carriages are opened by the guards, and we can step down, one by one, to relieve ourselves. Several girls are then permitted to bring snow from the ramparts of the rails. We share this snow hungrily.

Every time that one of us, the five companions, is permitted to step down from the carriage — she looks instinctively for the Tenzers, praying not to find them. We are almost certain that they are not on this transport.

After two days, at one such stop, I get down to relieve myself and bring some snow for many others. Hardly have I squatted — and what do I see? I catch a glimpse of Frieda. I don't even take time to lift my panties... I interrupt my physiological function and run to the carriage. "Damnation, the Tenzers are here" — I cry. Janka is not impressed. She says in her clipped calm voice: "There is a limit even to honesty. So, we have trudged this bread so far for these bread-robbers, but now no more. We shall cut and share their half of bread right now, before we die of starvation on this train of death." Nobody objects, and that's what we do. We share it among the five of us, terminally starving companions. By now we even look like ghosts. The fine dust of coal, covering the floor of our carriage, sticks to us. Even our faces are already smudged with it. Do souls in inferno look like us? A film costumer and characterizer couldn't conceive a better creation of infernal creatures. A station master at a village station almost faints at the sight of us.

Inside the train more and more women faint. We don't even discern who has fainted, who is asleep and who is dead. There sits next to me a nice girl by name of Babette. She is crying and fainting. Having quite recently arrived from Belgium, she is not underfed. She is simply not used to being hungry, she had no time to build up resistance. After she cries some more, she tells me her story. She came from Belgium. The moment she arrived at Auschwitz she was placed to work at the 'Effektenkammer'. She observed that the old-timers knew how to steal and even how to smuggle valuables out of the compound. She wouldn't dare to. Whenever she found a coin or a ring hidden in the clothes inspected and sorted by her, she only dared to throw it into the latrine situated within the precinct. Thus, she had no reserves when this evacuation started. Like us she didn't even get a slice of bread for the road. When her good friends who worked with her, noticed how destitute she had become — they dropped her like a hot potato, even though they were well equipped for the evacuation, having bought many victuals in exchange for diamonds. Touched to the core, Babette cried and fainted once more. Her example proves my theory that people getting gradually used to being hungry are less prone to collapse. Babette was exposed to hunger too suddenly.

Before she fainted, I had time to ask her several questions. I was mainly interested in the moods prevailing in Belgium before her deportation to Auschwitz. "Did you, over there in Brussels, know what was going on in the concentration camps, did you hear about gas chambers and all the atrocities?" — I ask her. Her answer is astounding: "Oh, yes, we heard. There were not only rumors; it was even on the radio. How did we react? We considered it effective and necessary propaganda, even if it couldn't be true". So, this was the atmosphere in Belgium in the end 1944.

I observe another case of fainting spells close to me on the floor of our carriage. It is the case of a woman going on fifty, who is said to have been working as a doctor in Birkenau. The color of her face is green. It is visibly a cardiac case. She is not fainting, she must be close to agony, seized by a heart attack. She will be dead any moment now. We sit and observe. Hardly able to breathe she draws from her garment a phial and a syringe. She crushes with her teeth the top of the glass phial, fills with trembling hands the syringe and injects herself. How clever of her to be equipped with poison — we think. She commits suicide and that's the best solution. We turn away so as not to observe her agony — It must be a dreadful sight. Several minutes later we throw a glance, certain that it must be over, she must be dead. But no, she isn't dead, she is even breathing calmly and seems to get better. So, it wasn't poison, after all, she injected herself with a life-saving medicament. What a surprise and what an instinct for survivals!

As for the others, we don't know who is dead and who is unconscious. We don't have enough experience in such matters.

"*RAVENSBRUCK*" AND ITS PURULENT APPENDIX

At long last we reach our destination point. The carriage is opened by SS officials, and we are told to get down. Many women don't move even when dragged or pulled by the hair by our oppressors. Now we know that they are frozen to death or dead of hunger or pneumonia. All the others climb down, swaying, seized by vertigo but alive. We discover that we have been brought to Ravensbruck. Every time we arrive at a new wimp, the same scenario repeats itself. We scrutinize the horizon, looking for chimneys.

In such a huge camp there must be a gas chamber and a crematorium. It is the usual logical speculation. We pass through what seems to be the main street of Ravensbruck. It is shortly before dark. The inmates are strolling in the street and gaping at us, the ghosts soiled with coal dust. They even venture some remarks: "You are from Auschwitz, you say? You have seen nothing yet. Over there it was paradise compared to Ravensbruck". Our hearts sink hearing this prognosis. We don't even dare to ask about the gas chambers. We just look around.

There is among us a giant of a girl by name of Halina Nelken. A bright and lively girl. When we are stopped in the street, she picks one in the crowd, one that smiled at her, and asks her in a whisper: "What is your name and your block number?" The girl answers. Halina whispers quickly in her direction: "Look here, I have in my hand a thin chain with an amulet, it is of no value except of a sentimental value to me. Would you guard it for me? If I survive the reception here, I shall come for it to your block" — and she quickly slips it into the girl's palm. So, I am not the only one with an amulet — I think. Should I do likewise? I reject the idea. Perhaps the amulet has to protect us from a selection? Perhaps it will serve as a passport to life?

We are brought in front of a building and it has... a chimney. Once more we face life or death. We undress, and I remain once more with a toothbrush in my hand and the ever-present amulet. I still hold in my palm this little slip of celluloid containing a bit of rouge that we use before a selection. There is no selection and the showers are real showers. Without soap it is not easy to wash off the traces of coal dust. We are ghosting no more, and we are alive. Our dresses have been disinfected and I can miraculously retrieve my own dress and my own shoes. Soon we are placed in a block and we are given soup and bread. Thus seems to end our Golghota, or one of several Golghotas. Counting back, I have consumed, in six days, three slices of bread, one glass of milk (in Pless), one bowl of coffee (in Loslau) and a lot of snow. Like squirrels in winter we can recuperate only by sleeping, but not at daytime. You cannot stay inside the block at daytime. The block is so densely populated that we sleep three in the space intended for one.

"Ravensbruck" was originally constructed for a number of six thousand prisoners. As we are informed, now it is actually populated by thirty-five thousand inmates. Bedding three in the space designated for one would only accommodate eighteen thousand. What about the rest? We shall soon discover how the problem is being solved.

As it transpires, we have been temporarily placed in the Polish block. There are only Polish gentile women, all of them deported to Ravensbruck after the Polish uprising in Warsaw. They are not underfed, not yet. They are proud and well organized, visibly a prominent element. They live and act in cliques. The strongest clique is this headed by Mrs. Cyrankiewicz, the wife of the well-known pre-war socialist leader. To prove to you what an important figure we are speaking of — it is enough to mention that after the war he would become the prime minister of the Polish government under the Russian occupation. It was explained to me some time ago that Mr.Cyrankiewicz had two or three wives. Was this his first or his second? How am I supposed to know? It is also not relevant to my story.

Hardly have we slightly recuperated, after the march of death and the train of death — we gradually get the picture. We shall be treated like vermin. The Polish ladies are given a certain measure of autonomy within their block. They have a royal court installed there. There is even a protocol and etiquette bestowing upon a happy member of the court — the privilege of handing a glass of water to Mrs. Cyrankiewicz... Though descended from middle bourgeois class they play aristocrats. Should I say socialist aristocrats?

They occupy the roomy part of the block and sleep only one to a normal space, while we are bedded three to the same space. They are patronizing — we are their slaves, their charwomen. They cut and distribute the bread ration as they please. They pour the soup, leaving the thick deposit for themselves. They have their personal effects, linen, sheets, towels. They stay inside the block, make fire and keep warm, while we have to stay outside, and it is the end of January by now. These socialist ladies are aristocratic in bearing and openly antisemitic.

Janka has, as usual, a philosophic approach to such a phenomenon. She knows that she is refined, aesthetic, lady-like, cultured and persuasive. She wouldn't let herself be abused by these Polish upstarts. She tries to work her charm on one of the leaders. She starts like a righteous person: "I am very sorry that we have been imposed upon you in such a manner. It hasn't been our choice, we are not guilty of it. There is no reason to consider us as an alien element, which we are not. No reason to treat us as intruders and pariahs. We have been planted in your midst, and you are kindly requested to bear with us. You have no reason to victimize us, especially not you, the proclaimed noble socialists. You are expected to treat us as equals, according to your credo". End of speech.

The socialist leader looks at Janka with icy grey eyes. She accents every word of her a riposte: "You are making a grave mistake. We are different from you in a thousand ways. You, you have reached your debased status by sticking to the wrong creed. You have reached the state you are in, by force of sheer inertia. We, on the other hand, we are not slaves but heroines of an uprising, now defeated warriors."

Janka doesn't give up so easily: "If we are the slaves and the sheep — where is your glorious Christian mercy? You gentiles, free to move in your occupied country, have risen to arms very late and merely by aping our example. We, the Jews of ghetto Krakow, organized the attack on café Cyganeria already two years ago. It was staged by our boys, acting bravely and escaping from a ghetto. Yet, you are taking credit for this action. It was the

Jewish uprising in ghetto Warsaw which made you move… it taught you a lesson. You were late-comers as heroes" — adds Janka. "I don't have to discuss it with you, you are simply impertinent" — says the lady socialist and retreats; Janka has achieved nothing, she has even provoked more hostility, but at least she has made her point.

The false socialists continue their policy. They even block our access to the washroom. When they go there, we are not permitted to enter. When they finish — the place is cleaned and locked. They make us look dirty and be dirty. It reminds me of the medieval policy applied in the Holy Roman Empire, where the Jews were ordered by a papal edict to wear a long garb. Because its long train was constantly grimy, being soiled by the mud of the streets — the Jews were declared dirty people, and this bad opinion stuck to them. That was exactly the aim of this edict. In reality, the Jews, being cleaner, were less prone to the contamination of pestilence. The explanation of this fact was attributed to Jewish sorcery.

As it is, we need to wash, we just have to. We are not too lazy to walk a great distance to the washroom of the French women. Why do we have to pick such a distant washroom? Here is a good reason; the French are "afraid" of draughts and of cold water. It is not a legend; I have seen in Paris many four-room flats without a bathroom. The French women in Ravensbruck used to enter the washroom, moisten a handkerchief, pass it over their temples and their nape, splash their face, and… walk out. Thus, their washroom barrack is never crowded, and we take advantage of it. We continue to wash our bodies from top to toe, even though we have no soap and no towel.

I have now to return to the story of Halina, who entrusted her talisman to the custody of one of the inmates, a total stranger. After we survived the 'showers', Halina retrieved her bauble. She now befriends this girl, Trude, who rendered her such a good service. This young woman is a German Gentile, and it is not clear why she is incarcerated in Ravensbruck. She tells some tall tales and Halina swallows them. Halina doesn't suspect that Trude used to be a freelance prostitute, evading the medical control and the extension of her services to the German soldiers. She has been incarcerated for this criminal lack of patriotism.

Halina and Trude make the rounds of Ravensbruck and Trude serves as a proud guide. The two walk hand in hand, but every time they approach a certain block — Trude does everything to avoid its proximity. Eventually Halina asks what makes her so afraid of approaching this block. "If my permanent girlfriend sees me with you, she may scratch out your eyes" — is the laconic answer. As it transpires, Trude is a lesbian, and that is where her jealous lover girl lives. Trude has now fallen in love with Halina and is afraid of a tragedy. We have a good laugh and tease Halina that being so tall and masculine, she is probably designated to play the male role in this relationship. Being so ignorant in the matter of lesbian practices, we prod Halina to accept the challenge for the sake of furthering our instruction.

There is no work for us in Ravensbruck, a bad prognosis for our fate. We are occasionally drafted to carry planks but whipped for being too slow. On the whole, Ravensbruck is for us a short episode. At the beginning of February, we are moved elsewhere. The powerful Poles have probably achieved our ousting. No train is provided for us, we have to march. Where to? It is not very far, it must be an appendix of Ravensbruck. Once more we go through the same ordeal. Is it an extermination camp with gas chambers and crematoria? Constituting a superfluous element, a burden — are we going to perish here, or survive with... a toothbrush in our hand? Because I am now recording my story, you may guess that we survived once more, the same Gehenna.

We find ourselves in what is called the 'Jugendlager', meaning a 'Youth Camp'. We don't understand the implication until... we see the permanent inmates. Most of them are old women, French, Dutch, Belgian, but not Jewish. With the typical German sense of humor, this camp for decrepit old women is, ironically, called the 'Youth Camp'. The Germans don't kill old Gentiles.

The whole camp consists merely of five barracks, but now it is populated by three thousand prisoners. You will soon understand how it is done. The old-timers, these old women, live on normal bunks. They are given one blanket to four women. As soon as one is dead of pneumonia or dysentery, she is replaced on the bunk by another. All this doesn't apply to us. We are brought into a barrack which is empty of bunks. The room resembles a school classroom empty of furniture. Into this classroom we are ushered four hundred of us, and no less.

The first ones hasten to occupy sitting places, the last ones tarry in the hope to be led to another barrack, an empty one. They are beaten and forced to enter. We are among them. The four hundred are expected to sit on the bare floor. Whoever remains standing gets a beating. We have to sit down one on top of the other. We try to wiggle our bottoms so as to make them reach down to the floor. Even then there is no room for our legs. We try to make arrangements between ourselves, take turns, shift positions. The Hungarian women quarrel with us no more, they simply viciously pinch our legs and our bottoms till we have to jump up and lose the sitting place. The least we can do is sit back to back, so as to be able to kick back when pinched.

Not all the girls of our transport are allocated to the same barrack. The lovely sisters Stenia and Dzidka are placed in a huge tent. It is no less crowded. When a woman cannot restrain herself and urinates close to the tent both sisters have their clothes saturated with her urine. It is February 12th and Dzidka says to Stenia: "It is now two days before your birthday. If you survive, you will be able to tell later that in 1945 you spent your birthday camping in a tent in a youth camp..."

I promised you, my grandchildren, to return to the problem of the Russians. I shall have to return to this subject several times, adding every time a new feature and dimension of their power over us. In this barrack, where we are so mercilessly squeezed in, there are also several Russian women. Where we can hardly sit, let alone lie down, they want more space for themselves. What they want — they achieve. They have a blanket and they spread it in the middle of this big room. They sit around its edges and leave in the middle an empty space like a table. Who can measure up to them? Try to touch one with a feather and all the others would trample you to death. Three hundred and eighty-five women are helpless against some fifteen of them. There is not one weakling among them, all are built like athletes. You would suspect that they are a handpicked team, and not an accidental cluster of average women.

I have already described how we are seated. When one of us has to get up and leave the barrack because of nature's call, she is never certain that she will retrieve her sitting place. Yet we go out every day to wash our bodies with snow. One day we wash the upper part, one day the lower part. It is not so much the body that freezes, it is mainly the palms. Call this washing-ritual a sadomasochistic self-torture, but we practice it daily for the sake of discipline.

As for food — it seems to us that the rations are reduced to the minimum. There is no water. We wash with snow and drink snow. We have now to gather it dangerously close to the perimeter. It goes without saying that we are constantly hungry. Suddenly it dawns on us that we still have the little bottle of methylated spirit given to me by Ulrique. Its color is bluish, and we realized way back that it is poisonous. That is why, when freezing during the march of death and on the death train we didn't open the bottle to fortify ourselves with alcohol. Didn't it occur to Ulrique? He probably never noticed its color in the dark. When we passed through the showers in Ravensbruck mother has hidden the bottle in her shoe. Now mother has an idea. She moves along the perimeter of the camp showing the bottle to one of the Ukrainian guards. He knows what kind of spirit it is, but he will drink it, nevertheless. They strike a deal and mother receives one single slice of bread. She could call me aside and share it with me, pretending that the Ukrainian took it away without retribution. But my mother is righteous. She cuts the slice into five tiny parts, and we share it with our partners.

Inside the barrack the wars for a sitting place continue. It is already the end of the second week of our 'sojourn' in 'Jugendlager'. The rain has melted the snow and we are constantly thirsty. We cannot wash. One day Janka goes out to relieve herself and I fight like a lioness to preserve her sitting place. When she returns, she can place her bottom in its former emplacement. Now it is my turn to go out. It is her turn to safeguard my place. When I return, I am not able to sit down. Janka has lost the battle without starting it. I am standing and standing, I feel faint. Mother, Rysia and Vela are in a bad spot, they cannot help. Nothing happens, I remain standing. Blood rises to my face. I turn to Janka: "Are you not going to help me? Am I to remain standing till I drop dead?" Janka doesn't budge. I am still standing… It is the first time that we are in conflict. I have to regain my place single-handed, bruised and half fainting. I turn again to Janka: "I shall never forget this incident or forgive you. There is a limit to passivity. It reeks of egoism". Indeed, from this moment our relations are so cool and distant that Janka knows that she has been rejected. She reads in my mother's eyes the same condemnation, and mother has nursed her throughout Plaszow, Birkenau, Auschwitz and Ravensbruck. From this moment we drift apart. Perhaps we would have patched it up, but fate is against us. It is eventually fate that separates us finally. Not only from Janka, also from Rysia and Vela. It takes but one single moment to separate the five of us who went through thick and thin. It happens in the following way: one day, after the distraction of rations, we suddenly notice that a group of Germans is chasing after women.

They are the 'leeches'... The men who take Jewish blood for German soldiers — the way they did in Plaszow. We have no time to think, mother and I escape from the barrack. We cut through the fields and out of breath we sneak into a barrack inhabited by old women. We hide in a corner behind the bunks. It is like finding oneself in a nest of vipers. The old French women look at us suspiciously and hiss: "What are you doing here? You don't belong here, out with you." Fortunately, I speak French rather fluently: "Mesdames" — I explain in French — "The Germans are all over our barrack. They chase us in order to take two pints of our blood. Permit us, please, to hide here for a while, perhaps for half an hour. We shall certainly leave before the head-counting, we shall not endanger you". It doesn't help; they want us out, these witches. We have to leave; they threaten us with their long fingernails. Outside we play hide and seek, we loom from behind the corners; once we even approach the perimeter and the Ukrainian guard points his rifle at us. He shoots and provokes general panic. We run, we get lost. In this turmoil we lose all our three friends: Janka, Fela and Rysia. Instantly after this blood-sucking incident we are surrounded and taken for transport. It is only later that we become very bitter over the loss of friends. We reach the sad conclusion that making friends in the Holocaust period is dangerous for your psychic balance. You get too attached, you get emotionally involved. You cannot cope with the tragedy of losing friends. But we are incorrigible. People need people and we are not egoistic enough to keep apart. Two weeks later we have new friends. But not here, it is elsewhere. Our fifth camp, the 'Jugendlager', is behind us.

It is mid-February and we are loaded on a train, but not one with open carriages, not this time. The moment you are prodded and whipped to enter a carriage of a train — you have to think very quickly. It is possible that you will never get a chance to sit down, and you have only an instant to adopt a policy. If it is a carriage open to the sky — you had better choose your place plastered to the short wall, the one in the direction of the train's progress, because it will shield you from the impact of wind. If it is an almost hermetically sealed carriage — you had better choose your place close to an air-providing crack. In both cases it is better to sit against a wall. It will prop up your back and let your feet kick, if the necessity arises. Having the wall against your back means having one enemy less. These are the technicalities of survival.

It occurs to us that we are a very valuable possession to the Germans if they go to such pains to shift us, to engage for us precious trains (so greatly needed in war time), to burn costly fuel squandered on our transportation. Does it make sense? It is still not clear to me, not clear to this very day. Incidentally, I have learned just this week that the German Department for Jewish Affairs had to pay the German Railway for these trains inserted into the railway timetable outside of the regular schedule... Ironically, this department paid to the railway with money obtained from confiscated Jewish property. Our train rolls, stops, rolls again. Sometimes I see through the cracks in the panels the name of a station, and it doesn't ring a bell. Sometimes we see ruins of bombed German towns, and we feel a grim satisfaction.

LIVING IN *MALCHOV* ON ONE SLICE OF BREAD DAILY

Once more we feel the pangs of fear. Is it for life or for death? That is to say — will we survive this trip? Didn't I promise not to describe it? Eventually, the train reaches its destination. The name of this little station is Malchov. The camp is a small one, probably raised initially for the slaves of a nearby factory. There is no factory, it has been bombed, and there is no work. There are no sanitary installations, no chimneys, and we do not pass through delousing and showers.

If we thought that the conditions in "Jugendlager" were subhuman, we erred. It can be worse, at least in one respect. We are not too crowded, it is true, we are two to a normal space on the bunks, but the rations are less than necessary for survival. There is warm water instead of coffee substitute in the morning, and there is one single slice of bread distributed in the evening. The soup is dirty warm water boiled on potato peels from the German kitchen. Once a week, on Sunday we are given a tiny cube of margarine, the size of a domino chip. We also receive, every Sunday, one potato boiled in its peel. The bread is the size and shape of a brick, to be cut into eight slices, one slice for one prisoner (In "Jugendlager" we were given two slices every day). The bread is baked from ground horse-chestnut and sawdust. It turns into crumbs the moment you touch it. It is often greenish from mildew, but we have to eat the only slice of bread as it is. (I had better stress at this point that we survived on this diet for seven weeks in the Malchov camp.)

No wonder that dysentery is rampant. Like in the two last camps there is no paper and no leaf for the basic sanitary use. There is in the primitive washroom a barrel with chlorine powder. We use it to wash our bodies and even our faces. Perhaps it will guard us from dysentery and typhoid, or so we hope. We delouse ourselves diligently every evening, inspecting the seams and cracking the lice with our fingernails. The same way we did in the ghetto and in all the camps except in Auschwitz 1, the lice-free model camp, where it was written on the wall: "One louse — your death". To our right and to our left, people lie sick with dysentery or typhoid, bunked next to healthy people. In "Jugendlager" they were spirited away and killed. The stench is terrible, but seeing people suffer and being unable to help them — is tragic. There is in the camp a woman-doctor who never forgets her vocation. She gathers little twigs of wood, burns them to coal and distributes them to those sick with dysentery. That is the utmost she can do. There is nothing we can do for the cases of typhoid, except changing cold compresses on their foreheads, if you are willing to sacrifice a strip torn from your dress and freeze in a short dress. As a matter of fact, you have already sacrificed a strip of your dress, that one to serve you instead of toilet paper. It has to be washed after every use and preserved wet for the next time. There is no nylon bag to keep it in; nylon has not yet been invented.

Let us return once more to the Russian women. How can these giants survive on one slice of bread? I happen to be the witness of a scene that I shall never forget. Behind the camp kitchen there was a huge wolfdog on a chain. It was a beast trained to tear people apart. It had a big juicy bone in its snout. Two Russian girls tried to overpower it. One held the beast's head, the second opened the terrible jaws and drew out the bone. Now they had to drag the beast all the length of its chain before they released it on command. Would they release the dog earlier — it would tear them to pieces. The operation ended, they sat on a stone and gnawed at the bone, taking turns. There was virtually no limit to their capacity for survival.

Another time their communist cells organized a whole gang for a single operation. It took careful planning. The minute the huge kettles of soup were carried to the barracks, they staged an upheaval. One group stroke with bear hands everybody in sight, including the two kettle carriers. Two giant Russians carried the kettle, running to their barrack. They distributed the soup in one jiffy, while the others were still beating everybody in the area, so as not to leave witnesses. Then, they planted the empty kettle next to another barrack, to erase all evidence. Thus, they gained for their group an additional kettle of soup. The commander of the camp must have been weak. There was no investigation and no punishment. As if it had never happened. The Russian communist cells were well trained to adapt to conditions and remain invisible.

We were, most of us, already swollen from hunger. Not all over, only in certain places. We had a crust of dry skin on our faces. Even chlorine could not rub it off. There was a chance to soften it with margarine, which would act as a nourishing cream. Here we had a dilemma; when we received on Sunday the domino chip of margarine, were we to spread it on our slice of bread and feed our stomach or rather rub it into the dead skin on our faces? There was still a third vital need for the tiny piece of margarine. Our new bosom friend, Sophie, a lovely young woman, was suffering terribly of hemorrhoids. She twisted on the bunk, she cried, she was weak from pain. Only inserting a piece of margarine into her rectum could relieve her. We decided to offer one cube of margarine to Sophie and share the second — rub it into our faces before they crack open into bloody wounds, as we already observed on others. Let our stomachs cry for this bit of margarine, they would get none.

We also got on Sundays, as I mentioned before, one potato boiled in its peel. Every prisoner devoured her potato on the spot. We did not. We decided to make a feast of it. We climbed on our upper bunk and sat down. We took our time. We peeled, each one, her potato of its paper-thin peel and ate it slowly, deleting ourselves on every bit of it. From below the Hungarians observed us with fascinated hungry eyes. They visibly begrudged us. It made us feel very proud. Is it a vice? We then took the few peelings and threw them ceremoniously down. The Hungarian women, waiting below, fought for the peelings like dogs. We enjoyed this scene. Today I know how foolish it was. The thin peelings could have filled our stomachs for a while and let the juices work on them. After all, we got this potato only on Sunday and were never sure to receive it the next Sunday. Was pride more nourishing than potato peel? It is sheer idiocy, but it was a psychological trick to make us feel human, as compared to the beasts fighting for our peelings.

Meanwhile we feel a strong urge to find other psychological tricks to keep us human. Anything goes. I find a stub of a pencil. I borrow a penknife to sharpen it. Has a pencil — will write. Still, there is not even a scrap of paper in this camp. There is only the cardboard of the margarine wrapping.

It cannot be used as toilet paper, but it could be used for a game. I cut it with the penknife into tiny squares. I mark on every square a letter of the alphabet. I distribute the squares among my partners. We play scrabble on our bunk. I never played it before, I didn't know that it existed... Somebody would invent it sooner or later. It reminds me of the aphorism coined by agnostics: "If God didn't exist — He would have to be invented". I cannot describe to you how happy can feel human skeletons, swollen from hunger, playing scrabble... Anything rather than succumb to apathy, inertia and depression.

We are sometimes summoned to dig trenches as shelters, but even the Germans don't believe that the Allied Forces would bomb Malchov. It is just to keep us busy and die sooner of starvation. Otherwise, besides the roll calls, all we do is sit on the bunks and wait for death. We save energy to such a degree that we refrain from speaking or speak in a whisper. Sophie says that scrabble assuages her hemorrhoid pains. We had to invent some other intellectual occupations instead of the abominable mental onanism of discussing cooking and eating. Since the ghetto we never stopped this nerve-racking game of surpassing each other in culinary inventions. It invariably ended with somebody saying: "Oh, leave it, just give me a big chunk of simple bread, and never using a knife I shall tear it to pieces and gorge myself on it".

We tried to explore our literary potential. Putting our heads together we decided on a competition: who would compose a better novel on the subject of the glorious "liberation". It had to have a high degree of probability and it shouldn't be literary trash. Not everybody participated. My mother didn't. I know that my father would, were he alive. Saving breath, we had only to render the gist of the story, without any stylization or embellishments.

One girl suggested a story: "A fakir endowed with the power of hypnotizing rats and mice and leading them out of town — hypnotizes the commander and all the guards. They follow him meekly out of the camp and far, far away. We are liberated. "Yes, yes" — added another girl — "and a regiment of fakirs enters the camp, carrying trays loaded with delicious food".

Another girl embroidered upon the same subject, but with a higher degree of probability: "The front is approaching. We hear a ferocious battle raging nearer and nearer. An Allie spy dressed up like an officer enters the camp with a (fake) written order: The commander and all the guards are ordered to abandon the camp immediately and follow him to an indicated registration point. They have no time and no authority to finish us of. They follow him into a trap and are all taken prisoners. He, our hero, a copy of Gary Cooper, comes back to open the gates..." We were all enchanted. "Yes, yes," — added the same girl — "And he is followed by American trucks loaded with delicious food".

I have already told you what our bread was baked from. It was delivered to the barrack in whole loaves, shaped like bricks, to be cut into eight slices and distributed by the prisoners themselves. Who was asked and empowered to cut the bread for our group? My mother, of course. She even had a nickname, 'The golden Hand', because she cut it expertly and justly. There were a lot of crumbs left after cutting. They were very precious, but how can they be distributed? How can one measure crumbs? Mother had an idea. There was among us a woman of splendid intellect, a former journalist from Lvov. Her name was Sidonia. She was willing, in the framework of our intellectual program, to tell the contents of excellent but less known books, and boy, she was a storyteller... It was a great effort for Sidonia, even though she did it in a hardly audible, weak voice. She was entitled to a reward, she burned up a lot of energy. Mother proposed to offer all the crumbs to her. The motion was approved. Sidonia did her story-telling every day for about half an hour. She had a large audience, listening to her stories in rapture and religious silence. She got the crumbs from several bread-cutters, and her listeners waited impatiently for her daily stories, sitting concentrated in a close circle, so as not miss a word of her whispered wonderful tales. She was ugly, but when she spined her stories she underwent a metamorphosis. With her thin, curled, reddish hair, she seemed to us like an angel.

In spite of this heavenly atmosphere, Satan was looming around the corner. There was another "client" aspiring for the crumbs, one that was not waiting to be offered them as an act of goodwill. As of late, we observed that the bread delivered to our barrack had been nibbled by rats. Several loaves had big holes and smaller holes. We made an investigation in other barracks, but it didn't seem to happen there. The rats wouldn't pick on us exclusivity, so it must happen somewhere between the 'Brotkammer' and our barrack. We discovered that bread was brought by volunteers. This in itself was strange. The volunteer who carried almost every day a heap of loaves to our barrack was the refined Parisian, Madame Przepiorka (pronounced

Pshepiourka). She could be the only suspect and we watched her from a hiding place. She took her time in carrying the loaves being apparently weak. But no, pay attention; she dug her fingernails into the bottom loaf of the pile, and breaking off chunks and a handful of crumbs — put them into her pocket. Then she shifted the position of the loaves and nibbled with her fingers at others. By the time she reached the barrack she had a pocketful of pieces and crumbs. We caught her red-handed. She should get a thorough trashing, but we looked at her and felt only pity. She had lost all her hair; she was bald after typhoid. Can one punish such a poor creature? Incidentally, the Polish name Przepiorka means "a quail", and isn't quail a thieving bird? From now on she was an outcast, but she had the gumption to pretend that she was still on the best of terms with all of us. I could not guess at that moment that a year later I shall meet madame Przepidrka in Paris, but that is another story.

Speaking of bread, I have to stress our policy — mother's and mine. The rollcalls took place between five-thirty and six-thirty in the mornings, the cold mornings of the end of February. Many women fainted during these rollcalls. We defended ourselves in our own particular way. We didn't devour our single slice of bread on the spot. We preserved half of it for the morning, so as not to faint standing attention. The Hungarian women who observed this custom hated us for our power of will and restraint. We felt it, but we didn't change our policy. One night we went to sleep as usual, putting the two half slices enveloped in a kerchief, under mother's head. She was, allegedly, a light sleeper. The next morning the bread was gone. We were miserable, hungry and furious, yet we did not give in. From now on we tied the ends of the kerchief to my wrist. I still cannot understand how one can steal bread from a brother prisoner.

Twenty years later, when I taught at the teachers' seminary in Tel Aviv, I befriended a fellow teacher, Mr.B. This lover of literature was very patriotic, idealistic, and very dedicated as a pedagogue. There was something crystal-pure about him, a certain aura. Yet, he once confessed to me that during the Holocaust, when he was detained in his native Romania in a labor camp (not a concentration camp), he was so hungry that he once stole bread from a fellow prisoner. I was shocked to the core. Am I that naive and such a poor judge of people's character? It was not so much the deception and disillusion with Mr. B. that hurt, I was more disgusted with myself. In retrospective I saw myself as Don Quichote, always striving to be righteous.

But let us return to Malchov. It is a small camp, yet it seems to be situated in a vacuum. When you approached the perimeter, you saw nothing but empty, barren fields of an endless flatland. I missed the trees. I am such a crazy nature-lover that I could cry out of longing for trees. (I hope that you believe me, my pets, knowing how I take care of my terrace garden in Tel Aviv...) It has been three years since I saw trees, if you don't count the march of death and the train of death.

One day a miracle happens, or is it a catastrophe? We are taken, a whole big group, out of the camp. Where to, what for? Destination unknown and we feel the fear in our bowels. I only notice that, as far as I remember, we are not led to the railway station from which we came several weeks ago. We try to ask a Latvian guard where we are being taken to, but he only smiles a crooked smile and shrugs his shoulders. Our guards now take a side-road and we see... trees. We find ourselves in the woods. I am so elated that I feel a tear under my eyelashes. I am breathing deeply as if I wanted to take a lungful of this pine-scented air with me. While I am beaming with happiness, one of the women whispers: "They will probably kill us in the woods". A second adds, looking at me: "You will be buried in the woods, you damn tree-lover". I don't mind anymore. To be shot in the woods is certainly better than to suffocate on Cyclone B... I watch the trees heavily capped with cushions of snow. The wind plays on the harp of pine needles the sweetest of melodies. I have only one desire: to hold a branch of pine tree in my hand. Here and there we see on the snow a few branches that fell off or were broken off by children. I must have one little branch — I whisper. Mother knows that I am incurable in this respect. She knows that I shall not give up, that I shall endanger myself by stepping out of line. She says quickly: "Let me pick it for you, I am on the outside of the column". Indeed, it is easier for her. The moment she spots a perfect branch with kitten-like, bushy clusters of pines and ripe pinecones, she steps out of line and picks it quickly from the snow. She hides it under her arm. She was quick like a squirrel, yet an SS warden, a vulgar, thick woman, has noticed. She jumped from behind, leveled with my mother and yelled: "What do you have here, what have you picked up?" My mother looked at her with her innocent blue eyes and drew out an innocent green branch. We heard some women giggle discreetly. The ridiculed warden took out her whip and flogged my mother from right and left like a fencing knight. Mother shrank but didn't emit a sound. The woman got tired and gave up. She must have felt how ridiculous was her reaction.

Mother straightened up and whispered: "Don't you worry, I am all right, and damn her, I haven't thrown away the branch..." I was deeply ashamed of my foolish desire and as usual very proud of my cocky mother. The green branch was a symbol of life, but the high chimney emerging in front of us gave a grim foreboding. Could there be a gas chamber and a crematorium here deep in the woods? Why not?

Besides the worry for our life, we had one worry more; if we survive, if this is simply a delousing installation — what are we to do with the branch? We cannot smuggle it in and out. It doesn't need delousing. We decided to hide it in the snow, right where we were assembled and waiting. We shall, hopefully, retrieve it on our way back if... if we shall not leave through the chimney.

We entered the building, disrobed on command and saw our clothes taken away. We were left once more with... a toothbrush. We passed through the showers and everything was alright. We washed gaily, though without soap. We also washed our hair and later passed a comb through it. Our ruined hair was so drab and dry that we were hardly able to untangle it. As usual, there were no towels, and wet and naked we were pushed into a waiting room, cold and damp. There were even benches to sit down, but we were ordered to occupy only the left side benches. We shall probably wait one full hour before we get back our deloused clothes.

Hardly ten minutes elapsed when the door of the shower room opened, and a group of naked men was pushed into the same waiting room. The men were no less shocked than we were. The consternation was indescribable. Never in our long concentration camp "career" have we faced a similar situation. The male prisoners had it better, they had only one private part to conceal under their hands, we women have no less than three — and only two hands. One joker who reminded me of the lost Reginka whispered: "Why cover our pubic hair and our tits...? wouldn't it be enough to cover our faces?" We were not amused.

Thus, we sat, naked women opposite naked men averting our eyes. Both sides were so ashamed that we sat shivering in stony silence. The German personnel of the sanitary installations found the situation most amusing.

They created it on purpose. They stood on the threshold, observing both groups of prisoners and splitting their sides with laughter. We felt frozen, we didn't dare to move, we hardly breathed. The tension was rising. My mother could not bear it anymore. She addressed the group of male prisoners in Polish: "Gentlemen, let us not give the Germans the satisfaction of putting us to shame and ridiculing both groups. Please, make an effort, pretend that you are not ashamed, and start a civilized conversation with us, as if everything were normal".

At first it was a lame start, then gradually, both sides seized the initiative and pretended to chat in a natural free atmosphere. We also asked them what camp they came from because Malchov was all female. The watching Germans were non plussed, they did not understand how we overcame the shame and broke the barrier of silence. We have spoiled their game.

After all, in spite of this degrading episode, we were elated that we were clean and... alive... and that we haven't left this building through the chimney. I was happy that I had a chance to retrieve my branch of pine tree. Indeed, I did and this time without incident. We retraced our steps through the woods.

When we entered the barrack, waving the green branch, there was a general jubilation. I suspended it on a blank wall in a visible place. I even took the stub of my pencil and drew a Magen David over the branch. The news about the trophy brought by us to the camp and the symbol of freedom drawn above it, made rounds and ripples. Soon we had visitors from other barracks, who came to admire the green branch and ask permission to smell it. One of the visitors made a fiery speech on freedom and intoned... Hatikvah.

Soon other voices joined in the Zionist anthem, and it sounded loud and clear. It was dangerous, but we risked it with a grim determination. Just imagine — Hatikvah sung in a forlorn camp in the depth of Germany!!!

Mother was less enchanted. She quickly transferred the branch to our bunk and tried to erase the Star of David on the wall. Its traces were still visible. How dangerous it was — you will soon understand. A day later two officers came to our barrack. Somebody must have informed on the Magen David, because they went straight to the emblem on the wall. "Who did it, who marked the Zionist symbol?" — they asked in a threatening voice. I intended to step out, I didn't want the others to suffer reprisals because of my deed. I knew that I shall die a tortured heroine. But my mother was swifter.

They haven't yet finished their question when she stepped out and declared: "With your permission, Sir, I know who did it. It is the Russian women who marked our barrack with the Jewish symbol, so as to know where not to distribute additional portions of soup". It sounded quite plausible because we were all Jewesses in this barrack. The two Germans accepted this explanation, why shouldn't the Russians be as antisemitic as the Germans? Fortunately, they were not informed about the anthem. It was such a narrow escape. While I was still trembling all over, my mother turned to me and addressed me with one single sentence: "I feel Like killing you with my own hands, you fool". I knew that I deserved it, still I answered back like a stubborn child: "I wish you would, I am quite satiated with this thing called life".

It was March and we had one girl marking the days on the wall. Thus, we knew that we have spent in Malchov seven weeks. Seven hungry weeks... Once more we were at the end of the rope. They were ordered to evacuate us. We were led to the station, having received two slices of bread each. First, we board a normal train with compartments and normal seats. The bliss didn't last. Several stations further, we were transferred to a cattle train of open carriages. Again, it took days and nights. There was no snow, and water was supplied only every second day. We tried to catch the rain into our soup bowls. It was a long trip, we only moved when the rails were free. We had been transported from Northeast Germany to the far South — to Saxony.

It took four days... and many victims. We saw and observed a whole cross-cut section of Germany and many, many towns in ruins. I said to a very sick girl: "If you could only see their towns in ruins, the bowels of apartments cut in two and exposing still visible beds and tables, the skeletons of multi-storied houses — you would be pleased". I knew it was foolish; she was beyond the stage of feeling satisfaction or caring. She looked at me sadly and answered: "I wish I could die from a bomb and not in a pool of my own shit". What could I say or do, I even didn't have a rag or water to clean her. When I moved away from her — I felt guilty and ashamed, when I kept close — I risked being smeared in her excrements. I chose to stand and to report to the others what is to be seen from the open train.

One evening we reached the Magdeburg station. Magdeburg was a big city and an important railway junction. Our train sat like a lame duck in the center of this station. Suddenly, we heard a loud, piercing sound of the sirens.

Finding oneself, during an alert and an air attack, in the middle of the railway station — was actually very dangerous. The whole town was in ruins, the railway station being the only target. The moment the sirens started to wail, our escorts, the SS men and women, the Ukrainians and Lithuanians and Latvians, abandoned us. They jumped from the train and ran to the shelter. One clumsy warden, a thick-set SS woman from Holland who supervised our carriage, had difficulty climbing down from our carriage with its door closed from the outside. When she managed eventually to touch the ground — the bombs were already falling on the station. It was now too late for her to run to the shelter. She crawled under the belly of the carriage. We were highly amused. Tova, the same Tova who made the whole way from Auschwitz with a bullet in her buttock, looked down from the carriage, observing the woman. "Frou-oifseherin"- she exclaimed from above — "Myn sehtaich di Fies!!!". What Tova believed to be German, was actually pure Yiddish, meaning: "Mrs. Warden, one can see your feet..." Our whole carriage exploded in laughter. We laughed so heartily that tears streamed down our eyes.

The night was as bright as day. Before the Allied Air Force started to bomb the Magdeburg station, they illuminated the whole area with hundreds of lights. Immediately after the alert a plane dropped over the station several clusters (or grapes) of light each similar to a Christmas tree. Attached to many balloons, these lights remain suspended in the air for almost half an hour. Only then arrived the planes which dropped the bombs. We stood upright in the wagon, we stared at the Christmas trees in the air... we were so excited that we didn't mind at all the bombs falling on the station. We didn't even shrink or cover our heads. We stood in jubilation, inviting the bombs to fall right on us. Why not, what better end could we expect?

Eventually the air raid was over, our guards came back from the shelter, and two hours later our train was in motion. There was one more observation that I made watching the landscape from the train. Wherever we pass a bombed city, everything was ruined except... the medieval churches in Gothic style. The stained-glass windows and the walls crumbled, but the skeleton with its pointed arches remained intact, like a stiff dentelle. Many years later, when I lectured on the intricacies of the Gothic construction, I could add my own testimony proving how the pointed arch could withstand high pressure and the collapse of the rest of the structure. As you can see, my grandchildren, one can learn a lesson even when observing the grotesque remnants from a train of death.

We were once more moved to another train. Here we were squeezed in, to such a degree that we could only stand. Not only those who fainted reclined upon the others; whoever fell asleep leant heavily on the others, who fought back to reject the pressure of the bodies that created a heap. There were among us standing corpses pressed into the crowd, but we didn't know it yet for sure. The men didn't open the carriages, not even for a moment, because the dead and the living bodies would spill out.

Thus, we arrived in Leipzig, or rather at one of the labor camps in the vicinity of Leipzig. It didn't seem to have a name, perhaps it had a number. We entered the showers with the same trepidation and question mark and… we emerged alive with a toothbrush in our hand.

THE LEIPZIG FAIR OF "GINGER" CREATURES

As we entered the camp, we saw a phenomenon that we had never encountered: Most of the inmates here were orange women. These women had a yolk-yellow skin, orange hair, orange eyelashes and orange fingernails.

Many of them had been transferred to Leipzig from the huge Skarzysko camp, where they slaved in ammunition factories. The chemical stuff, the substance that turned them orange was called picrine. Many of the orange women were from Krakow, they had been sent to Skarzysko from Plaszow about two years ago. Several of them were not orange — they were completely bald after typhoid.

We remembered that Aunt Mania, my father's sister-in-law, was among those sent to Skarzysko. Indeed, a day later we find her. She, the so beautiful, pretty, sport woman looked so emaciated and bald, but this didn't matter. She was the last remnant of our huge family — the last of my five uncles and six aunts.

We embraced, we laughed and we cried. Her husband was in Russia, her son had reached Palestine, but she had lost in the ghetto her little nephew Joseph and had no idea what became of him. She didn't know what happened to him (but you know, because I described his astounding story, how he escaped from the ghetto through sewage canals…). We had none of our former friends, we were separated, we didn't know what had become of them, at least we had now a bit of family.

In a new place one has to get quickly a basic orientation of the local constellation. This one here was very different from all the other patterns. Like

Malchov it was an all-female camp, and it was ruled by the Russian prominent. The center of the camp consisted of several solid blocks, four stories high. Here was the administration and here were the living quarters of the Russian women. On the outskirts of the camp were several barracks, inhabited by a dense crowd of women, the later-imported element. We were of course among them — we were three to one bunk. There was good news too. The rations were double of what they were in Malchov. The soup was thick and rich, at least for a while.

As for the Russians, they occupied here all the key positions. They didn't work in the ammunition factories; they were employed in the administration, in the kitchen, the bakery, the laundry, the sick room. It was very strange in our eyes because nowhere were the Russians a privileged element, but the old-timers knew the explanation. When, upon their arrival, the Russians were ordered to work at the ammunition factory — they refused flatly. The commander tried to break their spirit. They were kept standing in the courtyard for three days and three nights (like Henry the fourth at Canossa). After the three days had elapsed, they still refused to surrender. The local commander had no authority to let them be executed without notifying Oranianburg — his was not an extermination camp. Writing a protocol would constitute admission of his failure. He decided to hush it up and gave the Russians work inside the camp. That explained why they were so prominent. In the absence of Gypsies, we constituted here the basest element, and we could only wonder why we are still kept alive.

We tried to make new friends, we almost succeed, but then we lost them very quickly. They avoid us like pestilence and with a good reason too. We both stank, only mother and me. How come? Out of our whole transport, the two of us were picked for a very special job: to empty the latrine pits. The barracks of this section were overcrowded — and so were the latrines. Their pits were flowing over and threatening the camp with the outbreak of epidemics. A new latrine had been dug out, not far away from the former one. We, the two of us, were ordered to transfer the surplus of shit from the old latrine to the new one. Having to carry two pails of shit, this short distance, it doesn't seem so short. Try to be very careful while carrying two pails, again and again, all day long — sooner or later you will spill some of the contents on you. You don't have to spill much to stink like hell, a little bit is enough.

Both pails had to be full. You cannot carry half a pail, you would get a beating. Every day after this excruciatingly hard work we fell on our bunk like dead. Now we had enough space because everybody else was keeping their distance from us. We were like lepers. Who can blame our neighbors? We both felt like stepping out of our clothes and staying immersed in water for hours on end, using the strongest detergent. It was not to be. Day by day we stank more and more. Here I should write that we lost appetite, only we didn't. We were so hungry that our stomachs stuck to our backs.

On Sunday, the work-free day, we made a desperate attempt at cleaning our clothes. We scrub them till our hands were covered with blisters, but the stench of stool was very persistent, even if we had the luck to do it with soap. Our clothes didn't dry before the evening and we had to put them on, wet as they were, for we had to appear decently dressed at the rollcall.

We talked of nothing else, only how we could avoid soiling out clothes once more. We had a solution, or an embryo of a solution. If we could stretch a thick wire between two poles like a string, if we could suspend our pails on this wire — we could push them with sticks and make them glide, keeping our distance. After the rollcall we made the rounds of the camp. We found a long wire (that we have spotted previously), we made incisions on two poles of wood, that were situated close to the two latrines. We winded the wire around the poles not far off the ground and we stretched it to maximum capacity. We made several hooks of wire on which to suspend out pails. We also found two sticks to push the pails along the wire, which was slightly inclined to make the pails glide — or so we hoped. We were now ready for the next day.

In the morning we tried our 'patent' with much trepidation, but the excrements seemed to sing: "Has a rail — will travel". It was a delicate operation to lift the pails and suspend them on the hooks, but it worked. All we had to do now was to push the pail with a stick, to make it glide along the wire to the next and last 'station' — the second pole. Then we took the pail off the hook and spilled its contents into the pit.

When our oppressors came for an inspection and saw our ingenious patent, one of them exclaims: "Look at them, lazy Jews. Let them carry shit, and they will make it ride". They were so hilariously amused that they forgot to forbid us the use of our patent, to deny us this facility. They even brought other men to admire the invention and gloat over their own witty remark, repeating it over and over. The Germans were very repetitive people. We became the stinking heroines of the day.

Nothing lasts forever. The overflowing latrine was eventually closed and the new one accessible. After some ten days of this unusual occupation and specialization, we were at last exempted from shit-carrying. While it lasted, Aunt Mania commiserated with us so much, that she even gave me some coupons to the canteen shop (there was one in this camp). My aunt said that with these coupons, I could get soap, safety pins, even eau-de-cologne. How could I accept such a gift, knowing that Aunt Mania doesn't exactly smell of fresh soap? I refused. Nevertheless, I rushed to the canteen, just to check, and what did I find there? some detergent, some emetics and hair pins. Not even safety pins. It was sad disappointment.

The episode of the latrine emptying was behind us, but a souvenir remained: we still stank. Our clothes were permeated with the stench. We had to do something about it. We sneaked into the laundry and explained in Polish to a Russian girl that we had to empty a latrine with buckets. She didn't seem to understand, so we performed for her a pantomime of carrying... you know what. If she didn't understand our Polish or our pantomime — she still had a nose and could smell. She grasped our plight and took our clothes to a steaming cauldron with soapy water. We waited naked, squatting behind a huge boiler. There was no time to dry our clothes. Once more we wore them wet on our body, and thus, freezing, stood to attention at the long evening rollcall, in March.

We were stinking no more (we had some friends), we were even less hungry for a while. We were getting every day two thick slices of bread, a thick soup, a nugget of margarine. There was even a dining hall for the inmates in this camp. We no longer got our soup in the barrack, we had to queue up before being admitted to that hall where we could eat our soup seated at a table. What a luxury! It ended sometime after our arrival. The kitchen had run out of supplies, it had to cope with the afflux of a huge transport — our transport. It got "new provisions" for the prisoners' soup, this time some vegetables, allegedly curly kale, that normally constitute cattle fodder. This was the only ingredient of the soup. It wouldn't be so bad, but these vegetables were rotten and stinking. When we didn't stink anymore — the soup stank.

I was not able to taste this soup, let alone eat it. Day after day we queue up patiently in front of the dining room, and when we were eventually let in, I sat in front of my soup and could not swallow it. Mother implored me: "Give it a try". I tried, I cried and… I left it untouched. Mother got really angry. She felt like mopping my nose in it, as one does to a puppy. Then she offered me a deal: "You know well" — she said — "That I have always been a soup lover. If you hate this soup so much, let us make a deal. I shall eat your portion of soup, and you will take my ration of bread in exchange". Now it was my turn to fall into a rage. I turned to mother in a harsh tone and yelled at her: "I don't want you to starve because of your glorious deal. I am fed up with your eternal self-sacrifice, your bloody schemes and deals. We are not Siamese sisters. Let me be responsible for my own stomach and my survival. This soup is mine, not yours, and I shall not let you eat it. I want it all for me, it belongs to me".

A passing woman contemplates us for a while and remarks: "Look at them, just look at them, a mother and a daughter… and they quarrel like dogs over a bowl of soup". Hearing this remark, we both explode in laughter. The woman made a sign on her forehead and mumbled: "They must be both mad, beware of them, they are crazy".

The next day, we had a new grave problem, not the one of the soup anymore. After having stood for hours in a wet dress, I was sick and running a high temperature. It was our seventh camp and we knew something about camp hospitals, but here it seemed to be different. Mother was told that it is not dangerous to be hospitalized, they do not kill prisoners in this hospital and it is run very efficiently. It was on the fourth floor of a block. Hallucinating and only half conscious I could hardly make it to this high floor. I was admitted and got a bed, a real bed to myself, in a big sunny room. There was some medication and often a glass of hot tea. A paradise! In the morning when I felt a little better and my mind was clear, I had a lot of time to think. It was only here that I reconstructed some important conversations, a series of conversations that took place in Malchov.

We befriended in Malchov two wonderful women that I haven't mentioned so far because this encounter will have a bearing on our future, but not on the present. They were both French Jewesses, one from Lille and one from Paris. They were closer to my mother's age than mine. People in concentration camps make sometimes confessions that they would never make under normal conditions. Madame Ninette, the one from Lille, told us the story of her life. When she was about seventeen and dreaming of a prince on a white horse, her parents decided to marry her off to a rich man of middle age, highly recommended by a matchmaker. They didn't discuss it with her, they imposed their decision on her.

"How cruel" — I exclaimed "how could you bear it?" A bright smile illuminated her sweet face. "Never jump to hasty conclusions, dear — she said — "At first, I rebelled after the marriage, I even refused to look at him. Gradually, very gradually, he won me over by the sweetness of his character and delicate approach. I fell in love with him. Now, after twenty-three years of marriage, I am still in love with him, but fate separated us, and here I am longing for him like a schoolmarm". The story left a strong impression on me. I understood for the first time that a marriage arranged by a matchmaker can be a very happy one. Would you, my pets, believe it?

The second French woman, madame Sonia Arnaud, born in Russia, was to play a cardinal role in the story of my life, even though I never succeeded in finding a trace of her in Paris after the war. Sonia was a very clever woman and her green slanted eyes were far from cold. She knew how to induce me to open up to her. I told her that two years before my high school graduation, we already had it planned that my parents would send me to Paris to study history and anthropology. Would our destiny let us eventually survive, why not implement this old plan? We would hate to return to Poland after the liberation, we have no one left there, only ghosts. It would be too traumatic. We shall probably go straight to Paris, and I shall study at the university, as planned before the war.

Madame Arnaud listened attentively. Her reaction was instant: "Forget it. If you come to France without a visa and apply for an admission to the university — you have lost your game. You would be quickly deported to Poland as illegal immigrants. Only an accepted student, with graduation certificate and formal admission exams, gets a visa and a resident's permit to stay in France. You, Rosa, would not even be considered as a likely candidate for resident. That's the way it was before the war, and that's the way it will be. But wait… I have a suggestion. It sounds wild, but it would work. When you ask after the liberation to be sent to France, I am telling you to register as having been deported to the camps from France. Period."

My mother listened avidly, drinking in every word, but I reacted immediately: "Madame Sonia, I would never ride on a lie, not me. Anyhow, the balloon would explode very soon because there would be no evidence, not a trace of us in France dating to the period before the war. Now I am telling you to forget it. At least we are lucky, that your warning spared us a terrible mistake".

Sonia posed her strong hand on my shoulder and said after reflection: "Listen, dearie, listen to me carefully, I am not pulling a rabbit from my sleeve. You speak and write a rich, perfect French, and you Rosa, you speak a passable French. Thousands of Jews who have been living in France for thirty years are hardly able to communicate in French. I knew them very well in the "Platzl" quarter in Paris. As for the evidence, or rather the lack of it, this problem would be easy to circumvent and solve. You just have to register as having been deported from Abbeville. It is a coastal town that was totally wiped off the face of the earth after the war broke out. Its municipality, its police archives, its schools are non-existent after the bombing. You just claim to have been deported from there. So as to make things even safer, you have to state that your father (your husband, Rosa) came to France many, many years ago. Only after he had been firmly established and naturalized as full-fledged French citizen, did he bring you two to France. His naturalization embraces both of you, it is valid. It was valid before you were deported as Jews. So here you have the whole scenario, including your permanent address in Abbeville and the name of the school which you allegedly attended and finished. I can note it down for you, I happen to know Abbeville. Does it sound better now?"

Mother was enthusiastic. She was almost ready to adopt this convincing plan. I was opposed to it on the sole ground that I hate lies and would never think of entering France under false pretenses. "If you fight for your very existence and there is none for you in Poland, you will learn how to lie" — said Sonia firmly.

This series of conversations took place in Malchov. Since then we have lost the trace of Sonia Arnaud, she must have been detached from our convoy. Mother hasn't forgotten a word. When I cried carrying the buckets with excrements, she used to whisper: "Remember Abbeville". I pretender not to hear it, I was too exhausted to fight her. Now, in the hospital bed, prostrate and running high temperature, I probably subconsciously re-enacted the scenario composed by Sonia, because in the morning my sick neighbor asks me: "Why did you talk in your sleep in French? Are you a French spy or something?" I was much surprised at this disclosure. Did it mean that in my subconscious I was still thinking about this crazy plan? We were still so far from the glorious liberation and I was so sick that every afternoon my fever soared. Soon I relapsed into hallucinations — or so I was told later. My mother could visit me in this sick-bay and check for herself that I was well cared for, but very sick. There was no definite diagnosis, or it was not disclosed to us.

Hardly have I been two days at the hospital, when hell broke loose — Leipzig was heavily bombed. The sirens wailed very often, and every time when the alert started, we, the patients at the sick bay had to run down five stories into the cellars that served as bomb shelter. Eventually the camp commander ordered to move the whole sick bay into the cellars. The cellars lack air, light and commodities, my condition was deteriorating, my fever still very high. We heard the bombs falling on Leipzig. We were not interested, until one hit us. One dawn, I was sitting in my cellar cubicle, reclining on the wall behind my back. Hardly has the alert siren ceased to wail when a bomb hit our building. It passed diagonally and hit the cellar behind my back. Between me and the crater of the bomb remained only the thin wall. It was a sheer miracle that I was alive and unscathed. I didn't know how many victims were hit in this adjacent cellar, or for that matter in the whole building. I knew nothing, I don't know if I fainted or became catatonic in the aftermath of the shock. The next thing I remembered or seem to remember — was my mother, dragging me out of there. You have to understand that my mother was at the given moment in our barrack, some three hundred meters distant from me. She knew that the bomb had hit the building I was in. She could hardly hope to find me alive seeing the rubble and the crater of the bomb. What she found seemed to be a dead body that she cuddled and kissed. To make her understand that I am alive I gathered all my force and uttered one word: "Abeville". She dragged me out of the sepulcher and then ... we were on an empty bunk in some block, I don't remember how, where and why. Here certain things must be blurred in my memory because the next thing I remember was my mother telling me that there is an order for total evacuation of the Leipzig camps. Feverish as I was, I knew one thing for certain: I am not going to make it. I told my mother that I am not moving from this bunk, I begged her to let me die there. We could perhaps hide under the pallet or else — what do I care. It would be so cozy to die here and not in a second march of death.

Mother pulled me by my hair. Indeed, there was no one in the block, everybody was already outside, being formed into lines of five and into hundreds. We found Aunt Mania and some acquaintances. I could not stand or walk, let alone march. They supported me, they dragged me. The fresh air stroke my chest, it made me drowsy and drunk. We were given some bread for the way and we marched, or rather they marched and dragged me along. It was lucky that the guards were so nervous in the general panic and so afraid of being intercepted by the Russians, that they didn't notice how sick I was. My symptoms were too inchoate for any assessment of my actual state of health, but the fever seemed to abate gradually. There was only weakness and apathy. Miracle of miracles, the fresh air seemed to cure me. On the third day I was able to walk almost none sustained.

THE SECOND MARCH OF DEATH

The marching column seemed to be endless. There must be some five hundred woman-prisoners from the camps of the whole vicinity of Leipzig. It was our second march of death, only this one was going to last four times as long as the former one. Where were we being led to? Nothing was clear, only the general direction.

Judging by the sun we were moving westwards. There must have been a plan, a destination; was there indeed? One clever woman made a guess: "The SS men leading our convoy flee the Russian offensive without any specific orders, just as the situation dictates it". It was fortunate that we didn't know this march of death was going to last twelve days, twelve crucifying days. Had we known, what would we have done? Refused to move? Perhaps.

We have started with a bread ration for two days. Since then — nothing. Every three days we got something to eat. Once it was soup, once a slice of bread, very seldom water. Aunt Mania was marching at a good pace. We were, all of us, swollen from hunger. I was told that I was symmetrically swollen. Mother was swollen in a queer asymmetric way; her right cheek and her left jaw were protruding. We advanced less and less, which made our guards very nervous. They could not kill all their sheep, only the fallen ones. Whipping didn't help anymore. Often, we marched through the night. Sometimes we stayed in a field for half a day. It was not meant to make us rest and gather strength. It must be caused by lack of orders and confusion. One day they distributed raw rice. We had to form a line, extend our palms, and we were given a handful of rice each.

What can one do with raw rice lacking water and fire? We stopped on a large field, bordering the road on one side, and woods on the other side. Beyond the trees flew a stream. Mother said: "I shall bring water, "coute que coute" (whatever the price). It was very dangerous; the guards shoot at women who tried to break through the loose cordon of SS men and rushed to the woods. Who could stop my mother? Off she went. Hopefully, they shot in the air or on the ground. I was agonizing for a long, long while. Mother returned proudly with a mess-tin full of water. In spite of her protests I rushed to the forest to bring some branches of wood. A Latvian guard even lent me his matches. We made a fire and cooked our rice over the flame.

Two days later we were starving again and marching under a drizzle. Mother looked at the fields, or rather followed the glances of the Russian women. They seem to know something. They could discern that in those fields, potatoes had just been planted. The German peasants didn't put whole potatoes into the ground, they only carved out the "eyes" with a bit of the potato around them. While we were marching laboriously, several 'Ruskies' (as we called them) stepped out of line and rushed into the fields. They moved the earth with their fingers, dug with their fingernails and extricated these bits of potatoes. Mother followed in their footsteps... the Germans shot. They shot aiming at the legs to make the women jump and skip. They found it amusing... Mother brought several such potato carvings and we munched them as they were, dirty and raw. Nobody else dared to step out, only the giant 'Ruskies' and my diminutive mother. It didn't fill our bellies, but Aunt Mania said: "just imagine that you are munching crisp chips".

The next day, having nothing to eat for three days, at the seventh day we camped again in an open field. Our oppressors knew that nothing will make us move. We were finished. At least we could breathe and rest. It was mid-April and the cold was not so biting. We had one gray, simple blanket that we shared, some six of us, to rest on. The blanket was damp, but not as wet as the ground. We tended to the sick as well as we could. We fed them some rice, but that was three days ago. We had no water to quench their thirst, or ours. We dozed or vegetate on this blanket, everything was still.

Suddenly, we felt an earthquake. Our blanket was lifted, and we rolled over from it like meat balls. No, it was not an earthquake, it were the Ruskies. They wanted our blanket and they got it. Some four of them approached us on tiptoe, got hold of the long edge of the blanket, and in one swift movement, their eight hands pulled the blanket from under us while we rolled over. It was a sad loss, but we had lost more. In fact, I was full of admiration for them, the Ruskies. They were omnipotent. I would have to be reborn if I wanted to be like them. Was their secret buried in genes or in the web of communal cooperation induced at an early age? Was it simply their being used to privations, atrocities and a need for manipulation? Those who had been deported to Russia know the answers. As for now, all we had to do was to watch them and at least try to do likewise. They walked around the field and gathered the stinging nettle. We looked with round, unbelieving eyes. "Yes" — said Tova — "my parents told me that during World War I, they were so hungry that they used to cook nettle like spinach". We followed their example. One of us put her hand under her dress, and thus protected the picked nettle. A second one made a basket of her dress to gather the nettle into it. Then we shred it. What now? Once more we had to bring water from a stream and branches from the forest. Once more the guards shot, and they were sharp shooters. One woman was wounded, perhaps more. This time I managed to anticipate my mother. We had water and wood for one campfire, but we also had many 'clients' begging of us to let them boil their nettle on our bonfire. It was not easy, but I found a solution to accommodate them. In this empty field there were some heaps of junk.

Junk has always fascinated me since the Plaszow days. Out of junk we acquired a cooking pot and a basin. To this very day junk attracts me like magic. Now in the vast field I found a ruined hood of a pram. It was only a skeleton of metal bands, but it will serve the purpose. I found bits of strong wire and made out of it several hooks. I brought my trophies to our bonfire, which was protected by stones from all sides. I spread over the flames the skeletal hood of the pram and some seven mess-kits from Leipzig, which had a ringlet to suspend them from the hooks without quenching the fire. Everybody admired this communal, shared bonfire, even the Ruskies. Aunt Mania proudly eyed our "clients". Rely on Aunt Mania. She had already taken from one of our "clients" a match to start the fire, now she spotted another one who had salt. "'Listen, ginger" — said Aunt Mania — "you cannot take full advantage of our fire without contribution sometimes. We have endangered our lives (she hasn't), you have to give us some salt". A pinch of salt was very important, not for the taste of this substitute spinach, but for strength. You cannot live without salt or sugar in your system. We ate our nettle meal and it was a feast. Never had spinach tasted like this. The sting of the nettle was gone, it disappeared in cooking.

Our ordeal continued. We advanced once more, foot by foot, making very little progress. We protected and dragged some sick girls among us. The very sick or dead — remained on the field. We stopped to rest again in an open field. We were concentrated on a vast space, while the guards, all the SS wardens, the Ukrainians, Latvians and Lithuanians, guarded us, as usual, from all sides keeping their distance from us.

Suddenly, out of the blue, a plane appeared over our heads. We didn't pay attention. The pilot became obviously interested in us, he dived, low, very low…he understood. We didn't grasp yet that it was a plane of the Allied Air Force. The pilot returned, dived very low and …his gunner opened fire. He did it in an astute way; he aimed only at our guards… he overflew again the field where we were concentrated and shot again at the guards in the rear. He repeated this operation some three times, every time taking care not to hurt us, the prisoners. We were so impressed that we waved at him and blew kisses. Then he disappeared. As far as we know he missed our oppressors, but he was the first man from the outer world who intervened on our behalf.

The SS men were visibly shaken. They were so nervous that they became negligent in performing their duties. Meanwhile the commander of the convoy must have made an arrangement with the local head of the village, because food was delivered to us, after a lapse of several days. It was one single rural cart full of potatoes cooked in their peel. They were still steaming hot, straight from the cauldron. The confused men could hardly control the situation, they only squinted sideways looking for an opportunity to escape. Instead of forming us into a long line queuing for the distribution, they let the Russians play havoc. Seeing what is brewing many sick and weak didn't even get up, they knew that they don't have the slightest chance of getting a potato. The Ruskies rushed at the cart and took handfuls of potatoes from its top. They filled their pockets. Nobody else could even approach the cart. Only my mother could… She simply crawled between their legs. She could never reach the top, they wouldn't let her, but she had an idea. The side panels and the bottom of this cart were made of ladder-like rungs. My mother inserted her hand between the dense rungs and managed to pull out from there one potato, then another potato and one more. After a Russian kicked her, she withdrew. She didn't even notice that the steaming hot potatoes burned her palms, scorching them to the third degree.

Meanwhile I didn't lose time. I came closer but I didn't dare to come too close. Suddenly I was bumped and almost toppled by two Ruskie giants fighting like dogs and beating each other. Their fight was so ferocious that all I had to do was to grab some potatoes from the pocket of the one who was closer to me. When I almost dared to reach for the third potato, she seemed to notice that she had a pickpocket at her tail. She could tear me to pieces. I ran away and back to Aunt Mania. Mother arrived almost simultaneously. Elated as we were over this success, I noticed that mother was in pain. "What is it" — I asked. Only then did we see what happened to her palms. We didn't know yet how dangerously infected her burns will become.

We sat down and prepared for a feast, we had five potatoes for the three of us. It was then that my mother announced nonchalantly: "You eat them, I have no appetite...". Aunt Mania laughed, I felt like tearing to pieces this saintly hypocrite. No, not now. All right, so I shall play her game. I shrugged my shoulders and I said in the same tone: "Me too, I have lost my appetite inhaling the sweat of the two Ruskie... Aunt Mania, be our guest, you can have all the five potatoes". Mother eyed me suspiciously. After all, considering the state we were in, Aunt Mania could devour all the five potatoes. There was no place for niceties. Now it is only the question: to be or not to be. Our hearts pumped with difficulty, they were giving up. Soon, very soon, we shall join the women who died before our eyes.

Perhaps the end is nearer than we know or can believe. The German guards and their associates seem to sense it too. How do I know? When I watched a woman sitting on the grass, I notice that she was wearing under her uniform a flowery dress. She was visibly ready to throw off her uniform and vanish, mixing with civilians and pretending to be a simple innocent German refugee. Was the front that near?

It was the tenth day of the march of death. Being deprived by the Ruskies of our only blanket we could not sit on the wet ground, and it was raining constantly. We were so weak by now that sometimes we wept, sometimes we laughed. "Stop it" — said Aunt Mania — "weeping makes you weaker". How true. So I laughed for a change. "What is there to laugh at?" — asked Mania. "You wouldn't believe it" — I mumbled half audibly, saving every breath — "but when I was hallucinating, I heard the same tune all the time. I hear it now too, and the words are so funny". Here I must explain that it was a parody on the evening song sounded by the bugle in Plaszow. Somebody composed to it these funny words:

It is nine, and the whole camp is going to sleep
The latrine is closed, you are not supposed to... Shit

(The tune is registered on tape, once in whistle, once with the funny words in Polish, and once more in translation)

"Auntie Mania" — I continued — "if the front is that near, if we are going to survive, I shall one day sing this song to my children as a lullaby. It is a very soothing lullaby... they will like it". Aunt Mania only nodded her head. Everyone is entitled to his or her brand of hallucinations...

I heard strange sounds; I even seemed to hear thunder. Mother didn't participate in this exchange of hallucinating remarks. She didn't even seem to notice that I was saying queer things. Only then I discovered that her palms with burnt blisters were very swollen and festering. She didn't complain; she suffered silently. That is why I haven't noticed so far. Poor mother — that day was April 20th — her birthday and Hitler's too... I kissed her tenderly and made excuses that the liberation wasn't offered to her on her birthday, on a silver plate. I consoled her that it can now be only a matter of hours.

I didn't hear the funny lullaby anymore, but I distinctly heard thunders. Everybody heard, the Germans as well. It was not the thunder — it was the front, the Russian front. Is it that near? Planes flew over our heads, we didn't even discern if they were German or Allied planes. They dropped the bombs quite close to us. The artillery was shelling an objective that we did not see. It must have been the bridge over the river Elbe. Soon we heard the same sounds from the opposite direction. Was there not one front but two fronts, the Russian and the American? Were we caught in the middle? The noise became deafening, the two fronts seemed to close up on us. We were in the epicenter of two battles, fought simultaneously on both our sides: we were the target of the artillery and the bombs. It had to relate to the bridge.

Our escorts behaved like crazy. They even stoop to the point of explaining the situation to us. An SS officer said: "Have patience. All we have to do is to cross this bridge over the river Elbe. Beyond that we shall be secure". Who will be secure? He will be, or so he believed, because the German defense forces were going to regroup over there, beyond the Elbe. Why did he still stick to us? Was he afraid of a court martial if he would abandon us?

We had no time for contemplation. Things were happening so fast around us. When the shelling and bombarding were very heavy, we jumped into the ditch at the roadside. It was full of mud. Every time the shelling subsided for a while; our guards made us march to the bridge. When we eventually reached this objective, it transpired that we were not allowed to cross it. The bridge was reserved for the military movement or rather hasty retreat. The SS men speculated between themselves that once the German forces have crossed the bridge, it will be blown up to prevent the Russians from crossing. The Russians seemed to have chosen another tactic; they were set on destroying the bridge to trap the German forces before they cross to the other side. This posed a problem to our commander. He was afraid of being trapped here as a high SS officer, the tormentor of prisoners, the war criminal. He changed his policy; he decided to cross at another bridge, further down on the Elbe. We were whipped to harry and march there.

During a renewed attack we sought shelter again in a shallow ditch. The high officer did likewise, and I found myself head to head with him in the ditch. He dragged me to his side — his ribs under my ribs, his groin under my pelvis, as if he wanted my body to cover his body and protect him from the bombs. When the bombing abated, he got up, visibly ashamed. My mother got up too, but she was not the same person. The rainwater in the ditches must have caused her a lumbago attack. She was bent and doubled up like a penknife. She was in pain, she could not walk. We tried with Aunt Mania to catch her hands and drag her, but she screamed with pain. The blisters on her palms burst with pus. We could only hold her by her wrists and, supporting her elbows, drag her along. The Ukrainians whipped us to make haste.

Under a renewed bombing or shelling there happened something most unpredictable; we scattered so suddenly that we got lost. Everybody ran for his life, everybody in a different direction and thus a whole group of us (some twenty women) found ourselves far from the convoy, far from the escort, somewhere in Saxony close to the river Elbe and between two fronts pushing forcefully forwards. What were we to do? Where could we turn to? Were we liberated, were we free? No one was pursuing us, nobody cared. Who would shelter us, who would feed us if we survive this terrible shelling? Driven by a strange instinct we searched desperately for our convoy. We turned in circles without a sense of direction, we had only one wish: to go back where we belong, to go back into the line, to join the flock of martyrs and their tormentors. Today such a phenomenon has a name. It is called the 'Stockholm syndrome', meaning developing a dependence on the Hijackers — in this case the escort supervising the march of death.

We finally found them, we joined them, we entered back into the ranks and... we felt relieved. All this after we had been free like birds for some two hours or more. Perhaps it was less, but we were so frantic in our search for our tormentors that we lost sense of time.

Mother still had to be supported. She could not straighten up, not even halfway. Marching under a heavy shelling, we were driven along the Elbe River. The commander of our escort tried desperately to reach the other bridge on the Elbe and to cross it as soon as possible. At this point, he was trapped, and we with him, between two battles fought simultaneously on both sides of us. It seemed that the Russians and the Allies each wanted to gain more ground so as to claim later larger parts of Germany at the hour of partition, after the expected victory. Did they agree on a fixed demarcation line? In retrospective it seemed unlikely, or perhaps it didn't work, as I shall soon prove by the events.

These were not the thoughts that preoccupied us at the given moment. I only became curious much later, when I was able to analyze the events. All I was thinking of now was how to haul my mother along, while we were both, Aunt Mania and I, tripping often and hardly able to support her. Mother clenched her teeth but didn't utter a sound. It was the first time that our roles were reversed, that I was taking care of her.

Our column and escort must have split. There were hardly any guards marching with us, but the few were more menacing with their rifles. The rest of them must have been delegated to escort the other part of the column, but it is quite likely that they have escaped. We reached eventually the commander's goal, the much sought-after second bridge on the Elbe. Here too we were pushed off the road while the remnants of the German army escaped over from both battle fields and crossed the bridge chaotically. Our commander was frantic... Any moment now the two fronts would close up on us, squeeze us and crush us together with the rest of the German army.

It did not happen. The Russians and the Americans didn't seem to push any more. Were they afraid of clashing with each other? Had they lost their bearings or means of communication? Did they choose to let the rest of the enemy's army cross the bridge? What if the Germans blew up both bridges after traversing them? What would be our situation in that case, the lot of the sitting ducks?

Our commander was an SS officer. As such he was hated by the army. Now the army took its revenge on the SS. It rejected his plea; it didn't let him through. Only when the crossing of the army was reduced to a mere trickle and the check-post on the bridge was abandoned — we were, at long last, able to traverse this damned second bridge. It had taken us two days.

It was totally dark: we were in the middle of nowhere, but beyond the Elbe. Both battles seemed to be over. We were in a hamlet. We were on the grounds of an estate or a farm. "We" doesn't mean even half of the original column in the March of Death. We were now less than some two hundred prisoners left. What became of the rest — we did not know and hardly cared. The commander let us enter a huge barn filled with straw. We fell into a slumber or stupor, we were half-dead. We were beyond caring about life or death. Nobody said a word. One could only hear groaning from several directions. If we were dehydrated, we didn't feel it anymore. We haven't slept for more than fifty-five hours, nor had we drunk or eaten. We were in state of total blackout.

THE NOT SO "GLORIOUS" LIBERATION

In the morning, the commander of the convoy opened the heavy bolt on the door of the barn. He yelled at us: "Get up quick, on the double. Get ready, form the ranks". Nobody moved. Nobody tried to argue, to explain that we were "finished". We just didn't care how he will take it: we were beyond caring.

When we looked at him, we noticed that he was alone, all by himself. It was not so certain, but that was the impression. None of us moved. He stood forlorn in the door and said: "All right, I give you ten minutes to wake up and enter formations". He was gone and we didn't exchange a word. He came back, gave the same order but nobody moved. He said: "No problem, I am reporting you to the local forces, they will shoot you here right as you are". He was gone... silence. There was no fear, no speculation, just a vacuum.

The time passed and believe me, I didn't know if it is ten minutes or an hour. Then one of the Ruskies approached the door, looked out and said: "There is no one in sight, it seems that we are free..." Somebody went to the pump and brought water. Eventually, we crept out slowly into the pale sun of the morning of April 22, 1945. And that was the "glorious liberation" for which we had been waiting, six years less four months.

There was nothing glorious about this liberation except the quiet and the sense of nirvanas. The battle was over, the silence rang in our ears. We looked at the pastoral picture with tears in our eyes. The doves of peace and freedom fluttered their wings over our heads. The fat hens walked proudly in the courtyard picking worms and wiggling their bottoms in sheer provocation. They seemed to mock us. We looked at them sadly, we were helpless. Not the Ruskies. They knew how to trap a hen without effort. They had no strength to run after it, but they approached slowly from several sides till they caught one. They made a fire and roasted it.

Eventually, a frightened German woman emerged from the farm and took a few steps in our direction, as if she were facing some green creatures from another planet. She asked what she can do for us. Anything — we said — just anything to drink and to eat, and some soap too. She reacted cautiously, speaking slowly and distinctly as if addressing a bunch of imbeciles: "We ourselves are destitute, we have hardly anything to eat, but we shell do our best" — she added quickly, visibly afraid that we shall make a raid on the farm's pantry. Even the Ruskies had no force to do it.

Indeed, at noon we were served hot soup with a few vegetables and a trace of barley visible in the transparent liquid. We were so elated that one of us even ventured an old joke. She whispered the magic word "Amcha". I think I didn't mention this anecdote before, so I have to tell it now. Wherever there was in one of the concentration camps a Jewish cook distributing the soup, the Jewish inmates whispered the magic word "Amcha". This concise Hebrew expression means "of your people". Upon hearing this whispered code-word, the Jewish cook would dip his ladle deep into the cauldron and serve his co-religionist, thick soup from the bottom. Soon the gentiles picked and "borrowed" this Hebrew magic password and used it with Jewish "hutzpah". As far as I know, this was the only instance when the gentiles desired to parade as Jews.

Hearing now the word "Amcha" we laughed convulsively. The Teutonic matron distributing the soup suspiciously eyed the laughing skeletons mumbling an abracadabra word from another planet. Taking us for crazy, she said soothingly: "In Cavertitz... good people". The village Cavertitz was not empty as we thought. The local Germans crept slowly out of their farms and observed from safe distance the wobbly creatures. They were more afraid of us than we were of them. The mayor took things into his capable hands. To bake bread for some two hundred "invaders" must take some hours. Late in the evening we were given fresh bread and tea. It was not so much out of Christian mercy. This shrewd mayor was probably afraid of the occupying forces, were we to complain to them when they arrive at Cavertitz, as they certainly would.

We had no strength to stroll in the courtyard. We returned to the semi-dark, warm barn as to mother's womb. We remained prostrate on the straw. How drab and how different was this liberation from what we expected and imagined, in rosy colors, all those years. We thought that we would fall into the arms of our liberators, that they will carry us in their arms like brides lifted over the threshold, the threshold to freedom. Now, swollen and dizzy, laboriously catching air into our lungs, we fell into a fitful slumber.

I realize in retrospective how lucky we were that we got such skimpy supply of food. It took more than a few weeks until we were fed properly, and this gradual passage was our salvation. Many people died of overeating, being suddenly fed normally after the liberation.

Two days passed while we recovered a little. Some of the girls started to inquire from the local people what is going on. Where are we? In the village Cavertitz, district Oschatz — was the answer. There seemed to be a vacuum here. The SS, the army, the local militia were all gone, vanished. How far were the conquering armies? The villagers didn't know exactly, but the village Strehla was allegedly already occupied by the Russian soldiers — so they said. Here the Communist girls (but not the Ruskies) took over. So far, they kept a low profile, we were not even aware that there were several Communists among us. Now they raised their heads. Having heard that Strehla was not so distant, they decided to make a pilgrimage there. They had to greet the Russian soldiers, to embrace them and be taken into their custody as loyal communists. They left the barn, some ten of them. They dragged themselves on their own in the direction of Strehla, as pointed out to them. We exchanged glances and smiled a pale indulgent smile. Let them go. How strange that the Ruskies didn't join them.

We remained in the barn stretching our limbs and sore feet. We didn't even talk; we had difficulty digesting the fresh bread. We fell asleep. At about three o'clock in the morning we heard a commotion, people moving, groaning, trampling on us in the pitch dark. "What is it, who is it?" — we asked, suddenly awakened and frightened. "It's nothing, it's nothing, it is only us, we have returned. Go to sleep" — answered several shaky voices. We were curious, we asked questions, but the Communist girls who went to Strehla answered quietly in monosyllables, urging us to go to sleep. In the first daylight we saw that they were dressed in flimsy nightgowns. They remain non-committal, nonplussed, feeding us some malarkey in exaggerated detail. Eventually the truth emerged. It was now as transparent as their nighties.

They did reach Strehla, they did find the Russian soldiers stationed in a German posh villa. They were indeed received with open arms. They were fed, or rather, according to their version, wined and dined. The commander ordered a soldier to prepare for them a warm bath, clean beds and even gorgeous nightgowns (that must have been pilfered in German villas). Beaming with pride and happiness, they went to bed like sweet good children. When they were asleep, the Russian soldiers slipped into their beds and… tried to rape them. Only tried? I wondered. They ran away as they were, dressed in fancy nighties. They made all the way back to Cavertitz, to the safety of the barn, far from the Russians, raping on their way everything of the female gender, raping even living skeletons of professed loyal Communists. And that is the story of the first contact with the Russian bear.

We were still very hungry. We had to find some food. Having recuperated a little bit, we decided, three girls, to take a short walk and explore Cavertitz. Reaching a modest house with a lovely garden we knock at the door. We asked if we can get some food; the elderly couple received us kindly. The woman took out of the oven a terrine and a wonderful smell filled our nostrils. She served us something delicious. It was probably zucchini in a very thick white sauce that formed a brown crust on its top while baked in the oven.

"Are we not depriving you of your meal?" — I asked, hardly meaning that much concern. "It is all right" — they said — "we have some more of it and do join us please". Never have I tasted a more delicious dish. Whenever I tried later to imitate it — nothing came out of it. This old couple was not ashamed to ask direct questions. They were horrified hearing our answers. They had apparently and visibly known nothing of the German atrocities. "Yes, yes" — nodded the old man — "it is not like in the previous World War. It wasn't waging a war by torturing innocent people". I venture to mention that in World War I, my father fought in the ranks of the Austrian army and was stationed mostly in Bosnia and Herzegovina. I saw a flicker in the old man's eyes. 'Would you believe it" — he exclaims — "that I was stationed in the same area. How strange that you, my fellow combatant's daughter would come to my house as a victim of my own people. How cruel our world has become". He had tears in his eyes.

I noticed on the wall a photo of a young man in army uniform. It was framed in black. I didn't have to ask, I guessed that it was their fallen son. The woman followed my gaze and nodded her head in silent comprehension. We thanked them effusively and I found my hand gripped and crushed in the old man's handshake.

We returned to the barn. The supply of food was irregular, the mayor decided on a change of policy. He split us up and placed every little group in the custody of a farm. We were now in a small barn and the owners of the farm were ostensibly hostile to us, their new burden. They kept us on a very skimpy diet. We recuperated mainly by resting. There was on this farm another slave, an Italian boy, Pietro, about my age. He was conscripted to forced labor in Germany, as he had been evading military service or was it the tribute that Italy had to pay to its ally Germany — it was not clear to us. The farm owner made him work very hard. Pietro soon became my chum. His German was limited to the basics, I didn't speak Italian, so I tried my Latin on him, and it worked. I said in a funny combination of Latin and Italian: "Pietro, Io amoarbori, forresti. Io desidero allare con tui versus ripas de silva. Bene?" It was supposed to mean: "Pietro, I love trees and forests. I want to go with you to the border of the woods" — and I indicated with my finger.

Pietro understood. He said that on Sunday he has a free afternoon, he will take me. Sunday approached. The farmer's wife killed several hens in the courtyard. We observed her with hungry eyes, looking forward to the Sunday royal repast. Pietro perceived our hungry looks. He said: "You nix, zero". Don't cherish any illusions that you will partake of it, it is only for their family. Indeed, what we got on Sunday was a soup with some bowels and shreds of the chicken skin floating in it. Pietro wanted to recompense me for this sad deception. He stole for me an egg, he handed it to me discreetly and it was still warm. We managed to boil it, and we shared it among the three of us. We tasted our first egg after two years.

At long last Pietro was free to take me to the woods. They were quite close to the farm. The smells were divine. I wished I could walk into the depth of the forest, but I was too weak. I tried to pick some flowers; Pietro picked them for me. Hardly have we reached a denser area when we noticed something glittering in the shrubs, some crouching figures hiding in the bushes. Pietro started to sing nonchalantly and managed to whisper to me:

"Non spectare, soldati enemici". I grasped what he meant — "Don't look, the soldiers of the enemy". German soldiers...? hiding here in Cavertitz? My heart started to beat very fast, but I played the game of pretending not to notice them, the way Pietro played it. I whistled, I sang, I chattered. Pietro put an arm around my shoulder; we pretended to be lovers, engrossed with each other. Pietro whispered: "Pardone Maria, but I have to". He was a gentleman. We didn't change our pace, we didn't turn or took to our heels. We continued to walk turning gradually to the left and returning to the farm. It was a close escape. So, the area was not as empty of military forces as it seemed. The Germans took advantage of the absence of Allied forces around Cavertitz. Pietro suspected that these soldiers were clandestinely fed by the owners of the farm. I didn't tell mother of our adventure, I told her about birds and squirrels.

Mother's condition was getting worse. It was not so much her back-pain, it was mainly the festering palms. Was she endangered by gangrene? I showed mother's blisters to the farmer's wife and explained that she must be taken to a doctor. When I mentioned gangrene, the woman became afraid of her responsibility. She informed the mayor. He too didn't want to have a corpse on his hands. There was no doctor in the hamlet. The mayor decided that it is his duty to take my mother to the district town Oschatz, to the hospital. Soon his horse-drawn cart was ready. I had no time to say goodbye to Pietro and the mayor said that he was going to leave us at the hospital. We wanted to take Aunt Mania with us; he didn't let her come along. We insisted, but he remained adamant; it will be only the two of us or none. Thus, we found ourselves separated in an instant from Aunt Mania. She had only time to whisper with trembling lips, "Remember to write, as soon as you can, to my son in Tel Aviv, I shall not be able to..." She wouldn't be able to because she intended to return to Poland, which was under the Russian occupation. She had to return in order to meet her husband, Uncle Bernard, my father's brother, who will hopefully return from Siberia...

We were not going to return to Poland, that much we had already decided. It looked like we shall never meet her again. We didn't even have time to fix an address through which we could communicate. That was the final, sad separation.

The mayor swore and cursed his lot, he had so much on his hands, and now he had to drive us to the town Oschatz. He delivered us to a big hospital. The doctors looked aghast at my mother, this skeleton swollen from hunger. They had never encountered such a case. They exchanged observations on the effects of hunger. They speculated that it must be accompanied by stupefaction... Here my indignant mother interfered in her perfect, literary German. They were even more surprised and deeply ashamed. They finally gave my mother some care. They opened her wounds patiently, squeezed out the pus, cleaned the area and made elaborate dressings. They even equipped us with sterilized dressings as reserve. What now? My mother was not a patient qualifying for hospitalization, they said. We were handed over to a temporary camp for refugees. Under the term "refugees", the German civil authorities comprised all homeless people. In their eyes they were equal. Thus, we found ourselves in a school building turned into an asylum, a shelter for homeless people, and that included German native fugitives of all kinds as well as concentration camp survivors. It was a real cocktail, or rather a fermenting wine, composed of very ill-assorted elements. This society was not even divided along any lines. We were mixed with German civil population fleeing the heavily bombarded cities, having lost their homes.

The German administration had its sense of order. My mother was given a bed in the "Krankenstube" — the sick ward. I was placed in a bare classroom full of German civilians. I was the only ex-concentration camp prisoner, the only Jewess among some sixteen Germans, some of them children. We had each our own pallet. At first, I was depressed by this cohabitation, then being curious, as you know me by now, I tried to engage them in conversation. They felt very uneasy in my presence, they hastened to assure me, one by one, that they were no Nazis, just simple civilians. They were the victims of bombardment and homeless exactly like me. The slight difference didn't occur to them. I just said to myself "vive la petite difference..." After all, I have to live among them, I won't discuss it. The main thing was that my mother could recover in relatively good conditions. Good conditions meant a clean bed, soup, cabbage, bread, tea, some margarine, some jam — provided in this shelter. Being bedridden my mother could hardly digest this bread. There were no showers, but being given a cake of soap I could wash my mother and myself.

I was young, I was recuperating well, and I needed fresh air. Slowly, cautiously I started to walk in Oschatz and I was delighted. How many years I haven't been able to walk by myself, not in a formation. I tasted for the first time the real taste of freedom, I imbibed freedom, I bathed in freedom. I walked as if I had wings, I was so light that the wind could blow me sky-high; at least that was the feeling when you weigh only 28 kilograms (some four stones).

The alleys of Oschatz were bordered with magnolia trees, it was May and they were in bloom. I didn't see lilacs, but I could smell them. What a bliss! Though I was getting tired very quickly, I tried to walk, to explore some more. At long last I saw the occupying forces, I saw the Russians. They were spread over Oschatz, they commanded the town, but not for long. Soon they were replaced by the Americans. In one respect I was right in my assumption. The demarcation line between the Russians and the Allies had not been clearly established and we witnessed a strange oscillation, where even the district town changed hands within a short period. I observed the Russian soldiers. They had such heavy, square faces. Some regiments were composed solely of the barbarian Kalmuck soldiers with dark complexion, Mongoloid features and slanted narrow eyes. I had never seen such creatures. They could say the same of me: they had never seen a walking skeleton. At the crossroads the heavy military traffic was directed by Russian girls of the military police, only they did not look like girls in uniform, they looked rather like the tanks that they were steering. Strange people, the Russians.

I didn't have enough time or strength to stroll and observe. I had still to fight for subsistence. We were hungry and we were still dressed in the same rags that we were wearing in Auschwitz. Something had to be done. I enjoyed being on my own, but it was not safe or easy. I reluctantly renewed my acquaintance with some women familiar to me from several camps, who were now stationed in the same school turned into shelter. They tried to persuade me to join them in their outings and to try together to get some food and some clothes. I gave an evasive answer. I left the option open, but I didn't like the idea.

One day, I found myself in front of a baker's shop. There was white bread in the showcase. A long queue had already formed, and everybody had bread tickets and money. I had none. How I wished I could bring mother some white bread. As I stood so forlorn and sad, a man addresses me in Polish: "Excuse me, but you must be from Poland, aren't you?" I nodded in the affirmative. "You see, it is easy to guess that you have been incarcerated in a concentration camp. I have noticed with what longing you are looking at this bread. I can offer to help you". I felt ashamed that my greed was so transparent, I refused to accept his help, but I did so in a hesitant way. The man had his arguments; "I was lucky, as a forced laborer, I was getting my wages and my food tickets. Now I am free and going home to Poland. I have some worthless German Marks. I happen to know that these Marks and food tickets are not valid in Poland. I am boarding a train tomorrow. If you refuse to take them, I might as well throw them away. Watch me" — and he made a gesture of throwing the paper bills into the air. Now I believed him. He looked at me intently and uttered one word: "Amcha?" I was thunderstruck. So, this goy sent from Poland to force labor is in reality a Jew who had been concealing his true identity for several years. I was now the first person to whom he had revealed it. We laughed but we had tears in our eyes. I accepted his gift and we parted with a warm handshake.

It was not much money, but with it I could buy white bread for mother many a time. I was so proud and happy that I could take care of her and provide for her. In some respects, mother was in a situation similar to mine. She too was the only Jewess in a ward full of German women. The bed facing hers was occupied by a strange creature. Her whole body was cast in plaster, one could only see her beautiful face of a suffering Madonna. Mother told me what happened to this girl, Trudl. The Russian soldiers broke into her relative's house and tried to rape her. When they chased after her, she jumped from a third-floor window. Most of her bones were broken.

Mother used the story as a warning to me, admonishing me not to walk in town on my own. One heard every day new stories about the Russians raping even old women. "Being so skinny wouldn't save you"- said mother threateningly and made me promise to join the other Jewish girls who asked me to accompany them. Obedient daughter that I was, I had to comply. Just one visit into the town — I explained to mother. I have to go to the bakery by myself.

Having bought the white bread, I hasten back to mother when, suddenly, I found myself cut off. The street was blocked by Russian soldiers, it was curfew and nobody was allowed to pass. The mixed crowd tried to find out what was it all about. It was quite scary, what are the Russians up to? A German woman who was the last to get trapped in this narrow street knew to explain: "There is a rumor that a squadron of German soldiers is roaming the vicinity of Oschatz. The Russian forces occupying Oschatz are spread very thin, they are afraid that this German unit could reconquer Oschatz. That's why they impose this curfew". Did I hear pride and hope in her voice? A French prisoner of war in a tattered uniform, who hasn't heard her explanation, asked in his bad German: "What that is? Why we not permit to going out from that damnation street?" I answered him in French, translating the latest news as related by the German woman. We discussed the situation, we were even amused. With his French sense of humor, he saw the latest developments as a "hide and seek game": "So the mighty Russian bear is afraid of the hiding German fox?" — he quipped. Time passed and we were still cut off, trapped. I was able to walk but not to stand. I was going to faint. He had noticed, he understood. He said: "I have some French friends living in this very street. Let me see, it must be in this house, as far as I remember. Come with me, you can rest in their room". When I hesitated and didn't dare to impose myself on strangers, he laughed: "It is all right, mademoiselle, they are a family with a baby, not some merry bachelors. But let me introduce myself. I am Michel Houppe, a happily married man and by profession a customs inspector in my native border village in the Voges mountains, in France. Having passed the whole war as a military prisoner, I am now free, awaiting the first transport back home". All this was said as we climbed the stairs to the room occupied by his friends.

I found myself in a room full of French people gathered around this happy family with a baby. As the woman explained, letting me hold the baby, they were both sentenced to forced labor, they met here, fell in love, were married and produced a baby. They too were waiting for the first transport home. I basked in this warm informal atmosphere. I could not wait to tell mother that I held a baby, a real baby in my arms. That's life, that's freedom. I had only one worry: My mother must be out of her wits, not knowing what became of me, why I haven't returned. Eventually the curfew was over. I ran to the Hans Scheme school and found out that mother was informed about the curfew and did not suspect that I got raped.

In the next days, I met Michel quite often, he helped me to get some food. He was a good companion. Walking together, looking at me, Michel said with nostalgia: "You are as sweet and good as my wife. You even look so much like my wife, that my heart goes out to you". I can easily guess the reason. Liberated people are very confused in their feelings.

"Michel" — I said — "it doesn't take a psychologist to guess that you are longing for your wife with all your heart, and that is why you see in me, me the friendly soul, an imaginary resemblance to your dear wife". He admitted that it could be true in a way. Indeed, after I inquired a little, it became clear that his wife is much taller and has brown eyes. So here it goes for the imaginary resemblance. We laughed it off.

One day, as I passed through some side street, I saw a crowd running into a building. What could it be? "A la guerre comme a la guerre"- at war time, everybody is looting. The Russians looted compulsively, admiring the western luxury. What they could not plunder they destroyed with ferocious pleasure. The German mob looted from brother Germans. In one of the buildings was a shoe factory. The Russian soldiers had broken the locks, forced the door open and took loads of shoes to trade for other goods. The German mob followed in their footsteps. So did I, because I had to find shoes for us, ours were completely rotten. The storerooms were full of thousands of pairs, but I had a difficult task to find quickly exactly what I needed. I knew our size and number, I found it. Then I noticed shelves with children's shoes. The German family stationed in my classroom had a daughter about ten years old who also needed a pair of shoes, as I have noticed. I was looking for the right size. I was in a distant small storeroom; I seemed to be there all by myself, far from the crowds. No, it was a mistake, I was not alone, there was a Russian soldier in here, and he must have followed me. He was behind my back; he was breathing on my nape — he was going to rape me... He extends his huge hands, he encircles my thin waist, he said: "Come my doll".

When I am scared, I don't scream, I freeze. I didn't speak a word of Russian, so I simply said in Polish: "I am not a bloody German, I am from Poland and I am from the concentration camps". I showed him quickly the number on my arm. Thank God, it interested him; he studies it. I added quickly: "You would do nothing BAD to me, you wouldn't". The word 'bad' he understands. "It is not bad, it is good for you" — he quipped, showing his gold capped teeth. That's the end of me. I couldn't even jump from the window, like Trudl. The window was closed.

Believe me or not, I wouldn't mind admitting that I was raped (or so it seemed to me) now that I am registering this incident on tape — but it didn't happen. Out of my many traumas I am spared this one. My good guardian angel was watching over me. At the last moment some people came in, my persecutor hesitated, then he heard the voice of his superior and... I was saved. As usual mother was right, I was incorrigible in my lust for freedom.

All the shoes fit, everybody was happy and thanking me effusively. My mother wasn't. Though I didn't mention to her that I was almost raped, the very presence of the Russian soldiers on the scene was to her menacing enough to make her exclaim: "I forbid you to move by yourself, inviting an incident" (she could still say "I forbid you" to a daughter who was twenty-two years old). I was a good child, I obeyed. I had to join the group of girls from the concentration camps. They were more or less likable, rather less but what did I care. I was longing for a change of scenery; I hated these skeletal reminders.

Oschatz was now full of Russian soldiers. The first reinforcements were felt in town. We were looking for opportunities; we had to get something more nourishing and some clothe too. It was almost one month since the liberation, yet we were still wearing the same rags and had not tasted an egg (except the one stolen for me by Pietro). One day a Russian officer stopped in front of our group, in a side street, and whispered in Yiddish: "Yiden? Yiddische Kinder?" (Jews? Jewish children?) We answered in the affirmative. He opened his arms and embraced all of us in one bear's hug. This giant of a man cried like a baby and babbled: "Oh, my doves, my poor little ones, what have they done to you!!! Look at you so emaciated. I cannot bear it". His tears flew over his cheeks and fell from his trembling jaws on our heads. Then he composed himself, looked anxiously around and whispered: "I am a Russian officer, I am not supposed to make a display of my feelings, it is risky, you have to forgive me. But wait. I have to do my best. Wait here for me, right here, even if it takes half an hour". He was gone and we waited. He returned with a parcel full of goods. There was a bit of this and a bit of that, several cans of food, some butter, some sausage, coffee, half used soap — whatever he could get his hands on. He made excuses that it is so little, he kissed our foreheads and took his leave. And that was our first Jewish soldier, the first of our liberators, and we were shaken to the core. I didn't watch how they distributed the goods among the six of us, I still saw his tear-drenched face, and I shall never forget it.

Two days later, having achieved nothing, the five women decided to try in private houses. I was aghast, but I followed them meekly. Wherever they asked for food or clothes the German families quickly assured them that they were not Nazis, have never been members of the party... they were the victims of the regime and had nothing to offer. Actually, whenever you encountered German civilians and probed them a little to open up — you heard the same version. They were all very meek, subservient and fervently anti-Nazi. What has become of their pride, superciliousness and arrogance? Was it the aftermath or the counter-reaction to the brainwash? This reminds me of the story of an angelic woman of sweet character, who worked in a concentration camp under an elderly civilian German foreman. He told her once: "We know of course that you, Jews, are usurers, thieves, poisoners of wells and murderers. How could it possibly apply to you? You must be here by sheer mistake".

Once, my partners rang the bell of the first best flat, and an old woman opened the door. "Do you have something to eat for us?" — asked the leader. The old woman said that her pantry was empty, that they were a couple of poor pensioners and they could hardly subsist on what they get. "Is that so?" — said our leader, who was a beautiful, married young woman that I shall mention only as I.F. for a reason that will soon be obvious. She looked intently at the old lady's hand. She said in a commanding tone: "Give me your wedding ring". I was so shocked that I wished I could slip under the floor. The old lady twisted her gnarled hands, an angry spark plashed in her eyes and she reacted proudly raising her head: "Don't you have any respect for the marital sacrament?" I.F. had a ready riposte: "Do your people have respect for the marital sacrament? If so, where is my husband, where is my baby son? Do your people have respect for human life? You have no right to preach to me, to give me a moral lesson. Take off your wedding ring and hand it to me...". The old woman seemed to shrink in our eyes. In total silence, trembling all over, she twisted the gold ring and took it laboriously off her gnarled finger. I felt faint and nauseated. If that is revenge — I am shocked, disgusted and deeply ashamed. Never again shall I go out with them. The rest of the group must have felt awkward too, because they pretended to be tired and wanted to go back to the school shelter. I felt so faint that one of them had to support me.

I.F. didn't give up so easily. She gave a new order saying: "On our way home we pass next to the "Kommendantura", the office of the Russian commander of Oschatz. Why not go straight to the head? Are we not entitled to receive the basic commodities? We shall simply state that we are a delegation of the concentration camp survivors, we are still hungry and dressed in rags. He has to do something for us..." I tried to object but I was overruled. "It is a delegation; we have to go in as one body" — they said, and they were right in a way. We were already in front of the commander's villa and I had no time to separate myself from this clique before we entered the commander's office.

The room was big and long, his desk being at the other end of the hall. The vulgar commander sat there giving orders to some officers. Our delegation approached the desk and I.F. asked permission to speak to the commander. She was received with too amiable a smile. Hardly had this beautiful woman started her speech, when I noticed the commander's hand giving with his finger a very explicit signal to a petty officer. The "finger" drew half a circle, then the hand gave an imitation of turning the key. The delegation didn't notice, but I did because I am a hand watcher. I didn't wait for the officer to close the entrance door; I ran like a rabbit all the length of the hall and out of the villa. Now I could go slowly back to the school, back to mama and to safety.

I don't know what happened over there in the 'Kommendantura'. My former partners gave later reluctant, evasive answers, mentioned some vague promises and much too quickly changed the subject. The whole episode remained enigmatic. I am not saying for certain that they got raped. I cannot be sure of it. This time I related the whole episode to my mother with a grim satisfaction. Her Majesty was shocked and relieved me from my former promise of walking with a bunch of unreliable ladies for company. I now kept my distance from them. I was again on my own and even the magnolia flowers seemed to smile at me. Michel came to take his leave. His group was going to board the train the next day. He was so excited that he had tears in his eyes, the round eyes of a puppy. When he said that he shared with me the best, unforgettable moments of the newly regained freedom — it was not out of the famous French gallantry. I knew that it was true because I felt the same way. He asked me politely if he can kiss me goodbye. "Of course you can, you fool" — I said and it was a warm, friendly, sweet kiss, perhaps the most beautiful kiss of my life, just because it was not tinted by sexual overtones.

Mother was still in the sick ward, and in the next bed was a sick German woman surrounded by her little children. I was still in the big classroom among my German neighbors. One night, I heard a general commotion. The heavy boots of Russian soldiers in the long corridor, I heard their voices too. They were obviously drunk. We heard somebody screaming. All the Germans in my classroom were terrified, nobody moved until... they were eventually gone. The voices came from the direction of the sick ward. I ran to mother. In there, all the sick women cried and laughed. Some were in hysterics. Finally, when they quieted down a little bit, they all pointed to my mother as the heroine who saved them from rape. And this was the way it happened.

The drunken Russian soldiers did not know where they were and in what building, but they had a flashlight. The first room close to the entrance was the sick ward, and the first bed close to the door was that of the crippled Trudl. When they saw in the flashlight her beautiful face, they all wanted to rape her. They would probably have done it, one after another, and they would probably rape the other sick women as well. Trudl shrieked. My mother jumped from her bed straight to the light switch, she turned on the light and in one movement uncovered Trudl. The sight was frightful. Her whole body was, part by part, enclosed in plaster. The drunken soldiers sprang away as if they were shown a ghost. My mother yelled at them in Polish: "Don't you see that you are in the sick ward? All of us here are very ill". Then an idea struck her; when they leave the sick ward, they will go to the other rooms and... to the classroom where I was sleeping. She added quickly: "This whole building is a hospital, and the other rooms are the epidemic ward. There is typhoid, dysentery, cholera, you name it". Drunk as they were, they understood my mother's Polish, or rather the single most important words. It made them sober up and leave the building in haste.

From surprise to surprise... who would show up the next day if not Aunt Mania? Cavertitz got rid of the former prisoners, and of course they were directed to the district town Oschatz and to the school serving as shelter... We were happy to be together again, even though it was going to be a short reunion, because as I said Aunt Mania had the firm intention of returning to Krakow. She wanted to leave with the first train eastward to be reunited with her husband, who was interned in Russia. There was no transportation for her, and we were still in the same situation. No clothes, no food, except the white bread that I could procure for mother. I went out with Mania to provide something or at least to try. We had no plan, we just drifted. We were on the outskirts of Oschatz, there was a little farm and we entered the yard. The housewife looked at us, we looked at her. Everything was so quiet, and the hens walk and provoke us. Then we spot, both of us simultaneously, two eggs, two fresh eggs just laid by the hen. Without a word Aunt Mania put her big hand on the eggs. Without a word she grabbed them, and without a word we left the premises. It was the second and third egg that the three of us consumed and shared since the liberation.

One day we entered a villa. The door was not locked. The interior was splendid, but it looked too crammed with plundered furniture and valuables. It was noontime and the whole family was seated round the table. There was on this table a display of the most costly, rare and tasty dishes. We looked in bewilderment and didn't believe our eyes. The head of the family must be a big fish... Somehow, I felt that he was an SS man freshly out of his uniform. Indeed, I noticed on the wallpaper the trace of a big picture which had been recently removed. An insignificant little landscape was hung instead of it. Many pictures had been added haphazardly in this room, only this one on the main emplacement had been removed. The SS man followed my gaze. He knew that I knew... what picture it must have been.

The family sat like frozen, glued to the tall chairs. I inspected shamelessly the food on the table, and I did it on purpose, because I knew we shall not partake of it. Then I said negligently in German: "You should have replaced Hitler's portrait with a bigger picture, the marks are still visible. Anyhow, thank you for your cordial invitation to lunch (none was extended) but I think, Auntie, that we shall have to refuse it. This delicious food is contaminated, we shall not taste it". The owner of the house looked quite menacing, he could even kill us and nobody would know, but we took our retreat slowly and with dignity. On the doorstep I spell in a loud voice the name of the street and the number of the villa. Let this SS man stew in his juices — he will be afraid that we shall denounce him to the Russian authorities. He will flee his villa, he will strip it quickly of all the plundered treasures.

Aunt Mania was so furious that she cursed: "We could have taken out of this villa a whole load of food and clothes" — she said with regret — "were it not for your damned pride". I laughed it off. So, I have that kind of pride, and what of it. It is more nourishing than food. Mother will approve, she will understand. She may be very pragmatic but has her pride too.

The next day I was rewarded. While I queued up for the white bread, a German woman entered into conversation with me. She took me to her flat and gave me a change of linen and three old dresses for the three of us. She even added: "Don't mention it, we have enough between my mother, my daughter and me". She was even ashamed, that five weeks after the liberation we were still in the same rags. She was one of the few Germans who didn't proclaim loudly they had never been a Nazi. This woman simply didn't have to.

Eventually aunt Mania learned that a train was about to leave for Poland. This time we talked things over. We had decided to go to France. She had to return to Poland. Perhaps we should never meet again. Poland being under the Russian occupation, there was little chance that Mania could communicate with her only son, who reached Palestine in the first year of the war. We were now going to constitute the only link.

Here I have to fill in some details. When the war broke out it was rumored (as you may remember) that Jewish men were in direct danger. Uncle Bernard and their son Shlomo (Solomon) escaped from Krakow on foot and thus reached Lwow. Knowing that Krakow was under the German occupation they planned to cross the Romanian frontier and eventually, crossing illegally, reach Palestine. They tried it three times... with no success. Uncle Bernard said that fate must be against him, because he left his wife Mania behind. He just had to go back to Krakow. He wouldn't try any more to cross the frontier, but he gave his blessing to his son. A young man should go his way. Shlomo embraced his father, went to the shore of the river Prut, undressed, put all his possessions on his head and swam in the darkness of the night across the river, which constituted the border line. Once in Romania, he was robbed of the money that he had on him, but the Jewish center for help of displaced persons smuggled him with many others all the way to Palestine. Aunt Mania even received a letter from him, written in Tel Aviv. Uncle Bernard, finding himself under the Russian occupation and registering as a volunteer to return to Krakow (to the German zone) — was sent by the Russians to Siberia as an undesirable, suspect element. That's the story of this branch of my family.

Now, at the hour of parting, Mania imposed on me the task of communicating with Shlomo, after we reach Paris. "Yes, but what is his address in Tel Aviv?" — I asked the most crucial question. The answer was disappointing: "All I remember is that he is staying with the Munz family in Tel Aviv, and the street is Shderot Boulevard. The number I don't remember". Knowing no Hebrew, I couldn't realize that Shderot means boulevard and is not the name of the boulevard. The whole address was one nonsense (what I did about it will be related later in my story).

We took leave of Aunt Mania and we were very sad. All my mother desired was to get out of her sick-bed and go straight to France. I remonstrated with her that she was still far from being able to travel and start a new life. She was stubborn as a mule and wanted to leave with the first train provided for civilians — to France.

The situation in Oschatz has changed diametrically. The Russians were out, and the Americans were in. The American soldiers were all over the town, which changed hands under an unknown (to us) agreement. How different they looked from the Russians. Their presence changed all the local atmosphere, or so it seemed to me. Though I was supposed to try to get some food and less shabby clothes, my first thought was to contact my uncle in America, my mother's brother, Uncle Henry, Dr. Henry Rose. I approached the first best American soldier who looked passably friendly and asked him to mail my letter to Uncle Henry through military post. Unlike Aunt Mania, I remembered Henry's full address by heart, and it was in Wilmington, Delaware. I made it a short letter to inform him that only the two of us have survived the Holocaust, we have no address and we intend to go to Paris. As soon as we shall have a foothold there, we shall write again.

The soldier asked several questions and was moved by what he saw and heard. He was not stationed here, he was merely passing through Oschatz, but in the few hours left to him he was eager to help me as well as he could. He had nothing to offer, he was getting his food from the field kitchen; all he had were good intentions. He looked into shops and there was nothing that he could buy for me. The shop owners have hidden their wares, afraid of the pilfering soldiers and German mob following in their footsteps. All of a sudden, he saw a commotion and a crowd trying to enter a building. It was a storehouse of fine fabrics. This time apparently the German mob have broken the locks and looted. My brave soldier understood the situation and took advantage of his uniform. He ordered me to remain in the street and wait under the windows. Quick as a squirrel he penetrated through the mob and disappeared inside the building. Soon he appeared in one of the windows and called from above: "Mary, watch out, I am throwing to you a whole bale of good fabrics. Don't try to catch it, it is heavy, just don't miss it". He throw down a full roll of a most splendid velvet, the color of deep cherry wine. He came down all flushed, happy and proud. He would like to do more for me. Right then he found out from a fellow soldier that his squadron has left the town. He was in big trouble. He had hardly time for a handshake and... he was gone. I was sorry for him and at the same time elated to be left with a real treasure. I took it home, that is to the school, and showed it to mother. "Leave it in my bed" — admonished my cautious mother. "No, you have to lie straight, it would be harmful for your back to put it under your pillow. I'd better put it under my pallet" — I objected. "Your German neighbors will certainly steal it from under your pallet" — she warned me. I tried to keep my ground: "My German roommates won't steal it; they would never do such a thing to me" — I said indignantly making my voice sound firm. "I don't believe it!!! You must be mad!" exclaimed my mother in horror — "After all they did to us, you are still apt to trust them. Are you that naive or that stupid?" — and she turned her back on me. As she turned over, she howled with pain. Her backpains were far from cured.

I embraced her, cuddled her and caressed her cheek gently with the soft velvet. "It feels on to my cheeks like rose petals" — said mom who loved roses. "It feels like the cheek horse's nostrils or a kitten" — said I who love everything velvety to the touch. Mother sighed and seemed relaxed. I took the velvet to my classroom and put it openly under my straw-filled mattress.

The next day I stroll in the center of Oschatz. There seem to be more American soldiers in town. A group of them were discussing something and one turned to the passing people, asking if there is among them someone who speaks English. The Germans gaped but didn't react. I volunteered. "Do you speak German as well?" — asked the same soldier, for it is obvious to him that I am not of the superior German race. "Yes, I do" — I nodded affirmatively. "So please ask these people where we can find a watchmaker". I obliged, I inquired. Why not, these soldiers have probably one or more watches that need repair, why shouldn't I help them. I offered to lead them to the address indicated. A German boy showed me the way, I followed him, and my Americans followed me. We entered the little shop of the watchmaker and they were behind me, some five American soldiers now approaching the counter. "Tell him to hand over to us all the watches in his possession" — said the leading soldier. Paff!!! A hot wave of blood flushed my pale cheeks. I would have expected anything, absolutely anything, except pillage by American soldiers. Once more, like the time I accompanied the I.F. woman, I found myself, incidentally, linked to looters. I shrank; I swallowed hard and… I interpreted. "Tell the Americans not to be absurd"- says the watchmaker —"Don't they know that the Russian soldiers have been here before them and have taken away all the watches. I don't have a single watch left". I translated these words, whereupon the Americans left the shop without a word. A German observer quipped: "How stupid they are the Americans. The Russians didn't ask Questions. They searched the shop, they made a house-search at his home, checking from the cellar to the attic. Thus, they found the whole lot". I hardly listened, I was still ashamed that I interpreted for these base looters in American uniform.

It has to be stressed, however, that the American presence in town brought order and proper organization. We, at the school center, were told by an American representative that the former prisoners of the concentration camps are entitled to get proper housing in a German furnished flat, money as monthly allowance, food tickets (for eggs, sugar, meat et cetera), decent clothes and, of course, medical care. We shall receive all that soon after we register. (I saw myself already in the SS-man's villa, sequestered for us.) All that will be provided for a long period, until our problem is solved in a satisfactory way. It was such an attractive prospect that I was, for a moment, tempted to accept it, at least until mother will be cured or well enough to travel.

For the first time since we decided to go to France, I had a serious open conversation with mother. It was then that I discover a most troubling phenomenon: we, the close-knit unit, were concealing from each other that we were both helping the German people. I brought a pair of shoes for a German girl and rendered other services, meanwhile my mother was giving the white bread I brought her to her German sick neighbor. Indeed, I was happy that Mom could consume such a quantity of this bread, while in reality she gave the lion's share of it to this German mother with her little children, leaving for herself only a minimal part.

When we discovered the truth, we were both equally shocked. Where is our vengeance? What is wrong with us? Can't we at least keep our distance, keep aloof? Is our pattern of behavior anathema to sound, basic instincts of revenge? Is this the way to behave for us who have lost all our next of kin in the gas chambers? What a terrible guilt!!! We felt like throwing up, or like walking out of our own skin. Wallowing in this self-hatred we decided on the spot to leave Germany, at the first opportunity and with the first train for civilians.

When I went to my classroom with a heavy heart, torn by conflicting moods — I discovered that the roll of velvet under my pallet, has almost disappeared. My Germans, my friendly German neighbors, to whom I have been so helpful, whom I trusted — have stolen some fifty yards of this exquisite velvet, leaving for me only the exact measure for one dress... How considerate. Hardly able to raise my eyes, I went to mother like a little child with guilt written on my face. She didn't even scold me, all she said was: "Will it at least teach you a lesson for the whole rest of your life, not to trust strangers, let alone enemies". That clinched it. I don't want a villa or flat, I don't want money from American welfare, I give up medical care — I want out of here. Period.

There is a German proverb which states: "A man — a word — a woman — a vocabulary". Reverse it and it applies to us. We, women of this family said it in one word — "we go" and indeed we joined the first available train for civilians, going westward.

THE ODYSSEY OF THE SURVIVORS

It was not as simple as you probably imagine. This train wasn't going to take us straight to France. It was a long trip with many adventures, and there was time to make new friends on this train. As if was still used to forming a group of five... we were befriended by three strangers, none of them of our origin or creed. They were indeed strange strangers, the three women with whom we traveled for several weeks.

The most dominant figure among them was Henrike, a fortyish, thick-set, blonde woman from Holland. According to her story she was an orphan, adopted and raised by a Jewish couple. She never married and lived with her adoptive parents who left her a free choice of religion. When the Germans invaded Holland, Henrike, the Christian, rented a flat, and there kept hidden not only her parents but also several other Jews. An informer denounced her and she was deported to Ravensbruck and other camps. Liberated like us, she was on her way home, and she was a 'jolly good fellow': warm, caring and reliable. We loved her at first sight. We knew that we can trust her. The second new friend, Elisabeth, was a tall German gentile girl, almost twenty. She was well educated, lovely and likable. Why would we befriend a pure German? She had the following story to tell: Her parents, being of the old aristocracy, were openly hostile to the Nazi regime. Their vast lands and small castle were confiscated. They passed the war under a changed identity. Now her parents must return to claim and retrieve their possessions, but for Elisabeth they want a different future, far from this abominable country, somewhere in Holland or Belgium. That's why she was leaving Germany, she had some relatives in Belgium. Was it plausible? Who can judge? All we could say was that she seemed to have a positive character and fitted well into our team.

The third lady, and I must call her a lady, was fiftyish and she was from Denmark. Her husband was a German industrialist. They lived in Denmark, but the war caught them in Germany. They were unable to return to Denmark or rather her husband was not permitted to leave Germany, even though he was above recruitment age. Eventually, at the end of the war, the husband was killed in an air raid. All she wanted was to go back to Denmark, but there was no way to get there, straight from Germany, so she would rather try Holland first. She gave her name as Dorothea Hansen, but she had no documents, no identity card. Neither had Elisabeth. They both lost them in a bombardment. Sic.

What united us with the three women was a feeling of being cosmopolitan, of being the citizens of the world. Our long, erratic itinerary, interwoven with periods of waiting — cemented the unnatural bond. As it transpired, Elisabeth and Dorothea had some money to buy provisions and shared them with us, we had privileges and priority — or so they believed and hoped. Were we again naive and trusting? There will come a day when the clever Henrike will say to me: "After all, what do we know about our new companions? The older could well be an SS-man's widow, the younger could have been a Nazi warden in the camps. Both are very nice, very correct, but what do we know about them...? Perhaps they are simply 'taking a ride' on our good credentials — our genuine concentration camp numbers".

At a certain station we were told to get off the train, it went only that far. Most unexpectedly we discovered that we were again on Russian occupied territory. Over there were the Americans. "Over there" meant over the Elbe River. Once more we found ourselves facing the Elbe, once more we were not permitted to cross the bridge. There was a Russian commander, and he had his orders. He could only let the Russian soldiers through, but none were coming to cross the bridge. What a strange situation. Once again, we were sleeping in a barn in a German hamlet, in the middle of nowhere.

We waited day after day and there was no opening, no change, only hope and stagnation. Nobody cared for us, nobody provided food. Elisabeth and Dorothea insisted on sharing with us whatever could be bought with the money they had. We would prefer to sell the velvet, or rather the little piece that was left of it, but they wouldn't let us. "Don't be petty" — said Henrike. She didn't know how proud we are. Anyhow, there was very little that one could buy there, so all was for the best.

The Russian forces manning the bridge were a company of Kalmuk Russian soldiers. In our eyes they looked like some medieval Tartars. Indeed, they seemed to be on the same level of civilization. Only the commander was a white Slavic man, and so was his cook. The cook had set his eye on me. Why not on Elisabeth — I don't know. Perhaps she was too tall for this little man, perhaps he liked them petite and skinny. He was astute. One day he asked us, my mother and me, to come over to the commander's villa. The commander had caught a splendid fish on his rod, and he wanted it cooked in a special way. He, the cook, didn't know how, or so he pretended. Would we oblige? Mother could not refuse, our only hope to cross Elbe depended on the commander's goodwill. Mother went to the villa, but without me. The cook was disappointed. Mother explained lamely that I was sick. She herself was too weak to do the cooking — she assembled the ingredients and explained in Polish what is to be done with the fish. Anyhow, it was a plain subterfuge.

The cook didn't give up. He pretended to have some errands in the vicinity of our barn, and I had to hide. Henrike looked knowingly and said: "He will be back, we'd better do something about it." Indeed, at night he came to our barn with a flashlight. Before he got his orientation in this huge barn Henrike had already covered me with hay and moved over, her whole body was now upon mine. How long could I bear it? He asked for me. Mother pretended to be deep asleep, but Henrike said in German "Maria is away, she went to see a doctor in another village". She points far away, and he understood. There was nothing he could do; he went away. I was once more saved from rape. He was selective, this one, for some reason he wanted only me. The Kalmuks were not so selective. According to Aunt Mania's report, they raped all the women of Cavertitz, including the eternal old virgin, the local bigot Else. Only the former prisoners, sleeping in the barn were saved from rape. Here, in this village, the Kalmuks didn't rape, perhaps they were afraid of their commander. But just to look at the Kalmuks was scary, and the whole village was afraid of them. We didn't see any other soldiers, there was no military movement over the bridge, in fact nobody crossed the bridge because over there were stationed the Americans.

Fed up with inertia, we decided with Henrike to make a move. We asked formally to see the commander. He had someone able to interpret. We stated that we were a delegation of the former concentration camp prisoners, now displaced persons desiring to go home. Henrike was from Holland, I was (allegedly) from France, and there were others with us who were also bound westward in accord with their origin. Would he kindly let us cross the bridge? He was all smiles, he opened his big arms in a gesture of impotence and explained that his bridge is only for military passage. After a moment of reflection, he added that he will do his best to help us. Two stations farther on the railway (village so and so), there was a bridge for civilians. He gave us a short note of recommendation to the local commander. We thanked him effusively.

We returned to our companions, beaming with pride. But Henrike, the prudent, suggested to check it first before we drag along mother and the rest of the group. We had also to check if people without documents like Dorothea and Elisabeth would be permitted to pass. Our "documents" were printed on our forearm. The train stopped at the station only for one minute and we were almost too late. We jumped on the steps of the carriage and... we found ourselves facing some thirty Russian soldiers... How did we so foolishly fall into the arms of the bear? We felt trapped. The soldiers eyed us, exchanged some vulgar remarks and laughed. They seemed to draw lots who will be the first. We decided to get off the train at the next station, come what may, but the soldiers seemed to get a dressing down from their officer and stopped the lottery. We decided to reach our destination as planned. We alighted at the second station. The name was right, as indicated by the commander. We asked the villagers for the way to the bridge. "What bridge?" — they asked. As it transpired there was no bridge in the village, we had been duped by the smiling commander. We returned by the next train, angry, fuming and crushed by disappointment. Did the commander make a mistake? Possible, but not plausible; not with his luscious smile painted all over his face.

After a couple of days, we were allowed to cross the bridge; the instructions had been changed. Over the Elbe we were directed to a transit camp run by the American military forces. We were offered food and had to undergo a personal disinfection. What would it be? Dressed as we were, we had to pass in front of an America soldier armed with a powder sprayer.

(Now I know that it was D.D.T., but what did we know about its existence then and there.) The soldier sprayed some of the fine powder behind our collar, some into the decolletage opening, and some into the sleeves of our dresses. That's all. Some disinfection... We laughed. "Why are you laughing" — asked the soldier. As if by accord we laughed with Henrike in thin squeaking tones. The soldier looked suspiciously, as if he had to do with cranks, so we explained patiently that it is not us, it is the lice who laugh at his valiant efforts.

The administration of this camp registered all the incoming people so as to arrange transport to their destination. We could stay in Germany if we wished to — so we were told, but first we had to register and give our personal data. We three, with Henrike, had no documents except the tattooed number. When we queued up for the registration, we noticed that we had lost Dorothea and Elisabeth in the crowd. No, we did not lose them, they must have clandestinely left the transit camp. "Wasn't I right" — said Henrike — "that there is something shady and spooky about both of them. Now you see for yourself that they vanished when facing a registration. What did we really know about them? Could we check on Dorothea's mastery of the Danish language?" I knew that Henrike was right, I even remarked: "Dorothea's German accent is genuine German most of the time, though sometimes you can hear a foreign inflection. I wonder if this is genuine or an attempt at imitation. Elisabeth's story seems, in retrospective, as full of holes as a sieve. Perhaps she threw off a uniform a few hours before the liberation, like this SS warden whom I saw wearing a flowery dress under her uniform. Perhaps they used us... perhaps we served as their passport for crossing the frontiers to the American zone and out of Germany. I could only hope that we were wrong, perhaps they really were what they pretended to be, perhaps they had indeed lost their documents, I had heard here several authentic Frenchmen telling the same story". Mother kept unusually silent, without any reaction to my utterances. She must have been much ashamed that she didn't suspect a hoax. I used my advantage to point out, sarcastically, that it was the snob in her that put her vigilance to sleep. She pretended not hear me...

GOING TO PARIS AS FRENCH CITIZENS

There is in this camp some confusion in certain respects. We, being registered for "return" to France, had to take leave of Henrike, who was going to Holland. Little did we know that our transport to France will be sent through Holland and Belgium, and that we didn't have to separate, not yet. I took Henrike's address to keep in touch. She embraced and hugged us as if we were her old friends. The feeling was mutual. I couldn't know that I shall misplace and lose her address in the turmoil and never be able to renew the contact.

As a measure of precaution, I wrote another letter to Uncle Henry in America, and gave it to an American soldier to be mailed by military post. As it turned out, this was the only letter to reach him for reasons that would soon become understandable.

This transit camp was so well run that the next day we were already put on a train. We discovered that this train was bound for Holland first. We left behind the ruined cities of Germany and the remnants of camps. That reminds me that during our march of death and our former rides on trains across Germany, we learned to distinguish between the various small military camps for evacuated Allied prisoners of war. Wherever we saw a well-organized camp with adroitly constructed booths, caves, canopies, underground huts and shelters with well-built campfires — we knew it was a Russian camp of prisoners. Next in line were the camps of Canadian and American prisoners. The most haphazardly organized, neglected camps, with unshaved, haggard figures dragging their feet in mud, were those of Frenchmen. All these have already disappeared from the landscape of Germany.

Now, crossing into Holland, the contrast was striking. I felt like a tourist, I observed all the time not only the landscape, but the way people lived there. The neat houses, the well-tended doll gardens spoke — if not of prosperity, at least of cleanliness and a peaceful life in security. The pictures were so charming that I felt like getting off the train at any such enchanted hamlet and staying there for the rest of our lives. Were the local people as charming as their surroundings? Would they be friendly? I wondered. Belgium was less fascinating, especially when we crossed the industrial district. Still, close to the French border we watched the pastoral life of the Belgians, trying even to peep into the windows of the neat houses. The north of France presented a sad picture of dilapidation. The contrast was appalling. Filth, soot, poverty, neglect — was all we saw the moment our train passed the frontier. The gloomy picture added to my gloomy mood. The pastoral symphony was over, I had now to face the hardest test of my life; I had to tell a chain of lies and make them stick. Believe me or not, I had never before soiled my lips with lies. Now I had to spread them thick and heavy. I had to pretend that we were deported from France, after having spent several years in Abbeville, where father was allegedly naturalized. The border control was very thorough, especially for people without documents. As we shall learn later, this dense net was spread to catch a particular species of fish — those Frenchmen who volunteered to work in Germany. People like us were not the target.

At this frontier station, there was an office and a clerk in uniform of the border police received us at his table. He had on his desk a long form of many questions and blank spaces to fill with our personal data and itinerary. I was well prepared; I had memorized all of Sonia's instructions. I had to give prompt answers with exact dates, addresses, reception of citizenship and stages of our absorption in France. The rest was easy; it concerned the camps where we were actually incarcerated. There was not a flicker of suspicion in the clerk's tone. My voice was even, my answers perfect and to the point. My mother looked so sick that the officer let me answer all the questions directed at her, it was only natural under the circumstances. I passed the test with flying colors. I was now certain that this long protocol, filling the official form in several copies, will accompany us to Paris and serve as a solid base for further formalities. How smooth it had gone. How stupid it was of me to fight against this version constructed by Sonia and approved by my mother. As usual mother was right. Moreover, I discovered that lies payoff.

After the formalities we were invited into a canteen. We were given sandwiches and we could choose a drink. I asked for beer. Mother looked reproachfully, but was I not a hero, was I not entitled to a tough man's drink? I was sitting at the table and beaming with self-contentment. France looked less ugly through a golden mug of beer, and the future seemed almost rosy. Later we boarded the train to Paris. I hardly remember this trip, being still in a state of euphoria.

The civilians arriving from Germany to Paris were not allowed to leave the station, and thus we were all brought in busses to a splendid hotel, hotel Lutetia in the center of Paris. Here we were seated comfortably in the lobby at a table for two. The lobby wasn't crowded, there were probably several such absorption centers in Paris. A waiter in a white jacket brought us coffee and bread with margarine. What bliss! An elderly person approached our table to inform us that we have to wait for a while for a formal reception, but soon, very soon, we shall be given a room and be able to rest. We waited, there was no hurry, nobody was expecting us.

As we sat so comfortably, we were approached by a monster of sorts. This little, well-dressed Jew had only half a jaw, the other half was missing (he was injured in the First World War). He politely asked several questions about the camps we have been in, and then if we were gentile or Jewish, and where from. Here we didn't have to tell lies, we declared freely that we were Jewish and from Poland. So was he. He came to France twenty-five years ago. He now drew from his pocket several family pictures of his wife and two children. Had we seen them over there in the camps? Had we by chance met one of them? — he asked. They were all deported while he was in hiding. He survived the war here in Paris, but what is his life worth if his family will not return. We felt sorry for him, we studied the pictures but had no information for him, no consolation. He asked some more questions concerning us and our plans, then he told us about himself: he lacks nothing (he is thriving on the black market), but he is so lonely in his vast flat, and his family has not returned. Would we not like to join him, give him a sense of family? We can live together for a while — he said — he will buy the provisions, my mother will cook, otherwise we shall have the good rest that we deserve. We were moved by his offer, but we had to decline it. We said that we cannot impose ourselves on a total stranger; there must be some institutions like the "Joint" to take care of us. He persisted that it would be a good temporary solution for both sides. "Joint, Shmoint — who needs it, just move into my house" — he said. Here was his "carte de visitie" and some coins for the metro tickets, after we finish the formalities we should come straight to his house — he said and took leave of us. I took his visiting card, put it absentmindedly into my bag, we had no intention of using it. Little did we know how we shall need it...

The way things developed from this moment made us forget this poor-rich Mr. G... Shortly after this conversation we were invited to the last room in a long corridor. There were several clerks there, and we were asked to take a seat opposite a high official of the Security service. He asked to be excused that after such a long journey he had to incommode us with this interview, before letting us rest in a room of hotel Lutetia.

This opening put me in such a good mood that I even permitted myself a little joke: " It fits" — I said — "that we should make our first steps after our return to the French soil right here in hotel Lutetia, because Lutetia was the first name given to what is now Paris by the conquering Romans". He liked the idea and could start. It was almost the same routine as at the frontier, but he wrote it in a form of a long protocol. He asked a lot of specific questions and received all the detailed answers in fluent French. Our personal story was carefully noted, and it was stressed that we are French citizens by virtue of father's naturalization. After the long protocol was written down, I beamed with inward pride while the security officer, beaming with benevolence, applied his signature. Wishing us a quick recovery, he directed us to a young clerk who had to fill out the entrance visa or whatever it was. Like his predecessor the young man hastened to reassure us that all the formalities were over, we can rest now in the hotel room. I took the opportunity to check the weakest point of my deposition. "Yes" — I said, "all the formalities are over, but how shall I later be able to prove father's naturalization, having no documents and no certitude of finding them in Abbeville?". He continued to apply the appropriate stamps and answered without raising his face: "But mademoiselle, that's certainly no problem at all. A copy of every naturalization, all over the country is always preserved at the 'Prefecture de Police' of Paris. You will certainly find it there". I was thunderstruck. I could hardly utter the two words 'thank you' while taking the documents from his hand.

Here starts my tragedy. I somehow reached the lobby with mother following me and... I broke down. I almost fainted, I went to pieces. I was shaking all over and sobbing uncontrollably. "That's that" — I exclaimed to mother between sobs — "now it is all over. The whole building of lies has collapsed, crumbled. All is lost. The only salvation, before we get arrested, is to make a clear breast of it, to spill the truth". I was in a spastic shock. I shook so violently that... I got my menstruation. I haven't menstruated for a whole year. I lost my period in May, as a consequence of shock, when Witek was taken to Auschwitz. I now recovered it in May, because of another shock. Mother gripped my shoulders, then tried to cradle me. She tried to reason with me, to prove that nothing has happened so far, nobody could prove the lies, there will be just no confirmation of my statements, no evidence, and the case will be left pending. Her arguments could not reach me in my shock. I felt like vomiting the lies, and that is what I said to mother, and that's what I did, having fortunately reached the lavatory. Straight from there I ran back to the same security officer who took down the long protocol. Mother tried to catch me by the sleeve, but I just ran, blinded by tears. I reached his table, he was alone, or so it seemed to me. "Sir" — I said, trembling all over — "a couple of minutes ago you wrote down our personal data and our story". He interrupted me and exclaimed: "Of course, but what happened to you, mademoiselle? Tell me pray what is it all about? Has somebody offended You?"

I now stopped sobbing and tried to say distinctly: "See, whatever I told you — except for our names — was a pack of lies!!! We have never been to France; we couldn't have been deported from France... My late father has never been to Abbeville, or to France for that matter. We have nobody left of the whole family in Poland. We were desperate. There was only one purpose in constructing this monument of lies. We knew that without them you would send us to Poland... and that would be horrible. We couldn't bear to see the same sights, to see the country where we have lost all our family. We just couldn't face it. It would be that traumatic. Please, try to understand". He nodded his head and said quickly: "Mademoiselle, calm yourself, nothing happened, nothing indeed. Dry your tears. Watch me, I am destroying the whole protocol, I am shredding it. As of now we forget that you ever made such a deposition... Now your status is different. You are simply foreigners, and you will have to go to the 'Prefecture de Police' and register there".

I thanked him in a choked whisper and left the room with lowered head. Hardly have I crossed the threshold when I started to cry and shiver again. It was a new wave of shock. It was caused by one word, the single word 'Police'. Police is associated with inquest and arrest in the minds of persecuted people. Can you understand what it meant to concentration camp survivors to face uniforms, to be detained between walls and to be, eventually, sent back to Poland? I sat down on a bench and cried again as if I had a fountain of tears in my eyes. There was nothing mother could do, she had run out of arguments, she too was crushed. She too must have been scared of the police.

We both cried silently, both utterly exhausted. At last something happened. A young man wearing on his arm a band with the inscription "Voluntary civil service" approached us cautiously, asking: "Mademoiselle, what happened to you? Can I help you in any way?" I hardly looked at him, answering between sobs: "Nobody can help us, we have to report to the Police headquarters". The young man was taken aback. That was not an answer he was prepared for. He, the good soul, the good citizen was in conflict. The good citizen in him got the upper hand, and he felt it his duty to deliver these 'criminals' to the police.

He returned a while later and told us to follow him. There was in front of Hotel Lutetia a station wagon transporting vegetables. The young man must have stopped the driver asking him to deliver us to the 'Prefecture'. The driver cursed his lot, he was in a hurry, but he could not refuse. After all, it was a short trip. It was dark, and we faced a huge building or rather a bloc of buildings of the French Police. We were brought to one of the gates, and instantly taken over by a policeman on duty. Shoving us in front of him he approached the cubicle where every arrested person was registered. "What have you brought here, what merchandise?" — asked the policeman in the cubicle.

"How would I know. They have been delivered in a private truck without any protocol of indictment. They are just simply foreigners, I think" — he replied shrugging his shoulders. "So, what does it have to do with us?" — asked the registering policeman, visibly disgusted by the lack of evidence: "Why not turn them over to the police office for foreigners" — he suggested. Then the other interjected: "Have you forgotten that it is Saturday evening now and their offices are already closed for Sunday? All there is to do is to set them free and instruct them to report to this office Monday morning. They understand French" — suggested the policeman who took us in. "Are you a fool? Look at them, they are wetting their pants out of fear; they wouldn't show up if released. No, no, we have to detain them here in the depot till Monday morning" — was his final decision. While he took down our names, a whole bunch of women was brought in by a police van. One look at them sufficed to guess that they were all prostitutes. The policeman in the cubicle took down their names and ordered to take the whole batch, including us, to the depot. I had somehow regained my composure and protested vehemently, I demanded to be treated differently, ours was a different case — we had landed here by mistake. "Oh, yes" — smiled the policeman from his cubicle — "Of course you two, ladies, will get a separate room with a personal bathroom" — he mocked me and sent us all to a huge cell on the upper floor. Here we tasted the first sample of the French sense of humor and the style of work of the French police.

In this big cell we were some fifty women, each sitting on her pallet, and most of them seemed to be from the underworld or prostitutes. In the dim light we did not discern the others who were more like us. There was one water faucet in the corner and beyond it one WC cubicle. It was crowded in here, it was noisy, and there was fear in the air. We felt like having been trapped again in a concentration camp of sorts. We were too exhausted, too spent to look around us, we just dropped on the pallet, and I tossed on it with a splitting headache for the most part of the night. Only in the morning did we inspect the picture around us. One has to adapt first to the physical conditions. The only people who had access to this jail were the Catholic sisters of mercy. They distributed the meals, and in the morning, they gave us a strip of cloth that had to be used as a personal towel.

I approached the nun and asked her for some cotton pads, whispering into her ear that I have got my time (the word 'menstruation' is unspeakable here). 'What do you think that you are in a hotel?" — answered the nun shrugging her shoulders. Then she added that next to the toilet I can find some strips of cloth. Indeed, there were some dirty rags, good enough to clean the toilet. So, this was the mercy of the sweet servants of Jesus... I was enriched by one more experience. Here is the place to explain why the depot jail was so crowded, far beyond its capacity. As I have hinted, the French arrested many people, mostly among those returning from Germany, so as to catch those Frenchmen who went to Germany as volunteers. It was not yet clear to me at this stage. I had never been to a jail and I found it a fascinating experience. I knew that we shall be released on Monday, so I hurried to study the human element in here, in the depot.

The Frenchmen hate the Germans, but they hate even more Frenchmen who have collaborated with the Germans. There is a wide range of grades and shades of collaboration and most of them were represented in this place. There were informers, dealers or women who had slept with the Germans... there were volunteers who went to work in Germany by their own free choice, but there was also a marginal phenomenon of forbidden fraternization, not here, but over there in Germany. Many French prisoners of war who had been sent from their camps to work on German farms (replacing the mobilized German men) were openly flirting with the German women. This could be overlooked, but of them fell in love with a German girl and brought her back to France with the honest intention of marrying her. Some of these women were now detained at the depot. To render such a marriage more difficult, the French authorities were eager to release such a girl from jail only if the prisoner's whole family gave its written consent to the marriage. It was obvious that the family will object to it, especially in the present atmosphere after the glorious liberation of Paris. For the French prisoner, returning home with his fiancé, it became "mission impossible".

Soon I incidentally discovered one such German fiancée. She was far from beautiful, but she was delicate, reticent and glowing with a certain aura, A real flower in this human garbage. Her French was perfect but with a slight German accent. I knew nothing about her at this stage, but I was intrigued by her personality. I approached her cautiously without imposing my company on her. That's probably why she warmed up to me. Soon I heard her story and it flew together with tears. Emilia worked as a secretary on a big estate farm. When the French prisoners were sent to do the hard work and slave on the farm (in spite of the Geneva Convention), she tried to help them as well as she could, even endangering her position. A shy, well-mannered French prisoner attracted her attention. They were both so shy that it took them a long time to become friendly and much longer to disclose, eventually, their love for each other and to become engaged. This gentle Emilia was a German baroness, but she was afraid to divulge it to her fiancé, lest he feel overwhelmed, this modest, inhibited young man. He was a French marquis, a landlord, yet he never disclosed it to his fellow prisoners or to his new fiancée, so as to integrate and not to feel different or be nagged as a ninny while working as a forced labor slave. The truth emerged on both sides only after the end of the war, when he asked her to accompany him to France and become his wife. He told her so much about his parents, he was so sure that they would love her and hug her to their bosom.

He managed to smuggle her into France, but here things developed most unexpectedly; she was arrested and, as I said, could only be released if the family of her fiancé signs their agreement to the marriage. Apparently, his family, this proud, patriotic French aristocracy, could not swallow such a concession, such a disgrace. "I understand his parents" — she said — "I am not blaming them, but if only I got a chance to face them, to explain the political background of my family and prove it by Nazi newspaper clipping — perhaps their attitude would change. I cannot show my credentials because I am not summoned... we couldn't guess that such a situation could arise".

Emilia was desperate, she was in a vicious circle, and so were we. Monday, Tuesday and several more days have elapsed, and we were stuck in this jail like sitting ducks. We were kept there as if we didn't exist for the outside world. Nobody claimed us. Everybody else was called for investigation — we never were. Mother explained that the police must be busy with important cases, ours was not. Let her believe it, I didn't. I tried to be patient, haven't I messed up things by being too impulsive and hysterical? I took advantage of this situation by trying to learn more about the inmates. It was not easy. One cannot approach an intriguing woman and ask for what crime she has been arrested. Sometimes chance helped me in making contacts. One woman had overheard me speaking Polish with my mother. She introduced herself formally, she was from Warsaw, she was a writer and her name was Stefania (I don't recall her family name). We could guess that she was Jewish, but she must have passed the war in Poland with false, Aryan identity papers. She mentioned vaguely that she went through a hell of denunciations, yet she seemed reluctant to speak about it when I showed some interest. She tried to be ingratiating and it sounded false. She was still used to play a cold Polish noblewoman. For some reason she was set on sticking to us. She milked us for many details of life in the concentration camps, very specific details. She asked about dates and number of blocks or who didn't get a tattoo number in Auschwitz (only the transports destined for death). That in itself was strange. Wouldn't a writer be rather interested in the inner fabric of life in the camps?

Soon I discovered the reason for her inquiry. Once, when she went to the toilet, someone kicked her purse and all its contents was spilled on the floor. While I picked up for her the dispersed objects, I noticed her notes. They contained our itinerary with dates and relevant information. That clinched it; now I guessed the purpose of her questioning. For some reason she wanted to pretend to have been incarcerated in the camps rather than admit having passed the war with false papers. Was there something fishy in her past? Being blackmailed, did she turn into an informer? Perhaps I was wrong, perhaps she thought simply that it would be to her advantage to pass herself as a freed prisoner, a martyr entitled to special privileges. I didn't mention to her my discovery of her secret. We just kept our distance from her. Now see who was snubbing whom.

Another shady figure had her pallet not far from ours. This one was French. She was too plain and thickset to be a prostitute. Though it was stifling hot in the room she didn't take off her thick sweater. When she turned, I noticed that she wore on it a rectangular white cotton patch over her left breast. It bore a concentration camp number. The white fabric was too clean and neat, the number was clumsily penciled in, not printed like all the genuine concentration camp numbers. It even lacked the red triangle of a political prisoner. Most freed prisoners had, as a manifest of freedom, torn off this denigrating mark of shame (ours were still preserved as a souvenir), but she wore hers like an order of distinction. After all, she could have lost her real number, and she had no tattoo to prove it. Still, she was too fat to have been a prisoner.

It took me but one conversation to unmask her. I opened with something like "How nice to meet a fellow prisoner in this room full of prostitutes". I didn't ask questions so as not to scare her. First, I pretended to reminisce, then I asked: "Didn't we meet somewhere in the camps?" — I pretended that her face seemed familiar to me. Couldn't it have been in Leipzig, or later in Auschwitz, or still later in Malchow, and then in Ravensbruck? — I asked. As you noticed, I deliberately changed the order of camps, enumerating them in an impossible sequence. She nodded every time in the affirmative as if she had been to the same places, in the same absurd order. Then I mentioned Malchow again. "In what barrack were you living in Malchow, what number?" — I set the final trap. She replied without hesitation that it was twenty-six (was it her lucky number?). Now I got her. Now I knew for certain that she was a liar and dumb too, because there never were so many blocks in this small camp. It was enough for me to guess that she was one of those French citizens who volunteered to work in Germany for good pay. Hearing after the war about the net spread to catch such volunteers, she decided to pretend having been deported to the camps as a political prisoner. The French have a good nose, they must have smelled the rat and here she was sitting in the trap.

It was already Thursday, all the other women had been called for investigation, many were freed or transferred and left the depot. We had obviously been forgotten. No act of indictment — no inquest. We could sit there a whole year and never get a chance to explain that we got in by sheer mistake, thanks to my stupidity. I now sadly realized that all we had to do was to register at the Police Office for Foreigners and get temporary permit of sojourn, pending further investigation. Now we were really done in.

I decided to write a letter to the head of this Police Depot. Somebody gave me a sheet of paper and I composed a letter, short but explicit. All I am asking for — I concluded — is a summons. I printed in capital letters: "Monsieur le Directeur du Depot de la Prefecture de Police". I handed the letter to the nun, explaining how important it is. Through the iron fence I watched her marching along the corridor, then, at its end I saw her... dropping my letter into the wastepaper basket!!! Once more the servant of Jesus has deceived me. Was there no hope, shall we rot here in jail to the end of our days? Nobody was going to check the register where we were inscribed.

Something unusual broke my gloomy mood. A new figure crossed the threshold of our cell. Was I dreaming? Was I watching a fashion show? Entered a lady in an exquisite black dress of "haute couture" — a dress adorned with a glace white collar and glace white cuffs. A red artificial rose was cradled in the opening of the girlish white collar. Her impeccable hairdo was certainly in the latest trends (I was not aware of the new styles, I haven't seen the Parisian ladies yet...). The lady with the figure of a professional model looked around in disgust.

Every human congregation has its jester, even a jail. Here it was a merry prostitute, full of temperament, a real "comedienne". This Josette now assumed the role of a pompous major-domo of the cell, the master of ceremonies. She approached the lady most formally and said, bowing courtly, but not subserviently: "Madame, allow me to indicate to you your personal quarters, the suite that has been prepared for you" — thereupon she led the lady to a vacant pallet situated between the most disgusting cases. The cell inmates were roaring with laughter because on the pallet to the 'Lady's' left was a special specimen, whose background I have already investigated. She was a vulgar, big girl dressed in rags and in a visibly advanced stage of pregnancy. Her head had been completely shaved. I had learned that she was not a prostitute, but she was sleeping around with German soldiers. That's why, after the war, her patriotic neighbors shaved her head, so as to brand her as a traitor. On the pallet to the 'Lady's' right was prostrated a prostitute of the lowest rank, probably rotting with venereal diseases and jaundice. But the 'Lady' herself was not so enigmatic, as it transpired, she was known in Paris as the "queen of the black market"... "Just wait and see" — said a pleasant young woman to me — "this lady, moving in high society circles, is not going to stay here for a long time. Her influential friends will know where to pull the strings, where to grease a palm. She and her husband dealt in wagonloads of the black-market stuff. Compared to her, I am but small fry. I was caught selling two pounds of sugar on the black market. I did it only occasionally and could hardly provide for my little brothers and sisters". Indeed, she was right, the 'Lady' was set free only few hours later. That is justice for you.

More days passed, I was becoming restless, I have had enough of my research on the cross-section of human society represented here from a genuine baroness to the baroness of the black market. The young woman who informed me on the 'Lady's' background befriended me in an engaging way. I was very grateful to her because we felt very lonely here. Everybody played his cards close to the chest, each of these women was afraid of a planted mole. The French people hate foreigners. French is the only language that has a special word for foreigners. It is the term 'Meteques'. Its origin is in the archaic Greek word 'meteikos', designating strangers in Athens, who had no full citizen rights.

The world believes the French to be very liberal, progressive and tolerant. I was to discover just the opposite. The French bourgeois is a bigot, a prude and a misanthrope. Here is one example. We had our good habits from the concentration camps. Here was water and ordinary soap. We haven't had soap for a long, long time. Mother was first. She undressed completely, the way we were used to, and started washing her body. "Shame on you" — yell several hyenas — "are you not ashamed of such indecent exposure before the eyes of all of us?!!! Get dressed, hide your shame" — they cried, assuming threatening postures. Didn't we remember from Ravensbruck how averse the French were to thorough body washing. We should have guessed.

We had now many enemies and only two friends, the German baroness and the young woman who sold sugar on the black market. This one was now certain to be released very soon. I knew that I can trust her, that I can ask her to smuggle out a letter, but to whom? Here mother remembered that I still have the visiting card of the monstrous Mr.Grossbart, who invited us to stay with him. Perhaps he could help — what do we risk. I wrote to him in a short letter that I shall later explain what happened, but right now, through a chain of mistakes, we are detained without questioning here at the depot. Could he do for us just one thing: ask somebody at the Police headquarters to call us for an interrogation.

Called for her last hearing, the young woman concealed my letter in the opening of her décolletage. When released, she was supposed to mail it — and I believed her. She must have mailed my letter "express" because hardly a day later we were called out and led to the office... The clerk wrote and filled out all kinds of forms. I was intrigued. "Monsieur"- I asked him — "Are you not supposed to find out how it came about that we were thrown to jail and totally ignored for eight days? Is it not relevant to our case?" He looked from above the rims of his spectacles and said: " There is no case, it is none of my concern, I only fill out the forms... I am merely an insignificant clerk". What he meant by this strange statement — I understood only later. At the moment I was simply indignant that nobody cared why we were forgotten by the world. The truth was — as we shall learn — that this clerk got a phone call from a fat fish at Police headquarters, ordering him to release us at the greatest speed. He guessed that it is due to favoritism or a bribe, that's why he emphasized so angrily that he is only an insignificant clerk... Later, the aftermath of our detention will not end with this lack of interest. It remained noted in our dossier and will persecute us for a long time. Remaining suspects, our resident's permit will be limited to one month and be renewable every month. The clerk called a policeman asking him to accompany us to the metro station, to buy us tickets and to give exact instructions how to reach the Belleville station... and that meant the address of Mr.Grossbart.

Thus, we discovered how influential was Mr.Grossbart, acting on our behalf from behind the scenes. We shall later find out that he used to be a tailor, but that was a long time ago. He was not only thriving on the black market, he was shrewd enough to have the police commander of this district in his pocket, to make him a partner of sorts. That's how with one simple phone call, Mr.Grossbart arranged our immediate release.

ROMPING IN PARIS

We had never been in a metro, but with the help of the policeman's instructions we changed trains and arrived at our destination enjoying the ride. Mr.Grossbart lived at 156 rue de Belleville. It was an old part of town, nothing special to look at. But it was fascinating for us. We haven't seen a town, a normal traffic and a normal train of life for years. Everything seemed fascinating. We felt like Robinson Crusoe returning to civilization. We walked up to the fourth floor.

Mr. Grossbart was not at home. We waited for him in the street and enjoyed the sight of shops and the shoppers. We turned round the corner, and in this street side there was a little shop with vegetables and fruits. We admired every carrot, cucumber and tomato; we haven't seen them for years. We looked in enchantment at the fruits. We have forgotten that they exist. Then I spot a box with cherries — "Mama, look, cherries!!!" — I exclaim in Polish to my mother. It was like magnet, I stared like hypnotized. The shopkeeper didn't say a word. He filled a paper bag with cherries and handed it to me. I protested, I made excuses... it is a misunderstanding, I didn't intend to buy them, I have showed them to my mother... The shopkeeper said: "I know, mademoiselle, it is no mistake, I guessed that you desired them but cannot buy. Please, accept them as a gift". So, we were still the branded people, the martyrs, the walking skeletons. It must be clear to every stranger.

We walked some more and munched the cherries. There was a shop with a radio, and that's when I heard for the first time the sweet tune "Besame-mucho". It induced a special mood, it was so full of longing... Unfortunately I now have to think only about the hideous Mr.Grossbart.

At long last he arrived. We thanked him effusively, stressing that were it not for his intervention we would have remained for months in the Depot. We tried to explain what happened, but he interrupted us, saying: "First things first". He wanted us to eat, drink, take a bath and go to bed. What warm hospitality. I felt ashamed that he was so repulsive to me.

Days went by and we lived like at home. He brought the provisions, mother cooked, I cleaned the flat — like a real family. The man had a heart of gold, a real Jewish heart. Had he indeed? Soon we shall have our first doubts. Meanwhile we told him about Uncle Henry in America. I have written from the road three letters, but we had no address, now at last we have one. Upon Mr.Grossbart's suggestion we sent a cable to my uncle. We waited for his answer, like in a waiting-room.

My thoughts turned to somebody else. I was often thinking of Ulrique, my 'kochany' from Auschwitz. Perhaps he survived, perhaps he had returned to Paris. I remembered his address by heart, it was not far away, it was within walking distance. I went in this direction and I walked as if I had wings. When I was near his house, my wings seemed to get clipped. My heart was pounding and I sweated. I approached the door of the "concierge", the janitor. "Madame" — I asked in a trembling voice — "do you remember Mr.Ulrique Teitler, who used to live in this house before the war?" Yes, she remembered, but he didn't return. She had no letter, no information. She almost slammed the door at my face, then a little ashamed, she added that I may ask again. Who knows.

I could not ask every day, so I went down there twice a week, every time with a heavy heart. It was true, five months have elapsed since I saw him for the last time when we took leave of each other in Auschwitz. They were five terrible months that not many people survived. We, ourselves, passed through four more concentration camps and two marches of death. Is there still hope for his return? As I shall hear later, Rene of the rosy cheeks did not survive this ordeal. Like a pilgrim to holy places, I returned doggedly to Ulrique's janitor. We were already on friendly terms; I had won her over, this rough woman with a stony face.

Mr.Grossbart often had visitors, and we became part of this circle. One of the visitors was a lovely plump woman, aged well over thirty, by name of Anette. Another was Anette's sister with her husband, and the third woman was Natka, funny little communist who participated in the civil war in Spain. Natka informed us discreetly that Anette is Mr.Grossbart's mistress. Why should a beautiful young woman be the mistress of a monster? The answer was simple: she was too lazy to work, she had diabetes, had no means… and she had an appetite for luxury. Natka will play a role in saving us from Mr.Grossbart's clutches.

After a while we were getting restless. For how long can we live on Mr.Grossbart's mercy? We had to make contacts, we had to find the "Joint" or other such institutions. We had certain privileges of displaced persons. But whenever we mentioned the "Joint", Mr.Grossbart jumped and exclaimed: "Joint, Shmoint — who needs it. Don't you feel happy here? What do you miss? I shall buy you all you need, I shall buy you dresses, cosmetics, anything. Just look at how nicely you are filling up. What else do you need?" We protested but he wouldn't listen. "Never mind" — said mother to me when he left the house — "any day now we shall receive money from Henry, from America. We shall buy a handsome present for Mr.Grossbart and be free to start life on our own". Days passed in relative bliss and still no news from Henry. Wasn't it strange? Perhaps Mr.Grossbart doubted his very existence. Mother suspected that her brother must be gravely ill, otherwise he would immediately react to our cable.

We had to return to normal life. Mother was going to look for employment, and I was planning to prepare for the equivalent of "baccalaureat" exams. When mother heard about this plan she explodes: "How dare you present yourself for examinations so soon. You will most certainly fail. Couldn't you ask for a later term?" — I explained that I have my policy: "The sooner the better. The conditions now will be more lenient than later".

As you can see, my grandchildren, our lives are at this point almost returning to normal, and that's where I could eventually stop my recordings. But no, I can imagine you objecting, pressing me to continue. That reminds we of the Polish song with the refrain: "Don't stop, granny, continue you wondrous tales…" I can imagine you asking a lot of questions, each of you in his own style and range of interest.

Little Inbal, who always asked when watching TV — "are these the good men or the bad men…?" will want to know if, after all, Mr.Grossbart was a good man or a bad man? I have to answer that one. "No, Inbal, after all Mr.Grossbart was a bad man. You want to know why? Because he wanted and claimed from me something that I couldn't possibly give him — love.

How did he ask for it, you may ask. Oh, he had his ways. He wanted me for himself. He would tell my mother that something was missing for dinner, he wants some horseradish. So, mother would go down to buy some, meanwhile Mr.Grossbart would take my hands into his hands and apply his cheek to my cheek. Cooing softly and purring like a cat, he would ask me: "Aren't you happy with me my baby, aren't you? I would do anything for you, I can cover you with jewels if you make me happy, if you love me"... So you see, Inbal, beware of good uncles who pat your hands and your cheeks. They are not as good as they seem to be". Inbal might be puzzled, and I am uneasy, I haven't explained it as I should.

"But Grandma" — interjects Yasmine, the oldest, going on fourteen, and almost a woman — "didn't you say that he had a young mistress, Anette? Why would he try to molest you?" What shall I say, what am I to answer? "Yes, it was true, and he already had her for a long time. He got tired of her, bored, he wanted a change; he wanted to pick a new flower. Men are like that, Yasmine. You had better learn it so as not to be disappointed... So as you may guess now, we had to leave Mr.Grossbart's house at great speed. We had to accept Natka's offer to move in with her, after we told her my secret" — I conclude.

"But granny" — objects my little man Erel, aged eight, who is a born pragmatist — "how could you leave when you were expecting any day a cable from Uncle Henry, to be mailed to that address?" How clever of him! So, I have to explain: "We would have somehow managed through Natka, but a miracle happened, and the cable arrived the very morning when we were on the doorstep, about to move out." That's not good enough for my grandson: "So what took him so long to answer your cable?" — inquired Erel indignantly. "What happened was very simple. Five years earlier my uncle had moved to another town, another state. The post had a hard time finding his new address eventually. That was the reason for the long delay". Now my audience is reassured, the good uncle did not abandon us.

I will now describe how Natka shared her bed with us, how her mansard, her attic room with sloped ceiling, looked out on the roofs of Paris and a dove cot on the adjacent roof, how happy we felt there. We got sweet letters from Henry and his wife Helen, and also from my dear cousins Harry and Estelle. Henry was not rich, he was just starting on his own, but they were sending food parcels that we shared with the wretched Natka.

We didn't dare to move out because our resident's permit was still renewable every month, pending further developments.

Natka's communism oozed from her pores. She was a former combatant in Spain and communism was her gospel. She was such a fervent adherent to her party's creed, that one week she would come from her cell's meeting announcing that Zionism is sheer fascism... but the next week she proclaimed that an honest Zionist is better than a lukewarm communist. We were fed such nonsense almost daily.

I now have to tell you, my children, how I was preparing for the exams. But the exams seem to be a dull topic to my grandchildren. The romantic Yasmine wants to know if my romance with Ulrique had a happy end. "Oh, yes, it had a happy end, like in fairy tales. He came back, he received my message from his janitor, he came running to me, and we were moved to tears to be at last free and together. Our romance bloomed. His brother and family received me like a bride" — I reminisce immersed in sweet memories. "So why didn't you two marry?" interrupts my virtuous Yasmine. "Because fate plays all sorts of tricks on you. Because reality is very different from dreams... The reasons were very prosaic, very down to earth. I discovered, eventually, that Ulrique wanted to do a lot of travelling with me, and I was not up to it. I had, and still have this trauma about travelling. I feel faint in cars, on buses and trains. I have never been cured of it. A 'shrink' who treated me for a long time explained this phenomenon by proving to me that whenever I have to move to an unfamiliar place, it is to me like facing again the danger of entering gas chambers; a danger to which I was exposed eight times (we counted). So now you see...

"Yes, we do, but couldn't he do his travelling without you if he loved you so much and knew about your...trauma?" — suggests the practical Erel. Perhaps he could, but I also discovered that he was very pedantic, obsessively pedantic, and also fond of 'gourmet' intricate dishes on the 'haute cuisine' level, that I would never learn to prepare. It would have been a disaster. I saw in time that, after all, I was not for him" — I admit with shame. "What a pity" — concludes Erel — "marrying him, the French citizen, would solve your problem of the 'resident's' permit ". How shrewd my Erel is. Is he my grandson, this naughty little boy? I have to tell him now how I solved this last problem.

Going once more to the detested and much feared Prefecture de Police,

I said to my mother, "I have this distinct feeling that the amulet given to me by Kuba, the one I carried concealed through six concentration camps, constitutes a real obstacle and impediment in obtaining a permanent permit of residence. When set in motion, the hieroglyphs on it spelled: 'Come back'. This 'come back' draws me back to Poland like a magnet. I have to get rid of it. I have to do it right now; I am that superstitious". Afraid of a second's hesitation on sentimental grounds, I threw this little disc into the opening of a sewer. What do you know, it helped immediately. We left the Prefecture de Police with a permanent permit of residence in our hand...

I have to add here that we also got in touch with the 'Joint' and received some money and tickets to a canteen for displaced persons. The association of Jewish students procured for me a student's bursary, a modest grant. Sometime later my mother got a job as artistic designer and modelist of women's belts for 'Haute couture'.

My little Inbal is bored by such details. She has a strong sense of responsibility, and she has very strong family feelings. That's why she asks me: "Didn't you promise Aunt Mania to search for her son who went to Israel? Have you forgotten?" Fortunately, my answer is ready: "But I was just leading to it, my pet". First, I have to correct her mistake. Shlomo, after swimming across the river and crossing many frontiers, did not arrive to Israel... because the state didn't exist yet — it was Palestine. Then I remind her that the only address Aunt Mania was able to give me was "Shderot Boulevard, Tel Aviv". It was one big nonsense, because Shderot is Boulevard and Boulevard is Shderot. Anyhow, without the house number a letter cannot be delivered. Even though I wrote on the envelope: "The Post office is kindly requested to find the addressee in spite of the deficient address" — needless to say, my letter was never delivered. I tried through the Red Cross but to no avail. What helped me finally were the tickets to the canteen for displaced persons. How possible? The miracle happened right there, in the canteen.

One day, when we were taking our meal in this big hall, we noticed a general commotion. People left their tables and encircled somebody whom we couldn't see in the middle of this crowd. We were told that it was the first Jewish soldier in Paris, serving in the British Palestine Brigade. My mother jumped up: "Go to him immediately and ask him if he knows Shlomo" — was her order. Bashful as I was, afraid to ask a stupid question, I tried to ridicule my mother: "So because he is from Palestine he must — according to you — know personally Shlomo Sperling from Palestine. Don't be ridiculous, Palestine is not the size of a Pipiduwka (small village)". But my mother wouldn't give up, and I wouldn't give in. A gentleman, a Mr. Selig, seated at our table, took pity on us, and offered to push through the crowd and ask this absurd question. After a long while he returned all flushed, leading the soldier to our table. "Shlomo Sperling, do I know him?" — exclaimed the soldier- "I am serving with him in the same unit, and I am even stationed with him in Holland, in the same monastery and in the same room. I shall deliver your message this very night". That was a real miracle! And for you — it is a lesson never to oppose one's mother, never to be bashful and stubborn as I had been. How many times did it get on my nerves that mother is always right, or most often right...

But that's not the end of the miracle. The good gentleman, Mr. Selig, was going the next day to Belgium to visit his relatives. He had no visa and he had to cross the frontier to Belgium illegally. It made him very nervous. He was quite relieved spotting a Jewish Brigade soldier from Palestine at the crossing point. He asked him how one could pass without being apprehended by the border police. The soldier gave him good advice and before they separated, Mr. Selig asked, off handily: "Do you happen to know a certain Shlomo Sperling in your brigade?" The soldier, taken aback, exclaimed: "But that's me, how did you guess? I am right on my way to Paris to meet my aunt and my cousin".

That was still not the last miracle in this series of strange coincidences. Shlomo came to us in Paris. He embraced us, and we all wept for a while when we told him about meeting by chance his mother in one of the camps. Then this tall, handsome hardened soldier, my cousin Shlomo, said a strange thing: "You don't have to conceal it from me anymore. I know that my mother died. Don't spare me, tell me all you know about her death". We were thunderstruck. We hastened to reassure him that Aunt Mania was very much alive, that she was well and on her way to Krakow. "Look, the game is over, it is cruel of you to pretend. I know about my mother's death from the best source. I know from a young woman whom I met in Italy who said that my mother expired on her lap. So please spill the rest." We had a hard time persuading and convincing him that it wasn't true, that a month after the liberation Mania went to

Krakow to meet his father, my uncle Bernard, who would hopefully return from Siberia. The epilogue of their story is that they were reunited in Krakow. Shlomo went there and smuggled them with forged orders into Belgium. The three of them went to Palestine and lived here happily ever after.

Speaking of relatives reminds me that shortly before the liquidation of the Plaszow camp, we came across a distant relative, the divinely handsome Emil. He reached Plaszow after a long Odyssey. You won't believe it — he was hiding in a... chicken coop. A good Pole kept him there, locked in this cage. He had to lie in an embryonic position, covered by a heap of straw. Late at night the Pole used to unlock the coop, bring him food and let him out for a short while. Only then was he able to stretch his limbs and relieve himself. One evening a German soldier was romancing with a local girl in this very courtyard. He excused himself for a moment and went aside to... pee, straight on Emil, who was concealed under the straw. That's when Emil decided to leave the shelter of the coop, eventually, after having spent half a year there. When Emil emerged in Paris after the war, he became a very strange person, oscillating between breakdowns and euphoria. We tried to stay in touch with him, but he was withdrawn and doubled up on himself — still the man in a chicken coop.

There was another man who never forgot his former incarnation. We were once approached in the metro by a young blond man with round blue myopic eyes. Stomping from foot to foot he said bashfully: "Excuse me ladies, but since you speak Polish, could you indicate me how can I go..." to a certain institution. We were going to the same place, so he came along. Since then he never left us. He adopted us, or rather chose to be adopted by my mother. Because he was a rabbi's son from a provincial village, he never lost his Hassidic habit of swaying, as if he were constantly in prayer. This habit earned him instantly the nickname 'Kaczka' (a duck) and it stuck to him. Kaczka spent the war in the woods where he joined the Polish socialist partisans of the Armia Ludowa. I was very curious about the glorious exploits of the partisans. "What glorious exploits" — said Kaczka — "All we did was hide in the forest... We knew where the German soldiers were stationed, they knew where we were hiding. We had a mutual non-aggression agreement of sorts; we didn't attack them, they didn't touch us. Whenever we ran out of supplies, we would raid a nearby village and pilfer whatever we needed. There were no reprisals". So that was the kind of war waged by these proud partisans. This emancipated Hassid was to become later an eminent history professor (in the USA) and also... a titular rabbi.

The second friend from this early Parisian period was Joseph H. from Krakow. This lame medicine student survived several camps, and nobody noticed that he was limping — a miracle in itself. The three of us undertook to study and conquer Paris on foot. We walked for miles, admired buildings and thus learned to know Paris the hard way. The most curious among us was Joseph. He would never give up. Limping heavily, perspiring endlessly, he prodded us to see more, to go on and on. Thanks to him I came to know Paris better than the Parisians.

Once, we stood like transfixed in front of a fascinating oriental building, covered with tiles and mosaics. Very much intrigued we noticed the inscription 'Société Theosophique de France". I became pensive. I disclosed to my two companions that I had an uncle (Uncle Philip, my father's brother), who lived for seven years on the island of java and turned into a theosophist. He later lived in the United States, somewhere in State Oregon. That's all I remember. "If you have an uncle who is a theosoph — in we go", said Joseph in an imperative tone. In we went, and I reluctantly explained my problem to a secretary. She took my address, adding that my quest is not absurd, they had lists of members all over the world. Eight days later we received a cable from Uncle Philip. We started a regular exchange of letters; he even sent some food-parcels. Gradually Philip's letters became sermonizing, almost preaching. He suggested to me to make contact with the same theosophical society, and its books and pamphlets explaining the essence of the theosophical creed. I did. After all, I didn't want to remain an ignoramus, and I was sincerely curious. He asked about my impressions. It dawned on me that my uncle was trying to influence me, to make me embrace theosophy. I was indignant but tried to hold my horses. I answered honestly that theosophy is sublime, even though there is a strong penchant to ascetics, based on the belief that man shouldn't consume living creatures. The idea of transmigration of souls appeals to me, but on the whole, it is not my creed. We went through this Armageddon of Holocaust as Jews, and we wouldn't abandon Judaism after six million had perished on 'Kiddush ha Shem'...

Uncle Philip inflamed by his missionary zeal couldn't swallow this defeat. He wrote me a nasty letter. It spelled no more and no less but: "We in America know well how depraved and debased you had become in the concentration camps. It is even asked here what you, the survivors, had to do in order to survive. All this has to be forgotten, it is about time to return to the right path". Needless to tell you, how this declaration stabbed me. I filled my fountain pen with poison and responded with the harshest letter that I have even written. I wrote my uncle that I had never been so proud of myself as I was now, having gone through this hell without a blemish on my name. He, who was sitting on the veranda of his villa throughout this war, had no right to judge my moral standards. That was the end of the correspondence. Before he expired, he hadn't forgotten to leave to us in his will... a symbolic dollar.

I have however to admit that there were instances when we, mother and I, behaved very strangely. When we started to exchange letters with Henry and Helen, we never asked about my grandfather who used to live with them. I can imagine how they must have wondered. That was another trauma and aftermath of the Holocaust. Whoever isn't mentioned and is obviously dead — one doesn't ask about him, one doesn't dare to. Only much, much later did we dare to ask under what circumstances my grandfather died. This syndrome of silence is characteristic of Holocaust survivors, but in the eyes of the beholder it gives the impression of a protective shell of egoism. In the eyes of the beholder we must look like cold monsters, devoid of human feelings.

"Granny, stop philosophizing" — reprimands me my oldest — "you have still left some strings untied. Some five tapes earlier you promised to tell us what happened to the abominable Marcel Goldberg, who still wanted to punish you for his humiliation, when he was fired from his job because of your complaint". Yes, she is right, my Yasmine. I have to provide an epilogue to these confrontations. Well, Marcel Goldberg emerged in Paris. Some of the survivors from the Plaszow camp spotted him and denounced him to the authorities. He was arrested as a war criminal and four people from Plaszow deposed their formally written testimony. We were very glad that justice would triumph. It didn't occur to us to add our testimony, or rather we thought that we would be summoned because the four witnesses had included our names in their deposition as additional prospective witnesses.

Nothing happened for a while. Meanwhile we heard more details. I have already mentioned how Mr.Goldberg filled his pockets with diamonds, taking bribes from those who wanted to get on the Schindler list. After the liberation, fleeing from Brinlitz in Moravia, Goldberg was astute enough to surround himself with a company of people financed by him, who would defend him in case of an accusation. They traveled with him at his expense like royal courtiers. When he was arrested, this clique of his minions, numbering some thirteen Holocaust survivors, presented itself as one man at the appropriate office and testified that Marcel Goldberg was their savior, the righteous among the righteous, a man of a crystal-clear character without blemish. Marcel's wife had probably bribed a central figure of the French investigation because he was quickly released, and as quickly spirited away from Paris. He allegedly went into hiding somewhere in South America. The affair left us with a bitter sense of guilt. We have absolutely no talent for vengeance.

"Yes, granny, but you have a talent for long, loyal friendships. So, what became of your bosom friend Janka, because I hear you still mentioning her name nowadays" — says Yasmine. Indeed, friendship triumphed, and this story definitely has a happy ending. Two years after the end of the war we were reunited in Paris. We were both married by then, Janka was expecting a baby, but when we were together, we often giggled like girls, just like in the old times. Sometimes we exchanged glances, and instantly knew each other's thoughts. When Janka's time came, my husband, your grandfather, delivered her baby Louis in the Rothschild hospital in Paris. Janka was very calm during the delivery because I fixed for her a 'mantra' of sorts. I told her to concentrate on the most beautiful picture of liberation: a Russian prisoner leaving the concentration camp gate and mounting a white horse grazing nearby. It was a picture described to me by Ulrique.

Later, Janka with her husband and her baby emigrated to Australia, we went to Israel. We still exchange letters on a permanent basis. When you read a letter from her you may think that I received a letter from a lover. She 'keeps my head' from afar, she sends some wise quotations, and she tells me how much she misses me.

When my dear mother of blessed memory became an invalid in wheelchair, Janka came over for a visit. Nothing has changed between us in the last forty years.

"That's wonderful, but now you have to tell us, granny, how you met your husband, our deceased grandfather" — asks Jasmine. "Oh, that's another wonderful story, that I shall tell you some other time".

www.ingramcontent.com/pod-product-compliance
Ingram Content Group UK Ltd.
Pitfield, Milton Keynes, MK11 3LW, UK
UKHW020630130126
10066UKWH00004B/25

9 789655 754872